# The Grace of Shortstops

## ROBERT MAYER

DOUBLEDAY & COMPANY, INC.

GARDEN CITY, NEW YORK

1984

Library of Congress Cataloging in Publication Data
Mayer, Robert, 1939–
The grace of shortstops.
Summary: An eight-year-old Bronx boy from an immigrant
Jewish family makes his passion for baseball the guiding
force of his life.
[1. Baseball—Fiction.  2. Jews—New York (N.Y.)—
Fiction.  3. Emigration and immigration—Fiction]
I. Title.
PZ7.M465Gr  1984  [Fic]
ISBN: 0-385-19049-2
Library of Congress Card Catalog Number: 83-40146

To
Gene Smith
and
Bonnie Knickerbocker

*Come away, O human child!*
*To the waters and the wild*
*With a faery, hand in hand,*
*For the world's more full of weeping*
*Than you can understand.*

William Butler Yeats,
*The Stolen Child*

# PROLOGUE

THE CHILD'S NAME was Lisa Hirsch. She was not quite thirteen months old. She was asleep in a gray baby carriage outside 1707 Townsend Avenue, the Bronx, New York City: a two-story red brick house. The date was May 30, 1947—then called Decoration Day, now called Memorial Day.

The street in the afternoon sun was devoid of motion, devoid of people. Almost everyone in the neighborhood was three blocks away, on the Grand Concourse, watching the colorful Decoration Day parade, which featured an appearance by the President of the United States, Harry S Truman. With unlikely cunning, the kidnapper chose the moment of the President's passing to strike.

Unseen hands reached into the carriage, gently lifted out the sleeping child. Frightened eyes met one other pair of eyes, droopy-lidded, half-open, half-shut: the eyes of a woman in a wheelchair. There was an instant of electric pleading on both sides. Then the kidnapper hurried away with the child.

The kidnapping was discovered as the last of the marching bands passed, as the sound of drums and trumpets faded from the afternoon. Police could find no credible witnesses. They interviewed all those close to the child.

Mickey Hirsch, the child's father, was a policeman. He said he had been on duty at the parade at the time of the kidnapping.

Hindy Hirsch, the child's mother, said she had been watching the parade, along with her two older children, Phil, eight, and Annie, six.

Felice Greenberg, an upstairs neighbor who had been minding the child, said she had gone in to take some aspirin for a headache, had gotten dizzy and lay down on a bed for a moment, had fallen asleep for ten minutes, then had hurried outside and had found the carriage empty, the baby gone.

Ruth Brunig, Hindy Hirsch's sister, from in front of whose house the child was taken, said she too had been at the parade, along with her husband, Rabbi Louis Brunig, and their two sons, Eli, fourteen, and Benjamin (usually called Peewee), eight.

Miriam Lester, the child's grandmother—the wheelchair-bound victim of a stroke—could only mumble that it was snowing; and that Death came.

Of those interviewed, two were lying. This fact was not discovered then.

Neither of those who lied was the kidnapper.

When the infant had not been found for two weeks, eight-year-old Peewee Brunig put aside his preoccupation with baseball—with the Brooklyn Dodgers—and initiated his own childish search, unaware of the tangled motive behind the crime.

This book is Peewee's story, crossing seas and generations. It is a story of America at mid-century. It is a story of secrets.

# I

# *Opening Day*

No word can say what the Silence tells that
is all around and within us, this Silence that
is no silence but to be heard resounding
through all things, whether of waking,
dream, or dreamless night . . .

Joseph Campbell,
*Myths to Live By*

## 1

THERE WAS A corridor that stretched from the living room past three doors on the left and ended at an airy room that was his brother's. Down this long corridor Peewee and his cousin Phil liked to run in their stockinged feet and at the very end slide on strawberried thighs as if into second base. It was practice for the time when Peewee would play shortstop for the Brooklyn Dodgers: the heir apparent to Pee Wee Reese, as the *Sporting News* would say.

He was eight years old that spring, and still afraid of the dark. His own room was the front parlor, which looked out into the street with three tall windows that took in the humid air and in his nightly fantasies sometimes even the Rag Lady herself. His mother had indulged him until he was seven, but this year he was a big boy and it was high time he learned to sleep in the dark. So Peewee the shortstop developed his own magic chant with which to banish the demons of the night. Discovering early on that numbers didn't work, nor leaping sheep, either, he began to say to himself in the pillowed dark, "The Dodgers are gonna win the pennant! The Dodgers are gonna win the pennant! The Dodgers are gonna win the pennant!" Over and over behind his tight-shut eyes he would murmur that refrain, until it became as meaningless as the temple politics his father talked on the phone or the Yiddish newspaper his grandmother sometimes left in the house; until, deep with portent, it would lull him at last to sleep. No other refrain would do the trick, yet his homemade incantation rarely failed. The year was 1947, and the damnedest thing is, the Dodgers *were* gonna win the pennant, after all.

There had never been, as far as Benjamin (Peewee) Brunig could tell, a Jewish shortstop in the majors. Those few Hebrews who while God wasn't looking approached the Sinai of physical prowess tended to gather like scholars at the pitcher's mound, where they would set the all-important tone, where they could use their intellect to overwhelm. Or, unexpectedly blessed with brute physical power, they would plant themselves like the Eastern Wall at first base, à la Mr. Hank Greenberg, tall and stolid and proud: a home-run-hitting aberration, the exception that proves the rule. Or, most likely, the Jewish athlete would camp in right field, yet one more victim, his father might say, of the diaspora. So for Peewee to want to play shortstop in the majors—to be a Keystone Kid—the position in all of sports of utmost grace—this was hubris of a large order. Especially in one who was still afraid of the dark.

"What about night games?" his unamused mother would say.

"There's lights," Peewee would reply.

His mother didn't know much about sports.

Nonetheless, it *was* the spring of 1947, depending on your bias a season of horror or hope. All through the crocus days in the Florida training camps, the papers had been heavy with the news: Mr. Jackie Robinson, formerly of Georgia, more recently of Montreal, was going to break the color line. Mr. Rickey had plotted it in the towers of his lofty dome. More important, in Peewee's innocent view, the Negro first baseman himself (he'd move to second soon enough; he never really looked like a first baseman, not to Peewee's young discerning eye) with his woolly hair and his pigeon toes and his elbows tucked in tight at the plate, the bat held much too high and proud for any ordinary nigger—this Jackie Robinson himself had confirmed it on the field all through the spring, in the uniform of Montreal; his right to wear the Dodger blues, the Dodger grays. And if there would soon be a nigger in the national pastime, as Phil's father Mickey, who was a policeman, liked to say, then why not, down the road a bit, a Jewish shortstop?

Why not, indeed?

Jackie Robinson broke the color line in the majors (0–for–3, with one run scored) on the same day that Peewee's grandmother was brought to the house to die.

The first dark inkling he had of it was the night before, when his father, with muscled arms and thick wrists wielding a hammer and a screwdriver with forgotten expertise, pried up the worn wooden doorjamb that divided the long dark corridor from his brother's airy room. Pried up second base, as it were.

"Why ya doing that?" Peewee asked.

His father, round-faced, balding, wearing his yarmulke, looked up at him while still on his knees, prying at the stubborn jamb. His face was slightly reddened from the exertion. "Grandma Lester is coming home tomorrow."

"Coming here?"

His father nodded.

Grandma Lester had been in the hospital for three weeks. She'd had a stroke, they said, though Peewee had no idea what that meant. There had been some debate between his parents about whether Peewee should be taken to visit her, his father arguing in the affirmative, his mother stating flatly that he was too young yet, that there would be time enough for him to see her when she came home. His mother won out, as always.

"How come not to her own house?" Peewee said.

Her own house was an apartment just two blocks away that smelled of old paint and chicken fat.

"She's still not well," his father said, exerting, prying up the splintered wood. "Your mother will have to take care of her for a while."

Peewee nodded, understood, walked back along the corridor past the open kitchen where his mother was doing the supper dishes, then, pausing, returned down the corridor to where his father had just stood up with second base in his hands. A definite setback to your career, he could hear Phil saying.

"So how come you took off that?"

His father opened the door to the dark back room, switched on the ghostly light. Light brown cardboard cartons were piled from the floor to the ceiling at crazy angles on all sides.

"Eli will be sleeping in the living room for a while," he said. "We'll put Grandma Lester in Eli's room. She'll be in a wheelchair. The doorjamb will get in the way."

The crazy boxes began to cascade onto Peewee's head. He withstood their assault for several seconds. Then, turning, he hurried away to the bathroom and closed the door. He hoped a nervous stomach would never happen at Ebbets Field, in the middle of a big inning.

Peewee Brunig, at the age of eight, knew a great deal about life. More than most of his friends, to be sure. He knew that on a ball hit to left or left-center he must go into short left field to take the throw. He knew that on a ball hit to right or right-center it was his job to cover the bag while the second baseman took the throw. He knew that if a runner on first broke for second, with a left-handed hitter at bat, it was his job to cover second and make the tag. Whereas if a righty was at the plate, he'd hold his ground while the second baseman covered the base. (Unless they'd arranged beforehand to pull a switch, in an attempt to foil the hit-and-run.) He knew how to turn the double play by dragging his foot lightly across the bag, then leaping high to make the throw while avoiding the incoming spikes. He knew that although he liked to throw sidearm, overhand was the only way from deep short.

The only thing he suddenly didn't know was how he would survive for weeks, or even months, in a house with a person in a wheelchair in it. Even if the person was Grandma Lester.

It was an old baseball expression that the legs were the first to go. But wheelchairs, though he didn't know why, reminded him of the Rag Lady.

That night, the eve of Opening Day, he had to say "The Dodgers are gonna win the pennant" 248 times before he could fall asleep. And even then, for the first time in years, the shortstop wet the bed.

He hoped his mother wouldn't notice. It was possible that she wouldn't. She had seem preoccupied with odd things in recent weeks, ever since her mother's stroke. One curiosity in particular that bothered her was the flecks of paint from the ceiling that had begun to fall at times onto Peewee's bed.

"It must be the vibrations from the el," his father said. The el was the Jerome Avenue IRT elevated subway, which passed beyond a warehouse a block away, rumbling so loud at times that they had to turn the radio up.

"The el's been here forever," his mother said. "And why only in that room?"

"Maybe they used cheap paint," his father said.

Until one day she realized what was making the paint flecks fall, and she never mentioned them again. She'd shake the white-flecked blue cotton bedspread out the window, glance up at the ceiling, and put it back, dark and taut as a night without stars.

What was actually on Ruth Brunig's mind each time she found the flecks of paint would have horrified them if they'd guessed. It was the pain of passion, pure passion. The only love affair she'd ever had. Three months of secret meetings two afternoons each week at the Concourse Plaza Hotel. A wild affair she had broken off a week before her mother's stroke, for fear that of all the household, little Peewee was beginning to suspect. A passion whose strangulation left her every morning wanting to die.

There was no one she could discuss it with. She was, after all, the rabbi's wife.

Peewee's maternal grandfather, Max Lester, had been born somewhere in Russia around the time of the dinosaurs. He had even had a dinosaur name back then—Lestersaurus, Peewee remembered it as, though it was actually Lestrakovsky, which would be shortened with a few strokes of a pen on Ellis Island by an immigration clerk too dumb or too lazy to write out the whole thing. Fleeing the Cossacks or some other mongrel horde with his beautiful bride Miriam, in search of the streets of gold, Max Lestrakovsky paused in London while his wife delivered their firstborn, an unaccountably red-haired daughter whom they named Ruth, and then, when the child seemed sturdy enough to survive the ocean crossing, they put to sea, proud folks in steerage class.

Established in the New World, Miriam Lester obtained work sewing dresses in a convenient sweat shop, her baby at her breast, while her tall, handsome husband Max plied his own trade at home in their tenement apartment on Rivington Street, or on the outside steps thereof, or in the small restaurants where for three cents he could drink tea from a glass all afternoon, his trade being that of inventor. He spent most of his time doing nothing, staring into a dream. To work for a few

cents an hour was not the way to get rich in America, Max had decided. To make a big invention and strike it rich—that was the only
way. So it was the wife Miriam who worked in the garment shop by day
and, when she had saved enough money, purchased her own sewing
machine and sewed dresses for the uptown ladies at night, and by
sewing day and night gave food and clothing and shelter to the six
children who lived of the eight to whom she gave birth. And when the
eldest daughter, Ruthie, completed her bookkeeping course and obtained a good-paying job with a prestigious lower Broadway wholesaler,
and contributed most of her weekly earnings to the upkeep of the
family, Max Lester, still tall and handsome, with flecks of gray now
beginning to distinguish his hair and his mustache, continued to ply
unceasingly his trade, which is to say he drank his tea and stared. With
typical perversity, the six Lester daughters, all of them stunning except
for the youngest, Hindy, who had a heart as big as the city but ran to
fat—all of them except Ruthie the eldest squabbled like street peddlers
with their hardworking mother, and gave their love to debonair Papa
Max. Perhaps it would have been different if the two boys had lived,
but the two boys had died, one at two months and the other at two
years. Perhaps that was Max Lester's punishment, if there is such a
thing.

In the absence of boys of his own, Max turned his doting to his
grandsons. Not so much to Eli Brunig, the firstborn, or to Philip
Hirsch, the second, but out of an obscure and dreamy vision to little
Benny Brunig, the third and last of the grandsons he'd live to see. He
watched impatiently while Benny grew slowly in his carriage. When at
last he left the carriage and learned to walk, Benny became the part-
time property of Grandpa Max. Three or four afternoons each week,
when the weather was nice, Max would leave the apartment on Walton
Avenue and walk the three blocks to the Brunigs' to pick up little
Benny. To give Ruthie some time for herself, he liked to say, winking at
his own unselfishness. Together he and Benny—not called Peewee yet
—small hand in large, would walk to the corner, purchase for a nickel
three chocolate twists that were Benny's favorites, and continue from
Goldstein's Candy Store on to Claremont Park, to a certain green-
painted bench that was Max Lester's favorite. They would sit together
on the bench, Benny getting chocolate-fingered from the twists, till
when he was through Max would produce from one pocket a white

handkerchief with which to wipe Benny's hands, and then from his other pocket a brown paper bag stuffed with broken ends of stale bread, with which the boy and his grandfather-protector would feed the pigeons.

Then the visits stopped. For several days when the boy was not yet four years old Grandpa Max did not show up to take him to the park. At first he bided his time, at first he didn't ask, lest he had done something wrong, and this was some punishment he really didn't want to know about. Then, one afternoon, his mother knitting in the sunny front parlor, his Grandma Lester sitting nearby, reading her Jewish newspaper, he asked.

"Grandpa Max won't be coming here anymore," his mother replied. "Grandpa Max has died and gone to heaven."

Benny pondered that for a while. He knew, though he didn't know how, of this heaven. It was very far away.

"Now who'll take me to the park?" he said.

His mother put down her knitting, hugged him tight. "Lots of people," she assured him. "I will, your daddy will, Grandma Lester will. Don't you worry about that."

He pressed his face into her shoulder for a time, wool-sweater-smelling, mother-smelling. Then he moved away, found a toy airplane Uncle Mickey had sent back from the war. He sat on the floor, moving the plane on its wheels along the linoleum.

"What does Grandpa Max do in heaven?" he asked.

"It wouldn't surprise me," his mother said, looking up over her knitting, "if he feeds the pigeons."

His Grandma Lester glanced over the tops of her bifocals, over the top of her hieroglyphic newspaper. "Working he isn't," she said.

The toy plane strutted on the floor. Then it took off, began to zoom slowly upward. Toward the sky, toward the clouds, toward the ceiling; toward whatever lay beyond.

Probably some of the others did take him to the park after that. If they did, he didn't remember. All the boy would remember afterward was feeding the pigeons with his Grandpa Max. And if something else was going on then, unknown to both of them, who is to say? Surely in the spring and summer months, within earshot and eyeshot of the man and the boy, there would have been older boys playing ball after school in the park that surrounded the special bench. The sights, the sounds of baseball, at least in its city-park incarnations, could not have helped but fill the wartime air on every side. And if the boy in his later memories would recall only the struts and coos of the pigeons, only the comfort of the old man's lap and the bristles of his white mustache, who could argue that baseball hadn't invaded his being even then?

On the morning of Opening Day the world woke well before Pee-wee, which was a rare occurrence. It was barely seven when the bell rang long and hard in the outer hall, and Peewee, leaping from his narrow bed, sprung open the venetian blinds and saw a moving-van-size truck marked Ace Hospital Supplies. The rear of the truck was being opened by a large Negro. There was murmuring in the hallway, his father's voice and another's, and then another man, white, vaulted down the four brick steps. A moment later he and the Negro were negotiating down the ramped rear end like drunken tightrope walkers what looked like a heavy mattress folded inside gray metal bars. They carried it to the sidewalk, set it down, pushed it across on wheels. Bending slightly, they carried it up the steps and wheeled it down the corridor to his brother's room. Eli, who was fourteen, was already washing up in the bathroom. His mother bustled in and nodded to the men. Peewee flushed with embarrassment that his mother should show herself to these two stranger truckers wearing only her nightgown and her robe. He flushed again as his father gave the men a quarter each and hung back forlornly in a corner as his father signed a yellow receipt, and the two men disappeared outside, till one of them came back and left something in the outer hall.

Peewee's father went for the abandoned wheelchair and pushed it, empty, as if pushing some invisible ghost of the future, down the corridor into Eli's room. In the slanting morning light Peewee saw in the wax of the linoleum six long dull tire tracks, four from the wheels of the bed, two from the wheels of the chair. It would take a lot of slides to erase those marks from the floor. Peewee guessed that for the rest of the season he wouldn't be doing much sliding anymore, except in a fantasy world of dirt and grass.

With all the excitement he forgot to comb his hair before going off to school that day. No loss. His brown hair was unruly and tended to stick up in back and fall across his forehead in the front no matter how many times a day he combed it. He was a boy, he figured, and for boys it didn't matter what you looked like as long as you weren't fat like Phil.

He had dark brown eyes. His arms and legs were thin, his torso still slim and undeveloped, and he had a distinguishing triangle of space between his two front teeth. This small gap, through which he could squirt a mouthful of water for eye-popping distances, had enabled him to become the two-time and current champion of the Townsend Avenue Spit and Piss Club, even though he couldn't piss worth anything.

There was a rumor afoot that the Italian boys up the block, having gotten wind of this secret Jewish society, were forming a Spit and Piss Club of their own and were planning to hurl a challenge at this pint-size so-called champion. Italians, they reckoned, could outpiss Jews any day.

Peewee was unconcerned. He assumed the challenge would never actually come.

He was in fourth grade at P.S. 70 that year, and his teacher was Mr. Lemon. Mr. Lemon had a large round face of a bright fruity hue and should have been named Mr. Tangerine, which was what the kids sometimes called him behind his back. The nickname had been thought up by Beverly Rosenthal, who was nine years old and sat in the seat next to Peewee, on the right, and whose dark brown hair fell over her left eye in a way that made her the prettiest girl Peewee had ever seen. One day a few weeks before, as they were hurrying out during a fire drill, the girl in front of Beverly had tripped over an untied shoelace and fallen, and Beverly had to stop short to avoid stepping on her. Peewee, hurrying right behind, had been unable to stop in time and had bumped into Beverly from the back with his whole body and then had instinctively clutched her shoulder to keep her from falling. Ever since she had been giving him curious, smiling looks out of the corner of her visible eye. Peewee did not understand any of this. Girls could not play second base or even first; he had no use for them whatsoever.

School began with arithmetic that day, which he hated except for batting averages, and then spelling, at which he excelled for reasons his mother could not understand, and then geography, Mr. Lemon pulling down a multicolored map from a wooden slat atop the blackboard and showing them the outline of Africa, from where he said the first slaves came. Beverly Rosenthal, who unlike Peewee was not shy in class and had even played Queen Esther in the school's Purim play, raised her hand to ask a question. "Is that where Jackie Robinson comes from?" she said. Peewee had the distinct intuition she had asked the question specifically for him, to show him that she was up on the baseball news. "Jackie Robinson comes from Georgia," he wanted to say, but being too shy to speak in class except when absolutely called upon, he leaned several degrees in Beverly's direction and whispered it across the aisle: "Jackie Robinson comes from Georgia." Beverly tilted her head toward him and with a brush of her right hand flipped the hair off her left eye. "Oh," she said, in a voice that sounded impressed. Then as if from underwater the voice of Mr. Lemon slithered into his ear like an eel. "Benjamin, did you have something to say?"

He turned to face front, clasped his hands on his desk, felt his face flushing red. "No," he said.

"It seems to me you did," Mr. Lemon said.

Peewee, deciding the truth was better than any dirty thing the other kids might deduce from his whispering to Beverly Rosenthal, stood somewhat shakily beside his seat. "Jackie Robinson comes from Georgia," he said. And then, finding it wasn't quite so torturous when you actually knew what you were talking about, added, "Though he played ball last year at Montreal."

He could feel himself sweating as he sat, could feel the eyes of the others, especially Beverly Rosenthal, as Mr. Lemon said, "That's correct." Beverly's smile was certainly genuine now, as if he'd just tripled with the bases loaded. "Though his ancestors hundreds of years ago probably were brought in chains from Africa," Mr. Lemon said.

Fair enough. Peewee had no quarrel with that at all.

The story was part of the family mythology; how one winter evening old Max Lester—letting the *Forward* fold into his lap, watching his wife's skilled hands pull tight under the needle with needed tension the cloth she was turning into a dress, this ancient wondrous female alchemy—made a breakthrough. It had taken him years to realize it, but this was the part that irked. Both hands. She needed both hands to hold the cloth in place, or else it would bunch up and crumple and the thread in the needle would snag. There must, Max Lester thought, be a better way. A simpler way.

All winter long he watched, that winter of 1929, without anyone realizing that he was watching: not Miriam who was too busy sewing, not Ruth who after seven years of bookkeeping had been dating a dapper young Hebrew-school teacher she'd met at a dance and was sometimes out in the evenings, not the younger girls who had plenty of homework to do. All winter long Max watched, and then on an unseasonably warm day in March, that first inaugural day of false spring, he disappeared. He was not to be found in his usual places for tea; he returned to the apartment only to share supper with his family, then he was gone again, out into the dark. He was working on something, was all he would say, working in the shop of a friend. For five days and nights this continued. Was Max Lester having an affair? If this thought ever crossed Miriam Lester's mind as she bent over the sewing machine, she never once let on. The fifth night, a Saturday it was, with Ruth out with her Hebrew teacher, and the other girls except Hindy at a party down the block, Miriam slumped on the sewing machine and cried. No one had ever seen her cry before, not even when the two boys died, and only little Hindy saw her now.

"What's wrong, Mama?" the child said, frightened, pulling on her mother's sleeve. Miriam bolted upright, wiped her eyes with her arm. She'd forgotten the child was home.

"It's nothing, *bubbeluh,*" she said, hugging the child around the waist. "I was only thinking of Russia. It made me sad. It won't happen again," she added. "Now go to your room and play."

The child, satisfied, returned to her room, not asking what it was about Russia that would make a mother cry, content that it would not happen again.

Her husband, who returned to the apartment soon after, didn't even notice she'd been crying, though her eyes were still rubbed red. He was too caught up with excitement, with the gift of his lifetime dream. A gift for Miriam first, and then for the world.

Entering the apartment with his key, setting something heavy down in the hall, he swept into the living room like some Russian or Polish count, lifted his wife bodily from her seat at the sewing machine, turned her face to him and kissed her heartily on the lips, something he had not done in two American decades. Miriam, out of some long-dormant female reflex, kissed him back, long and hard, and then pushed him away from her.

"What's the matter, Max?" she said. "Have you been drinking?"

"Drinking the beauty of spring," he said (for he considered himself something of a gentleman poet, in addition to everything else). "Drinking in the wine of my love's fine hands," he said, taking her bruised fingers in his. For the truth was he had had a bit of schnaps with Hymie, in whose shop he'd been spending the last five days, to celebrate his victory. And then another little bit, a celebration Miriam had tasted on his lips. "If I am drunk, I am drunk with genius," he ventured. "Drunk on two little schnapses I am not."

"Why are you talking so crazy?" Miriam asked, just as another key turned in the hallway lock and Ruthie stepped into the room, returning from her date.

"How was your evening?" Max said with bubbly unconcern. Ruthie, he knew, could well take care of herself.

"Fine," Ruth replied, ending all discussion of her private affairs with a word, as she always did. "Who's talking crazy about what?"

Miriam found a handkerchief to better wipe her eyes. Ruth had noticed immediately what her father had not: that Miriam had been crying, perhaps for a long time.

"Your father's talking crazy," Miriam said. "Waltzing in here like some *goyische* gentleman. Like he just swallowed a cat. I think he got hit by a streetcar maybe, and fell on his head."

"The streetcars don't run this late," Ruth said. It was the kind of remark that had earned her a reputation for perfect logic, for total seriousness. Her humor darted past them like a bird, too slight to be seen.

"See," Max said. "My daughter believes in me, even if my dear wife doesn't. Where are the other girls, by the way? I want them all to see."

"Hindy's asleep," Miriam said. "The others are out at a party. Which you might know if you'd been around here lately. To see what?"

"Maybe we should wait till tomorrow," Max said, "to see what I brought home from Hymie's shop."

"Maybe we should," Ruth said.

Max got no satisfaction from Ruthie's face. "Maybe we shouldn't," he said. "The others can see it later."

Not till he'd hurried away into the hall to retrieve his package did Ruthie grin at her mother, and did her mother, buoyed as always by Ruthie's solid presence, grin back.

"You still like him?" Miriam asked.

The question referred to Ruthie's Hebrew teacher, of course. Ruth shrugged, looked down at the wooden floor swept spotless except for some bits of cloth that had strayed from the sewing machine, and nodded. Miriam knew her eldest daughter, if not very well, at least this well: that something serious was in the air.

In fact, Ruth's beau, Louis A. Brunig, had asked for her hand in marriage not more than an hour before. And Ruth, in the shy, bosomy flesh of her twenty-sixth year, had accepted. He'd taken her hand and then arm in arm the way God made people to fight off the world together, they'd walked through the warm yet breezy March night, all the way down from Fourteenth Street; from Luchow's, where Louis Brunig had taken her to dinner; and not a hundred yards from where, across the street in the evening privacy of a bench in Union Square Park, he had popped the ultimate question.

But Ruth didn't mention it that night. Full as her young breast must have been, she didn't say a word of her betrothal, not then or for two weeks after. Papa Max was excited about something. She would let Papa Max have his day.

On Monday, when Louis Brunig stopped by the store to say hello, which was his habit of late before going off to teach, she explained to him the reason for the two extra weeks of secrecy. If the Hebrew teacher was at all hurt by her priorities, he pretended not to show it. Ruth said she loved him, and she surprised him by kissing him full on the lips behind the closed door of her bookkeeping cubicle. She promised she would make it up to him.

Her father never realized the sacrifice. He was too caught up in himself. God had invented the *meshuganeh* universe in six days. Max Lester had invented the sewing-machine foot in five.

For a shortstop, one critical skill was the ability to sacrifice. He didn't need home-run power, but he had to be able to move a man along.

The important thing, Peewee knew, was not to jab at the ball with the bat. That would produce too solid a bunt, would lead to a sure force-out, maybe to a double play. The way to sacrifice was to slide your right hand up the bat and sort of catch the ball on the thick end, letting the bat go slack at the impact, even drawing it back. This would drop a nice, soft roller down the first- or third-base line.

That was when you were moving a man along. Bunting for a base hit was another matter. You couldn't telegraph your intentions by sliding your hand up the bat. That would bring the third baseman charging in to throw you out. To bunt for a base hit you had to wait till the last possible moment, then drop the bat straight down, pull the bat on impact, at the same instant lighting out for first almost before the ball hit the ground. As a righty, he was better off dropping it down the third-base line. Pushing it past the pitcher toward second was an especially tricky business. Better left for lefties to drag it there most of the time.

All winter long Peewee had practiced bunting: sliding his hand up the thick end of the bat, laying down an imaginary ball. He'd gotten, he knew, quite good at it. Though if anyone asked him how he could tell—as Eli once did—he was hard put to give an answer. It was something you just felt in your bones.

That morning, for the first time in months, there had not been a brown paper bag. His mother had had no time to fix a sandwich, what with the men arriving with the ominous hospital bed and she having to get ready to go to the hospital to bring Grandma Lester home. Instead of a paper bag she had given him the forty-two cents it would cost to buy soup, a sandwich, chocolate milk and a hated dish of raspberry pudding. He bought the soup, a sandwich (bologna) and the milk. The nickel for the pudding he pocketed, against some future use. Probably his mother knew he would.

What he might do with the unpuddinged nickel, he thought, was begin to save up for a diary for himself, like the diary of his mother's that he had accidentally come upon a few weeks before, buried deep in the bottom drawer of the desk in the dark back room. He'd been rummaging by himself one gray and rainy afternoon, sticking his nose in the silken womblike smell of bundles of faded talises, shooting paper clips with rubber bands at the higher boxes, yanking idly as he often did at the bottom drawer, which was not locked but somehow stuck closed by something that was caught inside. On this day he must have yanked extra hard. The drawer came suddenly open in his hand. In a box that had jammed the drawer he found nothing but old and half-used spools of thread, some one-cent stamps and pennies coated with grime, and one thin dime, which Peewee transferred to the pocket of his pants. Beneath the box and a stack of colored cloths he found a battered wooden roulette wheel. Of this he thought he might make a salvageable game, but the long-dormant wheel was too warped to turn and probably had been in that condition when it was placed in the drawer long ago, impossible to mend yet perhaps equally impossible to discard. He was about to stuff the stuff back into the drawer when he noticed stuck in the back, hidden almost as well as a false bottom, a book with its cover missing, the first page of which had turned through the years the same ocher color as the inner wood of the drawer. Picking up the book, its fragile naked spine a crisscross of ancient threads, he read on the first page the words: "The Wanamaker Diary, 1922." Beneath that, in the middle of a circle design of leaves and flowers, was a place for Name and another place for Address. Under Name a thin dark pen in his mother's handwriting had written: Ruth Lester. Under address, in the same hand, it said: 212 Rivington Street. Beneath these was a printed drawing of a lady writing with a quill pen, with her nose in the air.

Idly and with no great interest at first, he flipped through the pages of the book. The first half was filled, page after page, with the same thin, neat, lovely handwriting which he knew to be his mother's. Midway through the book the writing stopped. His heart began to beat faster beneath the Dodgers shirt he was wearing as he saw what he had in his hand: a secret diary his mother had kept when she was a still-unmarried girl of nineteen. An unpleasant feeling crept over him, spread through his chest like disease: a feeling he knew to be guilt. The same feeling he'd had when so far back he could hardly remember it, fat aunt Hindy had caught him and Phil in the bathroom of her house, both of their pants down, looking at each other's meckies. He knew at once what he had to do to make that feeling go away. He had to put the diary and everything else back in the drawer, just the way he had found it. He was about to do exactly that, or maybe he was about to do exactly that, when far away down the long dark passageway he heard his parents' key in the hallway door. Carefully he placed the diary back in the drawer, and the roulette wheel and the cloths on top. The box that had jammed the drawer he shoved behind the desk. Then the hallway door was opening. Standing, brushing dirt from the knees of his corduroy pants, he switched off the bald overhead light, closed the door behind him, and with studied casualness, as if he'd just turned a

3-6-3 double play, moved through the ghostly house to greet his folks. He hadn't done anything bad, he told himself, merely by making sure that some stupid old drawer would not get stuck again.

He did not know why anyone would write down secrets anyway, if no one was supposed to read them. What kind of secrets could an old mother have?

Carrying his dark brown tray with both hands, planting each foot carefully so as not to spill his tomato-rice soup, he moved toward the only half-empty table he could see and placed his tray and then himself at the empty end. Several spaces away at the other end of the long narrow table, a gang of rowdy sixth-grade boys were up to their usual dumb tricks.

He glanced across the table, far across the cafeteria, to where a gaggle of girls from his class were giggling their lunch away. Even as he looked he saw the one bright eye and the comma of dark hair of Beverly Rosenthal looking back across the room at him. Her one visible eye met his. Then she turned away to the other girls. An instant later Peewee studied his soup. It was interesting, he told himself, that you could hardly even see the rice, though it lay no more than an inch below the surface.

If he had a diary of his own, Peewee decided, the very first entry would begin: "Today Beverly Rosenthal wore a nice pink sweater. She liked it when I looked at her."

Then he crossed that out in his mind with a heavy pen. He had a better idea. "Today is Opening Day," it would say.

He looked at the large school clock on the wall, its great white face in the windowless cafeteria like a bleached mechanical mockery of the sun. It was thirteen minutes before one in the afternoon. The game, the season itself, would begin at 2:05. Pee Wee Reese, of course, would be at short.

# 2

SHE COULD NOT, or would not, or dared not remember what had happened before, or how she had come to this place. She knew only in some instinctive way, as a country bird knows where to build its nest, that this vacant darkness suited her: that here she could live, and that here most likely she would die.

Above the battered basement room, the cross-beamed quicksilvered tracks of the Jerome Avenue el curved sharply. The trains with their dimming interiors screeched and screamed as they slowed into the station. The screams passed above her head in time unnoticed, and above the old man in his bed, who was deaf in any case, and above the cats who buried themselves alive in the coal bin adjacent to her room, and above the white-haired nigger who slept in the alley outside her door. Unnoticed in time perhaps because there were other screams, closer to the ear.

To the left of the soiled two-story gray frame building was a lumber-yard. Stacks of beige and yellow and ocher lumber half as high as the house and solid as a fortress walled off in a great piled L the otherwise empty lot from the street. Twice each week great flatbed trucks stacked high with additional lumber held in place by iron chains shook and trembled over the cobblestones from distant parts of the country she had never seen, and rumbled into the lumberyard. When the great trucks, stripped of their burden, rumbled out of the yard and under the el, they made more clatter empty than full. And in their wake left the screams of the electric saw, cutting the sweet-smelling lumber evenly to

size. The electric saw whined and screamed from seven each morning
to six each night, never seeming to lose its appetite. The whine of the
saw struck her breast as mean-spirited and self-pitying compared with
the fire-hurling heroics of the train.

"Damn blasted saw," the nigger would say each morning. "How
they expect a person to sleep around here?"

She would cluck her gums several times in sympathy and agreement
and remembered habit and hand him a thick white enamel mug filled
with hot instant coffee she had made. He would raise the mug to her in
a toast of thanks, and he would drink the coffee standing outside the
basement door, because though she had given him coffee nearly every
morning for more than a year, she had never once invited him inside.

For his part, he was grateful for the coffee. He never questioned the
limits of their acquaintance. Sometimes in the mild spring evenings in
the surcease of the silent saw they would sit together in front of the
building on overturned milk crates and pass the time with random,
disconnected remarks, which seemed all she was capable of of late, as if
she were preoccupied. But whether she cared for him any more than
she cared for the cats who lived in the coal bin—for whom she set out
two soup plates of milk each evening, but otherwise showed disdain—
he did not know. He was comfortable in their silences.

The Rag Lady, they called her in the neighborhood. She knew this
without comprehending, certainly without caring. She had long since
crossed the border of abstractions. Living meant surviving. Surviving
meant the trash of the here and now, the sun-dappled dark delights of
the here and now.

"A pair of shoes," she'd say, for instance, referring to her most
valuable find of the day.

"How new?" the nigger might say.

"New," she'd say, if the rubbed-worn points where the previous
owner's little toes had gone were not entirely worn through.

"A dollar," the nigger would guess, putting delight in his voice. "I
bet he gave you one whole dollar."

"Thirty cents," she'd say, perhaps remembering with satisfaction the
way she had bargained Rudy the Junkman up from a quarter.

They might not speak again the entire night, sitting in the fast-
falling dark. Or they might. All the nights were the same. Just as all the
days were the same, as all days without hope or anticipation are the

same. And yet maybe it was not so. Perhaps in the recurring spaces between one garbage can and the next, in the five feet or ten feet or fifty feet, perhaps in these linear passages hope was born anew each time, hope of some useful new find beneath the greasy paper bags and the orange skins; and thus sustained however faintly the dim candle of life in her breast. Something there was that kept her going. Perhaps that was it.

The ship was called the *Jungfrau*. It was of German registry, sailing out of Southampton. They had a bunk bed, Max and Miriam Lestrakovsky, in a line of perhaps two dozen other bunk beds. Beside the bed were three cardboard cartons tied with string: all the possessions they had been able to drag with them, halfway across Russia to London, by horse cart and train and boat, and now to America. All of it was clothing—Max's spiffy suits, Miriam's house dresses, a few things for the child—except for one unlikely item: a green felt cloth with numbers on it, and a small polished wooden roulette wheel, its numbers 1 to 36 painted alternately red and black, with 0 and 00 painted green: a wedding gift from a rich distant uncle of Miriam's in Petersburg, which they had brought along thinking it would amuse them on their long ocean voyage—except that all during the voyage the painted ship dipped and bobbed so mercilessly that there was never a level surface on which to place the wheel. So it remained in one of the cartons, while Miriam seated at one end of the bed held the post with one hand against the rolling of the ship and her infant girl Ruth with the other, and Max sat at the other end of the bed, regaling his bride with tales he had heard of the life that awaited them in America. In America, he said, there were buildings on every street that were taller than mountains. These buildings were filled from top to bottom with offices, he said, and in every office was waiting three jobs for any man who wasn't afraid to work: a man could work around the clock if he wanted, to build up his family fortune overnight. His words hurried on in a rush. The tsar did not persecute the Jews in America, he said, and that alone would make the trip worthwhile, he told her, would make this seasickness one day seem a joke, a small price to pay. There was no tsar of any kind, he said, pulling from the back pocket of his trousers a folded, worn copy of the United States Constitution, printed in small Yiddish type, which he'd purchased in London.

Why, in America, he said, folding open the little booklet, showing her the Yiddish page, in America any native-born citizen who attained the age of thirty-five years could be president.

"You know what that means, Miri darling?" he said. Absorbed in swallowing, she closed her eyes and gently shook her head from side to side. "That means one of our own sons," he said. "One of our own sons who will be born in America can grow up to be the president."

Miriam did not at first respond. She waited till she felt a little better, a moment's passing, and wiped the sweat from her brow, and moved the blanket from under the baby's chin. Then she looked Max in the face, determined she would keep no unnecessary secrets from him. "The boys in the family were weak," she said. "It may be we'll only have girls."

"Posh!" Max said. "Nonsense! In frozen Russia maybe the boys were weak. In America they'll be strong." He saw her look down at the child, and he realized he had gotten her upset. "Listen to me!" he said. "A child of mine grow up to be president. Ridiculous! But maybe," he added, touching the child's thin hair, "maybe little Ruth here will bring forth a president!"

Miriam looked up from the child's face, looked directly at her husband, and smiled the smile she knew had won his heart. She thought: I settled for a dreamer. Maybe even a fool.

"I think he really believed it," Louis Brunig would say whenever he retold that story. "I think they all really believed it—that lie we heard over there. They just had to set foot in America, and poof! they'd give birth to the first Jewish president. No matter that they couldn't speak English yet."

Louis would take another sip of schnaps, or tea, or whatever it was he was drinking. He usually told the story after dinner, when people from outside the family were over, who hadn't heard it seventeen times.

"You know the first time I heard that story," Louie would say. "It was a freezing cold night before the war, February twenty-second, it was. The night little Benny here was born." (Benny's face would grow hot while his mother corrected his father: February twenty-fourth, she'd say.) "Whatever," his father would say, and then, noticing the look on Benny's face—a look much closer to tears than his father ever imagined—would add, "Of course, what am I saying, it must be the schnaps talking. February twenty-fourth. A regular blizzard it was. Me at the hospital pacing back and forth, just like in the movies, the doctors in with Ruthie, Max on a wooden bench in the corridor, Mama was here at the house, I think, taking care of Eli, who was only six years old."

He'd lean back in his chair and his eyes would glaze over a bit, from schnaps or fond emotion, and he'd see as if it were only last week the heavy snow falling all day, large thick flakes that did not sleet down but tumbled from the sky like feathers, turning the neighborhood into one of those smooth crystal balls you could win for a prize in Coney Island and in which, if you placed the smooth ball in your palm and shook, the whole calm interior would be quickly ablaze with snow; as if God had taken the universe into His hand that day and shaken it and made it snow: this feeling that all expectant fathers have on the day their son is born: that God has taken extraspecial measures; that God this day has done something new.

With Ruthie in the hospital since the night before, with the baby possibly due at any time, Louie had stayed home, canceling Hebrew-school classes because of the snow, studying his Talmud, calling the hospital every hour to see how Ruthie was, the nurse saying she would call him when the time was near. Till at nine in the evening the nurse did call, and with fourteen inches of snow on the ground and the snow still falling, Louie and Ruthie's father Max both pulled on galoshes, wrapped themselves in their overcoats and scarves, pulled their fedora hats low over their eyes and stepped out into the swirling whiteness of the night.

Sitting in the parlor window, watching the two men, her husband and her eldest daughter's husband, breaking the virgin snow with their galoshes, disappearing out of sight on the next block, Miriam Lester felt the chill spread inside her, the frozen night half remembered when they had come to the village and taken Alex away. The night she heard the shot she never heard.

She had thought she would lose her mind back then, till Max Lestrakovsky's kindness saved her. She won him with her smile, a smile born of some unconscious will to survive; she kept him with her body, she promised him her love; and she was as good as her word: she loved him still.

But after all these years she remembered the flesh of Alex, the way he filled her up, the things he made her do that she had never done since. Still, after all these years, only keeping busy gave her peace. Only the throbbing sound of sewing stilled the silent shot.

She knew what people thought through all these years: friends, neighbors, even, she suspected, their own girls. Max Lester, they thought, such a fine man in every way! But how could he be so selfish? How could he spend his life drinking tea, playing at his inventions, as if life itself were a game, while poor Miriam sewed her fingers to the nubs supporting all of them? She knew the way they talked. He must have heard it, too, and never said a word, but sipped his tea.

"Ach," she said, looking out the parlor window onto Townsend Avenue. Why do I remember this? Knowing why. Because in her memory, or more precisely in her invention, it was snowing just like this when they came. Knowing why. Because why should today be any different? Because every day of her life she remembered, this old Jewish lady in a window on a winter night.

Two blocks away at the corner of Mt. Eden Avenue Max Lester and Louie Brunig turned left and trundled up the hill, stepping high against the building snow. If Max knew she still thought all that, he didn't say. He didn't dare to ask. He didn't want to know.

"So," he said to his son-in-law, both of them getting breathless now, their noses stinging, breathing in with their mouths, tasting the wet flakes. "Will it be a boy or a girl?"

"A girl, I think," Louie said. "Ruthie wants a girl. One of each. Rachel we're going to call her, if it's a girl. Ruthie's made a little dress already."

"I saw," Max said. "I wish she hadn't done that yet."

"Ruthie's not superstitious," Louie said.

Higher and higher they had to lift their knees against the steepening hill and the ever-piling snow. "You're telling me?" Max said, his breath coming in short gasps now. "I know my little girl. My Ruthie."

"Anyway," Louie said, "Miriam says girls run in the family."

"That you don't have to tell me," Max said.

Then it was too hard to talk on the last and steepest block. All the way from the house they hadn't seen a soul in the streets in the bright and furry night, or a car that dared to move. The half-buried cars that lined the curbs had sunk to black and silent tortoiseshells. They reached the hospital steps and moved one behind the other up a narrow path an anonymous caretaker had shoveled on the steps, and reached the top and tall Max Lester, one hand on the snow-covered brass-colored bar, trying to catch his breath before he could pull open the door, said, "And if it's a boy?" And the shorter Louie Brunig, stamping the snow from his galoshes, banging his hands together against the cold, said, "Benjamin." A puff of white breath issued into the night with the word, as if in Rome they just had named a pope.

The ball was hit to his right, a hot smash between short and third. That was what usually happened when his father told boring stories about him for the seventeenth time, him sitting there like a ghost, blushing but invisible. The ball would be hit to his right, deep into the hole, the hardest play for a shortstop to make. The play in all of base-ball of utmost grace, except perhaps for the 3-6-3. The play that felt the best if you did it right.

The key, of course, was to know the hitter. A right-handed pull hitter up, you'd be shading toward the hole in any case, and playing back near the edge of the grass, unless he was fast and you had to cheat in a couple of steps. Next you'd pick up the sign from the catcher. A fast ball—especially if your pitcher had a good one—you had to hold your ground in case the hitter ripped it up the middle, made you flag it down to your left. But a let-up or a curve, a good hitter would slam it through the hole before you could leave your feet unless you broke with the pitch. Not exactly *with* the pitch—that would tip off the hitter to what was coming, he could murder it into the seats. But a split second after the pitch, a split second before the crack of the bat, too late for the batter to pick up on your movements, too late for him to adjust his swing. Then came the crack of the bat, and you could tell. A solid crack and it would be there, skimming along the grass toward the hole, pre-cisely where you were headed. The third baseman would try to flag it down but he'd never get there in time, playing shallow as he was. He'd cut in front of you, blocking your vision for a second, but it was the shortstop's play all the way. If it was a truly hot smash, you'd have to leave your feet, dive into the hole, try to choke it in the webbing, land in a splatter of dirt, scramble up and try to make the throw. He'd have to be real slow, an Ernie Lombardi type, for you to get him then. It was more a matter of luck than finesse, that diving scramble in the dirt. But with any kind of a bounce, with a bit of grasspull slowing it down, you could keep your feet, backhand the ball while running onto the grass— the pleasant satisfying weight of the ball nestling in the pocket of your glove—plant your spikes in two quick steps, turn, and fire rifle-armed, overhand all the way, an echoing strike into the legsplitting first baseman's glove. If you pulled it off you'd get him by half a step. Maybe less. And if it was the third out, you'd trot nonchalantly to the dugout, and in those five seconds with the cheers raining down all around, all would seem righter with the world than in any other five seconds imaginable.

There was quicksand and there was earth. Shortstop was solid earth.

"So, *nu?*" one of the listeners would say impatiently, Louie having left them stranded there in the snow on the hospital steps, without ever getting to the point. "What's the point? What was Max's great prophecy?" And Louie, his mind having wandered for a moment, lost in the falling feathers, having forgotten the point himself, was reminded of it again and resumed his tale.

"So we got to the hospital," he said. "It was snowing out, I think. Did I mention that it was snowing?"

"You mentioned, you mentioned," Mickey Hirsch or somebody would say, a weary groan in his voice.

"It was snowing," Louie would say. "So we went up to the desk, and the nurse told me Ruthie was in delivery already. Three whole hours we had to wait and then, a little after midnight, they wheeled her in, Ruthie with the baby in her arms. It looked like a boiled beet, like Mama makes. I said to her, 'It's a girl?' Ruthie shook her head. So I went out to the hallway and I sat on the bench next to Max, and I said, 'You're a grandpa again, Max. It's a boy.' And Max grinned and nodded his head and lit his pipe, as if he knew all along it was a boy. We got up and went in and looked at the baby. Then a nurse took it away and me and Max went back and sat in the hall.

"That's when Max told me the story. The one about on the ship coming over. How he touched little Ruthie's hair when she was only six months old—six months, mind you—and said that maybe Ruthie would bring forth a president. And he said that later, when his two boys died, may they rest in peace, his and Miriam's, he knew it was a sign. It was a sign that he, Max Lester, was not good enough to make a president, but that his own idea on the ship had been right, that maybe one of his daughters would. He thought it the night our Eli was born, he said. His first grandson. But Eli was born sick. The first two days they didn't know if he was alive or dead. So Max didn't say nothing. There was a curse in the family, maybe, a curse about little boys. Just let him live, Max wanted. Never mind about president. Knock wood, Eli got better quickly, after three days no more problems."

"The point . . ." Ruthie would begin to interrupt gently.

"I'm getting to the point," Louie would say. "So he didn't say nothing the night Eli was born. And he didn't say nothing the night Sarah's Johanna was born. She was a girl, you know. And then came Hindy's Philip, just a few months before Benjamin. 'How come not Hindy's Philip?' I said to him. Max shook his head. 'It didn't feel right,' he said, 'Hindy being the youngest. I didn't think it would be hers. Not with that name, Philip Hirsch. It doesn't sound to me like the first Jewish president. A millionaire maybe. Maybe Hindy's Philip will go into business and make the family fortune. And what he'll do with some of his *gelt*, he'll finance his cousin's campaign.'

" 'His cousin's campaign?' I told him. 'What are you talking his cousin?' And that's when he made his prediction. Like he was one of the Prophets or somebody. 'It came to me,' he said, 'when I was looking at the baby. Like a voice from outside it came. Like a voice from the snow.'

" 'What did it say, this voice?' I said to him. I thought he was feeling sick, maybe he should go lie down. And Max said, 'The voice said this is the one. This is Ruthie's boy who'll be the one. Six years she waited from Eli. A little girl she wanted, and she got a boy. So this will be the one. By looking at him I can tell. By the name you picked I can tell. Benjamin Alexander Brunig. The first Jewish president. It has a good ring, no? Like Bernard Baruch, a little.' " Louie shakes his head when he says that. "I looked at him there on the bench with this *meshuganeh* dream in his head. What can you say to a man like that? A smart man he was. But also a lummox. So I didn't say anything. I got up and I walked to the door and I looked outside. It wasn't snowing anymore."

And then came the worst part. One of them—sometimes it would be a man and sometimes it would be a woman, smiling, with manicured fingernails—would turn to Peewee, who was trying to shrivel up and disappear into a corner like a cockroach when you turn on the light, and would say, "Well, Benjamin, what do you think? You think you want to be the president?" to the amusement of all the others. And Peewee would say, mustering all his defiance, "I want to be a baseball player."

"The next Pee Wee Reese he's going to be," his father would say, and Peewee would ask to be excused and would leave the room. "Leave him alone, leave him be," he'd hear his mother saying when he left, and he would go to his room and take out his glove and ball, the glove a Pee Wee Reese model his father had let him pick out in a store in Brooklyn, the ball signed by the president of the National League, and he'd sit on his bed and pound the ball into the pocket of his glove, the dark oiled pocket of his glove, flinging it dead center, again and again, flinging it into the glove for half an hour, till his hand inside the glove was red. All the while flagging grounders to his left. Taking away base hits behind the bag. Practicing in front of empty stands.

On Mr. Lemon's desk was a large paper bag that had not been there in the morning. He did not say what it was. He had them practice their cursive writing for a while, and then, looking at his watch, said it was time for history. But as they reached under their desks for their books he said no, they should leave them there. Today they wouldn't need books for history, Mr. Lemon said. Today they would speak of living history. They didn't know what he was talking about, of course.

Mr. Lemon pointed to three chalk words he had printed on the board. "Who can tell me what these words mean?" he said. "What they have in common." He pointed to the first chalked word: LINCOLN, it said.

"Abraham Lincoln," several of the pupils chimed together.

"He was a president!"

"He freed the slaves!"

"Correct. Correct," Mr. Lemon said. "Abraham Lincoln was the sixteenth president of the United States, and he freed the slaves. That was the easy one. Now what about the next?"

DOUBLEDAY, it said.

Puzzled silence fell upon the room like the sunlight falling in through the windows. They didn't know. Not a single one of the others knew. Only Peewee knew. And he was not about to say.

His heart was thumping, the heat pumping outward now from his chest, up through his neck, his arms, till he couldn't sit still anymore and stood by his seat and did what he had never done before in four years of school. He spoke in class without being called upon.

"Doubleday," he said. He could hear his voice vibrating in his throat. "Abner Doubleday invented baseball."

Like a sudden boom of thunder, laughter filled the room. Hoots and shrieks of laughter as, red-faced and aflame, he took his seat. "Baseball!" someone echoed. What did that have to do with history? The laughter continued in swells across the room till Mr. Lemon rapped on his desk with his ruler.

"If some of you would not be so quick to ridicule others," Mr. Lemon was saying, "you might like to know that Benjamin is correct. Doubleday stands for Abner Doubleday, who invented the game of baseball."

"And now for the third word," Mr. Lemon said.

The silence again was broken by random titters.

Macaroni? Not even Peewee knew that.

"MARCONI," Beverly Rosenthal intoned. She had stood for some reason between her own seat and Peewee's right shoulder, her blue skirt less than a foot from him. "Marconi," she repeated, thinking aloud now, with less than her usual certainty. "Marconi . . . I think . . . was the man who invented the radio."

Beverly remained standing, as if waiting for the same waves of laughter that Peewee had received. Her small hand was hanging at her side, at the side of her blue skirt, limp fingers only inches from his own. An unaccountable impulse seized him, to reach out and take her hand. He clasped his hands on his desk lest they reach out and touch her on their own.

This time there were no laughs. They didn't dare. "Very good, Beverly," Mr. Lemon said, and Beverly sat down in her seat. As she did she kicked Peewee's ankle lightly with her silver-buckled shoe. It was not a hard kick; it could have been an accident. But Peewee didn't feel like it had been an accident. It was more a conspiracy, a "we-showed-'em" kick, which sent heat across his face and made it, he was sure, glow. A glow that the others would see, a glow that would light up the room.

But they weren't looking at him. They all were looking at the teacher as from the large paper bag on his desk he pulled out a dark purple plastic boxy thing.

"It's a radio!" several squealed.

"Correct," Mr. Lemon said.

"Now, who can tell me," he continued, "what is the relationship today between these three people we've been discussing: Lincoln, who freed the slaves; Doubleday, who invented baseball; and Marconi, who invented the radio?"

Peewee could hardly hide his excitement, could hardly trust his understanding. Mr. Lemon was going to do it! He was going let them listen to the game! Right here in school!

He didn't say this, of course. He had said enough for today. He had said enough, he thought, for a lifetime. Nor did Beverly Rosenthal speak, though the smile on the left corner of her mouth indicated that she, too, knew. But she also knew somewhere in the center of her fourth-grade nine-year-old femaleness that she, too, had said enough for today. Nobody liked a showoff, especially a female one. Peewee Brunig especially, she somehow understood, would not like a showoff. So there was silence in the classroom, for none of the other thirty-one pupils seemed to understand, until Elliott White, the only Negro boy in the class, stood by his seat in the last row of the last aisle by the window.

"If Abraham Lincoln had not freed the slaves—" Elliott White said "even though he did it only so the North would win—then Jackie Robinson might be a slave in Georgia today. And he would not be breaking the baseball color line, which is an important symbol for the Negro people, and for all America. And if you turn on that there radio, and turn it to WHN, ten-fifty on the dial, we will all be able to hear Red Barber and Connie Desmond tell us how Jackie Robinson will hit a home run his first time up in the majors."

"Very good, Elliott," Mr. Lemon said, because no words existed that would have encompassed his admiring astonishment. "Except the part about the home run. For that we'll have to wait and see. Though I concede," he continued, forgetting he was talking to eight- and nine-year-olds, lapsing for a moment into the language of the PTA, "that in symbolic terms a home run would be a fine gesture indeed. A very fine gesture indeed."

He kept talking, then—Mr. Lemon, not Elliott White—about Lincoln and slavery, and about Marconi and the radio. Peewee would have to think about that some other time. The only thing he knew about Italians (wops, Uncle Mickey called them) was that the ones who lived up near 176th Street carried knives, and once a gang—six against one —had taken away his brother's basketball. He did not know they had done things such as invent the radio, though he knew from Uncle Mickey that they weren't as bad as the niggers. Italians killed only for business, Uncle Mickey liked to say, whereas niggers killed for fun. Wops liked money and power, niggers liked the smell of blood. Thus spake Uncle Mickey, whose opinions on such matters were rarely challenged on Townsend Avenue, Uncle Mickey being a cop. Besides which, it fit in with what they wanted to believe; had been brought up to believe. The Chosen People were both above and below the others: above them in exalted intellect, below them in the somewhat dirty passions of the heart. Which left Peewee with two new questions, one of which he would ask his mother, the other of which he would not. The first being why hadn't some Jewish man invented the radio. The second being what was this pleasant but embarrassing glow that was radiating from his chest and out through his arms at the closeness of Beverly Rosenthal.

"And over these electronic waves," Mr. Lemon was saying, as if they didn't know what a radio was, which they both did and didn't, "we will be able to hear from Ebbets Field in Brooklyn, which is about ten miles from here, the voices of the announcers telling us what is happening on the field. Now normally, of course, we do not listen to baseball games in school, but today is different, as Elliott White has mentioned. Baseball is called the national pastime. This is because, I think, more than any other institution in American life except wars, it unites us into one people, one nation, North and South, East and West—everyone out at the ballpark or listening in on the radio, root-root-rooting for the home team. So when a Negro is permitted to play in the major leagues for the first time, that is a historic event. That is what I meant by living history. It is a moment, I think, that all of us who participate in it, even over the radio, will remember for the rest of our lives."

His words triggered in Peewee's mind a memory of a scene from a night perhaps four years before. It was a Friday night. His mother, he could see it still, was lighting the Friday-night candles, saying the quick blessing, and then, as she served the food, telling some story from long before, finishing the story, and then, cutting the *chalah* with the large bread knife with its saw-edged teeth, saying, "I'll never forget that as long as I live!" This concept—that something could happen that you would never forget even if you were as old as his mother, even if you were as old as Grandma Lester—something you would not forget as long as you lived!—this notion intrigued him. And here was Mr. Lemon invoking this memory magic in the name of baseball, of Jackie Robinson, of the Negro race. In the name of America. Peewee made certain he would pay close attention. Anyway, it was the Dodgers, for chrissake.

"A foot," Max Lester said excitedly. "I call it a foot."

He had carried in from the hallway the sewing machine he had brought with him from Hymie's shop, with his invention already attached. He moved Miriam's machine out of the way, her faithful old horse, and replaced it with the new.

"What's that thing hanging down?" Miriam asked. She and Ruthie were standing one on either side of him as Max sat down at the sewing machine and with surprisingly deft fingers began to draw the thread of a white spool through the needle.

"A foot," Max repeated. "I told you, a foot."

"Why do you call it a foot?"

"Because it looks like a foot. What do you say, Ruthie, doesn't it look like a foot?"

"Verily," Ruthie said. "Like a foot."

Max looked up at her, slightly askance, pausing in the final act of threading the needle. "Verily?" he said. "What this means, verily?"

"Nothing," Ruthie said. "Hamlet."

"Oh. Shakespeare," Max said, returning his attention to the last delicate threading. "Hamlet. I'll tell you something. If Hamlet's mother had had a foot on her sewing machine"—pausing to bite off the end of the thread and try again—"they might not have had such trouble over there."

Ruthie laughed, leaned over, kissed the back of her father's head.

"Who's got trouble over where?" Miriam Lester said. "You mean the Hamlisches, over on Delancey Street? She's a no-good runaround. A tramp. The butcher she sleeps with, they say, to get better meat. Too many feet she's got, not too little. Another foot that tramp doesn't need."

"Elsie Hamlisch isn't married," Ruthie said. "She can sleep with whomever she wants."

"Is that so?" Miriam said. "Is that your new attitude? You're not married yet, you can sleep with whomever you want?"

"I didn't say me," Ruthie said. "I said Elsie Hamlisch."

"Well the butcher, it so happens, *is* married," Miriam said.

"Touché," Ruthie replied.

"Hamlet again?" Max Lester said. "All right, enough already. I'm ready. You want to see my foot or not?"

"We want, we want," Miriam said skeptically.

Max took a piece of beige cloth from the side of the table. He folded it an inch from the end, as if to make a hem. He slid the folded cloth under the needle, under his new metal foot. With his right hand he turned the silver wheel that lowered the needle into sewing position. It was poised a quarter-inch above the gap in the metal foot. Then he took Miriam's hand with his left.

"Okay, show already," Miriam said, letting go of his hand.

"Give me your hand," he said, and he took it again. Miriam looked at him a bit strangely this time—he had said that once before, many years ago, with the snow from the blizzard still hiding the ground, the body, her life—give me your hand, he'd said—and she gave him her hand, now as then, and he squeezed it, as if for luck, and she squeezed back, squeezing perhaps not for luck now as for dear life then—and still holding her hand with his left, he lowered the needle ever so slightly more with his right, and he began to pedal his feet on the treadle. The needle began to bob, the machine began to work, the beige cloth to move beneath the foot.

"You can't do it that way," Miriam said, letting go again of his hand. "You have to hold the cloth with your hand."

"Is that so?" Max said. He took his freed hand and stuck it straight up in the air above his head like some daredevil on a trapeze, unafraid. All the while he kept pedalling with his feet, the needle bobbing up and down like a feeding horse, the beige cloth moving through in a straight line beneath his newly invented foot, kept in a straight line by the foot.

"Do it again," she said.

Obligingly Max took the cloth, folded down the other side, slipped it under the needle. Then he said, "No, you do it," and he stood from the chair and made Miriam sit. She found that her whole body was shaking as she sat. Her left fist pressed to her lips. With her right hand she turned the silver wheel that lowered the needle and foot to the cloth. She looked up at him like a child seeking encouragement, looked back at the cloth, and then, one fist still pressed to her lips, began to move her feet on the treadle, guiding the cloth ever so lightly with the other hand. The hem moved through, straight and true, as if she'd been hunched over the machine. As if she were pulling the cloth taut with both hands, as she had always done, as anyone in the world had had to do, until that very moment. When it was done she pulled the cloth from the machine and examined the stitches.

"A foot," she said to the cloth. "You made that?"

"No, the *moloch ha muvid* made it. Of course I made it," Max said. "Where do you think I been all week? Sleeping with the butcher?"

Miriam looked up at her tall, thin, mustached husband. The yellow lamp drew tears on both of her cheeks, suspended halfway down.

"My husband's an inventor," she said quietly.

"*Nu*, will you listen to that," Max said, with loud and mostly false outrage; mostly false but with perhaps an underbelly of truthful pain. "Twenty-six years we're married, she doesn't know I'm an inventor yet."

She stood up then, hugged him then, her face on his broad, thin chest, sobbing openly now. Ruthie, not knowing what to do with herself, turned away, then turned back, sat at the machine, took another piece of cloth, tried it herself. It worked as easily as it looked. Above and behind her, Miriam Lester sobbed in her husband's bony arms, his large hands sticking out well below the sleeves of his wrinkled white shirt.

"You know what Hymie says?" Max Lester was saying, stroking his wife's thick hair. "Hymie says we'll be rich. Hymie says we can sell this to a big company and make a fortune. Ten percent I'm giving Hymie, I told him, for the use of his shop. He's got a friend of a friend who works for Zenger sewing. He's gonna come around next week maybe and take a look. We're going to be rich, Miri. You won't even have to sew anymore."

Miriam, pulling back slightly in his arms, looked up sharply into his

face. "What do you mean, I won't have to sew anymore?" Ruthie,
turned in the chair, watching the happy banter, this talk of instant
wealth, thought she saw in her mother's eyes at that moment a strange
look; frightened, almost. Crazed, almost. Then her mother shook her
head, as if shaking away some ghost. In an instant the look was gone,
had become a joke. "Listen to him," she was saying. "He makes an
invention to make sewing easy. An invention for me, he says. And then
he says I won't have to sew anymore. What kind of gift is that? I'll sew
as long as I want, *Meilach,* and don't you forget it. Rich maybe we'll
be, maybe not. But I'll sew as long as I want." She paused, her voice
again seeming to have turned from a joke to an undercurrent of hyste-
ria. "You understand? I kiss your foot, Max. I kiss your wonderful foot.
But always I'll sew if I want. You understand?"

Max enfolded her again in his arms, pressed his lips to the top of her
head. "Of course, of course," he said. "You'll sew whenever you want.
All I meant," he said, "is that you won't sew with cotton anymore.
With silk, you'll sew. With silk instead of cotton. Like a rich lady can."

She looked up at him again, still in his arms, pressing between her
tight lips a smile, like a dry flower or a dead butterfly. In her eyes was a
look of brightness, almost of passion, a look Ruthie could not interpret,
but one she had never seen before.

*I'll never forget that as long as I live, Ruthie saying, fourteen years
later, around the kitchen table on a Friday night.*

Was that the one? Was that the moment his mother would never
forget? Peewee couldn't be sure. It wasn't so important, that moment.
Probably he was mistaken. Probably it had been something else.

Going to your left was another matter. Altogether different than
going to your right. Going to your right that stop was important, that
instant of planting your spikes, setting yourself. Whereas going to your
left you didn't have to stop; going to your left was fluid grace. Your
body low to the ground, gloved hand stretched out in front of you like a
tiny snow shovel; flagging the horsehide down as it tried to skip by into
center field; a quick hop-skip step to change the angle, to get your
shoulders lined up for the throw to first; then a smooth side-arm toss,
natural, unbroken. You had him dead, you'd taken a base hit away.
Except with a man on first, of course. With a man on first the toss to
second for the double play was easier going into the hole: you fired it

hard and true at the second baseman's glove and hoped he could turn it over in time. Whereas going to your left it depended on where you were. From the right of the bag it was a simple underhanded flip. But if you'd flagged it behind the bag, if your momentum was carrying you on by, you had to while falling away from the bag get the ball out of the glove and toss it behind you, in the direction from which you'd come, broken-wristed, almost; like the left-handed kids trying to write cursive. And the second baseman had to sort of come back for it. That was a pretty one if you could pull it off.

All in all, he'd rather go to his left. He didn't like relying on his arm. His arm, he somehow knew, would be the first to go.

Sometimes they moved you to second when that happened. You didn't need an arm at second; Stanky had no arm at all. But second was not for him. In the majors Peewee Brunig was a shortstop or he was through.

The grass was almost visible now, issuing like a vast green genie out of the purple radio, as the Dodgers in their bright white uniforms with the blue cursive lettering took to the field, fanned out in all directions, Hermanski, Reiser and Walker running out to the outfield, Stanky and Reese trotting to second and short, the unfamiliar shamble of the Negro, this Jackie Robinson, ambling down to first, a warm-up ball in his hand, tossing a grounder across the diamond to rookie Spider Jorgensen at third. Peewee seeing every last detail, the radio drawing it all on his retina, Peewee oblivious now to the sounds from the schoolyard below, to the other kids in the class. ("Do the girls have to listen too?" one of them asked. "Yes," Mr. Lemon replied, with his phrase for the day, "it's living history.") Peewee oblivious, it must be said, even to the nearness two feet to his right of Beverly Rosenthal. Beverly, for her part, unnoticed, watched his face, fascinated by this fascination that she didn't understand, this love between a boy and a ball.

From the purple radio came the sounds of the national anthem, Gladys Goodding at the Ebbets Field organ. Mr. Lemon had them stand beside their seats, hands over their hearts, as they did every Wednesday in assembly. "The Star-Spangled Banner" sung in assembly was boring, but now it stirred Peewee's blood. The true purpose of the national anthem was to open baseball games.

When the organ sounds faded into a noisy cheer from the ballpark far away, Mr. Lemon and the pupils sat, Mr. Lemon leaning back in his chair—something they had never seen before—placing his feet up on his desk, legs crossed comfortably at the ankle, Peewee out of good-boy habit clasping his hands in front of him, as if the better to pay attention, Beverly in imitation doing the same. Elliott White seemed to look out the window but was surely attentive nonetheless; some of the bored girls passed notes back and forth, Mr. Lemon not seeming to care just now as long as they were quiet. This subdued class of fourth-graders heard, but not too many of them cared, as the Braves went down one-two-three in the first before the tosses of Lefty Joe Hatten, who started for the Brooks.

As the field changed hands, there was a commercial for Old Gold cigarettes. (If Jackie Robinson did, indeed, hit a home run his first time at bat in the majors, it would be an Old Goldie.) Then it was the Dodgers' turn: Eddie Stanky leading off, Jackie Robinson second in the order, Pistol Pete Reiser batting third, Dixie Walker, the People's Cherce, hitting cleanup. Pee Wee Reese was batting eighth: an affront. It wouldn't stay that way for long, Peewee knew. Why bat a man eighth whose greatest skills at the bat were the bunt and the hit and run, the moving of a man along? Why move a man along with the pitcher up next? But Reese, at least for today, was batting eighth.

The cigarette spiel was done and Eddie Stanky was stepping into the box. Peewee could see him choking up on the bat, his squat form hunched over the plate, the perfect leadoff man, always looking for a walk, always a league leader in that department.

Stanky, true to form even on Opening Day, looking for a walk, took a ball, a strike, another strike from Johnny Sain, then, choking up even farther, tapped a slow roller to second and was thrown out by a step and a half. And even before the first-base umpire's right arm shot into the air signaling the out, the boos came rolling out of the stands, boos not for Eddie Stanky but for Jackie Robinson, moving from the on-deck circle toward the batter's box, boos mixed with vociferous cheers to be sure, but boos predominating nonetheless: the Ebbets Field faithful booing one of their own. He would change their boos to cheers soon enough; it was all a matter of acceptance; but in the beginning there was the boo. They continued as he stepped with those mincing pigeon toes into the batter's box, standing deep in the corner, bat held high, taking a sweeping Sain curveball that started toward his head and then broke over the inside corner for a strike, Robinson holding his ground all the way, watching the ball right into the catcher's glove. (They would test this nigger's guts many times with curveballs that started toward his head.) And then on the second pitch, a fastball down the inside corner, he swung and popped it up off the handle, toward the stands near third, the boos resounding even louder now as the third baseman easily put it away for the out. The boos continuing as Robinson started back toward the dugout, his baseball career only begun but the prime deed already done—the first Negro to bat in the modern majors. Though to give it lasting meaning, to make the deed stick, he'd soon have to shove his talent down their craw, his base-stealing, slick-fielding, .349-hitting International League–leading talent.

Peewee, dimly aware of this, found himself turning in his seat, looking toward the rear of the classroom, looking at Elliott White. The light from the windows near where he sat was glistening in Elliott White's eyes, glistening more than normal, glistening off extra moisture, Peewee thought. He did not know if Elliott White was fighting back tears because the deed had been done, the major league color line had been broken, or because Robinson had popped to third, had not hit a home run his first time up. Maybe a little of both, Peewee thought.

As Peewee turned back in his seat, his eyes met Beverly Rosenthal's. She, too, apparently had turned to look toward the rear of the room, perhaps to look at Elliott White's reaction, or perhaps only to see what it was that Peewee was looking at. Then he swung around and stared with instant outrage at Mr. Lemon, who, with legs dropping from desk to floor, had just leaned forward and turned off the radio.

"Wha—" Peewee started to say, and then remembered that he was in school. He kept his quiet but still he couldn't believe it. You didn't shut off the radio in the middle of an inning. You didn't turn off the radio with Pistol Pete Reiser coming up.

Mr. Lemon looked at his watch. "I don't think we need to discuss anymore what we just heard. Not today. It was an important moment. I want you all to think about it. It's twenty minutes till the bell. You can leave quietly as you think about it. But don't make any noise in the halls. I don't want you disturbing the other classes."

Peewee gathered up his books and followed the first departers. Beverly Rosenthal stood by her seat a moment, watching Peewee's vanishing back. Then, her thoughts apparently elsewhere, she joined a gaggle of girls who were giggling at the rear of the room.

# 3

WHEN RUTH HAD signed the forms necessary for her mother's release from the hospital, she sat on a dark bench across from the nursing station, waiting while her mother completed one last therapy session upstairs. She waited and watched the nurses come and go, her unoccupied mind straying against her will as it always strayed now to two times: the first time and the last. Sitting in the hospital where Peewee had been born and which she had not visited again for eight years, till the day of her mother's stroke, she saw again the facade of the hotel, forbidding and beckoning at once; the room he took, its fresh-made bed smooth and inviting as an apple yet unbitten; recalled kicking off her shoes as she might have done for Louie long ago, and he holding her, shorter now in her stockinged feet, their first tentative kiss, the heartbeating undressing opening of buttons each for each, kissing again naked to the waist, his chest hair blonder than Louie's was, is, and then of a sudden the abandon bursting forth on the bed, their ferocious playing fiercer than it had ever been with Lou, even when that had been good. And then—but she cuts off the and then. An elderly man has caught her attention, hobbling to the nursing station in a faded bathrobe. A nurse appears, answers the old man's question. Seeing he is in no real need, her mind wanders again, not to where it left off but to the last time, barely a month ago when in the same room at the Concourse Plaza Hotel she had after their lovemaking, instead of smoking a Pall Mall, which she always smoked after their lovemaking, said, "I can't come here anymore." He had looked at her uncertainly and said, "We'll go someplace else, then." And she had said no, that was not what she meant: they had to stop it, everything, altogether. He had looked at her with pain, as if she was out of her mind, which perhaps she was, and asked her why, what was wrong.

"It's because of Benjamin," she said.

"Benjamin?" he said. "Who's Benjamin?" And then, "You mean Peewee? What does he have to do with it?"

"I think he suspects something."

"He's eight years old. He's always in school. How could he suspect?"

Sitting on the side of the bed, pulling on her underthings quickly, ashamed for the first time, now that it was over, she talked while half-naked of her boy. "He suspects. Can't you see it? You've heard the things he says: 'Why do you come over so much, you've got your own house?' 'You're not my dad, you know.' You've heard him say those things, more and more each week."

"That doesn't mean anything. That's just a kid talking. He probably doesn't know what sex is."

"He probably doesn't," she said. "But he knows something's going on. He knows something's wrong. That's why we've got to stop. Before he finds out."

"And Lou—Lou doesn't suspect?"

She shook her head. "Lou doesn't suspect." She rubbed her eyes, her cheeks, with her hands. She stood and went to a chair and pulled her dress over her head. "Lou thinks I'm too good for this." She looked across the room into his face. "I used to think so, too."

Lying naked, he swung his legs off the bed. "I don't believe this," he said. "You're not worried about Lou but you're worried about the kid?"

Her eyes flashed angrily. "Yes," she said. "I'm worried about the kid."

She turned from him, straightened her dress, combed her hair. They had, each time till now, showered together afterward. Some days that had been the loveliest part.

He approached her, stood behind her, placed his hands on her shoulders. "You're just upset. We'll skip Thursday this week. Think about it. You'll change your mind."

She wanted to remain angry, because it would be better, easier, angry, but she was touched by the pleading in his voice. She turned to face him. "I won't," she said quietly. "I can't." She kissed him lightly on the lips for the last time and turned away to hide her despair.

"Mrs. Brunig?"

She looked up, as if in a trance. The nurse at the station was calling her. Shaken but hiding it, as the remembrance always left her shaken, she approached the nurse.

"The ambulance service just called. They'll be late in picking up your mother. There's an emergency somewhere. Perhaps you'd like to get some air, or get coffee someplace. I'm afraid it will be a while."

"Yes," she said, half hearing, and then, regaining control, said, "Yes. Thank you. Perhaps I will." And not hearing the echo of her steps, she walked down the corridor, out into the warm and mocking sun.

Near the schoolyard fence Peewee met his cousin Phil after school each day, so they could walk home together. On this Opening Day, let out of school a full twenty minutes early by Mr. Lemon with Pistol Pete Reiser stepping into the batter's box, Peewee felt he had adequate excuse to hurry home by himself, without waiting for Phil: so as to hear as much of the game as possible. But he decided not to do it. Phil would not know he'd gotten out early and gone. Phil with his stolid fat loyalty might stand there half an hour waiting for him to appear. So instead he put his books on the ground and leaned against the fence and watched the guys his brother's age playing stickball in the yard.

"How'd you get here so fast?" Phil said, sweating, trotting up to him.

Peewee reached down and picked up his books. "Mr. Lemon let us out early. You know what? He let us hear the game in class."

"The game?" Phil asked. "The Dodger game? He did not!"

"He did," Peewee said nonchalantly as they walked toward the corner amid crowds of other kids pouring out.

"He couldn't have," Phil said. "The game's still on."

"Only the first inning," Peewee said. "One-two-three for the Braves. One-two for the Brooks."

"And then? A homer by Dixie?"

"Don't know. He shut it off after Stanky and Robinson. All he wanted us to hear was Robinson. Walker's batting cleanup, by the way. Reiser's third."

They were waiting for a streetlight at the corner of 174th. A crossing monitor was holding them up. Phil looked at the Mickey Mouse watch that encircled his fleshy wrist, the watch a payoff from his father the week after Baby Lisa was born. "We can hear most of it on my new portable at home," he said. "While we're having a catch." The portable radio was another present from his father, a week ago; the day that Lisa was one.

Peewee did not reply right away. The light turned green and they walked.

"Something wrong?" Phil asked.

"Don't know," Peewee said. "They brought Grandma Lester home today. To our house. Don't know if I can have a catch. Don't know if I can listen to the game, even."

"What they expect you to do? Take care of her?"

"Don't know," Peewee said.

"We can listen at my house," Phil said.

"Yeah," Peewee replied. But his voice lacked its usual enthusiasm. If you couldn't listen to a Dodger game in your own house, what was the point of anything?

"I can put the radio on the stoop," Phil said. "Maybe we can play some I Declare War and hear the game at the same time."

"I guess," Peewee said. "If they let me."

Phil was somewhat unhappy of late, Peewee had noticed. It was because of Baby Lisa, his mother said. Phil had a sister, Annie, who was six years old and whom Peewee absolutely adored. She had been born on the same day as Peewee, February 24, only two years later, and this gave them wishing stars in common. Peewee and Annie had a blushing if unspoken understanding that being cousins and born on the same date as well, one day they would marry.

Between Phil and Annie there was a normal brother-sister relationship, sometimes fighting and sometimes tolerating. But the previous spring, six years after their family had seemed complete—no one else of all the Lester sisters had had more than two children—Aunt Hindy and Uncle Mickey had had another; had had Baby Lisa. Jolly Hindy, who had been depressed before the baby came, he'd heard his parents say, had taken on new life with the new child, often sitting on the stoop or in the front parlor of their house, knitting booties or whatever it was that new mothers knitted, while the baby slept peacefully in her carriage outside by the stoop, the same gray carriage that had been used, in their infancy, by Phil and Peewee and Annie. Little Annie was enchanted with her baby sister, helping her mother change the diapers, helping to give her her bottle. It was like having a real live doll to play with. Not so Phil, who since the baby came had felt neglected, his mother always with the infant, his father the cop away at all odd hours, which was the life of a policeman, his life and work shifts never his own, he said.

Neglected in his own home, Phil hung out more than ever in Peewee's, two houses away. He and Peewee had become inseparable. And if the price Phil had to pay for this was to allow Peewee, who was shorter and lighter and nearly a year younger, to be the leader he was willing to pay that price. He was willing to crouch endlessly at the entrance to Eli's room, swiping imaginary tags as Peewee raced down the long dim corridor and practiced stealing second. Phil had no ambition to make it to the majors. He was glad to help Peewee toward his goal. Peewee (he felt deep down) would never make it without him. While to Peewee being the leader of the two though he was nine months younger was perfectly natural; it was a question that never came up. It was the grace of shortstops.

Now, as they walked home from school, the grace of shortstops was being squashed by fear that had settled onto Peewee's head: the dark presence of a sick and wheel-chaired and probably dying Grandma Lester in his house. Phil did not seem concerned by Grandma Lester's arrival. But she would not be staying in Phil's house, to be seen in her infirmity every day. Phil was not afraid of the dark, either. The only fear Peewee knew for certain that he and Phil shared in equal measure was the fear of the Rag Lady, who prowled the neighborhood like an evil witch, a secret sack on her back.

*"If you don't be good, the Rag Lady will take you away."*

This flat, dark warning they and all the other children of the neighborhood had heard from their parents so often the last few years that it had become a truth beyond question. Else why would the warning be ubiquitous? Jews were smart, Italians were tough, and the Rag Lady stole boys and girls who didn't behave themselves. Merely seeing her made children believe.

But the Rag Lady was out of doors, the Rag Lady you could run from if you saw her coming in time. Grandma Lester was something else. From her he would not be able to run, would not be able to hide.

And though he could project onto her no evil intent, her forthcoming presence was beginning to loom in his mind like some eclipse of the baseball sun; as if the demon-filled dark of night would settle in at three each afternoon, and on weekends all day long.

"Hey, I heard a good one today," Phil said, determined to shake Peewee out of his withdrawn mood. It wasn't like Peewee, not on Opening Day. "You want to hear it?"

"Nah," Peewee said, and then looked over at Phil to be sure he hadn't hurt his feelings. "Let's get a move on," he said. "We're missing most of the game. They got Reese batting eighth, can you believe that?"

Phil could believe it. "Not for long," he said, though secretly he was pleased. Eighth was where Pee Wee Reese belonged. He was a good fielder, but who did Peewee think he was? Dixie Walker?

"Let's move it then," Phil agreed.

As they hurried toward Townsend Avenue, Peewee wondered about Beverly Rosenthal. Probably Beverly Rosenthal would want somebody rich, he thought, seeing that she lived in the swanky Lewis Morris. She wouldn't want the shortstop for the Dodgers. Whereas Annie wouldn't care; Annie would follow him, love him, anywhere. As he would her. Though they might have been rich themselves one time, all of them. Lived on Easy Street. He'd heard Grandma Lester tell it a hundred times. How Grandpa Max had given away his foot.

"For nothing he gave it away," Grandma Lester used to say. "For nothing! A rich man he could have been! But not Max! He had too much pride to bargain. 'I'm not a businessman,' he used to say. As if that was an answer. 'We do nicely the way we are,' he used to say. What did he care, drinking his tea with his cronies, and me sewing my life away? A rich man, he could have been. But not him! A gentleman he wanted to be. A gentleman! But not rich.

"For five hundred dollars he gave it away, his foot. Would you believe? Don't do it, Ruthie told him. Advice from Mr. Loeb himself she'd gotten. Don't do it, she told him. Get a patent on it first. But would he listen? Of course not. That skinny *goy* came from the Zenger Sewing Machines—Mr. Schmeed, his name was, I'll never forget it— and put down three hundred dollars cash. Max was ready to take that till Mr. Schmeed heard what Ruthie was saying and went up to five hundred. Take it or leave it, he said, now or never. And Ruthie said never—the nerve she had—but Max took it anyway. Five hundred dollars for his lifetime invention! The biggest sewing machine company in the world they became, and all because of Max's foot! And what did he have to show for it! *Bubkus!* When I think of the life we could have had!"

Then her voice would trail off. And no one would ask her about the life they could have had.

Peewee turned on the yellow plastic radio that sat on a shelf in the kitchen. At the end of three innings, Red Barber was saying, there was still no score. He poured himself a glass of milk, took some Oreos from the closet and sat at the kitchen table to listen to the top of the fourth. And noticed—it was the first time he had ever consciously noticed this —that his mind could think of two opposing things at once: that while he was listening to Lefty Joe Hatten dispose of the Braves in the fourth, he was also thinking of wheelchairs.

As the top of the fourth ended, Phil came through the left-open door and down the corridor, his turned-on portable in his hand.

"I rounded up the other guys," he said. "We're gonna play I Declare War on the corner. You got any more cookies?"

Peewee went to the closet and took out two more Oreos and handed them to Phil. He would have rather played punchball, but there wouldn't be time for a whole game before he had to go to Hebrew school. Perhaps that was why there had never been a Jewish shortstop, he thought. They were always being packed off to Hebrew school.

Sometimes he was asked by aunts or uncles why he was a Dodger fan, living as he did in the Bronx, only a mile from Yankee Stadium. "Because the Dodgers are the best," he would say. The truth was that he did not know the answer. Being a Dodger fan seemed to be inherited somehow, like his muscles and his bones, although his parents knew nothing of baseball and wanted the Dodgers to win only so that Peewee would be happy and eat his entire supper.

The fact that Peewee was the only passionate Dodger fan of all the younger kids on the block clearly made life more interesting. It kept the pavement outside alive with arguments over who was better: Reese or Rizzuto, Reiser or DiMaggio, Hugh Casey or Joe Page. Life without those endless arguments would have been unimaginable. Life without the Dodgers would cease to be. He was proud, too, that it was the

Dodgers who were bringing up Jackie Robinson, that it was the Dodgers who were breaking the color line. Why he was proud of this he didn't consciously know. He did not know any Negroes personally, if you didn't count Elliott White, who was only a boy in his class. He had never heard a good word spoken of any of them.

Perhaps that last, when you got right down to it, was the reason. Though he certainly didn't think that then. He only knew that whatever the Dodgers did was right. He was a Dodger fan in much the same way that he was Jewish, almost by birth and certainly without complaint.

Noticing Phil's impatience, he drained the dregs of his milk, and he placed the white-coated glass in the sink. He left it there without washing it—without even filling it with water, which his mother hated him to do. This act of rebellion was conscious, though its motive was not quite clear. Perhaps because the Dodgers were not yet winning. Perhaps because Grandma Lester was coming here.

He remembered quite clearly the day it happened. A Tuesday afternoon, three weeks before. With a light drizzle falling outside, he was sitting on the floor of the living room, doing his arithmetic homework. It was long division, the thing he hated most about school after speaking out in class. Hindy had taken Baby Lisa for a checkup at the doctor's, so Annie was visiting with them, sitting on the floor a few feet from Peewee, playing with her jacks. His mother was sitting in the flower-patterned wing chair, knitting something white. His grandmother was sitting in the easy chair, the *Forward* open in her lap.

"Did I tell you," his mother said to his grandmother, moving stitches along her knitting needle, "Morris's girl Andrea got engaged."

"Engaged?" his grandmother said in a slightly hoarse voice. "She's a child, no? How old is she?"

"She's away at college. She's twenty-one already."

"*Oy, vey.* How time flies," his grandmother said.

Which made Peewee wince. It was not his favorite expression, though he figured he heard it from his mother or his father or his grandmother at least once a day. It was his own personal opinion that time crept along, slower than a caterpillar.

Annie, pausing in her jacks after twosies, looked up at Peewee's mother. "What's engaged?" she said.

"Engaged to be married," Ruthie said.

"Oh."

"Aunt Ruthie?"

"What, dear?"

"How do you know when it's time to get married?"

Ruthie counting her stitches and Grandma Lester looking at but not really reading her newspaper both smiled. Peewee, pretending to concentrate on his long division, felt his cheeks grow hot, as if Annie were slyly looking at him.

His mother lowered her knitting to her lap. "When you fall in love, I suppose," she said.

"But how do you know when you're in love?" Annie said.

His mother resumed her knitting. "You'll know, dolling, you'll know," Grandma Lester said.

Peewee was having a difficult time with 12 into 136. Especially amid all this female chatter. If only the rain would stop, he could go find Phil and have a catch.

"Aunt Ruthie?"

"What dear?"

"Did you and Uncle Louie know each other a long time before you got engaged?"

This time Peewee was sure that Annie was looking at him. He could feel his brain hairs tingle. Twelve into 136 was 17.

"A very long time," his mother said. "We went together for three years before Uncle Louie proposed."

Annie contemplated sixsies but didn't think she could make it. "How come he waited so long?" she said.

"He was just shy, I guess."

Peewee, hot-faced, couldn't stand the silence that followed. He was grateful when Grandma Lester, giving up the pretense of her newspaper, set it aside and spoke. "I'll never forget that night," she said.

"What night?" Ruthie said, counting a row of stitches.

"The night you told us you wanted to get married."

Ruth shrugged, the memory dim if present at all. Grandma Lester smiled her big smile, the one that Peewee hated because it revealed the plastic gums of her false teeth.

"It was the week after Max sold the foot," she said. "Or gave it away, I should say. You brought Louie home with you from work. He was wearing a nice blue suit, I remember, and a green tie. Can we have

some privacy, you said, so we shooed all the girls into the bedroom.
And you took Louie's hand, right in front of us, and you said that Louie
had asked you to marry him, and that you had said yes. And you
wanted our blessing. Well, of course! Max said right away, whoever my
Ruthie wants is the one we want her to have. And he shook Louie's
hand and welcomed him into the family. Never asking him could he
support you right on a Hebrew teacher's salary, nothing like that. Max
didn't think of such things. We all hugged each other, I remember.
What a nice night that was. And the girls came bursting out of the
bedroom—they'd been listening at the door, of course—and they lined
up in front of Louie, a perfect straight line, I remember, and one after
the other they kissed him on the cheek. And then you. Louie's face was
red as a flag the whole time."

She paused as if finished, her eyes far away on the wall between the
living room windows, seeming to see the scene reflected in the glass of
a Vermeer print that Ruth had bought at the Metropolitan Museum of
Art a month before, a picture of a not-old woman, alone, her elbow on
a table, her hand supporting her weary face.

"And then they wanted the present," Miriam said.

"What present?" Ruthie said, not looking up from her knitting.
"Who wanted a present?"

"That roulette wheel," Miriam said.

Peewee's point broke as he pressed too hard on his pencil. His heart
started pounding, his chest filled with barely explicable guilt.

"You said you'd be sailing to Europe on your honeymoon," Miriam
said. "And Max said wonderful, that would be your wedding present,
two steamship tickets to Europe. You asked him where he would get
the money. He was a rich man, he said. He'd buy it with his money
from the foot. Which you had helped him get from Mr. Schmeed, in
any case. You said no, you wouldn't take that money, that Louis had
saved up for the tickets before he proposed. So I said fine, we'd think of
something else. Something practical you needed, for a new apartment.
And then the girls started jumping up and down. A present, a present,
they said. We have to give them an engagement present, tonight! Tonight? I said. How can we give them a present tonight? We didn't
know till just now. Though I had suspected, of course, knowing you.
But a regular party it was becoming. A present, a present, the girls
shouted, while Max broke out some schnaps. Then he says, I have just

the thing! What it is? I say. You remember! he said. And he went into
the bedroom, and climbed up on a chair, and poked around, and came
back with a box that was covered with dust. I looked at it and I think I
turned white. Like I had seen a ghost. I closed my lips and I shook my
head no. What no, why no? your father said. It's like brand new, we
never used it. It's the perfect thing. He wiped the box with a rag, and
then he turned to you and Louie. I can hear him like it was yesterday.
This gift, he said, was given as a wedding present to your mother and
me, twenty-seven years ago. The roulette wheel. It needed a little polish, maybe, but it was still brand new."

"I remember," Ruthie said.

Peewee wanted to ask if it was the same one. The broken one in the
drawer in the dark back room. The drawer that was always stuck, the
one where he'd found the diary the week before. He wanted to ask, but
something told him he shouldn't. It had to be the same one. How
many roulette wheels would one family have?

"From Alex it came," Grandma Lester said.

Ruthie had only half heard. "From what?"

"From Alex the roulette wheel came," Miriam said. Her gaze had
shifted from the glass in the picture to the drizzle on the window
beside it. Some strange extra hoarseness in her voice, as if she'd been
speaking too long, but not exactly, made Ruthie look up from her
knitting.

"Alex was your rich uncle? In Petersburg?"

Her eyes were still off in the distance, looking at ghosts. She shook
her head. "Alex was—" She caught herself, where she was, looking
down at the children on the floor, both of them looking raptly at her
now, caught up in her story. "Alex was one of my suitors," she said.
"Before Max came along."

"What's a suitor, Grandma?" Annie said.

"A boyfriend," Peewee said.

Ruth had set her knitting in her lap, was looking with new curiosity
at her mother. "You never mentioned him before."

Miriam shrugged. "From Alex it came," she said. "I thought maybe
Max would be upset. That maybe he wouldn't like that. So I told him it
came from my uncle, in Petersburg."

"A little white lie," Ruthie said. Both children laughed. And then something in her mother's face made her wonder. "For forty years you never mentioned this Alex."

Grandma Lester did not seem to hear. Her eyes again were away in the gray outside. Her voice was oddly flat.

"All the way from Alex it came."

They were, Peewee recalled, the last words he'd heard his grandmother speak.

"I Declare War On—Germany!"

The circle widened like a fierce ripple as the boys ran in six directions. The ball soared high into the air, growing smaller, hanging motionless at the apex of its ascent like a planet on the roof of the planetarium, then plunged back toward the earth. The boy who was Germany stopped in flight, realizing that he had been called, and he raced back toward the descending ball. He caught it at waist level. It popped from his hands briefly, but he caught it again in the air.

"Halt!" he shouted.

The others stopped running and froze where they were, each thirty or forty feet from the boy with the ball. The boy looked them over like a surveyor, trying to decide which of them would be the easiest to hit.

The girls, chattering and laughing, clutching their books to their barely budding breasts, were taking longer going home from school, having no ball game to hurry to. A small boy too young for school ran up behind them, looking for his sister. The girls sang out in unison:

> *"Georgie, Porgie, puddin' 'n' pie,*
> *Kissed the girls and made them cry!"*

George's face flushed red. He turned and ran from them, up the block, and crashed headfirst into the bandaged legs and black dress of a woman who had just turned the corner. He stepped back to go around her. Then he looked up and saw who it was.

"Mama!" he shrieked, and he ran away, across the pavement, into the street. The brakes of an automobile screeched. The street was filled instantly with the smell of burned rubber. The car skidded to a halt, its bumper less than a foot from the frightened boy. The boy looked at the car and continued running, stumbling, screaming for his mother.

The girls, frozen in place by the near-accident, a tableau of horror, thawed quickly. They looked at the black-draped figure moving slowly toward them up the block.

"The Rag Lady! The Rag Lady!" they cried.

They stood their ground in defiance, prancing like young fillies, their blowing skirts forgotten as she approached. When the shuffling woman was less than twenty yards from them, fear won out. Real terror filled their screams.

"The Rag Lady!"

They turned and ran.

The woman in black continued on her rounds.

The boy with the ball at last had chosen his target. He took aim, pulled back his arm, threw the ball, low, at Switzerland's feet. Switzerland, who was Phil, jumped fatly out of the way.

"Hey, you moved!" Germany shouted. "No fair, he moved!"

"The Rag Lady! The Rag Lady!"

They were all shouting at once. Switzerland turned and saw the woman behind him. "The Rag Lady!" he shouted, and he ran away across the street. They were all running in different directions, up the block or toward their own homes, pushing open heavy hall doors, pressing hard on bells or fumbling with keys on lanyards attached to their belts, running into apartments through mercifully opened doors.

Peewee, his chest heaving from flight, kneeled on the floor of his room and peered out the window. Not a soul was left visible in the street except Baby Lisa, asleep in her carriage, still too innocent to run.

# 4

WHEN SHE WAS gone, when he had made sure that she was gone, when he had followed her through the window with his wary eyes, followed her out of the alley and up the block, up the block as far as he could see, Peewee's pounding heart slowed. He went into the bedroom and checked the alarm clock on the night table between his parents' beds. It was 4:08. He'd have to leave for Hebrew school.

He snapped on the radio in the kitchen, knowing that he shouldn't. He had heard on Phil's portable during I Declare War the Dodgers take a 5–3 lead into the seventh. He listened now to one more inning, heard them keep their lead before reluctantly turning it off. He had, he knew, already made himself late.

He hurried outside, unchained his bicycle and with a faltering running start hopped on, sped off, waving as he did to Aunt Hindy, who was lifting Baby Lisa out of her carriage. Down Townsend Avenue he pedaled to the Mt. Eden Center, the grandest temple in the Bronx. There was a smaller synagogue in a storefront on 175th Street, only a block and a half from their house, but it did not have a Hebrew school. It was of this smaller temple that his father was the rabbi. His father, in Peewee's view, had never quite made it to the majors.

As he chained his bike to a sapling tree outside, Peewee heard Mr. Pinski's voice already intoning the lesson through the second-floor window. Mr. Pinski, who was well beyond retirement age and whose hands shook when he held the *sidur*, usually acted as if coming late to class was an affront not only to himself but to all Jews who had ever lived and suffered, and even to God.

"Brunig!"

He had opened the door to the classroom and closed it quietly behind him and slid noiselessly into his seat in the third row and without a sound sat with his hands clasped in front of him while for two whole minutes Pinski read in Hebrew from the black-bound *sidur* without once looking up. Read for so long that Peewee began to hope, even to believe, that for once at least his lateness would go uncommented upon. Till his name blasted forth from the old man's upturning face as if his arrival had been divined and not seen. He even thought for a moment that he might deny having arrived late. But there were witnesses.

He did not reply at first.

"You're late, Brunig."

"Yes, sir."

"Why are you late, Brunig?"

"The clock stopped." It was a lame lie but the only one he could think of with Pinski looking directly at him and the other children in the class trying out of mercy not to.

"That's why you're not wearing a yarmulke," Pinski said. "Because the clock stopped."

His hand flew to the top of his head. He fumbled in the pocket of his jacket, pulled out his yarmulke, flattened it like a doily on his head.

"And your *sidur?* I see you have your hands clasped in front of you, just like in military school. This isn't military school, Brunig. This is Hebrew school. Suppose you take out your *sidur.*"

Peewee couldn't believe it. He'd left the house so fast that he'd forgotten to bring his books.

"I forgot them," he said weakly.

"It's a good thing you didn't forget your head," Pinski said. And then the ultimate clincher, which Peewee could see coming. He'd seen it come before, like a screwball you could see coming and still couldn't hit. "The rabbi's son!" Pinski said, shaking his head as if in pain. "An example you should be for the rest of the class. And look at you!"

Fuck you! Peewee wanted to say. It was the only time those terrible words came leaping to his brain: when someone hurled "the rabbi's son" like that. Instead he said nothing, squeezing his clasped hands on the desk in front of him until his fingers became red and white from the pressure. Pinski got up from his chair and walked across the room and looked out the window for a moment.

"We've been reading, Brunig," he said, "about Abraham and Isaac. Do you know who Abraham was?"

Peewee responded without standing. It was the only thing about Hebrew school that was better than public school. You didn't have to stand when you spoke. As a target of ridicule, you were much less visible. If your knees started to shake, no one knew. "Abraham was the first Jew," he said.

"And Isaac?"

Mr. Pinski never credited you with being right. He only corrected you when you were wrong.

"Isaac was his son."

"His only son, Brunig. That's important. His only son. Do you know why that's important, Brunig?"

What am I, the only kid in the class? Peewee wanted to say. But he didn't.

"I don't know," he said.

"Ah," Pinski said, "you don't know. Maybe next time you won't be late, you'll know."

Peewee breathed deeply again for control and also for relief and let it out. Already Pinski's eyes were roaming the room, seeking a new target.

"Who knows why that's important?" he said.

Peewee, off the hook now, couldn't have cared less. AbrahamIsaacandJacob. He had heard the trio mentioned as far back as he could remember, mentioned by his father in the house or in his sermons. They had become, in time, the first double-play combination: Abraham to Isaac to Jacob. Preceding by many years Tinker to Evers to Chance. If he closed his eyes he could see without trying, and sometimes did, Abraham turning his back to the plate, racing out into short left center in pursuit of a pop fly, hearing, feeling as he did so the thundering hooves of the left fielder and the center fielder charging in. It was their ball if they called it, but if they didn't, then Abraham had to keep going, risking a powerful goy knee in the balls. It was the only shortstop's play in which for one fleeting instant fear invaded the baseball field. Then they went speeding past, and either they had it or you did or it was lying in the grass for a double. Either way the fear was gone.

"Shapiro, what do you say?" Pinski said.

"Because of what God told Abraham to do?" Larry Shapiro asked rather than answered.

Pinski took it as an answer. "And what did God tell Abraham to do?"

Emboldened now, Shapiro's voice was firmer. "God told Abraham to kill his only son. To kill Isaac."

Peewee's attention was brought abruptly back by this image of fatherly violence. He waited for Pinski to knock it down. But Pinski didn't. Pinski let it stand. Affirmed it, in fact, with his next question. "And why did God tell Abraham to kill Isaac?"

Peewee thought, Maybe because he was late for Hebrew school. He bit his lip to stop himself from smiling at his own joke.

Pinski looked around. No one seemed to know the answer. He did not repeat the question. Instead he read aloud in Hebrew from his book, and then in English he painted the scene for them.

"So Abraham went into the hills," he said, "taking Isaac with him. And he made an altar, and he tied Isaac his son to the altar. And he took a knife, and he was about to sacrifice Isaac on the altar . . ."

Peewee couldn't believe this. He couldn't believe this at all. This was the God of—never mind his forefathers—this was the God of his father! His own rabbi father!

". . . when an angel came down from heaven and stopped his hand, and said, 'Halt! Do not kill your son, but unbind him and let him live. You have shown your faith in God by preparing to kill your only son. I know that you fear God now.' And Abraham unbound his only son, and found a lamb instead, and sacrificed the lamb to the Lord."

Pinski closed the book and looked around at the breathless silence. It may have been his imagination, but it seemed to him that a few of them at least had paled. Brunig especially it seemed to him had paled.

"It was only a test, you understand?" Pinski said. "God really didn't want Abraham to kill his son. It was only a test. To test his faith in God."

He let them chatter a bit to break the tension; chatter with relief. They pretended it was all over, they pretended they understood.

Martha Schwartz raised her hand in the back of the room. "What if the angel from heaven had been late?" she said.

The others all murmured in agreement, young Isaac's blood flowing across the floor, flowing in among their seats.

"What if, what if?" Pinski mimicked. "The angel wasn't late, that's what counts. Angels from heaven aren't late."

He didn't look at Peewee. Probably he had already forgotten. But Peewee thought it anyway: only rabbis' sons are sometimes late.

She clutched tight to a railing as she moved down a waterfall of steps. To passengers in the trains that passed on the el overhead, she must have resembled a large black bug.

She moved down the street under the rattle of a disappearing train. People were flowing toward and past and around her on the sidewalk, faceless rush-hour riders who had debarked at the Mt. Eden station. She moved slowly but in a straight line past their curving-away steps. She did not look at them or they at her, but what the children who feared her did not know, what she had divined, was that these adults feared her, too, though they did not admit it even to themselves. If they avoided her path it was, they told themselves, because she was dirty; because she was probably a carrier of some dread and catching disease. But she knew the real reason. It was because hobbling in black through their slanty-sunned streets, the sack upon her back, the bandages concealing her legs, she represented something too fearsome to think about. She represented the senile or even mad old age that would come to inhabit all of them, unless they had the good or bad fortune to die first.

This she represented to the adults who moved quickly past her on the street. If they had understood they might have set upon her in a pack, like vicious dogs, but instead they merely looked away and made up stories with which to make their children behave.

Half a block from the food store, she stopped. She did not remember all of it. She did not remember what she needed the nigger to do. But she needed him to do something. A favor. She remembered now only that she would have to pay him; reward him with something. She thought she'd perhaps reward him with a peach. Slowly under the burden of the sack she turned and moved toward the store. Wearily she approached the counter, wearily yet with some dim plan burning.

"What do you need today, missus?" the proprietor said.

She set down her burden and with unshaking hands opened the clasp of her purse. "A peach," she said. "I need to take a peach."

He placed the peach in a bag for her. She paid for it with coins. She lifted her sack and the bag with the peach and moved toward the door, which this Ben-Al in his dirty-socked feet held open for her.

"Come back soon," he said.

She did not reply, but as she moved down the street in the gray of the departed sun, the sack somehow felt lighter on her back. It was as if by buying the peach she had set in motion some plan, which was rolling now on tracks of its own.

They were there with his sick and wheelchaired grandmother when he got home. He could tell by the shadows occasionally moving on the wall of the corridor, shadows cast from the living room, that they were all gathered there—his mother and father and Mickey and Hindy and probably some of his other aunts and uncles as well, and dying Grandma Lester in the wheelchair. They would all be gathered in the living room while the lights burned brightly and unusually in every room in the house. It was as if, he thought, on this spring evening even the adults feared the dark.

He rolled his bicycle down the alley and chained it to the fence in the back, walked around to the front and up the four steps. He had not yet digested the sounds coming from inside when Eli came out, almost bumping into him.

"They're here," Eli said.

"It sounds like a party."

"Yeah."

"So where you going?"

"Got to go to Schlomo's to bring back food. Mom didn't have time to cook for all of them."

"How is she?" Peewee said, with an apprehension he didn't want to show before his big brother. "I mean—how does she look?"

Eli shrugged. "Like Grandma." He took the four steps two at a time and disappeared into the street, calling back, "Your yarmulke looks real pretty." Peewee closed his eyes, put his hand on his head, pulled his yarmulke off, stuffed it angrily into his jacket. He hated it when he did that, forgot to take his yarmulke off and rode on his bike that way all the way home.

Seething at himself, he stepped inside and walked down the front hall to the living room. All the seats were filled with his mother and father, Mickey and Hindy, Aunt Clara and Uncle Leo down from Westchester, Mr. and Mrs. Greenberg down from upstairs. Everybody here for the freak show.

The chatter stopped as he stepped into the room. Mickey, Clara, Leo and the two Greenbergs all had drinks in their hands. It was a goddamn party.

"Hi," he said in a small voice. The response burst forth from all sides at once, like an ambush: Hello Benjamin Hello Benny Hello Ben—these from his relatives—Hi Peewee from Mr. Greenberg, Mrs. Greenberg with her glass to her lips not speaking but sort of pursing her eyebrows over them in greeting, hiya kid an intentional split second late from Mickey the cop, his voice booming. Him and his new-grown pencil-blond mustache, as if, he'd heard Hindy say the other day, he was God's gift to the Bronx.

He looked around the room. She wasn't there. As if she had died already and gone away.

"Where's Grandma?" he said, managing his voice better than before.

"She was tired," his father said. "She's asleep, in Eli's room. She'll come . . . we'll bring . . ."

"She'll come in later," his mother finished.

He took off his zippered jacket and hung it on the back of a vacant kitchen chair and sat, feeling somehow exposed before these adults who had softer, deeper chairs in which to sink. Not knowing what to do with his hands, he clasped them on his knee as if ready for their questions, which soon came.

Mr. Greenberg: "You just getting back from Hebrew school, Peewee?" Peewee says yes.

His father: "Where are your books?"

"I forgot to take them," Peewee says, saying it more easily to his father than he could to Mr. Pinski. His father does not reprimand him, merely raises his eyebrows questioningly.

His mother: "We'll eat soon. Eli went to Schlomo's to get some herring." Peewee merely nods.

Uncle Leo: "The Dodgers did good today, eh Benny?" Peewee nods again, smiles, grateful for the mention of the Dodgers, which casts out nervousness. He looks at Mickey, at Hindy with Baby Lisa asleep in her arms. "Where's Phil and Annie?" he asks.

"They're at home, dear," Hindy replies. At home two houses away. So they will not have to see Grandma Lester, he thinks.

Then there was quiet in the room. Already they were finished with him. Bored with him. It was as if his presence was an embarrassment.

"So," Mickey said, clearly the most impatient. "What was that story you were going to tell us, Lou?" His use of the name Lou falls as a slight affront. The rabbi is Rabbi Brunig to the community, Louie to his family and his friends. Only Ruthie calls him Lou. The affront passes unremarked upon, attributed perhaps to the whiskey and soda.

"Just a story I heard," Louie said. "I was thinking of maybe using it in my sermon Saturday. There's no rush; it can wait."

"It can wait?" Leo said. "Wait for what? Where we got to go?"

Peewee wondered if his father would tell a joke at a time like this, with Grandma Lester sick in the unlit room at the end of the corridor. His father, as if reading his mind, looked at him and shrugged and winked. He felt glad to be included, acknowledged.

"There was a ship that went down in the ocean," his father began. "Everyone drowned except Heschie. Heschie clung to a life raft for three days, till he was washed up on a desert island. He slept on the beach, and then he got up and looked around. There were no ships in sight, so he decided to build a little hut in which to live. Little by little he made himself comfortable. For five years he lived alone on that desert island, till one day a ship came and rescued him. He thanked the captain of the ship and said he would be glad for a ride back to civilization. But first he would like to show the captain around the island, show him how he'd been living the last five years. The captain agreed, so they began to walk along the beach. 'Over there, that's my hut, where I been living,' Heschie says. 'Over there, behind it, that's my garden, for food. That little building over there, that's the outhouse. And that one across the field, that's a temple I built.' They keep walking farther along the beach. 'Up there, on top of the hill, that's a lookout tower, where I would look for any ships passing by. Over there, that's a boat house, for boats I go fishing in. Over there, by the trees, that's a temple.' The captain stops walking. 'Waiting a minute,' he says. 'That's a temple? I thought you said the building near your hut was a temple.' Heschie makes a sour face. 'That one?' he says. 'That one I don't go to!' ' "

They all erupt into laughter except Mrs. Greenberg, who doesn't seem to get it, and Mickey, who says he's heard it before. "Yeah, that's a good one," Mickey says. "I heard it last week." Peewee smiles uncertainly, wanting to align himself with those who got it, wanting to support his father.

"That's a good story," Leo says. "You got another one? You said you got two you wanted to try out."

"Wait a minute, my turn first," Mickey says. He is holding his drink high. He seems to be talking through the drink.

They are looking at Louie. "Go ahead," Louie says. "Your turn is correct."

"It goes with the other one, see," Mickey says, as if apologetically. "These two men are standing in the street. Across the street they see two ladies talking. 'You see those ladies?' the first man says, 'The fat one is my wife. The beautiful blonde is my girlfriend.' The other man looks at him. 'Your girlfriend?' he says. 'What do you mean, your girlfriend?' The first man takes his arm. 'You know,' he says. 'My girlfriend. I fuck her—' "

"Mickey!" Hindy interrupts angrily. "Watch your language. Benjamin is here." They all look toward Peewee, who is trying not to blush.

"Benny's a big boy, right, Benny?" Mickey says. "Benny knows the facts of life. Let me finish my story, for chrissake. So he says, 'You know, she's my girlfriend. I fuck her, I eat her pussy, I let her lick my dick—' "

"Mickey!" Hindy says again.

"Quiet," Mickey says. "I'm almost finished." He takes another drink of whiskey. "So the second man says, 'You fuck her, you eat her pussy, you let her lick your dick? What about the other one, your wife?' 'That one?' the first man says. 'That one I don't go to.' "

Mrs. Greenberg erupts into laughter, spilling some of her drink on her green dress. Leo laughs, too. "Another good one," he says. "Two good ones to tell the boys at the office." The others are silent. They all seem to be red in the face, as if embarrassed by the story, embarrassed by Peewee's presence. He thinks perhaps he should excuse himself but does not want to call attention to himself, to their embarrassment. In any case he did not understand the joke. He sits, perspiring, sees eyes glaring at Mickey: Hindy's and his mother's especially.

"You've had too much to drink," Hindy says, perhaps more for the benefit of the others than for him. Peewee too now glares at Mickey. He thinks there may be tears in Hindy's eyes. Perhaps because he said the wife was fat.

In the awkward silence that followed, Mr. Greenberg came to the rescue. "So, Louie," he said. "How goes your wars with the Mt. Eden Center? Any new battles looming?"

"As a matter of fact, there is," Louie said. "That no-good Goldenbaum is trying to lure away my cantor, Larry Paltz."

"Was he the one who sang last Yom Kippur?" Felice Greenberg says.

"He's the one," Louie said. "A gem. And Goldenbaum is offering him assistant cantor—assistant, mind you—for twice the money that I can pay."

"If I was him I'd take it," Mickey said. "The Mt. Eden Center's like playing Radio City Music Hall. How could he refuse?"

"Sometimes you find the best acts in the smaller clubs," Mrs. Greenberg said with authority now, the authority of someone who at nineteen had had a brief singing career in the nightclubs of Toledo, Ohio. "Also," more softly now, looking across the room at the rabbi, "sometimes you find more God in a smaller temple."

"What do you pay him?" Mickey said.

The rabbi looked at his brother-in-law with anger and sadness. Even a dummy who uses obscenities in front of women and children should know: you don't talk about your income to anyone, or how much you pay your help. "As much as we can afford," he said. "Half of what he's worth."

There seemed to be discomfort in everyone's eyes. Peewee had the sensation that the room was turning around him, that they were playing musical chairs with their words, that their words were going around and around without anyone saying what they really meant. He felt that soon the music would stop and one of them would not have a chair. One of them would be out of the game.

He did not know why he was thinking this.

In the kitchen Ruthie unstuffed the bulges of the bag onto the table. She took silverware from the top drawer. The smell of the herring made her mouth water, her stomach rumble. She had not eaten since her morning coffee, had not eaten at the hospital all day while waiting for her mother to be released.

"Ruthie's upset by Mama's illness," she had heard Lou tell his brother on the phone long distance from Chicago the other evening. Which was of course true, also.

The spread of food from Schlomo's made her think of simpler, happy times. She remembered standing on the deck of the *Napoli*, looking out over the rail as the boat passed Ellis Island going out, passed the Statue of Liberty, their arms linked, till the boat left land behind, and there were only the walls of their cabin and the vast blue sea outside the portholes to witness their first attempts at making love. They had made love sufficiently these seventeen years and, more important, had raised two sons. Times were easier for them than for most, Loeb and Loeb secure in the knowledge that people needed cheap clothing to wear even if a depression came, she even more secure in her job. Bookkeepers were needed for red ink as well as black. Louie teaching Hebrew school also secure, people needing God more in hard times than ever, Louie planning even then to study for the rabbinate. They fantasized about it together at night: the quiet, scholarly life they both wanted. She would go to college at night, she thought for a time, but she never had, though they had in fact till lately made the life that they had planned, mostly. They had failed or not yet succeeded in some particulars. Louie, for instance, did not yet have the leather-book-lined study he had always envisioned in his house, the dark back room being needed for storage, for the extra prayerbooks and talises and folding chairs needed for the *shul* for the High Holy Days; she long since having page by page departed from a life devoted to Great Books, shriveled in the face of cooking and cleaning and raising two boys from the full-bodied swellings of *Ulysses* which she had read on the boat going there and coming back, Molly Bloom's soliloquy touching her in depths she dared not admit she had, even to herself, not then—not so much dared not admit back then as dared not know she had, back then —and the *Hamlet* they saw on the stage in London, thrilling to its eloquence—had shriveled imperceptibly through the years from these to Daphne du Maurier and the crossword puzzle in the New York *Times*, taking like rainwater the path of least resistance. And so they had made it—a quiet, respectable life. An eleven-letter word for "proper in character and behavior." *Respectable.* She was the rabbi's wife. You could not get more respect than that. But it felt now as a burden: reminded her of the donkeys they had seen in Italy, their backs piled high with wood or produce on both sides, piled so high it seemed that surely they would collapse under the weight. And yet they climbed the hills, moved through paths among the olive trees, the burdened donkeys never missing a step, the villagers no longer even noticing the outlandish weight they asked the donkeys to bear.

A three-letter word for *donkey.* Much too easy. More worthy of the *Post* than of the *Times.*

She wondered if ever a donkey just quit. Just lay down and died, out of boredom with being a donkey. Or, more to the point, she thought, if God ever made mistakes. If God ever put a gazelle in a donkey's flesh.

"You need any help?" Hindy said.

She knew the voice and did not look up at the broad figure in the doorway but kept fussing instead with the food. "No, it'll be ready in a minute," she said.

They had, she recalled, cut quite a figure in the capitals of Europe (to use a phrase of the day), she and her Hebrew teacher. Young and in love, they had danced fox-trots closely if awkwardly on the boat going across. Hand in hand they had climbed the moss-grown cat-infested ruins of the Coliseum, where the Romans had thrown the Christians to the lions. "Perhaps not enough," Lou had joked dryly, puffing on his pipe. Arm in arm they had walked the streets of Paris, had prowled especially le Marais, the old Jewish quarter, Lou delighting in digging out of junk shops old Jewish artifacts, explaining in a blend of Hebrew and English and pidgin French their significance to the uncaring owners of the shops while Ruthie waited patiently. Drinking wine in outdoor cafés and then repairing to their hotel room to make love. And always in each city unpacking and then packing again their engagement present from Papa Max, that sad Russian roulette wheel once bright and shiny and red and black whose sad fate it seemed was to go through life unused. This same gift Mama had been speaking of a moment before her stroke.

"All the way from Alex it came." She had told Lou Mama's last spoken words, lying in bed that night. "All my life, I never heard her mention any Alex. I had an eerie feeling, that she wanted to tell me more. Then she had the stroke. Do you think they could be connected?"

"A stroke is a stroke," Louie had replied. "It's a blood clot in the brain. A physical ailment. It could happen anytime."

He was right, of course. Down through the years, succeeding in the rabbinate, Lou had become more settled, more comfortable, less questioning as his hairline receded and a small potbelly grew. He had gradually become more practical as the middle years passed, she less so, she the headstrong, practical young woman still projecting this image, the rabbi's wife, yet in the privacy of her thoughts more prone now than before to wonder at the mysteries of life, of wild sad humanity. To become less certain of everything, even as Lou had become more so. So she accepted his word; a stroke was a stroke: but not entirely. And when in the hospital the doctors said that she could talk if she worked at it, she looked at her mama lying crushed and depressed in her bed and wondered if she should risk it, should ask her about this Alex. For the doctors said she could hear just fine, she only made believe at times she couldn't when she didn't want to respond. Should she ask her about this Alex and study her face for a response? But she dared not risk it. Another stroke might be her death. For three weeks in the afternoons she sat abject in the hospital by her mother's bed and looked into her unspeaking face and somehow knew that she was right, and then walked home in the early spring air to solid Lou and the solid kids and knew that she was wrong, that she was much too prone to fantasy these days. That she, like her mother, was ill with a festering ingrown poison, a painful infection; and that she must become again what they thought she was, what she herself had always thought she was. She must regain control of herself, without them ever knowing she had lost it. She must become, once more, their donkey, and smile through the pain.

"Ruthie?"

"What?"

"Are you okay?" It was Hindy again, in the doorway.

"I'm fine. Why?"

"You looked a little lost, standing there. You're sure?"

"Of course I'm sure. Send the others in. Buffet style. Tell them to come, the food is getting cold."

Hindy squinted at her. All the food on the table was cold food.

"Don't worry, Mama will get better now," Hindy said. "Here at home, with you to take care of her. All of us, I mean."

Ruthie leaned over and kissed her sister's cheek. "Maybe you're right," she said.

They filed into the kitchen in ones and twos and heaped their plates with food and returned to the living room and sat in their same seats, in that curious way most people have of always returning to their same seats, as if life were merely theater or a movie. Ruthie the wife set coffee to perk on the stove. Ruthie the mother sliced a bagel in half and put it on Peewee's plate.

"Louie, what was that other story you mentioned?" Leo said. "You said you had two new stories to try out."

"I think we've had enough stories for tonight," Hindy said, glancing bitterly at Mickey, who was starting on his second bialy. She was no longer encumbered by Baby Lisa, had set her down asleep in the bedroom in the middle of Ruthie's bed, the light burning brightly above.

"No, this one is okay," the rabbi assured Hindy, adding, glancing at Mickey, "as long as there are no second acts."

Mickey, his mouth full, raised his drink in Louie's direction—instead of coffee he'd poured another rye—as if in toast to no second acts.

"So *nu*, tell it," Leo said.

The rabbi set his plate on the arm of his chair, as if he needed his hands to tell the joke. He tugged up the longish sleeves of his white shirt, as if, Peewee thought, he was getting ready to pitch.

"It was Yom Kippur," he began, "in the biggest synagogue in Moscow."

"Like the Mt. Eden Center," Mickey interrupted.

"Shush," Hindy said angrily. Ruthie too glared at him.

"He's right," Louie continued. "Like the Mt. Eden Center. The temple was packed to overflowing; half the Jews in Moscow were there. Then it came time for a certain prayer, where we prostrate ourselves before the Lord and beg for His mercy and forgiveness, because before God we are as nothing. So the chief rabbi turned to the congregation and asked, who will be the first? Who will be the first to prostrate himself before the Lord? A great hush fell over the temple. There was a stirring in the very first row, and then Max Rothschild, the leading banker in Moscow, stood up. He was six feet four inches tall, dressed in a fancy blue suit, with a talis with real gold lettering. Rothschild the banker approached the altar and prostrated himself on the floor before it and said, 'Have pity on me, O Lord, for I am nothing.' He stayed on the floor for a moment, then he stood up to his full height and walked to the eastern wall and took his place there. Again the temple was quiet. Again the chief rabbi approached the lectern and said, 'Who will be the next?' There was a stirring in the second row, and then Axel Rabinowitz, the leading merchant in Moscow, stood up. He had on a new brown suit, and a talis trimmed with real silver tassels. He approached the altar, and he prostrated himself on the floor in front of it, and he said, 'Forgive me, have pity on me, O Lord, for I am nothing.' Then he stood up and he walked to the eastern wall, and he took his place next to Rothschild the banker. Again a hush fell over the vast temple. Who would be the next, everyone was wondering. Who would be the next? Finally from the very last row there came a stirring, and a little man came walking down the aisle. He was so far back at first that hardly anyone could see who he was till he reached the front. He was Yussel, the tailor. His clothes were patched; his talis was worn so thin you could almost see through it. As he reached the altar, as he prostrated himself in front of it, Rabinowitz the merchant, standing by the eastern wall, turned to Rothschild the banker. 'Look at that,' he said, in outrage. 'Look who thinks he's nothing!' "

They erupted again, each in his own laughter, Leo and Mr. Greenberg and also Hindy laughing heartily and vocally so that their entire chests shook, Ruthie grinning broadly, Clara the next oldest sister grinning in a mirror image, Mickey smiling as if in spite of himself, Eli laughing loudly but an instant late, as if, Peewee thought, he was just trying to join in, Felice Greenberg smiling uncertainly, just as he, Peewee, was smiling uncertainly, feeling a common bond between them, he and the long blond Mrs. Greenberg, as if somehow they two did not belong, were outcasts by race and by youth. He *did* think the joke was funny, but he could not say precisely why.

"You've got to use that one on Saturday," Mr. Greenberg was saying. "That's a wonderful story."

His father was smiling. "It's a good one," he concurred. "I think I will. In a way, you know, I think that's the most perfect Jewish joke."

"You're damn right it is," Mickey said. "That's the trouble with it. It's that kind of joke that keeps the Jews in their place."

"What place is that?" Ruthie said. She seemed to be calmly biting out the words; calmly forcing herself to speak.

"Downtrodden, that's what," Mickey said.

"Oh, the poor dear," Hindy said, touching her husband's face. "You feeling downtrodden tonight?"

Mickey brushed her hand away with annoyance. "I didn't say me," he said.

"You said the Jews," Hindy said.

Faces were getting red. Especially, Peewee thought, Felice's. It accented the lightness of her hair.

"I think enough of this," the rabbi said.

"I think maybe Mama's up now," Ruthie said, standing. "I think we should bring her in."

As she edged past his chair, as she walked down the corridor where Peewee would not be sliding for a while, his eyes followed her back, her navy blue dress: this taken-for-granted bulwark of his life. As if he was somehow counting on her to return with something not nearly as horrible as he expected. To protect him from evil; which was, he assumed, a mother's task.

He watched her open the door and vanish into the darkness behind it as totally as into a grave. Soon the distant door reopened, revealing in garish silhouette backed by a bright yellow rectangle of light this unimagined crippled centaur shape, his mother's familiar hair and shoulders and arms, and then where her hips should be instead of hips another set of invisible-headed shoulders, sloping not in to a waist but out to a broad box, all of it resting, propelled, not on legs but on wheels. As in some vivid nightmare this violent-seeming shape moved toward him, inexorably, growing, gliding larger as it did, through the dim light of the hall, till together it, they, burst into the lamplit living room, Grandma Lester in the wheelchair looking wan to be sure and somewhat off center but not grotesque, not all that different than she looked on any healthy morning when she had not yet fixed herself for the day, the way old people have to; and behind her his mother, sturdy, familiar, pushing the wheelchair with not much more difficulty than she pushed a cartful of groceries when she and Peewee did the weekly shopping in the A & P under the el.

In the light his mother left her, the wheelchair completing now the ring of chairs in the living room, a circle within a square. "How you feeling now, Mama?" from Hindy. "She's looking much better now," from Leo, questions, statements hurled into the air in her direction, questions and statements not expecting answers or responses, hurled rather like a ball against a wall, with no batter to swing at them, hurled merely as exercise, to fill the air. Peewee, half hearing, studied her face. Her gray hair was pulled down more severely than it used to be on both sides, thinner than it used to be. Darker-than-usual blotches under both eyes, as if she had been struck. Her nose the only feature perhaps the same, her mouth hanging open slightly to one side. But mostly he looked at her eyes. One of them was half open and the other was half closed. That was the way it seemed. The lid on one hung high, the lid on the other hung low. It was this, he thought, more than her drooping mouth that gave the sense of imbalance, the impression that she was off center somehow. Her eyes were like two window shades in the same room lowered to different lengths. And yet it all was not as terrible as he had feared.

"Say hello to Grandma," his mother said.

"Hello, Grandma," he said nervously.

She did not respond. There was no flicker of knowledge in her face. He thought he was in her line of vision, but he could not be sure. They said that she could hear him. From her lack of response, he found it hard to believe.

His mother approached the wheelchair, took her mother's hand. "Say hello to Ben," she said. "Do you recognize Ben?" Still there was no response. "Don't you want to say hello to Ben?"

The eyes, the mouth remained inert, as before.

"Maybe you should leave her be," Louie said.

Ruthie let go of the hand, stepped behind the wheelchair, turned it slightly so her mother would have a better view of everyone in the room. They resumed their talking, ordinary things, as if she weren't there, as if she were normal, as if she still were one of them. Peewee, hardly listening, kept sneaking looks at his grandmother's languid, drooping face. And the same odd thought kept returning: she had somehow become, instead of a person, a secret.

"Keep talking," Hindy said into a silence that had fallen over the room. "The doctor says that we should try to talk a lot around Mama. The more words she hears, the easier it will be for her to talk again, when the time comes. Isn't that right, Ruthie?"

"That's what the doctor said," Ruth said.

But Hindy's words had made them all self-conscious. They began to measure their words before speaking. So no one had anything to say, not even Mickey now, and the silence began to take root in the middle of the room like a tree of lead, casting its heavy shadow over them all.

From the kitchen in the dead-quiet pall came the rocking sound of the coffeepot, rocking on its burner, perking violently, preparing to erupt. Ruthie, grateful for the excuse, hurried into the kitchen to turn it off.

They left two by two in matched pairs. Mr. and Mrs. Greenberg first, then Clara and Leo, finally Mickey and Hindy, Hindy carrying the baby, seeming to lead Mickey now with some invisible leash, Mickey somehow without saying anything seeming both half drunk and half contrite, Ruthie, watching them, convinced somehow that he was neither. It was, she had noticed, a pattern of behavior that he had developed, perfected: overly boorish and aggressive at the beginning, overly sheepish at the end; a pattern, she reckoned, designed to cover a myriad of sins. She hoped for Hindy's sake that it worked. It made her loathe him just now.

Peewee watched without speaking as his mother pushed Grandma Lester down the corridor past second base and into Eli's room, closing the door behind her. From the sounds breathing now through the quiet house he could see, envision, her hauling her loose-skinned mother out of the wheelchair and into the hospital bed. Then he thought: they are putting her out for the night, the way he had read in books people put out a cat for the night. It had always seemed a cruel way to act, to put something out for the night, but this he saw they would do each evening now to Grandma Lester, who used to be a person like any other. They would push her down the corridor and put her away for the night.

He did not know what else they should do.

When he had washed his face and changed into his pajamas and crawled into bed, with the light in his room still burning, his father came in and sat on the edge of the bed, as he did almost every night, for a moment or two of talk. Usually it was his father who took the lead, asking what had happened in school that day, or with his friends, or with the Dodgers. But this night Peewee spoke first.

"Dad?"

"What, son?"

The sleeves of his white shirt were rolled at the elbow, his dark tie loosened, his dark gray vest unbuttoned. On his head of course he still wore his yarmulke.

"If God told you to kill me, would you do it?"

Louie's brow furrowed; his expression became nonplussed. "What kind of talk is that?" he said. "Of course I wouldn't kill you." He leaned over and hugged his son's thin body under the covers and kissed him on the cheek, hard. "How could you think such a thing?"

"Not even if God told you to?"

Louie looked at his son's inquiring face, the familiar bone structure, the hair unkempt on his forehead, a face of utter innocence and trust. He had consciously ignored the first part of the question. He could not do so again.

"God wouldn't ask such a thing," he said. "Why would God ask such a thing?"

"He told Abraham to kill Isaac," Peewee said.

Louie nodded, relief relaxing the muscles in his face, almost as if he'd drunk a glass of whiskey. "Mr. Pinski told you that," he said. "You're studying about Abraham and Isaac."

Peewee nodded, still awaiting an answer, feeling not so much dread as curiosity.

"That was a long time ago," Louie said. "God doesn't ask such things now."

Peewee hesitated, listening as in the dark night behind them, behind their punchball field, behind the looming warehouse, a train rumbled by on the el toward the Mt. Eden station.

"How do you know He doesn't?" Peewee said. "Isn't God still alive?"

"Of course He's still alive. He just doesn't ask those things anymore."

"But He could if He wanted to, couldn't He?"

"I suppose theoretically He could," Louie said.

"Then what would you do?" Peewee said. "If He asked. Would you kill me?"

Louie felt a tightening in his belly. "If He asked anyone to do that," he said, "He wouldn't ask me. You don't have to worry."

"But He might ask you," Peewee said. "You're a rabbi. You might be the first one He asked."

Louie, who sermonized about such dilemmas every week, was stuck now for an answer.

"What would you do?" Peewee insisted. He thought he had been just curious, but now, unexpectedly, tears began to roll from his eyes. Louie, shaken, brushed away the tears with his fingers.

"That was only a test," he said. "A test of Abraham's faith. God never intended for him to really kill his son. He didn't lay a hand on him."

"But what if He asked?" Peewee said. He was crying now, it seemed unstoppably. "What would you do?" Tears now surrounded his nose, his mouth. "You couldn't be sure if it was a test this time."

Louie felt tears welling in his own eyes. "Benjy, Benjy," he said, taking the boy's small hand in his. "You don't have to worry. I wouldn't hurt you. I wouldn't ever hurt you. Not me, not Eli, not your mother. Never."

"Not even for God?"

"Not even for God," Louie said, uncertain if this was blasphemy. If it is, he thought, so be it. When God becomes fear, then love must be the stronger.

But this he couldn't explain to the boy. This he himself must ponder.

"You don't have to worry," he said. "God loves you. God loves everyone."

Immediately he regretted the last. He had set it up; he could anticipate the boy's next question. What about Grandma Lester? the boy would ask. If God loves her, then why did she have a stroke? Certain as he was that the boy's questions were somehow related to the sad, despairing fate of his grandmother. And what could he say then? He could only fall back on the clichés with which the wise men through the ages had beggared themselves: that God works in mysterious ways. That we cannot understand God's will. It was true, perhaps, but it was still a cliché. It was no answer for a father to give his son.

The boy was wiping away his tears, sniffling in the rest.

"You go to sleep now," Louie said, trying to avert at least for now the question that lay unasked.

"Okay," Peewee said.

Louie, relieved, stood from the edge of the bed, prepared to turn off the light.

"Can I ask you one more thing?" Peewee said.

There was no escape. "What is it?" his father said.

"Ask Eli if Hal Gregg got the win. I didn't hear the last two innings of the game."

Louie smiled. His son was back again. "Be right back," he said, and he went into the living room, and then a moment later he came back. "Hal Gregg got the win," he said. "Five to three. With help from Hugh Casey in the ninth."

Peewee grinned through the remnants of his tears. "Good old Hugh Casey," he said.

His father turned off the light. Peewee started to protest, out of years of habit only recently broken, but did not. "Your mother will be in to kiss you good night," Louie said, "as soon as she finishes the dishes."

Peewee waited. The brown-white light from the street lamp outside clawed its way as usual through the venetian blinds, spread its claws on the walls. Peewee said to himself with firm conviction, The Dodgers are gonna win the pennant, more than fifty times before he dared to close his eyes; and another fifty after that. When at last his mother came to kiss him good night, pressing her lips gently to his forehead, he was already deep asleep.

# II

# *Decoration Day*

We are in danger of losing the past itself . . .

> Hannah Arendt,
> *The Life of the Mind*

MUMBO JUMBO MUMBO jumbo his father mumbled on. Mumbo jumbo *adonai elohenu adonai ahod.*

He did not know what this daily *tfilinn*ing accomplished: not for his father and not for God. He knew that all Jewish boys and men beginning at age thirteen were supposed to do this every day, but that was a rule and not an explanation; and a rule that he knew was mostly broken. He knew that when at age thirteen he himself would be bar mitzvahed his supposedly most important gift would be a set of *tfilin*, in a blue or maroon cloth bag with golden lettering; the kind of bag, he thought, in which he would much rather keep his Pee Wee Reese–model glove. He knew that Uncle Mickey never *dovan*ed; he was pretty sure that his other uncles didn't either. He knew that Eli, who was fourteen and a half, didn't. He had done it for the first week after his bar mitzvah and then stopped. He figured when he was thirteen he would do about the same as Eli: try it for a week to see what it felt like and then put the things away, deep in some drawer where he'd never look again. He could not imagine himself as the shortstop for the Dodgers, sitting in some hotel room in Cincinnati or St. Louis, putting on *tfilin* in the morning while his roomie second-sacker, who probably would be Catholic or Protestant, or maybe even Negro, looked on.

His father was still *dovan*ing, getting near the end. Peewee got up from the bed and went to the bathroom. When he returned to the bedroom, his mother was telling his father about a trip to the cemetery. They would be taking grandma along. His father was unwrapping the coiled black strap from his arm. As he did so the strap left in his flesh under his uprolled sleeve a row of red indentations, like welts. Peewee watched as his father rolled down the sleeve of his white shirt, under which the pressure welts would slowly disappear. Then with swift, deft, rolling strokes his father coiled the leather around the twin boxes, the arm box and the head box, and shoved both of them into his faded brown bag with the faded silver lettering.

"So," his father said as Peewee pulled off the tops of his pajamas, preparing to dress, revealing in his mother's long mirror his scrawny, rib-lined chest. "What are you going to do today, before the big parade, while we're at the cemetery?"

"I don't know. Play some punchball, I guess," Peewee said. He was thinking that maybe he'd practice some sliding in the hallway while Grandma Lester was gone.

Mickey was wearing a brown suit, Hindy a green dress and a hat with flowers on it. Even Baby Lisa, in Hindy's arms, had on a bright pink dress and a tight sunbonnet that matched. People seemed to get more dressed up to visit the dead, Peewee thought, than they did to visit the living. They came into the house and halfway down the long corridor encountered Louie wheeling Grandma Lester out. They backed up as if in a traffic jam and after exchanging hellos—"How are you feeling today, Mama?" Hindy said to Grandma Lester as the wheelchair passed, Grandma Lester, her mouth drooping down in its ever-present scowl, as usual not responding—Mickey took one side of the chair and Louie took the other and with apparently little exertion by either one they carried her, chair and all, down the four brick steps of the front stoop, Mickey with his typical policeman's strength, Louie with his unaccountable rabbi's strength. But she wasn't very heavy; she had withered to less than a hundred pounds. To eat meant to live, and for months now she hadn't wanted to live.

Mickey and Ruthie maneuvered her out of the wheelchair and into the rear of the car. Mickey slammed the door, folded the wheelchair, the sun glinting off its chrome, and put it in the trunk. Ruthie walked to the other side of the car, climbed into the back beside her mother. The others arranged themselves appropriately. As the engine turned over and caught, the two mothers spoke in sequence to Peewee, Phil and Annie lined up at the curb. "Be good," Hindy said. "We'll be back about one," Ruth said. "In plenty of time for the parade," Hindy added. And then, the three kids waving as if at some departing army, Mickey eased the Olds away from the curb.

"Look at all the flags," Ruthie said, leaning across her mother, pointing out the half-open window. As if grudgingly, more perhaps following the direction of her daughter's arm thrust in front of her than because she had heard or understood or cared about the words, Miriam's head lolled toward the window. Her eyes peered out, but she made no other response. Her body inert in the backseat was like a doll's. Beneath her dark kerchief Ruthie had dressed her in her best dress, light blue silk with purple irises, which she wore only to weddings and other occasions, and around her shoulders her mink wrap against the breeze, the wrap a present from all the sisters on her seventieth birthday in March, a wrap which, if Ruthie remembered correctly, her mother, always saving it for a special occasion, had never gotten to wear until today.

Mickey drove in silence through the flag-draped Bronx, moved to real emotion by the colorful display, though he denied this even to himself. The others, too, were silent, less perhaps because of the flags than because of the unusual presence of the half-living Miriam in the car. Ruthie, holding her mother's frail, cold hand in hers, found her eyes drawn magnetically to the small blond hairs on the back of Mickey's neck. She had not wanted this arrangement. She would have preferred they go in the Chevy, Lou driving and her beside him, Mickey and Hindy in the back, because she knew this would happen, this magnet, her eyes, but it was true that the Olds was roomier. There was no way she could object. Sitting now in the silence, she let it happen, let her eyes rest where they would, because she had no will just now to resist: let them rest on the small blond hairs on the back of his red-scraped neck, always trimmed close as the police department required, just as three years before the Air Corps had required. The close-cropped hairs that reminded her of all that had been, of the journal through which she had discovered at the age of nineteen that she would like to be a writer; of the poems and short stories she had tried to write from time to time. How she had given up the girlish dream when Lou came into her life, and then the kids. She had become the practical, down-to-earth person that everyone thought she was. Then the war had come, the men had gone away, Mickey had gone to war, Sarah's David had gone to war, lots of the men on Townsend Avenue had gone off to war, though Lou had not. Lou was slightly too old to be called, was also by his rabbi status exempt. "There are things to be tended to here at home," he'd said, showing no apparent guilt, and, she thought, feeling none, serving as an air-raid warden, the chief warden of the entire neighborhood, in fact. In his way, in emergencies, she knew, Lou could be a leader of men. As she sat at home through the war minding the kids, watching Hindy and the other women around her waiting with hidden desperation each day for uncertain news from the front, from Europe or from the Pacific, her old writing dream had been rekindled. Here was something worth writing about, something she could observe firsthand: the quiet bravery of the home front. It could be a novel, she thought, a novel of waiting women, quiet and brave and true. And so she began to observe more closely, began at night to write down notes, thoughts, observations, began to draft an outline, began in the afternoons to actually write her book, to interweave the quiet lives of the waiting women around her, those who got good news and those who got bad, and mostly those who day after day got none. She wrote and read and rewrote and read again, liking much of it but never really satisfied. Something was missing, and she didn't know what it was. She read the letters Hindy got from Mickey from the Pacific Theater, censored letters in ink on onionskin. Reading these, incorporating her own versions of them into her budding novel, she felt they nonetheless underlined the fact that something was missing, though what it was eluded her.

Then in the summer of '44 Mickey had come home on a two-week leave. She had gone out to the airfield with Hindy to welcome him. She had watched him come down the ramp of the military plane with his khaki duffel bag slung over his shoulder, looking spiffy in his light brown uniform. She had watched Hindy run to greet him, had watched him drop the duffel bag and grab her in his arms and spin her around, the two of them kissing passionately right there in the middle of the strip. She had seen Hindy's nails pressing deep in the back of his neck as they embraced, this image somehow sticking with her more than all the others, and then they had kissed, too, a welcome home, sister-in-law and brother-in-law, and then that night and for many more nights in the next two weeks they had sat around, all of them, friends, cousins, neighbors, listening to Mickey tell tales of what it was really like out there in the war, his adventures in the planes that flew the Hump. And listening to all this, she knew what was wrong with her book; or at least she thought she did. She'd been telling only half the story.

Listening to Mickey's tales, hers seemed dull. The real novel to be written was away out there in the war. So she changed the working title of her book from *The Home Front* to *On Two Fronts*. She decided to keep most of what she had written about the women but intersperse with it the story of the war itself; to insert real action that would make the book more exciting. She invented a hero: a dashing bomber pilot flying dangerous missions in the cruel South Pacific. She made him look a lot like Lou, or like Lou had looked when they were young, substituting for his devotion to God and Judaism a pilot's devotion to danger; and to Lou's personality and devotion she would weld Mickey's stories, changed and dramatized, of course, since Mickey was only a corporal, a mechanic. She never let it interfere with her wifely or motherly duties. But in her spare time, instead of knitting now, she wrote. And found another obstacle: while the home front, however unexciting it might be, had an authentic ring to it, the war parts sounded false. With Mickey gone, she had taken to making up stories out of newsreels at the Surrey. She tried to think it through. She thought perhaps her first idea had been right after all. Confused, she put the book away altogether, as she had done with her diary at nineteen. But like the diary, she couldn't bear to throw it away. She put it in a bottom drawer.

For more than a year the two hundred pages she'd written had lain untouched, in the excitement of the growing Benny coming of school age, in the excitement of the endings of the war: the fall of Germany, the atom bomb and the surrender of Japan. It was a happy time, those weeks, the soldiers coming home—happy, too, perhaps, because she was no longer one of the few women on the block who had her man. And when Mickey came marching home, the same scene repeated, Hindy's nails as they embraced digging into the short blond hair on the back of Mickey's neck—always this for some reason the image that stuck with her—and when night after night he would regale them with his tales, would unwrap presents of silk kimonos and trinkets he'd brought back from the Orient, the tales rekindled once more the thought of her book. Now the war was over. Now there could be perspective. Now perhaps by picking Mickey's brain she could learn firsthand from him without the censorship the little details she needed to get it right; to make Captain Elkhorn—for that was his name in the book—to make Captain Richard Elkhorn and his fighter-bomber adventures come alive, a vivid symbol of the fighting half of the book. With Benny in school now, with Mickey taking a rest to let a thigh wound heal before going back to his policeman's beat, there would be time in the afternoons to pick his brain. To get it right. And she found that her comic character, Jim Jameson, the overweight tailgunner, was always complaining that all he got to see of the war was the small bleached hairs on the sunburned back of Captain Elkhorn's neck.

The Olds bearing five separate silences had left the bannered Bronx, had crossed the gleaming water beneath the Whitestone Bridge. Ruthie, returning her gaze from the pale green spring trees beside the parkway, saw now on Mickey's neck large open ugly pores. She wondered why she had never noticed them before.

The dream of the grace of shortstops. In Peewee's case the dream was largely his own, but the coaching came from his brother. Hour after hour, as far back as Peewee could remember, he had come charging in for grounders: skimming the pavement or bouncing normally or kangarooing high, Spaldeens or worn and faded tennis balls or gleaming new fat softballs, or hardballs lumped now and wrapped in sticky black electric tape, all of them tossed, looped, dropped, fired underhand, overhand, sidearm in big-brother conspiracy by Eli's whippet left arm, alternating at times with looping pop flies that made him, breathless from a grounder, hit the brakes of his black-and-white sneakers, turn and go charging back taking the pop over his left shoulder or right or even directly ahead with his glove outstretched, his webbing pointed as far as he could reach, sometimes a split second after the catch crashing helplessly into the brick wall of the warehouse, some of these catches so spectacular or at least feeling so that indeed they remained as clear in his mind as if he had made them yesterday; as if, in fact, he'd made them at Ebbets Field. He could name his top ten catches lifetime, made in the street between breaks for passing cars or in the paved backyard. Not so with the grounders, which blended together, punctuated by Eli's first shrill, then cracking and now more manly voice: "Two hands! Two hands! None of that backhand crap, you should have got in front of it! Charge it, charge it!" And an occasional "Good one" —that was Eli's highest praise: "Good one"—or "You better take a rest now," and over his objections, though his ribs hurt from breathing so, they would sit against the wall, Eli toying with the ball in his long-fingered hands while Peewee, heart pounding as if it would burst out of his chest like a flapping bird, tried to sit, to let his body calm, to not go for a drink of water until his body cooled. Not knowing that these moments of two brothers sitting side by side on the pavement, their backs against the wall, hot, breathless, knees almost touching, wanting water but waiting for their parched throats to cool—not knowing that these not-quite-taken-for-granted moments would be the closest they'd ever come in their lives: that soon, entering high school, Eli would discover his own vision of the future, would discover reality, would, even worse, discover girls, and Peewee from the moon around his, Eli's, earth, would fade to a distant, still visible but not very necessary star. Brothers they still would be, sharing a house, a dinner table, common parents, yet their galaxies were already moving apart, like the unstoppable, ever-expanding universe. Though they would still occasionally—rarely—have a catch—and only if Peewee asked—and only if Eli had nothing more important to do—Peewee was losing him, had lost him already, even if he didn't know it, accept it, or couldn't articulate it. And yet in some way beyond words he knew, because in the vacancy he had turned to Phil, trimmed him down, switched him from the Yankees to the Dodgers, taught him—without Phil realizing he was being taught by this young snippet of a shortstop—how to play first base, from where it was only natural he would spend his hours tossing grounders. Cousins they were, inseparable they had become, Phil thinking he was the coach now, emulating Eli's words, Peewee showing gratitude with his camaraderie. Together against the wall it was they who would sit now, hot, dripping, though Phil always got a soda and cookies from the house before sitting down, not waiting for his body to cool. And on rainy days Phil obligingly making the tag, swipe after swipe, as Peewee in his stockinged feet, practicing his steals, ran down the long dark linoleumed corridor and slid into second base. All this was part of it, he somehow knew, even at eight years old: the way a shortstop became what he was.

They haul me now like a sack of flour, she thinks. They are pushing her in the chair down narrow ways. The ways are lined with trees in spring bloom. Beyond the trees in every direction is grass, and peopling the grass in every direction are gray or white stones, upright, rectangular. There is something they call these stones, she thinks. As they push her along, she works at what it is, and then she gets it: to-whom stones. That is what they are: to-whom stones. She knows that is not quite right, but she will settle. Floating along in the chair without propelling herself, propelled by one of those behind her, unasked, she is aware of a kerchief tied around her head, tied under her neck. She is aware of fur that covers her shoulders, that covers the flabby places where once there were breasts that Alex liked to suck. That Max liked to fondle. The fur is like the grass neatly mown in front of all the to-whom stones.

The wheelchair hits a rock, upsetting the feeling of floating. Then it resumes. There is another word for the stones, she thinks, and this time she gets it right away: *monuments.* Though it is a false word, she thinks. In what way are these stones monuments? Soon, for instance, she will have a stone. (She wants to be dead, yet shivers now at the proximity.) In what way can a stone lay claim to being Miriam Lester's monument? Because it will bear her name? *"Feh!"* she says aloud into the breeze, but none of those behind her responds. Perhaps they did not hear. Those behind her, who haul her around like flour, who push her places she doesn't want to go. Those, she thinks. Those are my monuments. And thinks again, *feh,* but doesn't think she said it aloud.

They make a turn into another way. Along it are low black iron railings, perhaps a foot off the ground, enclosing family plots. Before long they stop in front of one. On the railing in front of it the angel sits, just as she knew he would. The angel had been visiting regularly of late.

"It's you," she says matter-of-factly, without pleasure, also without pain.

"Whom were you expecting?" the angel asks.

"You," she says.

The others are stepping past her, stepping over the rail: the two men, the two women, one of them carrying the child. The rabbi one is putting on a yarmulke, is handing a yarmulke to the other.

"How've you been?" the angel asks.

"How should I be?" she says.

The rabbi is bending, picking up pebbles, putting them atop the monument. LESTER, the monument says, carved in the center.

Several feet in front of it, much smaller, off to the side, is another one. A to-whom stone. "Max Lester, 1871–1943." Beside it there is space, tended grass. This space she knows is for her.

"*Nicht* today?"

"No," the angel says. "Not today."

The others do not hear. They are standing in the plot in front of her, two on each side, heads lowered while the rabbi prays. They are gazing at the grass that covers the box that contains whatever is left of Max after four years.

"So why did they bring me here?"

"They're trying to help you," the angel says.

"How can they help me?"

"They can't. But they think they have to try."

"Not they," she says. "One."

"Yes. Your daughter."

"Ruthie."

"Yes."

She lifts her gaze, looks at Ruthie's eyes, staring down at the grass. There is darkness under the eyes. There is pain in her face as never before until these past few months. It was there, she thinks, even before she herself got sick. She had felt it in a womanly way. It was why, she thinks, she began to speak of him that day. Began to speak of Alex that day.

"You want to tell him now?"

The angel has been reading her mind. As always.

"No."

"It might make you feel better."

"No," she says again.

"Why not?"

"Because it would kill him."

"He's already dead."

"It would kill him again."

The angel tries not to laugh, but laughs anyway. "People don't die so easy," he says. "Not even the first time."

"So easy?" Her voice is bitter; the taste in her mouth is vile. "Easy for you, maybe."

The angel looks down at the ground, saying nothing, accepting, perhaps, the criticism.

She looks at him without remorse. She hesitates. "If I want to tell him . . ." she says. The angel looks up. "I don't mean today. I mean sometime. If I want to tell him some other time . . . does it have to be here? Where he lies?"

"It doesn't have to be here. You can talk to him anywhere. Besides . . ."

But she isn't listening. Her head is resounding with her own last word. *Lies* . . .

# 2

A holiday. She tried to remember, sitting on her milk crate beside the nigger on the pavement, holding her almost-empty cup of now-cold tea, what it was she did on holidays. On holidays she didn't sift the trash. On holidays when she was not performing she went to her home in the country, where on the bright lawn that drifted away to the sea the men in their white jackets and white pants played croquet, the children rolled their hoops across the lawn and the servants set out lemonade and petit-fours. She in her famous way surveyed it all from the depths of her white wicker chair, protesting when at evening they drifted into the large music room that she couldn't play, she really couldn't play, she really had to take her rest, she had a major concert coming up next Saturday, in Prague, or Berlin, or Budapest. The king would be there, or at least a prince, the train ride would be long, she really had to take her rest. But this pupil or that of hers, visiting for the holiday, would be charmed to entertain them, she was sure. And sitting alone far back in the music room, she would listen with her dreamy eyes closed to the young fingers of this or that apprentice playing Bach or Mozart or Brahms. She would listen till a soft hand on her shoulder told her that madam's bed was folded down. No, she was quite certain of it. On holidays she didn't prowl the trash.

A loud riding of brakes led her to open her eyes, to look up the block where under the el in front of the lumberyard a large, windowless truck had rolled to a stop. From the back of the truck where twin doors swung open, the men in their uniforms were jumping down, guns, holsters visible in their belts, nightsticks in their hands. The old fear, time remembered, hooped like barrels around her breast. She clutched the nigger's arm.

"Nazis!" she said.

The nigger in his plaid shirt rubbed the doze from his face, looked up the block after her gaze. "Po-lice," he said. "New York City Po-lice Department."

"Nazis," she said again, mumbling now. They were pouring out of the truck like rats from a building someone had set afire. "What do they want?"

"Now don't you worry, they don't want nothing," the nigger said. "Big Decoration Day parade today, over up on the Concourse. The President himself and everyone. Be lots of po-lice all over the place today. These is only the first. Just parking their trucks here, I'd say, and walking on up to the Concourse."

The Nazis formed up on the sidewalk, leaving their truck at the curb. On the el above a holiday train screamed, only the second one of the day. She remembered once being on a train, winding through a deep dark forest. The train had come to a stop; there was a long delay.

"What is the problem?" she'd asked the conductor.

"Sorry, madam," he'd said. "The rain seems to have washed out a bridge up ahead."

"But my concert," she'd said. "I have to—"

"You are Mrs. Wiedkowski," he'd said.

"Yes."

"We have a message for you from the emperor," he'd said. "He has dispatched his private car for you. He assures you the driver will get you to the capital in time."

"That's very kind of the emperor," she had said.

This remembering, coming back to her in vagrant and perhaps unwanted glimpses, then disappearing again, like dreams. Ever since she gave the nigger the peach. Ever since the nigger brought the box.

"What you want that for?" he'd said, but she didn't answer him. She hardly knew herself. But he had done it that very night, climbed after dark over the fence to the lumberyard, prowled in the back, in the place where the coffins were made; found the kind she wanted, brought it back for her. Ever since, with a sense of mission she only dimly perceived, her remembering, also dimly perceived, was coming back;

only to leave again, to come and go with a will of its own. It gave her pleasure, but she also waited in fear.

The Nazis in a double column in front of the lumberyard marched off in the opposite direction, turned the corner and disappeared from sight. The street under the el was holiday-quiet again, holiday-empty.

"Yessir, be lots of po-lice around here today," the nigger said.

Her back was aching from sitting too long on the milk crate. She went inside. The old man, inert on his bed, was staring at the ceiling. Only the even rise and fall of his chest revealed he had life.

She went over now and looked at the coffin. It was black. At first she didn't recall why it was black, but she remembered with her new re-membering how it had gotten that way. She remembered it was wood-coloredwhite when the nigger brought it to her. She remembered the next day taking a large lump of coal and rubbing the coal on the outside of the coffin. She had rubbed it all over the outside, till the coffin was blacker even than the nigger. While the inside still gleamed woodcoloredwhite, like the nigger's teeth. It was while doing this that the white patches had begun to show through the dark of her un-remembering.

She touched the black of the coffin. It no longer came off on her hand. She looked at the coffin and wondered what it was for.

When the kettle screamed, she poured more tea for herself, more coffee with milk for the nigger. She took the cups outside and sat on the crate again. A cat came over and rubbed her leg for milk. She kicked it away tiredly with her aching foot. At night the cats got milk, not before. The nigger took the coffee, at once grateful and as if it were his due.

"Maybe we should walk up to the Concourse later," he said. "Maybe go see that parade."

She didn't answer. The nigger stared glumly into his coffee. He thought perhaps he had overstepped. He had never before suggested that the two of them go anywhere.

"Goddamn!" he said, looking not at her but at the el above. "I'm a man, ain't I?"

She did not respond. She did not hear him, or if she vaguely heard she had no idea what he was talking about. There was something she must do today. In the darkness of her remembering she could not remember what it was. But there was something she must do, before the Nazis did.

Peewee raced down the corridor and hit the dirt, slid on the linoleum under Phil's tag, into his grandma's room. He lay sprawled on the floor and looked at her empty bed.

Sometimes the play that looked the simplest was really the most difficult. The ball hit directly at you, for instance. Going to your left or right, you needed speed, but you could see the trajectory of the ball quite clearly, you could time the perfect hop. Whereas with a grounder hit straight at you, the pace was difficult to judge. You had to charge it immediately, as if to show it right off the bat that you were in control. Charging it, you could avoid the indecisive halfhop that was the cause, he estimated, of ninety percent of all shortstop errors. The worst thing you could do was wait for the ball to come to you. Almost every time you did that, the ball would assume control. It would leap unexpectedly off the edge of the infield grass and strike you in the chest. Or it would skip low, for one perverse bounce hugging the ground, scooting under your slow-reacting glove, turning what the onlookers thought was the easiest of outs into an E-6. Perhaps worst of all, these scary possibilities ran through your mind the instant you made the decision to stand flatfooted. The instant you made that decision you could see the error coming, as if it had happened in the past instead of the future. Standing there flat-footed instead of charging in, you knew in your gut that you were waiting not for a ball but for an error. And ninety percent of the time that's what you got.

Still, for no reason he could understand, sometimes you made that decision: not to charge the ball but to stand and wait.

Louie clutched his prayer book in his hand, tighter perhaps than was necessary. His hand clutching the prayer book pressed between his own thigh and Ruth's was sweating in the closeness of the car. For some time his hands had been growing moist unaccountably whenever he touched a prayer book, or a *sidur*, or even the polished wooden handles of the torah. It had begun soon after the war, when the patriotic fervor was over and the magnitude of the horror became known. When people in the congregation began to ask that new impossible question: "If there is a God, if there is a God of the *Jews*, then how could it have happened? How could the Nazis, the holocaust, have been allowed?"

He had thought about it after the war for long, agonizing nights and had received no satisfactory answer. "I don't know," he would reply. In the street or in the pulpit, in response to that question, he would always say the same. "I don't know." It was not a response that pleased the congregation.

One Sunday night he had gone to the Mt. Eden Center, had sat inconspicuously in the back, to hear Goldenbaum speak on "God and the Holocaust." Goldenbaum's ideas were the usual: The Jews had suffered all through history. This was maybe the worst, but nothing new. They were being tested, again and again. It was part of being the Chosen People, the keepers of the world's morality. God worked in mysterious ways.

He had heard it all before; he had thought it all himself. Maybe Goldenbaum could buy it, but he could not. It was too easy; it was just as unsatisfactory as and less honest an answer than "I don't know." What troubled him about it was the problem of the individual. The Jews were a people, perhaps, but they were also individual men and women, and the religion honored that. Sacred was the scholar who honored his mind, who became a repository of the past. A rabbi was not like a priest, through whom Catholics related to God. A rabbi did not give punishment, or sacrament, or absolution. He merely led the prayers, in which each man spoke directly to God. Each *individual*. And if each individual was sacred, then to permit the killing of six million individuals amounted to nothing less than God blaspheming; no matter that the Jews as a people had still and yet again survived. So Rabbi Brunig felt, and though he dared not accuse God from the pulpit, he would not, could not, excuse Him, defend Him, either. And so he pleaded the truth: "I don't know." And little by little he saw his congregation dwindle, saw especially the young ones with children shifting to the Mt. Eden Center, to the glib, comforting words of Goldenbaum. Louie from his dark, cramped study watched them go, but couldn't offer words of comfort.

It was not his faith that was slipping away, as it did so often with priests in the movies. He still believed in God as much as ever. *Something* had created all this. He had merely broken with God, he told himself, on the issue of the holocaust. *That*, he felt, had not been necessary. And so his palms had sweated, and he had agonized. He had had the idle notion at times that it was his marriage that was slipping away and wondered amazed and not really frightened from where that thought had come. He loved Ruthie as ever; the boys were more precious to him than anything in the world. The thought was merely the devil's work. Then one day Benjy had come home from Hebrew school, from old Pinski's class, with a book of raffle tickets to sell for the Jewish National Fund, to raise money for the future state of Israel, conceived but not yet born in Palestine, in the ancient Holy Land. And though he himself had been distributing the same raffle books, it was only upon seeing Peewee going from door to door selling the tickets, giving up his precious baseball time—only then in a moment of inspiration that he had understood what was slipping away, what it was he had to relinquish. It was his own passivity. To talk was not enough. To say "I don't know" was not enough. He had to act. If God for reasons of His own would no longer do His work, then men had to do it for Him.

Action was not his line. But he remembered the nights during the war, when the air raid sirens shrieked; remembered how he felt as the chief warden of the neighborhood, prowling in the dark of night and war to come, ringing doorbells, asking them, ordering them, to please turn out the lights, never knowing if this was just another drill or if the bombs would soon be dropping, as they had on London, where Ruthie had been born, as they had on . . . so many places. The bombs had never come, but he could still feel in his bones the strong-marrowed tingling of the night. It was a feeling that he no longer got in *shul*, perhaps had never truly gotten in *shul*. And so he had begun the Wednesday night men's discussion club, which Ruthie thought lasted from seven to ten, which lasted only from seven to eight-thirty, which gave him an hour and a half for the other. An hour and a half to let them move the guns. He did not want her to know, lest the FBI in their blue suits or anyone worse came around asking questions.

He didn't let anyone know. Secrets must remain secret.

Bumper to bumper the Olds inched in the Decoration Day traffic through the narrow streets that led to the highway that would take them back to the Bronx. On almost every corner there seemed to be an Italian bakery with long, narrow breads in the window. These were almost the opposite, it occurred to him, of the fat braided *chalah*s of the Jews. Such cultural differences, he imagined, could be traced back millennia, to differences in climate and crops, perhaps even to artistic tastes. But why in the cemetery were there so many young and why there on the streets watching all the cars inch by so many old, why even here in the car such old and apparently hopeless living death? He pondered as the car inched along, idly wondering also why the Jewish dead in the Beth David cemetery had been buried among the Italian living. Some pointless circumstance of real estate, of economics. Not that it mattered very much where you buried your dead. The past was prologue, but it was also past.

Except perhaps for the apex of extermination the Nazis had reached. This he could not conceive of as ever being prologue. Nor perhaps of ever being past, in the sense of being dead. These dead, he thought, of all the dead in history, would be among those who, though nameless, live forever.

He had come to believe in recent years that each person's life was a story that he or she was destined to live out: a story predetermined, perhaps not by God-the-novelist but in much the way that a small dark bulb would bring forth an iris, or a tulip, but not both, the future story —the flower's myth—already encapsulated in the seed. But the holocaust had called this belief into question. It did not seem likely that the life stories of six million Jews—of twelve million people—were destined for no higher purpose than the gas chamber.

The others were making conversation, idle remarks to pass the time. He did not feel compelled to join in. It was as if by saying *kaddish* at the cemetery, he had been present in his professional capacity and not as himself. Gazing at the slowly passing houses on the road that led to the highway, he saw as he often did the feathers falling through the shafts of light in the pillow factory in Austria, which, he often felt, had been his home. Of his mother he had no memory, and little of his father, who had outlived her by several years. Only his bachelor uncle Yussel remained in his mind as the bulwark of his early years, Yussel the largest pillow merchant in the region, telling him from the time he was old enough to push a broom and sweep the stray feathers on the foot-worn floor that if he swept well, if he did each new task to which he would graduate well, then it was inevitable that one day he, Louie, would be the manager if not the owner of the whole pillow factory. This as near as he could recall had been his childhood goal. But such was not, it seemed, in the seeds. Uncle Yussel had taken a trip to America, had liked what he had seen, had come back and spoken with the boys, with Morris and with Louie. "I have taken an apartment in America," he'd said. "It shall be my new home. There is great opportunity there. You are welcome to come with me if you like." Morris had agreed at once. Louie had wandered off—it was a *shabbas,* he recalled —had walked the winding path to the wooden factory, had stood in its vast main room with the sunlight falling through the windows. For a long time he had stood there in the silence, and then he had marched back down the winding path and told Uncle Yussel yes, he would go.

They had sailed off to America, they had shared a room in Yussel's new apartment on Hester Street. Uncle Yussel, as he had promised, had gotten the two of them jobs in the industry, carrying sample cases from store to store, twelve hours a day: their stepping-stone into the business of dry goods. Morris had moved up the ladder as prescribed, was now one of the largest wholesalers in Chicago. But as he had learned English with an accent he would never quite lose, he would also never quite lose the image in his mind of the wooden pillow factory with its white feathers falling on the pigtails of the village girls. When he began to borrow books and then more books from the English teacher who lived around the corner, he came to see the old pillow factory as an odd, silent symbol of the past, the past of the Jews. As if the falling feathers were silent tears. He heard in the passing years the voices of assimilation fill the teeming streets. He was not against this. He wanted as much as anyone to be American. He still could recall with modest pride the day standing in front of the Stars and Stripes that he had recited the Pledge of Allegiance and had earned his citizenship in this grand (as the Decoration Day speakers would be saying all over the land today) in this grand and glorious republic. But as his arms grew heavy with year after year of carrying the sample cases, he felt as if his head grew lighter with its emptiness. He was devoting his life to dry goods, and this he decided was not enough. And so with Uncle Yussel's agreement if not his encouragement, he had decided to become a Hebrew teacher. He had taken his own apartment, and there in a small room arranged as a miniature classroom he had begun giving lessons. He found satisfaction in this work. He thought he had found his role in life: to do this, perhaps one day to continue doing it as more than a Hebrew teacher, as a rabbi. And when at a Saturday-night dance at the temple he had met Ruth Lester with her stunning red hair and her solid intelligence, he had been smitten at once, and he had asked her to share his dream.

He looked out the window of the car at the stark, incredible image of Ruthie on their honeymoon, that one image still so vivid now after seventeen years. In the harbor at LeHavre, standing on the deck of the *Marseille*, watching the last trunks being loaded aboard by the seamen, not yet having gone to their cabin, a suitcase with some of their recent purchases on the deck between them, when a drunken party celebrating too much sendoff lurched past and sent the suitcase scudding through the rail, falling through the air, the snaps opening as it did, scattering the contents into the port-black sea, dresses floating, a jewelry box sinking, another box floating, Ruthie crying for someone to help, Louie trying to calm her, telling her there was nothing to do, the clothes could be replaced; nearby strangers sniffing commiseration, till Ruthie in the one reckless act he knew of in her life took off her hat, handed it to him, then before he could stop her jumped fully clothed into the sea, swam, to the gasps and consternation of hundreds of onlookers, toward the small wooden box still afloat, swimming in a pink dress, gathering up the box and swimming to the pier, where the seamen helped her up, dripping wet, while the crowds on the deck and down on the pier cheered. Louis did not recall or never knew if his face was red with embarrassment or white with fear. It was a moment both heart-stopping and confused. Minutes later Ruthie's clothes were making puddles on the cabin floor as she stripped them off, as she washed off the seawater, as she sat on the bed wrapped in his robe, as he held her to stop her shivering, to calm his fright, and she told him, when he asked why she had jumped, "It's the roulette wheel," pointing to the box on the dresser, a box he hadn't even recognized. "Papa's engagement present. I couldn't bear to lose it like that." In time they had laughed about it, had mourned with mockery the lost clothes, had decided the last night at sea to take out the roulette wheel, to play some games, if only so they could tell Max that they had. But when they opened the still-soggy box on the dresser and took it out, the wheel would hardly turn. The sea had done its work, had warped it well.

They had looked at it sadly and then had laughed again. For this she had leaped into the sea; for this she had risked her life. And holding ruefully the sad, soggy wheel that would now forever go unused, she said, "Don't tell Papa. Promise me you won't tell Max." He said of course he wouldn't, he hugged her close, and soon on the bed that last night at sea they were making love. When he looked back upon that night he believed it was the best night of love they'd ever had. They had, he knew, been landlubbers ever since.

His mind returned to his frustration after the war. Seeing Peewee ringing doorbells in spite of his shyness, selling raffle tickets for the Jewish National Fund, he'd suddenly understood what he must do. He had the very next afternoon taken the subway to Manhattan, to Fifty-seventh Street, had gone to their offices. "The best thing you can do is raise money for us, Rabbi," they had said. He had shaken his head. He would raise money, yes, but that was not enough; he wanted to do more. They had given him an address, down on the Lower East Side, not far from where he'd lived with Uncle Yussel so long ago. It was a plain, drab apartment in a tenement, a secretary in the front room, a redheaded man at a desk in the back younger than himself. "Sit down, Rabbi," he'd said. "Tell me what you want to do." He had sat on a folding chair. He had looked at a large black-and-white poster taped to the wall behind the desk. The poster was of a girl, a young woman, dark-haired, dark-eyed, her long hair unbound, flowing loosely behind her, as if in freedom. Her eyes were bright and shining and declared a fierce dedication to her cause. She was wearing a man's shirt, the top of a dark uniform. The sleeves were rolled, and clenched in the hand raised above her head was a rifle. The whole of it was superimposed on a pale Jewish star.

"You tell me what I can do," he had replied to the young man. The man had stood and paced. "You have room in your temple to store things? Where no one sees?"

He thought of the cramped space. "Yes," he said. There was a small room in which they stored old talises, old *sidurs*, folding chairs they needed only on the High Holy Days. If necessary he could move these out, store them in the house, in the dining room in the back. They rarely used the dining room; mostly they ate in the kitchen.

"What would you store there?" he had asked.

The young man had hesitated, had looked him in the eye, as if deciding whether to trust. "Guns," he said.

The mere word had sent tremors through Louie's heart.

"With the money we buy guns," the young man said. "To send to Palestine. To the Hagganah. We need places to put the guns when they arrive. To keep them till they can be shipped."

Louie's chest was throbbing. He did not know what it was he had expected, what it was he wanted to do. He noticed too that his palms were dry.

"I want you to understand," the young man said. "It's quite illegal. But necessary."

The rabbi nodded. The rabbi understood.

"No one must know," the rebel said. "Not your sexton. Not your cantor. Not even your wife. Can you arrange all that?"

Louie found, with a cool comforting courage inside himself, that he was not afraid, that this was what he wanted. And so they had talked, had worked out the arrangements, the code words. And so it was done. The young man wrote a phone number on a plain slip of paper while Louie looked at the poster, the Sabra girl with the rifle in her hand.

"Tell me something," he said, taking the slip of paper, folding it and putting it into his wallet. "Who is that girl?"

The young man had glanced idly at the wall. "A freedom fighter," he'd said. "In the Hagganah."

"Yes, I can see that," Louie had said. "But who is she? What is her name?"

"What does that matter?" the young man had said.

"It doesn't," he'd replied. "I just—I just would like to know."

The young man hesitated, frowned. "Her name is Rebecca," he said.

Louie stood, looking at the poster, then at the rebel. "I'll call next week," he said. "As soon as things are ready."

On the subway ride home he had found himself smiling.

And so it had begun. For himself. For the future *Eretz Yisroel,* a homeland for all Jews who wanted to live there. So the holocaust or anything like it could never happen again. Remembering now in the cruising Olds, he rubbed his weary eyes, his tired cheeks. For Rebecca.

Because today his palms were sweating again, for the first time since that day. Because of what Larry Paltz, his cantor, had told him yesterday. Sweating, as if something else was slipping away.

"So," Mickey was saying, looking over his shoulder while driving. "What good did it do, dragging your mother out there? She didn't even know where she was."

"You expect miracles?" Ruthie said. "Overnight recoveries?" She seemed to hesitate for an instant. "Some things take time to heal." She looked at her mother's face beside her. "I think you're wrong, anyway. I think she knew where she was. Didn't you, Mama?"

She squeezed her mother's hand, languid and limp in her lap.

"Max," her mother said.

There was sudden excitement in the car. Hindy twisted in her seat to look back. "See, Ruthie was right!" she said. "It worked! Mama's better! What about Max, Mama? Where were we just now?"

They waited expectantly. But there was nothing more forthcoming from Miriam. She sat alone, her eyes behind her drooping lids, one half open the other half shut, staring straight ahead again, awash in her distant and stroke-trammeled world. "Tell us, Mama, tell us where we were!" Hindy seemed to be begging, almost frantic.

"Leave her be," Ruthie said. "That's enough for now. She must be very tired, the first time out like this."

Miriam stared straight ahead. Hindy looked into her face pleadingly. Finally, the baby squirming in her lap, she gave up and turned around, faced the front of the car again as they began the long, gradual ascent of the Whitestone Bridge.

"She's improving," Louie said, and squeezed Ruthie's hand. Ruthie nodded, took a deep breath, as if she could not get enough air into her lungs, wearily let it out. "A little," she said.

From the crest of the bridge of cabled steel he could see the sun glinting madly off the furrows of the bay, as off an infantry of rifles. Near Great Neck gilded sailboats glided, holiday sport for the Gatsby class. Six feet above the water a lone gull cruised in freedom or loneliness or private search. Through the window the breeze brought the smell of the sea, pungent and not quite fresh.

Always there are choices that must be made, he thought. Life is a ceaseless series of difficult choices, stern and irrevocable.

Now there would be another.

He remembered the serene, useful feeling when nearly a year ago he had begun to prepare for the guns. He had told Ruthie that the dining room in the back, which they had been talking of converting into a study for him, he would have to use instead for storage: that the *shul* was overcrowded, he would have to bring home some cartons of books and talises. Which he had done, the rarely used room becoming now a dusty place of hide-and-seek for Benjy and his friends. The storeroom at the *shul*, not much larger than an extended closet, he left looking the same, boxes of prayer books and talises in front, folding chairs on the sides: but invisible behind them now some empty spaces, for boxes that not even the sexton would likely notice. They had agreed on the phone, he and the redheaded young man—he and Rebecca's friend—on Wednesday nights.

He had formed the Men's Discussion Group as a cover. For an hour and a half each week he led them in a discussion of one or another esoteric point of the Talmud. Then they would leave, and he would stay behind, to catch up on his paperwork, he'd say. And wait for the dark green truck.

And then yesterday Larry Paltz had come by, had come into his office to talk, had called it all once more into question.

Louie had stood and motioned him to the chair beside the desk, thinking: it's about the Mt. Eden Center. He's decided to leave, he's decided to go with Goldenbaum. Feeling disappointment even before Larry spoke.

"It's about the Mt. Eden Center," Larry said.

Louie nodded, as if to take the rejection casually, but then decided that would be false, a cruel pose. He leaned back in his chair, met the young man's eyes. "You've decided to take the job over there," he said. "I can't say that I blame you."

"No, that's not it," Larry said. "It's something else."

"Something else?" Louie, who was in his shirtsleeves, the white sleeves rolled to the elbow, leaned forward, clasped his hands on the desk. Through the open window that looked out on the vacant lot, they could hear children coming home from school. "What's on your mind, then?"

"I haven't decided yet about the Mt. Eden Center job. I enjoy working with you. I'm reluctant to leave."

"I appreciate that," Louie said. "Still, the money, the prestige—I don't want to stand in your way."

"That's not the point," the cantor said. "They know how I feel about that. I told them I hadn't decided yet. Then yesterday they called me. Someone from the board of directors. He asked if we could talk. I said certainly, I'd come right over. He said no, not at the temple. So we met in a deli over on 174th Street. Near P.S. Seventy."

"In a deli? Spy business?" Louie, recalling the guns in the closet, regretted his words. But they seemed to pass unnoticed.

"It seems that Rabbi Goldenbaum's wife is not well," the cantor said. "They're planning to move to Florida in the fall. After the High Holy Days. He's lined up a small temple there. It's a growing place, Miami Beach. Lots of older Jews are beginning to spend the winters there."

"Goldenbaum leaving the Mt. Eden Center?" Louie said. "He practically built the place."

"The important point is this," the cantor said. "There's a division on the board about how to look for a replacement. Some of them want you."

"Me?" Louie leaned back in his seat, the front two legs of his chair off the floor now, his heart *dovan*ing slightly with disbelief. "Why would they want me? They know how I feel about country clubs."

"Some of them," the cantor said, "feel the same way. They don't like the reputation the place is getting. They want you to come over there and turn things around. Put things back in perspective."

"It's maybe a little late," Louie said. "They've let things go pretty far. The sisterhood practically runs the place, I hear, with their dances and outings and such." He paused, looked up at the ceiling, then down again. "This is a majority of the board speaking?"

"I don't think so," Larry said. "Not a majority. But a strong minority. They'll fight to get you, the man said. But first they need to know if you're interested. On the qt. It would take a majority to make a formal offer. And they don't want to start a fight if you'll turn them down. They want the new man, whoever he is, to look like their first choice."

"So that's why the deli," Louie said. "And you're the go-between." He placed the tips of his fingers together, let the chair fall forward, stood and walked to the window and looked out into the vacant lot. A bunch of Italian boys were choosing up sides for a baseball game. His heart continued to *dovan* at the sudden possibility of achieving his secret dream, his dream known only to Ruthie: to become rabbi of the Mt. Eden Center: not as it was, but as it could be; as he would make it if given a free hand. Gone or greatly reduced would be the parties and the dances and the politics that somehow always weakened temple life. Gone the trips to baseball games, the summer outings to the zoo. In their place the Mt. Eden Center, already the largest temple in the Bronx, would become what it ought to be: a respected, even sacred center of learning, staffed with the best Hebrew teachers he could find. A repository of tradition and faith, containing, if they gave him adequate funds, the best biblical library in the country. Hebrew scholars from all over the world would come to use it and could be induced, perhaps, in return to lecture there, to the students in the afternoon or perhaps to adults in seminars or an auditorium at night. Over this place of wonder and brilliance and ancient memory he, Louie Brunig, in a quiet and low-key and self-effacing way, would preside, requiring no self-aggrandisement as Goldenbaum did, serene in the knowledge that to the history of his people he had contributed something lasting and meaningful. This which he could not do at his little Temple Beth Shalom, his storefront *shul* where at times they could barely pay the rent, this he had long dreamed of doing at the great stone Mt. Eden Center, if they would let him. It had always been a pipe dream, he knew. The chance would never come; he certainly would not seek it, could not without appearing quite ridiculous. They had made it a country club because that was what they wanted over there.

He turned back to the cantor, still seated beside his desk. "It's a flattering offer," he said. "I appreciate your role in this, Larry. I'm sure they only want me so that you'll come and sing there."

Larry smiled. "That's nonsense, of course. But it would be nice. Wouldn't it?"

"Yes," Louie said. "It would be nice."

And so he had left it. That he would have to think about it. He would let them know. And only after Larry had left, only after he had spent the next half hour recalling in his mind the great stained-glass windows of the center, the pulpit on a velvet platform in the main temple, reveling in his dream—only then did it occur to him: you could hardly run guns in secrecy through the Mt. Eden Center. Even if it came to pass, even if he got the job, even if they gave him a free hand to do as he wished, to build the monument he wanted: even if all this was possible, there would be a terrible price: as more and more, it seemed, there always was. He would have to relinquish the guns for the

Hagganah that gave him such deep serenity. His secret rebel flame would sputter and die. He'd have to turn his back on Rebecca.

All this ran through his mind because he had not yet told Ruthie of the offer, would have to tell her, discuss it with her, and he did not know how to discuss it with her without breaking his word of honor. Without telling her about the guns.

Tonight, he thought. He would have to find a way tonight.

# 3

WHEN SHE HEARS the drums and trumpets, that will be the time. This she has figured out. When she hears the drums and trumpets, the soldiers will be marching by, and all eyes will be turned their way. Then she will be able to do it. Then she will be able to pass, unnoticed by tattling eyes. This she knows now with the instinct of an animal, thoughtless and cunning and heedless of consequences. This day she is living now she has lived before. She knows it without knowing, without remembering. The shadow of the past is conjuring this day, like the gloved white hands of a magician.

She feeds the old man in his bed from jars of baby food. She does not know who he is. Today he is no longer part of the past. He is not yet a hero; not yet a relic, either. He is merely there, like the cats are there in the coal bin beside, like the nigger outside the door. She does not know who the nigger is. She does not know why he is black. Perhaps he is black because he is the negative image of the old man in the bed.

Sitting, listening, attentive, like an animal, she waits for the rumbling sound of the next train, and then the scream. She hears none now. But sooner or later, she knows, there will be another train. She must act before the next train.

Then she remembers that is wrong. The music will be the key. When she hears the sound of drums, of trumpets. That will be the time.

In the alleyway the nigger knocks on the door. He has never done this before. When she does not answer, he knocks again, and when after a time she still does not answer, he pushes open the door. He has never done this before. He sees her sitting on the paint-scarred straight-back chair beside the old man's bed, her eyes seeming like ears to listen. He does not enter the room—that much he does not dare—but talks to her through the now-open door. "I want you to come up with me to that parade." She does not answer; she does not seem to hear.

"Well, damnit to hell, then," he says. "I'll go by myself, then."

He stares for a time at her. Then he turns and walks up the alley, willfully leaving the door open behind him. Then he stops. Regretfully he hesitates. He turns, he goes back down. Gently, though without apology, he closes her door.

For a long time she sits in the straight-back chair, waiting for the music. When after a time it does not come, she stands, uncramping the tenseness of her muscles, shuffling in slippers she has made from old newspapers to the dresser, and peers into the mirror above the coffin. It is very important she look her best today. That is the only way she can carry it off, she knows: walk tall and erect and unapproachable. The cracked mirror refracts her face into many faces. She looks at them and they are good. She has chosen today to wear her black dress. She thinks that black will be best.

With remembered motion she pats her stringy hair. She sees in the mirror seven images. She turns and watches the old man breathing. She sits in the straight-back chair and pulls off the newspapers from her feet. She forces her blistered feet into her shoes. She waits once more for the music, for the trumpets and the drums. When the music starts, it will be time to go. There are Nazis storming into the neighborhood. Today she must take the child: before the Nazis do.

Captain Richard Elkhorn was Mickey and Mickey was Captain Richard Elkhorn, and why this had come about, this illusory turning of base metal into gold, Ruthie didn't know. It was a trick of the mind that went back, perhaps, as far as the Garden of Eden. They had in the months after the war spent almost every afternoon together, all quite innocently, right here in the kitchen where Ruthie was now preparing tuna fish sandwiches that they would eat before going up to the parade: Ruthie seated on one side of the table, her back to the stove, writing notes on a yellow legal pad as she interviewed her brother-in-law, who

sat on the other side, endless war stories spilling under Ruthie's prod-
ding from Mickey Hirsch's lips. Some were things that had happened
to him, some were things he had witnessed, some were things he had
heard about. All of them went onto Ruthie's pad, to be transformed
before long, she hoped, into the missing parts of her book. Into the
stuff of literature. Mickey as brother-in-law had never been a person
she especially admired. He was not as bright as Lou, or as tender, or as
scholarly. There was an edge of grossness about him that did not even
seem quite Jewish. He was rude to Hindy at times, and she was quite
certain, even if Hindy refused to see it, that he played around with
other women on nights he claimed to be working overtime, silly wives
foolish enough to become enamored of a policeman's uniform. It was
all, she felt, somehow not quite Jewish. His life was his business, but
she didn't have to like it. But when the war came, and he had gone off
to fight, his absence made her judgment grow lenient. She saw how
much Hindy missed him, how much Hindy loved him. With the passing months, years, his faraway wartime life, his exploits seemed gallant.
And when he returned at the end of the war with shrapnel in his leg
which he had never mentioned in his letters so as not to upset Hindy,
with a wound that needed time to heal before he could resume his
policeman's beat, he seemed an altogether better person than he had
been when he went away. And so they had spent nearly every afternoon
for weeks, months, sitting in the kitchen, drinking fresh coffee, talking,
while Ruthie absorbed the stuff of her book. And in the course of this,
in a way she even now did not understand and certainly then could not
have predicted, her brain turned the corporal's stripes on his uniform in
his closet, which she had inspected to get the details right, into captain's bars, turned his mechanic's skills as he sat in the belly of a
transport flying over the Hump into Captain Richard Elkhorn. The
creature of her brain became more real to her than this man across the
table, this brother-in-law. The creature of her brain was the missing
link in her book, the piece that would make it work. And so she fell in
love with this gallant myth of her own creating: as perhaps, in a way, all
lovers do. Never for a minute in all those months did she confuse the
two, she thought, until, one Thursday afternoon, shopping in Saks
Fifth Avenue for some shirts for Lou's birthday, she began to look at
the silk ties and thought that for all the time and help he had given
her, she ought to give Mickey a present, and she bought him an expen-

sive tie, pale blue. And buying the tie and paying for it, she did not yet
know it, and walking down Fifth Avenue, she did not yet consciously
know it, but felt a strange, brewing excitement mixed with peace, and
then, only then on the D train riding home, did she know that when
the next afternoon in the kitchen she would give Mickey the tie, he
would put it down and kiss her cheek: a simple brotherly touch of the
lips. And yet—she saw it clearly—this time his lips would not stay on
her cheek. This she envisioned and this she knew amid uncheckable
excitement would happen, and this made her understand all the rest on
the D train riding home: that amid all their time alone together she
and Mickey had fallen in love.

It was, that ride on the D train, the last moment of peace she had
known.

The next afternoon when she gave Mickey his present, it happened
precisely as her brain had drawn it on the train, had continued to draw
it through a long, sleepless, anticipatory night. Setting the tie on the
table, he put a hand on her shoulder and kissed her cheek. And when
she, although taking no forward action, did not immediately pull away,
he moved his lips gently over and touched them to hers. And when she
still did not pull away, he put his other hand on her shoulder and they
touched lips again, again—for ten seconds perhaps, no more—till the
loud ringing of the doorbell interrupted them. They pulled apart
quickly and she, as flustered as she could ever remember being, hurried
down the hallway and let in the seltzer man.

Mickey hurried out. When on the weekend they met in the company of Hindy and Lou, their eyes at once sought each other and
turned away. In both there was the same knowledge, the same anticipation, the same misgivings; and when on Monday he came to the
kitchen again, they started to talk of the war in the South Pacific, but
then stood and took each other's hand, and kissed, lightly, and said how
they shouldn't do this, and kissed again.

The next few weeks she remembered as agony and ecstasy in alternating currents: the joyous anticipation of seeing one another, even if
only for kisses in the kitchen; the agony that this was all it could be
when they wanted, needed so much more. Emotions changed and blew
across her from minute to minute like clouds in a summer sky. They
were already, they knew, being unfaithful in their minds, each thinking
of the other when at home with Hindy and Lou. Their thoughts were

beyond control. Why then not share ecstasy, in secret, if no one got hurt? And that became the key: that no one else get hurt. Fidelity fell in time—but not without a mortal struggle—to one condition: that no one get hurt.

They talked this way and still the reality remained to both of them unthinkable.

Until, one day when they both knew it would happen, without prearrangement, it happened. A walk to get some sunshine, out of the house, out of the neighborhood . . .

And no one, she thought, mixing mayonnaise into the tuna fish, no one, she knew with triumph and despair, no one had gotten burned: except themselves.

Why was she reliving it all so vividly, so painfully, today? Perhaps because of the day itself, Decoration Day, Memorial Day: the hordes of policemen they had seen marching up toward the Concourse to protect the President, the military men who'd be marching, the bands, the flags that flew from nearly every house. The war was in the air today, as if it were still being fought, or the victory at least still being celebrated. She had lived a lie during the conflicted, agonizing pleasure of their love. She was living a lie now in the barely endurable pain of its strangulation. She must live this lie forever. This secret. She had discovered with Mickey that she was somehow different than she had always believed herself to be. It was a monstrous truth, yet also, somehow, appealing; but a truth she must shield from all those she loved, a truth that she must hide for the rest of her days, this touch of Molly Bloom in Eli and Peewee's mother, this touch of Molly Bloom in the rabbi's wife.

"Hey, Mom, when we gonna eat?" Peewee said, peering into the kitchen. "It's almost time for the parade."

"The parade doesn't start for an hour. Go wash your hands and face and get your brother, and come sit down."

Peewee looked at the round-faced electric clock above the stove, saw that it was exactly one, switched on the yellow plastic radio on the kitchen shelf. Then he went into the bathroom to wash his hands. Often he only faked this. He liked to leave the smell of his baseball glove on his hands, the gritty feel of all the grounders he had scooped and thrown that day. But today he actually washed, actually in fact used soap, while his mother, setting the tuna fish sandwiches on the table, hearing a steady blast of static from the radio, did not adjust the tuner but let the static crackle on.

"Whyn't ya fix the radio?" Peewee said, returning to the kitchen, heading toward the shelf.

"It's your ball game," his mother said.

Peewee edged the dial till the voice of Red Barber came in clear and true in his southern drawl, all the way from Boston, giving the starting lineups. Adamsapple Spahn was hurling the opener of the doubleheader, just as he had figured. It could be a long, quiet day for the Brooks.

His father came into the kitchen and sat in his accustomed seat. Then Eli wandered in and sat.

"Too bad you can't come to the parade, Mom," Eli said.

"Your mother is coming," Louie said. "We're all going."

"What about Grandma Lester? Who's going to watch her?"

"Mrs. Greenberg has a headache, she's not feeling well," their mother said. "She's going to stay home. She offered to watch Baby Lisa and also to check in on Grandma. So we can all go see the parade."

"You see all those cops out there?" Eli said, drinking from his tall glass of milk. "Whydaya think they need so many cops?"

"It's just a precaution," their father said. Though a precaution against what wasn't clear.

Stanky out, Robinson out, Reiser out. A one-two-three inning for Spahn. His mother, pushing most of her sandwich away, lit a Pall Mall.

"Is Grandma really getting better?" Peewee asked. He had heard them talking about that with Dr. Greenberg and Felice in the hall when they got back from the cemetery. His mother didn't answer but took a long puff on her cigarette.

"There seems to be a little improvement," his father said. "It's difficult to know what it means."

"You mean maybe she'll get better?" Peewee said. "Where she can walk and talk and everything? Like before?"

"No," his mother said. "We can't expect that."

"But maybe some improvement," his father said.

Peewee drank his chocolate milk. He wasn't sure how to say what he needed to say.

"Mom? I mean, Dad? I mean . . ."

"What is it, son?" Louie said, seeing his embarrassment.

Peewee ran his finger back and forth along a curlicue pattern on the green plastic tablecloth. He spoke with his eyes down.

"This—this kid-in-my-class who lives in the Lewis Morris. Who's got windows that look down on the Grand Concourse—invited me to watch the parade from there."

"I think that's very nice," Ruthie said. "Which boy is that? Do I know him?"

"I said I couldn't," Peewee said. "I said I had to watch it with my family."

"You can watch it wherever you like," his father said. "From the Lewis Morris if you want."

"No, I don't want to. I want to be with you. And Phil. But then she said, well, how about coming up for milk and cookies afterward."

His eyes were still looking down. He felt his cheeks grow hot, glow red. Ruthie and Lou exchanged glances, eyebrows raised.

"I said maybe. If you said it was all right."

"Well of course it's all right," his father said. "She sounds very nice."

"What's her name?" his mother said.

His cheeks he felt were burning now like coals in the furnace below. Why was it so hard to say her name?

"Beverly," he mumbled. "Beverly Rosenthal."

Eli reached across the table with his long thin arm, faint red hairs beginning to show tangles on it, and bopped Peewee on the head with his fork. "Look who's got a girlfriend!" he said.

Slowly Peewee raised his head, was glaring into Eli's face. "Look who's talking!"

He looked at the table again. He wished he were out playing ball. Things like this didn't happen when you were out playing ball.

One by one as they finished their sandwiches, they put their plates in the sink and scattered through the house. Only Peewee remained at the table, gnawing slowly at his tuna fish, leaving the dry crusts he didn't like, listening to the game, kicking the heel of his left shoe into the ankle of his right foot under the table until it hurt: wishing he hadn't mentioned Beverly Rosenthal.

He sat there listening to the game until it was time to go. Ruthie had pushed Grandma Lester in her wheelchair up the long hallway into his own room, where, she explained, Grandma could look out the window into the sunlit street if she wanted; where, too, if she happened to cry out for something, Felice sitting outside would surely hear her. Hindy came by with Phil and little Annie, pushing Baby Lisa in her large gray carriage, parked the carriage next to the hedge in front of the house, for Felice to keep her eye on. In front of the house they gathered, all except Mickey, who was working, assigned to parade duty.

On all sides, from the row houses and from the apartment buildings, people were streaming. Felice bid them all a good time. "Say hello to Harry for me!" she said. Hindy showed her where the baby's bottle was tucked under her blanket and off they went, joining the knots of people in the stream.

Soon Townsend Avenue was all but deserted. Felice sat on a canvas chair in front of the house, crocheting in spite of her headache. The baby was asleep in the carriage a few feet away. Through the wide open windows of Peewee's room Miriam Lester was visible in her wheelchair, her head nodding slightly to the side. But everyone healthy who lived on the street was gone now, gone up to the Grand Concourse to watch the parade, to see President Harry S Truman ride by in a motorcade, right there in the Bronx. Not a car was moving on the street, not a bicycle. On a normal Friday afternoon there would have been a steady flow of traffic, children riding their bikes, older boys trying to get in a stickball game between the runs of cars, younger boys playing Off-the-Stoop or I Declare War. On alternate Fridays the seltzer truck would be there, the seltzer man delivering a case or two of the blue and clear bottles to almost every Jewish apartment on the block, along with jars of U-Bet cherry or raspberry syrup for the kids. Sometimes on Fridays the vegetable man would be there, his wooden wagon pulled by a broken-down horse with a concave back and a convex belly, the wagon laden with wooden crates of fresh string beans, broccoli, cauliflower, carrots, peaches, strawberries, other fruits and vegetables depending on the season, the housewives of the block crowding around the wagon, squeezing the fruits, putting them in paper sacks, the horse and wagon, perhaps the last in the Bronx, eventually moving on, the horse in his hard shoes clomping resignedly along the asphalt. On a random Friday every few weeks or months the knife sharpener would have his truck parked in the street, passing cars having to edge around it while the women brought their pairs of scissors and their poultry shears and their best big knives out to be sharpened. The knife sharpener, too, used to have his machinery on a cart pulled by a drooping horse, but on his last visit a month before the horse and wagon had been replaced by a used and already battered truck. On a normal Friday any one of these might have appeared. In autumn and winter the coal truck might have appeared, too, the coal man bridging his silver chute from his truck like a sliding pond across the hedges into the small cellar windows at pavement level, opening the latch, letting a hard, fast, black river of coal roar down the chute into the coal bins. On a normal Friday any of these might have appeared. But this was not a normal Friday, this was May thirtieth, Decoration Day, Memorial Day. This was a holiday, the day of the annual parade, a day, too, when the President of the United States would be riding in the parade, right there in the Bronx. Since there would be no one in the houses, no one in the streets, since it was the duty of patriotism in any case, the seltzer man had taken the day off, and the vegetable man, and the knife sharpener as well. Chances are that all of them were up there on the Concourse, somewhere along the route from Kingsbridge Road where the parade would begin down to 149th Street where it would end at the main Bronx post office, watching in and among the hundreds of thousands of other people who would be watching, just as Peewee and Phil and Annie, Eli, Ruthie and Hindy and Louie and Dr. Greenberg, climbing now the great stone steps leading up from Walton Avenue to the Grand Concourse beside the Lewis Morris, would soon edge forward among the earlier arrivals to get a better view. Leaving behind in deserted Townsend Avenue only Miriam Lester, who was beyond caring, and the year-old Baby Lisa, who was before knowing, and the beautiful blond Felice Greenberg, who seemed unperturbed by the headache that was making her miss the parade, unperturbed by anything as she crocheted in the sun, glad perhaps to be able to do this double favor for her two casual friends Ruth and Hindy, by watching over their respective wards, she in the meantime betraying only occasional anxiousness by every few minutes glancing up the length of the silent and deserted block, as if perhaps she were waiting for someone to come and share the emptiness.

For twenty minutes she crocheted that way, while in the carriage the baby slept and in Peewee's room visible through the window Miriam watched or daydreamed or slept. Till, turning again, Felice saw him shambling up the block, his nightstick in his hand, looking to any stray observer like he was all business. She gathered up her crocheting, went into the hallway to wait for him out of sight. When he came up the steps, she touched the dark sleeve of his uniform. "Did you have any trouble getting away?" she said.

"Nah," Mickey said. "There's five thousand cops up there. I told my buddy I gotta take a shit. They won't miss me for hours."

Felice hid her distaste for the excuse he'd used. "What about the baby?" she said. "You think she'll be all right?"

"She's fine, she's fine," Mickey said, trying to nudge Felice along. "If she starts crying, we'll hear her upstairs. Since you insist on that rickety cot instead of your nice double bed."

"I told you, I won't use my husband's bed. Aren't you ever satisfied?"

"You ought to be glad I'm not," he said. "Or I wouldn't be here, would I?"

She looked at him coldly, wanted to say something but didn't. Instead she turned and walked up the inner stairs. Mickey, following behind, ran his nightstick lightly up the bottom of her orange skirt, along her thigh.

All they could see was the people lining the islands on both sides, the policemen standing about every fifty feet, the apartment buildings towering behind. In the street itself there was nothing yet that they could see, and yet they could hear it, ghostly, angelic, the faintest of the faint at first but growing louder every moment, the music of invisible bands, the skirling metal sound of trumpets, the boom of drums. The music was like a breeze that riffled the crowd, turning the heads of the adults in its direction, focusing straining eyes on the horizon, lifting the seated children from the curb in a rippling wave. And then finally visible where the distance met the street, the first of the flags of the first color guard, the first of the marching bands. The high-prancing drum majorettes drew applause. The booming bass drums, the snapping snare drums rapping breathless insistencies, the blaring brass bugles vibrated the soles of feet and the bones of chests. The bands strung out for miles—bands from the Army, the Navy, the Air Corps and the Coast Guard, bands from the police department and the police auxiliary, the fire department, and even the sanitation department, bands from every high school in the Bronx; and interspersed between the bands the shuffling phalanxes of uniformed marchers, from every branch of the armed services, from veterans' groups, the veterans of the Second World War, the veterans of the First World War, even aging veterans of the Spanish American War, most of these in civilian suits but with ranks of ribbons on their chests. For two hours they came and came, drum majorettes blowing whistles, bands marking time in lock-step, playing all the tunes of glory, followed by countless color guards leading ranks of anonymous marching men.

It was, like all parades, a diversion from the rut of daily life. And then toward the end a great roar swept down the Concourse, beginning in the north and rolling down the street between the tall rows of ocher-brick apartment buildings like thunder down a western canyon, and in the wake of the thunder, a series of automobiles, of Cadillacs, and in the next to last, a convertible with its top down like a pretty lady hatless, he stood in a white linen suit, holding his familiar fedora in his left hand, waving to the crowds with his right: President Harry S Truman, S for nothing, who couldn't hit, couldn't field, couldn't run and couldn't throw, but who somehow was getting the job done. He had so much nerve that, according to the newspapers, he was even thinking about running in 1948, running in his own right, the clothing salesman from Missouri, a prospect that, Peewee had heard, made much of the country giggle. The Eddie Stanky of presidents. But they weren't giggling here, not in the Bronx. They were clapping and cheering and shouting their approval for the job he was doing, or for his presence here today, perhaps for something altogether different, for the flags and the music and the wartime victory, which, though it had come nearly two years ago, still on days like this tasted sweet. They were at this moment in the center of the universe, and they were pleased to share it. Like playing shortstop, Peewee thought, in the World Series. He wore a smile and rimless eyeglasses and had an unpretty wife at his side, but he was all wrapped up in the flags and in the music, in the bugles and in the drums, and because of this there was respite in the minds of the watchers for some of the time at least, respite from decisions to be made, from the strains of uncertainty. In the music and in the flags and in the proximity of him there was excitement, and there was peace. The parade was magic masquerading as gravity. The parade was doing its work. Peewee even forgot for a time the milk of the Lewis Morris he'd have to drink.

"Give 'em hell, Harry!" someone yelled. And someone else. And someone else. And someone else.

In the slowly passing Cadillac Harry Truman raised his fist and smiled.

While in the little room the snow was falling. Miriam Lester though she could not see it could feel it on her hair, her arms. Looking out the open window through perhaps the closed half of her eyes, she could see it there, covering the village with white, the roofs of the houses and the barns, the woodpiles and the animal huts, there in the late Russian spring, on the day that Alex was shot and left to die. The snow falling to hide his blood on the day they took him away. The snow falling to hide his footsteps on the day he abandoned her. Snow to hide her shame.

"I'm going away," he said. "To Petersburg. To do my work there. There's a revolution to be made."

"But I thought . . ."

"I have to go."

"Take me with you, then."

"What for?"

"What for? Because we love each other."

"Love? Who said anything about love?"

His words echoing now in the heaviness of tears behind her hardly working eyes. Now, after fifty years.

"Alex!"

She grabbed at his shoulders, his chest, tearing at his clothes. He pushed her away. Then, reversing, he pulled her to him. He kissed her on the mouth, long and fierce and rough, till she bit her tongue and her lip started to bleed. And then with equal passion, or so she remembered it, he pushed her away and turned to go, in the direction of his house at the far edge of the village. In the direction of the outer world. The light snow started to fall even as she stared at the vanishing back of his wrinkled white blouse.

She watched, stupefied, her life at an end, till he vanished past the end of the road. Then she ran to the side of the barn, hurled herself alone into the place they had made love and wept. She was still there, delirious, hours later, when they found her half frozen in the snow.

Their neighbor, Max Lestrakovsky, whose young wife had died the year before, was one of them.

"They took him away," she babbled, inventing on the spot to hide her shame. "The men of the czar. They took him away with guns. I heard a shot." And she ripped herself away from them and hurled herself again into the snow, to weep again, to stop the flowing lies.

It snowed for three days, and when, weeks later, the snow was gone, they could not find his body.

Her delirium lasted for weeks. Looking through it now, she sees a figure dressed all in black who is staring at her. The figure must be Death, she thinks. Death come to get her at last, Death with pleading eyes, Death with a sack on its back. Somehow she had never expected this: that Death would be a woman, like herself.

"Hey, angel!" she calls.

The angel perches there, on the edge of her chair.

"So, you've brought him at last."

"Me? Brought who?"

"The *muloch hamuvid*, of course. The Angel of Death." And she lifts her hand and points, there, out through the window, only half aware that she is moving her arm, this arm she could not move.

"That's not one of mine," the angel says. "That's one of yours."

"What do you mean, one of mine?" She does not understand. She turns to look at him. But he is gone. She turns back to look at Death. Death, too, is gone. She places both hands over her eyes, not aware that she could do this. Again, she thinks. For the second time in my life I'm going mad.

She came out of it then in the spring. Under Max Lestrakovksy's gentle attentions. He was nice. He was kind to her.

"I'm going away," he said.

"What? Not you! Not you, too!"

They were seated on a bench. He put his arm around her shoulder. "There is no life for me here anymore," he said. "I am going to America. It will be lonely there. I want you to come with me. I want you to be my wife."

The muscles in her neck had collapsed. Her head had rested on his shoulder. An unknown peace had fallen over her. *I want you to be my wife.*

She had thought it over. So it would be. There would perhaps again be life to live. And so it was arranged.

Months passed. The snow was falling. It was early summer, but in her head the snow was falling.

"I have to go to Petersburg," she said a week before the wedding.

"Petersburg? What for?"

"I have an old uncle. He will die soon. I must see him once more before we leave."

Max had looked deep into her eyes. "If you're sure he will die soon," he said, "then perhaps you must."

And so she had gone. Had asked about until she found the house, the nerve and the shame leaving dueling scars in her chest. She had waited around the corner. Then she had gone to him, had found him at his books, had bothered him, had taunted him, had pleaded with him, had actually gotten on her knees in front of him, had begged; until as if to get rid of her he had thrown her to the floor and leaped on her, had through her bitter tears split her apart, had given her what she asked. This one last painful memory.

When she awoke, still on the floor, he was gone from the house. Daylight still hung in the windows. Beside her was a box, with a note in his writing on it.

"A wedding present," it said. "Do not come again."

With tears in her eyes, her hands shaky, she pulled open the box. Inside it was a gambling game. A wheel of roulette, shiny and never used.

She clutched it to her naked breasts. A gift from him.

Max, with the horse and cart he would soon be selling, met her at the station, helped her down. "How is he?" he asked.

"He will soon be dead," she said. "It's good I went."

Max looked at the ground and merely nodded.

"Look, he gave us a present," she said brightly. "For our wedding." And she opened the box and took it out.

Max took the wheel in his hand, then gave it back. "It's very nice," he said.

She looked through her half-open lids into the sunlit street. On the corner of her chair, the angel perched. "You want to tell him now?" he said. She shook her head. She brushed the angel away with her arm.

"I'm tired," she said. "Not now." The angel vanished as quickly as he had come.

She lolled her head; she closed her eyes. In the air above, as if across fifty years, she could hear again the whimpers and cries of passion. They sounded as if they were real, in the falling snow.

She followed out of habit and cunning and simple common sense her usual route, right at the corner for a block, then left. She walked at her usual slow pace. Wherever there were garbage cans, she stopped. This she had not planned to do, but decided now that she must. She took off the cover of each, she poked her scarred hands in the trash. As always. This she must do, she decided, in case they were watching her. This, she knew, was her coat of invisibility.

The neighborhood was a village abandoned, silent, desolate, all of them up on the Concourse, there at the parade: men, women, children and police. Even the nigger was up there, she remembered. That was where he had wanted her to go. She had not been nice to the nigger, she remembered. She would have to make it up to him. She would listen to his tales, as no doubt he would have tales, of trumpets; of drums. And then she would show him what she had done. And then he would understand.

She measured this journey now in garbage cans. Once she had measured it in butcher shops, in candy shops, in passing streets, in the dwindling size of houses, till houses were replaced by countryside, and countryside by trees. But that she did not remember; that had become now this: one journey, one and the same. Then it was the child that had slowed her down, had kept her to a prudent measured pace. Now it was the past, the throbbing legs, the bandaged feet.

She peered behind her at the el now a block away. The tracks still were silent, and the screams. But at any moment they might screech to life. To death. She turned and hurried on, faster than she ought, and the quickened pace made her breathless, made her pause, made her lean for support against a streetlight, feeling faint. Holding on to the post as to some strong man, she let her breath slow and gathered her resolve once more. Shouldering again the weightless sack that she had set on the ground, she started off again through the sunlit empty streets, streets that suggested that some impossible bomb had removed all the people but had left everything else intact. The houses still stood, but there was no sign of life around them. Automobiles were parked along the curbs on both sides of the streets, but none was moving in the middle. There was no one left to drive. This was the work of the Nazis, she decided. A neighborhood of Nazi paradise.

One more block. And still no sign of people anywhere. The music was louder now, the trumpets blasting down out of the heavens, the drums rumbling up out of the earth. Military music. This much she recognized, though she didn't know the tunes. The world had been conquered by them.

Crossing the last street, she thought there should have been trees. This thought intrudes from the past. She does not know why she thinks this. Ahead are only houses, tenements, a few scraggly trees spaced far apart, each standing alone. One small tree per house. She looks around in fear. She does not know what happened to the forest. Where will she hide? Thinking this, she stumbles on the curb, twisting her bandaged ankle. She does not know why she thought of forests. She thinks it must have been a waking dream. She knows again where she is. On a twice-painful ankle she is crossing now the last street before the child.

She remembers something else. She remembers how they always run from her. The children mostly, but also the adults, shrinking away, running from the blackness of her rags. Perhaps she and not the Nazis is responsible for the emptiness of the streets. Perhaps they have run for the last time, run to a place without returning, taking the child with them, to save it from *her*. But she rejects the thought like foul food. Her mind retains its dark integrity. It is God, not she, who invented the place without returning; and the Nazis who perfected it.

She reaches the far curb at last. She is herself again, or at least the remembered part. Today she will save the child, or die trying.

She passes the first house. There is no one there.

Breathless with the daring of it, keeping her eyes straight ahead, afraid to look from side to side, she approaches the second house. The second house is where the child is. Always the child is there, in a carriage near the second house. Now, approaching, her heart plummets. The carriage is not there. The child is gone. She wants to cry. She has not cried since the days she cannot remember: the days when crying died. But she does not cry. Not yet. She stands alone and mute in front of the house, bewildered. And then she sees it. Two houses away. The carriage. The same gray child's carriage in which on every other day she knows the child lies, the child sleeps.

She shuffles on, painfully and with great thought. Pausing perhaps five feet before the perhaps empty carriage, she looks up and down the block. There is no one there. And across the silent street. There is no one there. With a summoning of will she approaches, peers down. Inside the carriage beneath a pink baby blanket the soft child sleeps.

With instinct timeless and tender, she gazes for an instant at the baby-soft cheek, the pale blue eye, the wisp of thin hair sticking out from beneath the pink baby bonnet. Allowing herself a moment of pleasure. Knowing that in this instant she risks being caught. She cannot move her eyes. Then, summoning again the ironness of her will, she sets her sack on the pavement. She leans with an aching back into the carriage, lifts out the sleeping child, blanket and all, and sets the whole of it like a sacred treasure in the sack. It occurs to her that the child might wake, the child might cry, here. For this she has not made provision; this could spell her doom. For all else she has provided, she thinks. But not for this. But the child doesn't cry. The child with a small fist rubs its eye, then settles in again, to sleep in the sack.

She hesitates. She must lift it now, carefully. This she thinks and this she does, slowly lifting the sack, stooping under it, letting the sack rest gently on her back, slowly standing then under its weight. Thinking: it is done. But even as she thinks this, before she has taken a step, she sees them. She sees the eyes staring out at her through the open window of the house, the window not six feet away. The eyes, the face, the woman have seen what she has done. An old woman like herself: with one eye that seems half open and another that seems half shut.

She looks unblinking across the top of the carriage, across the dark green hedge, into the open window where the other woman sits. She notices the chrome of the chair. She notices too odd flecks of white on the woman, as if she is a statue, perhaps. As if she needs to be dusted, like something inanimate. She sees all this and, subduing it again, the crying feeling, thinks: one old woman to another: let me save the child. We both know what the Nazis do.

This she tries to say in an instant, with the pleading of her eyes.

The woman in the window does not respond.

Then she knows she must go. With all of her remembering, she knows. The sack on her back is heavy, the child asleep in it. She looks, throws, darts her pleading one last time. Tearing her gaze from the eyes of this other woman is like tearing flesh from frozen metal. Without looking back, she moves on, leaving the empty carriage behind.

Slowly but without faltering she walks up the block. She moves through the sunlit and still-deserted streets unchallenged. She moves past the tenements at the upper part of the block, holding her head higher than usual because of her precious burden, and sees for the first time the flags, the red and white stripes, the stars in a blue night sky, the flags hanging from windows on every floor, flags hung out as if by grateful citizens to welcome some long-awaited liberating army, and she wonders, she wonders if it can be true. She wonders if the Americans are coming, if they are here at last. She wonders if it's safe to leave the grave.

Turning left, walking on, she throws away this thought. The streets are empty; there are no more people. The flags she knows are a Nazi trick. A trick to lure her out. A trick to get the child.

Turning again, she walks under the el. In the cloistered air of the warehouse blocks the light falls dappled, broken by the tracks above. She looks no different, is not yet any different, than on any other day: the Rag Lady, trudging home under the burden she always carries.

For a moment she is apprehensive as she nears the store marked Ben-Al Foods. She is afraid the man will see her, Ben, or Al, the man with the tumored neck, will see her and will know, will know what she has done. That he will inform, perhaps. But then she thinks: no, he will not inform. Then she thinks: no, he will see nothing but the usual sack on her back. Then, slowly, approaching, she sighs a tortured sigh. The store is closed, locked. He, too, must be up there with the trumpets, up there with the drums.

In sight of the lumberyard now, she trudges on. Above and behind her she hears a noise, a distant rumbling. Louder and louder it grows until across the dappled sunlight frantic shadows rush. She pauses, waits, and then she hears it: the piercing metal scream of the train. She adjusts the sack on her back; she smiles with broken teeth; and moves on.

# 4

A YOUNG WOMAN, of childbearing age, who couldn't have a child and desperately wanted one.

In the absence of a ransom note, such was the profile of the kidnapper the police were looking for. It was the textbook motive in such cases.

Mickey was the first to see the carriage after the child was taken. But he did not realize it was empty; he did not discover the theft. He was in too much of a hurry. Dressing quickly when he was done with Felice, noticing as always his body hairs arrayed like souvenirs on her skin, he did not bother to shower but donned his uniform, did up his black tie while Felice watched, languid and naked, from the cot. Securing the gun in the leather case on his belt, he nodded a wordless good-bye and hurried out, down the stairs and into the empty street. The carriage was there. He noticed it idly as he hurried past, but it did not occur to him to check on his child. He was formulating what he would say if his absence had been noticed: he'd gotten the cramps, perhaps; the runs. He didn't like this lying, this subterfuge. He often felt it wasn't worth it, certainly not for Felice. But he felt he couldn't help himself. Not after Ruthie. His passion for her had uprooted his soul. Felice was good, she knew all the moves, and so he kept coming back as often as he could, when he knew the house below was empty, their passion slamming the cot against the wall again and again, he wondering at times as he slammed into her if this had anything to do with it, the knowledge that it was Ruthie's house below. He didn't know much about psychology, but he wondered sometimes what a headshrink would make of that. If all the times with Felice, he was still making love to his sister-in-law, but with violence instead of joy, banging away with a vengeance, to forget. Whatever his motives, Felice never questioned them, never pried into his state of mind. She seemed content with it. Of Ruthie, she did not know. No one knew. For a time after Ruthie, he had been desperate to confess: to tell Hindy all. Keeping it going, banging away, now with Felice, perhaps next month with someone else, was a way to prolong his shame, and thus a way to avoid confessing. And so the room at the Concourse Plaza, three blocks up from Yankee Stadium, near which he was often assigned traffic duty during Yankee games—this room made available courtesy of the Yankee brass—remained a private memory, his and Ruthie's alone, along with the wet laughing games they had indulged in those two afternoons a week. This room whose memory he would not profane by taking Felice there.

Diarrhea he'd had, he'd tell them. The craps. But the parade was still on when he got there, the extra cops strung out all over. They didn't even notice he'd been gone.

So it fell to Felice to suffer the full instant impact of the absence, the horror of the theft, the thudding strike of guilt. Showering quickly after Mickey left, massaging his body hairs off her breasts, she dressed as she had been before, wanting to put on fresh clothes but not daring to, picked up her crocheting, and with studied casualness, as if even God could be fooled—the only weapon she had found against her lapsed Catholic girlhood in Toledo—she descended the inner stairs and then the stoop, placed her crocheting on the canvas chair and went to check on the baby, this wonderful baby, she thought, who always slept so long and peacefully. And saw that the baby wasn't there.

Her reaction was twofold, the two almost but not quite simultaneous: first a terrified and terrifying plunging of her innards toward the ground; then a desperate thought that Mickey must have taken the child, Mickey must have put her in the house.

Reluctantly, as if the pavement were miles long, she walked the sixty feet to the Hirsch house, reluctantly because, if ringing the bell, she discovered he wasn't there, her panic would be inescapable.

She knew she should have gone to the parade. She had wanted to go to the parade. Even as a child, she'd loved parades. And in her panic now all she could think to do was keep her finger pressed as hard as she could on the doorbell of Mickey's house. For a full minute she leaned on the unanswered bell before she acknowledged that Mickey wasn't home, that probably it wasn't he who had taken Lisa and that she'd better start looking herself.

On shaky legs she walked back toward her own house, toward the silent gray carriage, and looked inside, as if perhaps whatever elf or genie had taken the baby might already have put it back. She felt with the force of a slap across her face what a rotten person she must be. She had never felt this before, not even on those few occasions when she had betrayed her husband. Not even with Mickey had she felt a sinner, though he had come the closest, Hindy being a neighbor, if not exactly a friend. But this: leaving the child unattended—someone else's baby! In this she felt she had sunk to the depths. She felt suddenly as if her life had been a steady downward curve of degradation leading to this. It was as if the theft had revealed to her a truth about herself that she had always deeply believed. And standing in front of the house now in the empty street only confirmed this feeling, moment on passing moment. Because here she was, thinking about herself again instead of about the missing child. Instead of even searching for the child.

She thought: my headache got worse. I went upstairs to take some aspirin. I felt dizzy, I lay down on the cot for a minute, just for a minute, to let the dizziness pass. But I must have conked out. I must have fallen asleep. When I woke up ten minutes later—it couldn't have been more than ten minutes—I came rushing down to check on the baby. And she was gone.

This she would tell them. This they would have to believe. All this ran through her mind, and as it did, she began to relax. This they would have to believe. And thinking this, fixing it in her brain, she thought for the first time of the question at hand: who could have taken the baby? For the first time she looked up and down the block as far as she could see. There had been no one in the street. She walked down the alley to the backyard, then up the block, peering into every alley, every hallway; not knowing what she expected to find. The baby could not have gone by herself. And whoever took her, whatever the reason, was not likely to have left her nearby. Frantic and frazzled, she thought to call the police. And then thought: Mickey *is* the police. The police are all over the place, for the parade. And as she stood, pondered this, whether to call the police or run to the Concourse to find one, as she stood frozen with inaction, she began to hear a hubbub, voices, and remembered the music, the fading music that now was gone, and then from around the corners small knots of people began to appear. The parade was over. The people were coming home, Ruthie and Hindy and all the others. She grabbed for support at the stone flowerpot overhung with morning glories that flanked one side of the stoop; clung for support against the made-up dizziness which now had become real. How was she going to tell them about the baby?

The word *kidnapper* tolled in her brain like a bell. If the baby had been kidnapped, then soon, perhaps, there would be a ransom call, a ransom note. But why kidnap Mickey and Hindy's baby? They didn't have any money, she knew. It was altogether strange, kidnapping a policeman's child. And then she thought: the baby was taken from in front of her house. Perhaps the kidnapper thought it was hers. Perhaps they were after the dentist's gold that Morris had hidden away in various corners of the house, to avoid the income tax on bank accounts. But that made no sense, either. No one that she could think of knew of the gold.

And then she began to cry. Arms crossed in front of her on the great stone pot of morning glories, she pressed her forehead into them and sobbed, twisting vines and purple morning glories caught up now in her rarely uncombed, distraught and distressful hair.

When, still sobbing, Felice told them what had happened, Hindy collapsed.

"Come in," Mrs. Rosenthal said, closing the door behind him as she did and leading him down a short corridor into a great bright tan-carpeted tan-painted living room. He walked behind a sofa, pressed his fingers to a great glass window, and looked out at the stunning view. Too late he realized he should not have touched the window with his sweating fingers, pulled his hands down to his sides, saw with chagrin his fingermarks on the glass. He turned and found to his horror Mrs. Rosenthal watching him from the middle of the room, pretty Beverly walking up behind her, wearing a pink party dress and a pink ribbon in her hair.

Mrs. Rosenthal was smiling benignly.

"Hi," Beverly said.

"Hi," he managed, hoping the brightness behind him would blot out the redness of his face. "I . . ." He found himself stammering, not knowing what to say. "I'm sorry I messed up your window."

"Don't worry about it," Mrs. Rosenthal said.

"Janet will clean it up," Beverly said. "Janet's our cleaning lady. Let's have milk and cookies, okay?"

"Okay," he said.

Mrs. Rosenthal, still smiling in the middle of the vast room, a living room larger than any he had ever been in before, said, "You children enjoy yourselves," and then she turned and walked under an archway, disappearing into some nether region of the apartment, an apartment which suddenly felt to him like Madison Square Garden, until, when she was gone, Beverly, who had taken his hand—not shaking hands, clearly holding his hand!—led him through a couple of hallways into a kitchen as large as their living room at home, in which on a gray-curled Formica table—Formica was the newest thing, he'd heard his mother say—were neatly arranged two blue cloth napkins, two filled glasses of milk, and in the center an inviting plate of chocolate cookies.

"I watched the parade from downstairs," Peewee said as they took their seats. He watched as Beverly took her napkin from the table and placed it on her lap, and he did the same. At home they used paper napkins. They always slid off his lap onto the floor.

"Yes, I know," Beverly said. "I think I could see you from up here. Help yourself," she added encouragingly, and she moved the plate of cookies closer to him.

"I liked the bands best," he said.

"Me, too," Beverly said. "The view from up here was terrific. You could see them coming all the way from Fordham Road. It sort of took forever for them to arrive. Like a snail. A marching snail of many colors. You should have been up here to see it!"

"Yeah, well," Peewee said. "I had to be with my family. You know."

"Yeah, I know all about families," Beverly said. "But the bands were probably better from downstairs," she added. "You could probably hear the bands much better in the street. I mean, up here seventeen stories high they sounded sort of tinny."

"Down there they sounded great," Peewee said. "De Witt Clinton High was the best. Then maybe Evander Childs."

"You could really tell the difference?" Beverly asked over her glass of milk. "Gee. From up here they all sounded the same. I wish maybe I'd have been down there."

"The President, too," Peewee said. "The President was probably a better view from downstairs." Immediately he realized his error, however, and added, "But I would have liked to see it from up here. It's really neat, that window over there. You can see everything. We just have a warehouse out back."

"What did the President look like?" Beverly said.

"Like Eddie Stanky," Peewee replied.

"The baseball player? The shortstop for the Dodgers?"

"Second baseman," Peewee said.

He started to reach for another cookie. "How do you know about Eddie Stanky?" he said. "I mean, most girls wouldn't."

"I like to keep up on things," Beverly said.

Peewee wasn't certain what she meant. He thought of telling her about Eddie Stanky, about what he meant, about how he'd heard that President Truman, like Stanky, couldn't run, couldn't hit, et cetera. But he decided that would be too complicated. He bit into his cookie instead, embarrassed at the crumbs that sprayed the table. He pushed them together with his hand.

"My dad says that Dewey will get in next year, in any case," Beverly said. "Then we'll have the man on the wedding cake."

When Peewee seemed puzzled and did not respond, she added, "The way he looks, all starch and stiffed. You know what they say."

"Right," Peewee said, though he wasn't sure what it was they said. Governor Dewey as a ball player would be what? A boring Yankee, that much was certain. Governor Dewey might be Johnny Lindell.

The thought made him remember what day it was: the big doubleheader with the Braves. He wondered how they'd made out against Spahn, how Rex Barney would do in his first start. He wished at once that he was home and could turn on the radio. He didn't dare ask to do it here.

"What are you thinking about?" Beverly asked.

"Oh. Sorry," Peewee said. "Nothing. Just baseball."

"That's not nothing," Beverly said. "Not if you like it." She took her napkin and wiped her mouth with it and put it on the table.

"You ever seen television?" she asked.

"Once, in a store window," Peewee said.

"Would you like to see it now?"

"You got one?" Peewee said. "You have a television?"

"We got it last week," Beverly said.

"Really? I thought only rich peop—" He checked his swing, but not nearly in time.

Beverly didn't seem to mind. "My father works for RCA," she said.

"Oh . . . I thought . . . I thought he was a lawyer."

"He is. For RCA. All the executives got a chance for a terrific deal on these new sets last week. They want to get as many in use as they can. That way there will be more advertisers, and more shows. To get the whole industry rolling, Dad says. Someday television may be as big as radio, Dad says."

"You think it really will?"

"I don't know. Dad says. Of course, the price will have to come down a little before most people can afford them. You want to take a look?"

"Sure," he said, and he stood up as she did, placing his napkin on the table. He picked up his milky glass and looked about for the sink to put it in. "Never mind that," Beverly said. "Janet will take care of that."

Beverly strode briskly along some carpeted turns, Peewee following, till they entered a smallish room with no windows: just two plush armchairs and several folding chairs, set in a semicircle around a dark wooden cabinet taller than he was that faced out from the wall like an altar; like the *aron kodesh* in his father's *shul*. Beverly went to the cabinet and pulled open the double doors.

She turned a knob. At first nothing happened. Then a bunch of wavy black and white lines lit up the screen. "It takes a while to warm up," she said. As he watched, the lines began to stutter, to slow down, to slowly straighten out. All was settled except for a thick black band across the middle. Then with a sudden leap it jumped into place, the black band was gone, and there on the screen was a gray picture of a man on a horse, with a lot of empty land in the back.

"It's a cowboy!" Peewee said excitedly.

"It's Hopalong Cassidy," Beverly said.

"Who?"

"Hopalong Cassidy. He's the best of the cowboys, so far."

"What kind of name is that?"

"I don't know. It's just his name, I guess. There's another pretty good one named Bob Steele."

"I think I like Bob Steele better," Peewee said.

Beverly shrugged. "Anyway," she said, "you don't want to watch cowboys now, do you?"

"I don't?"

"I mean, you can see cowboys every Saturday at the Surrey."

Now it was Peewee's turn to shrug. "I guess."

Beverly gave him a sly, mysterious smile, doing something with her lips, this closed-mouthed smile, that made his blood run fast. Without taking her eyes from his face she reached back and clicked a dial. The Hopalong cowboy vanished. In its place for a moment was the thick black line again. Then, as before, it leaped into place, as if at some master's command, revealing—Peewee's heart jumped in his chest; he couldn't believe it at all—revealing Jackie Robinson, pigeon-toed, taking his lead off first.

"It's—it's Jackie Robinson—it's baseball—it's the Dodger game!"

"Brooklyn versus Boston," Beverly intoned. "Holiday doubleheader. I thought you might be interested."

"It's—" he stammered. "I didn't—I never heard they was broadcasting baseball yet!"

"It's experimental. To see how it works. Today is one of the games they're doing. So the cameramen can get used to the job and stuff. Next year they're planning to show lots of baseball, my Dad says."

Peewee forced his eyes from the screen to look at Beverly. She had known this when she invited him. It was a surprise, special for him.

"I think it's the very first transmission from Boston to New York," she said.

He looked back at the screen. Robinson was dancing, dancing. He couldn't tell if Jackie was going to go. It depended on the score.

"One out in the top of the ninth," Red Barber was saying, as if in answer to his thoughts. He hadn't been paying attention to the voice, which was tuned down low. Voices he'd always heard on the radio. "The Dodgers are trailing, six runs to three. Dixie Walker is at the plate."

The news sank in slowly. The Brooks were losing again, to Warren Spahn. But it was mitigated, was eased just now by the miracle of this picture on the screen in front of him. Also by the smile of Beverly

Rosenthal as she continued to watch not the screen but his face. Also because it was a doubleheader. They could easily bounce back in the second game.

"Swung at and fouled away," the Redhead said.

Warren Spahn was standing at the top of the screen. Dixie Walker was standing at the bottom. It was as if the field had been stood up on end. This he would have to get used to. The grayness, the absence of green, didn't bother him. It was the same grainy gray as the pictures in the newspapers every day.

Spahn checked Robinson at first, threw over easily. The picture swerved wildly as the camera followed the ball. Robbie stepped back quickly. They both knew he wasn't going, but Spahn wanted to keep him close. The camera swerved again as Torgeson threw the ball back to the mound.

Then it steadied, Spahn at the top of the screen again, Dixie Walker at the bottom. Spahn went into his windup, fired a sweeping curve. The damn ball curved a mile, Peewee thought. Walker hit it off the end of his bat, an easy fly ball to left center. The cameraman had some trouble locating Johnnie Hopp. He finally found him just as he caught the ball.

Two down.

One out left.

It was up to Furillo.

Peewee had sat on one of the chairs, was watching the screen intently. Beverly was gone from his mind. So too was the Lewis Morris, the apartment he was in, the parade. Gone even was the miracle of television. He was looking past it, through it. He was watching baseball.

Beverly, respecting his silence, watched too. Though she was beginning to hope it wouldn't go on too long. Baseball was an acquired taste, she figured. You had to work at it. Unless, like Peewee, you somehow had been born into the game.

"One ball, one strike," the Redhead said.

On the next pitch Furillo swung. A sharp rap headed up the middle. But Spahn speared it backhanded, tossed it easily to first. The game was over. The Dodgers had lost, 6 to 3. For an instant Peewee wanted to cry.

On the screen was the empty pitcher's mound, the empty home plate. It stayed that way for perhaps a minute, the way baseball lingers after the season ends. Then with a shudder of lines it was gone. In its place was a circle of light with stripes coming out. Red Barber's voice was replaced by a buzzing sound.

Peewee continued to stare. To see what would happen next. Nothing happened but the pattern and the buzz till Beverly got up and turned off the set. Peewee continued to stare at the now-dull vacant screen, his mind grasping at thoughts it could not contain. He felt as if something special had just happened, as if he had been present at some creation. The notion that before long he—everyone—would be able to sit in his house and not only hear baseball on the radio but actually see it: this seemed a paradise too enormous to contemplate.

"I'll let you know when they're showing another game," Beverly said. "If you like."

Soon without knowing how they had gotten there they were at the door. He thanked her for the milk and cookies, and for the television, and then, knowing that if he stood there a moment longer she might lean across and want to kiss him, which he was not sure he wanted her to do, he with a perfect instinct that surprised him beyond all measure reached out and lifted the comma of hair from her eye. Her left eye was there all right, a perfect duplicate of the right, and as his hand lingered a moment, holding the hair above it, it winked. The wink like electric current lit his face.

Shyly smiling, he backed across the hall, into the waiting elevator; and, seeing through the closing grate her other eye wink, he plummeted toward the center of the earth.

By the time he got home the police were all over the place. They were prowling the pavement and the alleys, the hallways and the basements, the street and all the surrounding streets, in search of Baby Lisa. They were spreading apart hedges, peering into garbage cans, even lifting the manhole covers from the sewers on the corner, the way the big kids did when a ball went down: peering anyplace someone could have ditched a policeman's kid.

In the house he found Hindy stretched out on the couch in the living room, under sedation provided by Dr. Greenberg. Upstairs, he was told, the distraught Felice was similarly sedated. His father filled him in on what had happened: how Baby Lisa had been stolen from her carriage.

"It's the Rag Lady! The Rag Lady must have taken her!" he burst out immediately.

His father merely smiled and hugged him with his arm.

"Have they checked the Rag Lady's house?" he insisted.

"They're checking everywhere," his father said.

He went into his room, his chest pounding with the excitement—he was far more excited than upset—and looked out the wide-open windows. The dark blue uniforms were everywhere: a cluster of them outside the house, where a command post seemed to be operating under the direction of a plainclothes detective, who at the moment had a walkie-talkie at his ear. Nearby the gray carriage remained unmoved, so that, he assumed, they could check it for fingerprints and other clues. Neighbors stood silently or in gossiping groups across the street, while uniformed police prowled everywhere, like ants on a hill, some of them even up on the roofs, checking in every corner, looking for the child.

"It's a good thing the parade was on," he heard his father saying. "So many police already in the neighborhood. They would never have sent so many. Especially on a holiday."

"It's because it's Mickey's," he heard his mother reply.

The voices stopped and then he heard others: the detective from outside with the walkie-talkie, his mother, his uncle Mickey. They came into the small room hardly noticing him, just as he until now had not noticed his grandma Lester tucked away in her wheelchair in the corner of the room, her head tilted down, apparently asleep.

"She had to have seen who did it," Mickey was saying. "She was facing right there, out the window."

"I've talked to her three times," his mother was saying, retreating in front of them. "You know she doesn't see much. You know her mind isn't there."

"It won't hurt to try again," the detective said.

They clustered around the wheelchair, Ruthie kneeling in front of it, taking her mother's hand, slowly rubbing it, fondly. "Now, Mama," she said slowly, articulating each word. "You understand what this is about? Baby Lisa is missing. You understand that? Hindy's Lisa was taken from her carriage. Do you hear what I'm saying?"

Miriam moved her right hand in annoyance, nodded her head with seeming impatience, as if to say: I understand. I understand.

"You were facing the window. The carriage—did you see anyone near the carriage? Did you see anyone take the baby?"

In the room the snow had been falling, but that is impossible. It does not snow in rooms, only outside there in the cloistered village where Alex was saying good-bye, Alex was leaving her, there in the falling snow turning his back and then a shot her hearing or making it up, they shooting him or was it she shooting him for leaving her, the face of death coming, a woman all in black, she had not known that death was a woman's face. A baby was taken, they say, they are speaking of taking babies, or do they mean making babies, making babies on a floor in Petersburg, Alex splitting her apart to make a baby, giving her two last presents, only one of them a wheel of red and black. That must be what was taken, the wheel of red and black. The baby nobody took. The baby was hers, the baby they brought with them across the sea. The one with the red hair. Sometimes she did not remember its name but now she did. Ruthie was its name. Her baby.

"Try to remember, Mama," Ruthie said. "Try."

Try to remember. But she can never forget.

"It was snowing," she says. "Death came."

His mother stood. "It's useless," she said. "I told you. She didn't see anything. She doesn't know anything. She must have been asleep, dreaming."

"Bad luck," the detective said. "She's the only possible witness we have so far. It seems the whole block was up at the parade. As if it was planned that way."

Mickey paced about in the room. "How can it be?" he said. "How can someone steal a baby and nobody see? And why?"

"We'll know when the ransom call comes," the detective said.

"There won't be a ransom call," Mickey said. "Not on a cop's salary."

"Maybe someone you collared once?" the detective said. "Revenge?"

"I never thought of that," Mickey said. "I can't think who."

"Well, think. Make a list for us. It's not likely, but you never know. Personally I think it's some frustrated woman who wants a child of her own. She's been watching the baby, parked out there every day. Today she made her move. It's too bad Mrs. Greenberg went to lie down. You people are too trusting around here." He paused before leaving the room. "I think I want to talk to her again, when she's able."

The detective left. Ruthie stood staring at or above her mother, absently—as if absently—picking flecks of white off Miriam's hair, arms.

"And where were you when it happened?" she said.

Her eyes were on her mother, but her quiet, bitter voice was aimed at Mickey.

"Me?" Mickey said. "What do you mean, where was I? You know where I was. I was up at the Concourse, working the parade."

"Yes," Ruthie said. "You were working." She peered into her cupped hand, where a small pile of white now rested: a pile of flecks of paint from the ceiling. When she looked at Mickey, her voice remained soft, but there was ice in her eyes.

"Mama said it was snowing," she said.

And she hurled the flecks of paint in Mickey's face and ran from the room.

Mickey stood, red-faced, wiping the flecks from his skin.

"What she do that for?" Peewee said.

Mickey glared at him, noticing him for the first time in the corner. "What the hell you doing here?"

Peewee fought an impulse to slink away, to disappear. "This is my room," he said robustly. Already he was on his mother's side, even if the attack seemed unprovoked. "You can get out if you want."

Mickey stared at him, uncomprehending, then ran his hand once more across his face and left. Peewee, standing in the corner, found his knees turning rubbery. He slid down along the wall and sat on the floor. Across the room his grandma Lester seemed to be sleeping again. He tried to understand what he'd seen and heard: why his mother threw the paint from the ceiling in Uncle Mickey's face. He thought till his head began to hurt. It didn't make any sense.

"Why don't they just go get the baby?" he said to his grandma's back. "Why don't they find the Rag Lady and get Baby Lisa back?"

But his grandmother didn't answer, didn't hear.

"Look everywhere!" a Nazi voice is shouting angrily.

"But Sarge, there's a million little crannies in this place. All these stacks of wood. No one could get in here. The gate was locked."

"I said everywhere," the Nazi voice barks. "Make believe it's your own goddamn kid!"

She hears their footsteps, occasionally hears a plank of lumber fall as they shove it aside. In the room where she is, it is quiet as a grave; until, as if on the downswing of a baton, the cats in the coal bin beside begin to howl as if to wake the witches of the night.

She closes her eyes to listen to the music. She sees a poster pasted on a wall. Concert Tonight, it says, above a picture of a woman seated at a piano. She cannot see the woman's face, though her posture seems familiar. Sold Out! a sticker across the woman's face says. And then, beneath the woman, on the lower part of the poster, she sees the words. Simple and stately they are. Olga Wiedkowski, they say.

So that is it, she thinks. Olga.

It has been several years since she has known her first name.

She is trying to ponder this unexpected return when above and outside she hears a frightful scream: the metal-curving scream of the train. She permits herself a meager thought of gratitude. Another train has come and gone, and still the child is safe.

And then she hears them, the footsteps in the alley, and her heart begins to thump in her chest as if she has been buried alive. Hears voices above, in the always-vacant house, feet stepping on broken glass, and other voices, closer, coming down the alley. "Check down there, that's where that garbage lady sleeps." The last word pains her, a surprising stab, for she has not felt pain for some time. *Sleeps*, instead of *lives*. A word from a stranger, a Nazi, yet, oddly, it causes her pain. And then the pain is cast away by the banging on the door.

She shuffles across the room to open it. They push in past her, two Nazis, three. They begin to look about. "What it is you want?" she says.

The room feels crowded with the three of them, and her, and the old man in his bed. One of them is crouching, looking under the bed. Another pats the bedclothes beside the old man.

"A baby is lost, missing," the leader says. "We're looking for a baby. Have you seen it?"

"A baby?" she says. She shrugs. The leader pushes past her, looks about. Eyes narrowing, he strides to the table, picks up an almost-empty jar of baby food.

"What's this?" he barks.

She shuffles toward the table, looks. "Food," she says. "For the old man. He has no teeth. No stomach. Is all he can eat."

"Where did you get it," he barks again.

"The store," she says, fearful now. Wishing the store were open so they could check. "The man with the big neck."

"Ben-Al Foods," one of the others says, coming over. "It's true. She buys it all the time for the old man." This one seems familiar. She has seen him in the neighborhood.

"You're sure?" the leader barks.

The other, kinder Nazi nods.

They seem to have looked everywhere. There is nothing here.

"What's that?" the leader barks, pointing to the other door, behind which the cats are screaming.

"The coal bin," she says.

The leader strides across the room, yanks open the door to darkness. The startled cats halt momentarily, then scream louder. One of them brushes out into the room. The leader takes a flashlight from his belt, sprays its beam into the room, up and down, back and forth across the coal. A cat leaps up through the small coal passage to the street. The others cringe in corners from the light.

The leader snaps off the flashlight, closes the dark door. Annoyed, he brushes from the bottom of his dark trousers invisible coal dust left by the cat that passed. It has fled across the room, out into the alley through the open door.

"Let's go," he says. "There's nothing here. We got two more blocks to cover."

With one last look around they leave. The kind one closes the door behind. She hears them kicking the nigger in the shoes. "Hey, you, wake up," one is saying. "We're looking for a baby. You seen a baby around?" She hears the nigger mumble something, but it is a half-hearted attempt to question him. In a moment she hears them leave him be. In a moment she hears through the door his breathing, his sleep.

Shakily she collapses onto her chair. She touches her hand to her hair, pushes a few hairs off her forehead. A few loose strands are wet. This remembered motion, this remembered wetness, makes her feel young again.

Danielle, she remembers. That is the child's name. Danielle.

# III

# June 16

In one fairy tale the hero comes to the witch's house and has to go in and kill her or he is done for. The next fairy tale tells him: Come to the witch's house, but as soon as you see her you had better turn around and go away or she will kill you. The next tells him: You have come to the witch's house, and you have to go in and sit with her and eat with her and be nice to her. One time the hero has to kill the beast, another time he has to avoid it—it may be the same animal.

Edward C. Whitmont,
*The Symbolic Quest*

167th Street Cafeteria and then going to a movie at the Mt. Eden or
the Surrey, not caring much what was playing, sometimes seeing the
same double bill three nights in a row, to get out of the hot apartment,
he would say. Phil and Annie moved through the house like Peewee,
ignored by the adults, the three of them sometimes going up to Phil
and Annie's to play in an almost conscious attempt out of the vision of
the unseeing adults to recapture their missing substance, to hang on to
their children's souls.

It was out of this sense of his own disappearing, perhaps, that Peewee felt compelled to act, to try to find the child himself and reaffirm
with a grand triumph his right to space in the house.

He began with the assumption that it was the Rag Lady who had
taken the child. What else could he assume? That was what the Rag
Lady was *for* as she prowled the streets, a messenger of God or of the
devil: to spirit little children away. Why else, as he had heard, did every
neighborhood have one? She was the weeder-out of little souls who
were bad. All his life he'd been told this, had spent a bit of most every
afternoon keeping out of her reach, her sight, with the at-least-passive
approval of the adults. Why, now that a child had actually been taken,
the adults gave little credence to the notion that the Rag Lady might
be the culprit, he could not understand. He had heard what Mickey
and the other policemen said, that the Rag Lady's dingy room somewhere in a basement beneath the el had been thoroughly searched
twice with no sign of Baby Lisa. But it seemed to him that if the Rag
Lady was really an agent of God or of the devil, then it would be an
easy trick for her to find a good place to hide a baby. He began to
suspect from their casual attitude that the adults did not believe in her,
and that perhaps to find her hiding place, it would take someone who
did. This was a concept of faith the enormity of which he did not yet
conceive. Far more troublesome to him just then was the question of a
reason: of why, of all the children on the block, the Rag Lady would
have taken Baby Lisa. How badly could this infant have misbehaved to
merit such an uprooting? To this question Peewee had no answer. He
could only assume that in the world of agents of God or of the devil,
some things were beyond an eight-year-old's knowing. Yet with each
passing day the need for him to act became clearer. If the adults early
on had relinquished the notion of the Rag Lady as actual kidnapper,
the image of little Lisa twisting and crying in that filthy sack grew

stronger and stronger within him; an image that, like a recurring dream, would not go away. It was as if she were crying out to him for rescue; specifically to him—Benjamin Peewee Brunig—the future shortstop of the Dodgers. With each passing day he became more convinced that the child would not be found unless it was he who found her.

And so he evolved his plan. He, with Phil as his accomplice, would search the alleys and warehouses and basements that lined Jerome Avenue under the el until they discovered where the Rag Lady lived. Alone and unknown to the adults they would have to go. They would have to seek her out at whatever cost and force her in some way he had not yet devised to give the baby back.

"We have to do it," he said to Phil that Saturday.

"We do?" Phil said. His pinkish face had turned white at the notion. His neck had begun to recede turtlelike into his chest.

"We do," Peewee said. "It's your sister, for chrissake!"

"I know it's my sister. But the cops have been looking for two whole weeks. My father, too."

"They haven't found her," Peewee said quietly.

"If you're so sure the Rag Lady has her, why don't you tell them, then?"

"I told them," Peewee said. "They don't believe me."

Phil did not respond. He, too, had been raised with the Townsend Avenue tales. It made simple sense that the Rag Lady had taken Lisa. He did not know what people did with common sense when they grew up.

"I think you're right," he said.

The words had come blurting out before he could stop them.

"It's up to you and me," he added, compounding this unexpected bravery. "We've got to go and get my sister back."

Peewee looked solemnly at Phil. He stuck out his hand and they shook. Both of them noticed that their hands were sweating. Neither of them mentioned it. Both of them rubbed their palms on their pants.

And so the bargain was struck. On Monday morning they would start out for school as usual. But instead of going to school, they would stash their books somewhere and set out on the search for the Rag Lady; and, through her, for Baby Lisa.

"Can Annie come too?" Phil asked.

"Annie's too little," Peewee said.

"We can use her as a lookout while we go exploring," Phil said. He was not certain why he was suggesting this. He usually was happy to leave his little sister out of things. "It might be good to have a girl along," he added. "The Rag Lady might be nicer to girls."

"I doubt it," Peewee said. "Baby Lisa who she stole is a girl. But it doesn't matter, anyway. We already got a lookout who's a girl."

Phil cocked his head to the side. "What do you mean 'we already got?' "

Immediately Peewee realized his mistake. "I don't mean we already got, exactly. I was thinking of asking someone to come help us. This girl, Beverly, who lives in the Lewis Morris."

"What do we want her for?" Phil asked.

" 'Cause her father's a lawyer," Peewee said.

"Oh," Phil said. He adopted an aura of deepest concentration. "Good thinking." Beverly Rosenthal was pretty damn cute, he recalled, and if Peewee couldn't hold her, if Peewee succumbed instead to his obvious infatuation with little Annie—they both had the very same birthday, after all—then he, Phil, might get her instead. "I guess she can come," Phil said, "since you already asked her before telling me the plan."

Peewee looked at the ground, red-faced but unapologetic. "I didn't want to call her on the weekend," he said, "with her parents around and all. So I sort of asked her yesterday, in school. I told her it wasn't definite, though. I told her it depended if my cousin Phil thought it was a good plan."

"You did?"

"Sort of," Peewee said.

It was the most the one would give, the most the other would get.

"Okay, then," Phil said.

"Okay, then," Peewee said. "She's gonna meet us by the tunnel. On the way to school."

"Okay," Phil said.

"Monday, then," Peewee said.

"Monday, then," said Phil.

Ruth lies alone in her bed in the warm June evening thinking: you do not really need sex. When a woman is forty-four years old and has two growing boys and has not had sex in any liberating sense for all these many years, then the need for it dwindles. You can fill your life with preparing breakfast and lunch for the boys, with shopping for groceries, with the crossword puzzle in the *Times*, with mah-jongg with a sister and friends on Wednesday nights, with a movie with Lou and Mickey and Hindy or Felice and Sam at the Mt. Eden or the Surrey, with a monthly dinner at the Lobster Box in Times Square. You do not need sex. The mechanical kind with Lou had become an unpleasant chore until both of them in unspoken agreement let more and more time pass between until it was months and then actual years and they had not bothered with it, feeling at first that this was a guilty secret, until even that feeling fell away. They have been married seventeen years. What more do they have to prove? It is a fact of life.

You do not need sex, Ruth thinks, lying alone in her bed. She has put Mama to bed in Eli's old room, Mama seeming slowly to be improving, though where she gets her strength from, Ruth doesn't know. Eli is at the kitchen table, bent over his books, studying for final exams. She has shooed Hindy away to her own house. It is Sunday night, her family needs some time alone; she actually had the nerve to tell Hindy this tonight. Hindy pretended to understand but cried as she left. Lou has gone to his office at the *shul* to catch up on some paperwork. To get away from the madness in the house, she knows. To wrestle again with his conscience, she knows, with his agony over whether to stay put or to accept the job at the Mt. Eden Center. There is more to it than that, this she can sense, but Lou has not said what the more to it is, and she hasn't pressed him, not with all the chaos over the theft of Baby Lisa. Perhaps, she thinks, he is not at the office at all. Perhaps her Lou has found himself a girl to *shtup*. Maybe, she thinks, she will call him at the office to make sure he is really there, find some pretense. But she knows she will not do this; this is unworthy, Lou is not the type. Lou is busy with *shul* work, busy with his private agony. Besides, she thinks, if Lou has found some willing young girl it would be only fair. It would be more than fair, it would be good. It would help ease her own dark soul.

You do not need sex Ruth tells herself, lying alone in her bed, the twisted sheet thrown off. In the next room through the wall she can hear Peewee tossing and turning in his own narrow bed, unable, it seems, to sleep. The Dodgers have lost five straight. This curious trauma of an American boyhood: he cannot eat, he cannot sleep, because nine men in flannel knickers halfway across the city, or now on a road trip halfway across the country, are not hitting the ball well, or catching it well, or pitching it well. Whatever it is that the Old Redhead has been bemoaning this week over the yellow plastic radio when it is not turned to the hated news. "We have a late bulletin from the newsroom: Mrs. Ruth Brunig, wife of Rabbi Louis Brunig of the Beth Shalom Temple, and her brother-in-law, Patrolman Mickey Hirsch, are no longer fucking each other's ears off in a secret hideaway in the Concourse Plaza Hotel, under the mournful eyes of a picture of the late Lou Gehrig. Now back to Bing Crosby singing 'When You Wish Upon a Star.'" The Old Redhead, she thinks. The Old Redhead is me. And the thought leaps into her mind for the first time in weeks of the moment of her mother's stroke. She wonders again who the mysterious Alex was.

You do not need sex, she tells herself, awkwardly pulling in the dark her nightgown above her knees, high above, until like a white cat in the night it comes, until with a rhythm all its own, unstoppable as the rain, Mickey's thick prick is in her, Mickey's thick tongue is in her, and hers on him, licking, sucking, loving it as if it were a part not of him but of her, until with the unasked-for unsought yet hardly unwanted love and unstoppable passion they fuse with this terrible beautiful secret between them: a secret they must take to the grave. Until then you do not need sex. And then when it starts it is the falls over Niagara, the terrible beautiful all-encompassing mist which she has seen in pictures in *Life* magazine, love-passion suffusing her middle years, or year, or three months, more precisely, these stolen meetings, assignations, guilt free because they did not seek it, did not ask for it, neither he nor she, it simply stole upon them like a robe of God, and how to shed a robe of God? Better to wear it over naked flesh. Better to revel in its glory. This breasted, nippled, warm-balled naked gift. This heat.

She tries but nothing happens. She tries thinking of Fredric March, of Clark Gable as Rhett Butler, of the kid Frank Sinatra, even of young Larry Paltz over at the *shul*. Nothing. Only the thought or rather not the thought but the memory of Mickey's face in her thighs arouses her. And this she will not do, this she dare not do, this she must get over, even in memory. She must turn elsewhere or die. And so with the willpower that everyone thinks is the center of her being she pulls her fingers away from her own dryness, pulls the nightgown down with the petulance of a child, wrenches herself onto her side and tries to sleep: tossing and turning even as Peewee is, hearable through the wall.

"Dear Lord," she says, as she has said in bed every night for months. "Let me die tonight and never wake."

And takes advantage of being alone, and lets the tears come pouring out. Loses control, all consciousness, of the sobs that wrench her chest.

Peewee, hearing through the wall, thinks: I have to find the baby and bring her back. So Mommy won't cry anymore.

The rabbi sat at his cluttered desk in his office at the *shul*. From the moment he unlocked the door he had seen the angel sitting there, perched like some Chagall creation on a quarter-moon in the stained-glass window that looked out over the vacant lot. He had left Peewee getting ready for bed early because there was school tomorrow, Eli studying for his finals, Ruthie taking aspirins, rid at last for the night of Hindy's moans, and had walked up the warm June block through the streetlight pools past people sitting in front of apartment houses, hoping for an evening breeze, "Hello, Rabbi," some of them saying, even the Italians, he nodding, saying good evening, keeping on his pace. Tonight was not for being nice. Tonight he needed to be alone.

He pulled open the lower drawer of the desk, placed both his black-shoed feet on it, leaned back in his gray swivel chair with both hands flat on top of his head: his favorite posture for thinking, born long years ago, perhaps out of constant insecurity over whether his yarmulke was still on his head. On his desk was a note the sexton had scrawled and left for him Friday afternoon, while he was home for lunch: that a Detective Marion Cole of the Bronx north division had phoned, would like to speak with him in person, would stop by on Monday morning if that was convenient. He had not given it much thought, did not do so now. It had to do, no doubt, with Baby Lisa. He had told them all he knew, which was not very much, several times. In his thoughts now was the decision he had to make about the Mt. Eden Center. The minority on the board of directors had prevailed, at least for the moment. He had been offered the job. No guarantees could be given about his various demands, they'd said. About his dream. They would, of course, try to accommodate the ideas of a new director, within reason, of course. But no guarantees. Their only request was that he give them an answer within a week, so that if he decided not to make the switch, they could initiate their long-planned nationwide search for a rabbi of stature. Louie listened to all this with faint disgust, leaving the meeting in a modest fury, and yet, after a few hours, calmed down, trying to be reasonable, trying to see their side. It was an offer that in his lifetime would not come again. Seeing what the directors in their shortsightedness—a curiosity amid all their pompous talk—did not seem to realize: that the job carried with it stature. That whomever they chose—even he, Louis A. Brunig—would instantly become, upon the public announcement of his appointment, a rabbi of stature.

"So," the angel said, breaking his bemused silence. "Is that what you want? Is that what it's all been about? Staturehood?"

"Don't *hock* me," Louie said. "You know that's not what it's about."

"What, then?" the angel said.

Louie reached up behind him, switched off the lamp, hoping the angel would go away.

"I'm not afraid of the dark," the angel said.

"I know, I know," Louie said. "My eyes are tired, okay. Do you mind?"

"Me? I don't mind nothing," the angel said.

"No? Sometimes I think you mind everything. You mind everybody's business but your own."

"Ah. But that, precisely, is my business," the angel said.

To which Louie did not reply. Instead he posited a question: "So. What do *you* think I should do?"

"Me? I don't give answers. Only questions I give."

"Very Socratic," Louie said.

"Don't knock it," the angel said. "Shlomo was a good man."

"Shlomo?"

"Socrates. His Jewish nickname."

"Socrates has a Jewish nickname?"

"Most smart men do. Not all. But most."

"Who's to argue?" the rabbi said.

He dropped his hands from the top of his head, rubbed his eyes, his cheeks. He leaned his elbows on the desk, propped his face in his hands.

"Ah," the angel said. "A picture of rabbinical Confusion. Rabbinical Consternation. With a capital C."

"Screw off," the rabbi said. Then, looking up quickly in the dark, "I'm sorry. I didn't mean that."

"It's all right," the angel said. "Maybe that's what you all need around here. A little effing off."

The rabbi, without lifting his head, raised his eyes over his hands, glanced toward the opalescent half-moon. Not exactly startled but bemused. He had, in fact, been thinking of Rebecca, the poster girl.

"If you'll excuse me," the angel said, "I've got to go for a moment. I'll be right back."

"Go?" the rabbi said.

"You don't need me to fantasize."

"Showoff," Louie muttered, but the half-moon was already empty, the angel gone.

To the foot of Miriam's bed, where she lay unasleep in Eli's room. With her returning health she was growing slightly more self-confident, more crotchety. Her hands were clasped on her stomach, outside the bedclothes.

"You're late," she said. "Where were you?"

"Me?" the angel said. "I'm never late."

"You weren't here," Miriam said. "So you're late."

"I am where I am," the angel said.

"Hoo-hoo-hoo," Miriam said. "Angelhood is getting close to Godlihood."

"Of course."

"Of course nothing," Miriam said. "That's not what I heard."

"Ah," the angel said, crossing one knee over the other. "You've been talking to Max."

"Yes."

"And?"

"I want to tell him."

"About Alex? About Ruthie?"

"Yes."

"A secret, you said. A secret you would carry to the grave."

"I know what I said. But the grave is going away again. You—they—are taking the grave away from me."

"It'll come back, one day."

"You're telling me something? Angel wisdom is that? That much I know without you. But there comes a time, I think maybe, to give up secrets."

"In return for . . . ?"

"I'm not sure. Other secrets, perhaps."

"Maybe worse ones."

"Maybe. That I thought of, too. But there comes a time, you come to my age, you take a chance. Don't you think?"

"I have no opinion."

"I've noticed that lately," Miriam said. "Maybe you should see somebody."

"See somebody?"

"A specialist."

"Ah. In what?"

"Vacillation. Anyway, enough chatter," Miriam said. "I'm going to tell Max. Part of me always wanted him to know. A good time now to tell him, now that he's dead and gone."

"Gone where?" the angel said.

"I said enough! Enough religion. Enough philosophy. I want to tell him everything!"

The angel sat at the foot of the bed, crossed his legs. "Miriam?"

"What?"

"I have to tell you something."

"What?"

"He knows."

"He knows? Who knows? Who knows what?"

"Max knows. Max knows everything."

"I don't believe it!"

"Believe," the angel said.

"You told him? Why did you tell him?" Her hands clenched at the bedclothes, then went slack, anger giving way to disappointment mixed with relief. "It was up to me to tell him," she said weakly.

"I didn't tell him," the angel said gently. "He knew. He always knew."

Limp in the bed she lay. She felt as if all her life a secret steel spike had supported her backbone, and now it was giving way.

"He knew?"

"All along," the angel said. "He wasn't a dummy, you know, your Max. When you went to Petersburg that one last time, he knew. You wouldn't go to see an uncle. When you came back with that box, that game—"

"Roulette."

"Roulette, he knew where you had gotten it. From Alex."

"Impossible! Alex was dead. Everyone thought Alex was dead. I told them so."

"No one thought Alex was dead. Only you, sometimes."

She felt as if she were dreaming: a dream she had dreamed many times before.

"Why, then? Why did he let me go? If he knew I was going to see Alex again?"

"One last time, he thought. To get it out of your system. If he forbade it, he thought, you would think of Alex all the days of your life."

"He was right," Miriam said. "I would have."

"He was wrong," the angel said. "Because you did anyway."

Miriam placed her hands over her eyes, closed them as if she were closing the eyes of a corpse.

"Yes," she said.

She lay in silence in the dark, taking deep breaths, afraid to continue, knowing that she must. Knowing she must face the impossible.

"And Ruthie? He knew that, too?"

"Of course."

"The hair. The red hair. But it was in my family, too."

"Not like that," the angel said.

Miriam nodded, her head still on the pillow, her eyes still closed, nodded, eyes closed the way men do when saying certain prayers. Certain Yom Kippur prayers.

"But he loved her," she said. "He loved Ruthie more than the others. Why, if he knew? If he knew he would have hated her."

"Because she was better than the others," the angel said. "Because he felt your Alex was a better man than he. That he was only a poor substitute. And Ruthie was the proof."

"But that's not true!" Miriam said loudly, vehemently, louder than she had spoken in months. "Alex was a shit, a fraud. Max was the better man."

"Yes. But not in Max's eyes. Alex was a revolutionary, a man of action. You remember what Max said. None of his children would grow up to be president. But Ruthie's—one of Ruthie's, perhaps. You remember?"

She lay with her arms at her sides, trying to remain calm, trying not to shake. "A poor substitute," she said. "How could he feel that way?"

The angel said nothing, tried to remain expressionless.

"Because I made him feel that way," she said. "Because I thought of Alex every day."

She sighed, wiped at her eyes with her hand. "And he put up with it," she said. "Such a good man. *That* he put up with, *that* knowledge, every day of our lives. And never said a word. And never took revenge."

The angel couldn't help smiling. "Bullshit," he said.

"Yes," Miriam said, beaten and emotionless. "Bullshit. That was why he was *shtupping* every hussy on the Lower East Side. With every *shtup* he was getting even."

"And this you knew all along," the angel said.

"Of course."

There was silence in the room for a long time. Miriam surprised herself by smiling.

"You know what I used to tell myself," she said, "after he made that invention? I used to say to myself: everybody else he gives his prick. Me he gives a foot."

The angel, too, smiled, nodded. "Maybe the foot was more important."

"Maybe," Miriam said.

While in his office at the synagogue the rabbi paces about, waiting for the angel to return; knowing he will not return tonight. Even angels break their promises, he thinks: knowing this is not the case. Angels aren't interested in poses, only in truth; the best available truth, at least.

Pacing about, he pushes open the stained-glass window, looks out into the June night. Beneath the window and slightly to the left a couple of teenagers, a boy and a girl, are pressed against the temple wall, pulling and poking at each other. So young, he thinks, to be doing things like that; and in such a place. In the near-darkness the boy resembles Eli; the girl even looks a bit like Gloria from upstairs, with her fluffy hair. But he knows they are not. Eli is home in the kitchen, bent over his books, studying for final exams. The rabbi is glad of this at least: he is raising good Jewish boys.

In late spring and summer Peewee did not like sleeping in the front room. To get enough air you had to leave the windows open, the venetian blinds pulled several feet up. This left too much black un- guarded room through which monsters could leap in. Not to mention the Rag Lady.

To keep his mind off her, he told himself again and again that the Dodgers were going to win the pennant. But there was doubt in the air this night. The Dodgers were in fourth place. Pee Wee Reese was hitting .241. That was a dead weight in the starting lineup of a pennant contender.

Peewee had given much thought to his hero's slump the preceding week. He had studied over and over again a picture in Wednesday's *Times,* a picture of Reese smashing a double off the wall. It was one of his rare hits of late, but something about the picture was wrong. Pee- wee cut it out of the paper, pasted it on the wall near his bed, studied it on and off for two days while Hindy moaned on the sofa in the living room. And then he saw: Reese was not choking up on the bat. Reese was swinging from the end: a sin, a blasphemy in the fraternity of slick- fielding shortstops, whether eight years old or twenty-nine. This swing- ing-from-the-end, swinging-from-the-heels swing may well have pro- duced the smashing double described in the picture's caption. But it had also produced, Peewee was certain, many a routine fly ball instead of a slashing line drive. It was, he knew at once, responsible for Pee Wee's meager .241.

The next question was why. Why was Reese, a bunter, a hit-and- runner, a confirmed choke hitter, swinging from the end of the bat? This, too, he figured out quickly. It was because they had him batting eighth. With the pitcher coming up behind him, Reese did not want to walk, did not want to slap out singles only to have the man behind him ground into a double play. So Reese was going for the long ball, swing- ing from the end to clear the bases, to knock in runs. Which was not a shortstop's role. Which was why Pee Wee Reese was hitting only .241. Which was why the Brooks were mired in fourth.

All this Peewee saw illuminated, the way some people see angels, or God. Like those people, he believed implicitly in what he saw. And like them, he did not know what to do about it. To tell others was only to invite doubt or, at best, bemusement. And yet some action was clearly called for, or what was illumination for?

He could, he thought, lying asweat in his bed, hearing Eli leaving the house, through with his studying, going out no doubt to palm like a basketball Gloria Greenberg's tits, hearing his mother crying in her bed, he could, he thought, desperate to shut this out, write a letter to Pee Wee Reese, point out to him what the shortstop himself may not have realized.

He could do this, but he could not. An eight-year-old does not give advice to a major leaguer.

He stared closed-eyed at the ceiling, drifting at last toward sleep. The monsters, real or potential, from the lower half of the windows were only half forgotten.

# 2

THE CHILD IS in the coffin, asleep. Daylight has come but with great reluctance. Dark clouds brood over the city.

Her remembering has returned increasingly since she took the child: mostly the bad memories that in the past months, years, had been hidden. But also good ones: the white godlike curve of the Matterhorn sweeping heavenward above Zermatt; the black lake at Lucerne dotted with white swans; the opera house at Milan; a boy on a bicycle who tossed flowers to her after four different concerts in four different cities, always the same boy. With these memories she tries to offset the terrors of the bad; though these, too, she must face, she knows, in order to be whole again.

The baby she calls Danielle, though when the nigger asks her how she knows this name, the question confuses her. Danielle was someone else.

Her memories alternate like moods, black and white: like the keys of distant pianos. Deceptive phrases by Beethoven, leading up to the expected and then veering off.

"Coffee ready yet?" the nigger asks. The nigger has knocked on the door, opened it without waiting for a response, poked his head inside. The nigger has become more familiar with her ever since, the night of the parade, he found her with the child, as if sharing this secret has made him more than just a neighbor, has made them comrades.

It had become different that first night, when she told him of the police visits, and then showed him the child.

"I used to live in Poland," she had said. They were sitting in the street as usual, on their overturned milk crates, the child asleep in the coffin deep inside.

"In Warsaw," she continued. "A nice city, very pretty. Till the Nazis came."

She paused then, as if her mind was off somewhere else; as if it was not struggling with itself. He did not question, merely sat and waited. Overhead on the el a holiday-night train screamed.

"They started disappearing. Neighbors. Friends. On the trains. Being taken to farms in the country, the Nazis said. To help on the farms. Being taken away each week. On the trains. Sisters, brothers, my husband. Then they took my daughter. It was time to leave. To save the child. My granddaughter. I told no one. I walked away from the ghetto. The Nazis did not stop me; I came and went all the time. I was Madam Wiedkowski, who played for the emperor. She was three years old. I clutched her hand and we walked away through the city, out in the countryside."

She stops, hearing the black notes inside her, then the white. "I was very good," she said. She stops again. "The child's name was Danielle. She's here with me now. In the dark she sleeps. I think I should go check on her."

He watches, says nothing as, standing up from the milk crate, she seems to grow shorter: to shrink from the piano player into the broken creature who shares his alley, his life. He watches as she shuffles down the alley. A minute later she returns, sits again.

All day long they had walked, away from the ghetto, across the city, out into the countryside. Always away from the ghetto, away from the trains. Past houses at first, then fewer houses, then fertile fields, then empty fields, until at last they were passing forestland. Hungry and tired, they walked until the child could walk no more; until she could carry her no more. The sky in late afternoon was growing dark, as dark finally as the shirts the Nazis wore. They would hide in the forest, she thought, and pray; but as they crossed the road she saw atop a nearby hill an old Catholic cemetery. "There we will spend the night," she thought, thinking no further than that, and under the lowering clouds they climbed the hill.

The cemetery had no gate. It was a simple gathering of hundreds of stones, marking for eternity the final resting place of many hundred people once alive. Each stone had a name, a date, an inscription. This she would remember later. Names, dates, inscriptions. They moved amid the stones until, too tired to go farther, she lay down behind one of the larger ones, hugging the child to her. Hugging Danielle.

And then under the el she pressed her fingers to her eyes; to press away remembering.

Beverly was waiting under the tunnel. She had sent her girlfriends on ahead, had pretended she had to go back, get something she'd forgotten, some pretense or other at which girls were so clever and boys were so inept. She had also, Peewee noticed, convinced her mother that because of the impending rain she be allowed to wear dungarees to school instead of a skirt. Peewee liked her looks in dungarees. He could almost imagine a baseball cap on her head. B. Rosenthal, third base. Where he could back her up, when necessary, on grounders into the hole. Dungarees because there was no telling what climbing or squirming or running they might have to do today.

Their greetings weren't spoken, were merely nods.

Peewee looked at Annie, then at Phil.

"You go on to school," Phil said.

Annie squinted, looked from one to the other. "What about you?" she said.

Under the tunnel where they had paused it was always gray, even on sunlit days. Now with the sky lowering on both sides it was darker still. Rush-hour people on their way to work pushed past them on all sides into the station doors, hardly noticing the children. Passing cars filled the humid tunnel rotunda with exhaust.

"We've got something to do," Phil said.

Annie, without hesitating said, "I'll do it too."

"This is only for boys," Phil said. Peewee closed his eyes, winced.

"What about her?" Annie said. She jerked with her thumb toward the intruder in their midst, this girl who she could already tell was after Peewee.

They looked from one to the other. Annie would not be disposed of easily.

"Let her come," Beverly said. "I'll keep an eye on her."

Annie smiled slightly at her a-little-too-pretty new friend.

"I'm Beverly," Beverly said.

"I'm Annie," Annie replied.

Peewee looked at Phil. Phil shrugged his fat shoulders. Peewee shrugged back. He looked for no reason at the underside of the high tunnel, above which the Grand Concourse ran, the underside of which for some reason was always wet, even when it hadn't rained for weeks. Then he looked solemnly from one face to the next, establishing his leadership.

"Let's do it," he said.

Again they looked from one to the other and nodded nervously, as they had seen soldiers do in war movies before the last tough assault.

"Let's do what?" Annie said.

"Never mind," Phil said.

"You just stay close," Peewee said.

"Yes, sir!" She threw him a mock salute. Beverly fought hard not to giggle. For a moment there was a sternness in Peewee that she had never seen before. Then, as quickly as it had come, it passed.

"Okay," he said. "First we got to stash these books."

"What for?" Annie said.

Peewee looked at her, a flash of his sternness returning.

"Sorry," Annie said.

"I'll hide them," Peewee said. "You guys wait here."

He held out his hands, his books. One after the other they piled their books on his. Without a word he left them standing under the tunnel, walked to its edge and disappeared around it into the rocks behind the vacant lot, slipped into and up a crevice he had climbed many times before on days when there were no baseball games. About fifteen feet up, he placed the books in a foot-deep niche in the rocks. Then, looking around in every direction as if to be sure he would not be seen, he unbuttoned and pulled off his brown-and-white plaid shirt and stuffed it into the niche above the books. Beneath the shirt he was wearing the top half of his baseball uniform: gray flannel, with the word *Dodgers* emblazoned in red—not blue—across the front. He stood a moment among the boulders. Then, slowly, he started down. Phil, he realized, would be upset.

He found them standing where he'd left them. As he approached, he saw the hurt in Phil's blue eyes.

"Where'd you get that?" Phil said.

"Where'd you get your baseball shirt?" Annie said.

"Had it under my other shirt," he said.

"Whyn't you tell me?" Phil asked. "I could have worn mine, too."

Peewee had no answer. He shrugged, looked at the pavement; then at Beverly's face. What he found there was not admiration.

Peewee, she was thinking, was a bit more complicated than she'd thought.

Embarrassment flushed Peewee's face.

"The hell with goddamn shirts!" he said. "Let's go find the kid."

"Let's go what?" Annie said. Her eyes rolled heavenward; her cheeks filled with air, making them as fat as Phil's, till slowly she let the air out. She was squinting with new excitement at her cousin. At the future shortstop of the Dodgers. (Whatever it was *shortstop* meant. A fielder without a base: like a book she'd seen in the school library: *A Man Without a Country.*)

"Screw it," Phil said. "Let's get a move on."

For a moment they stood immobile, frozen in the tunnel gloom. Then, as if with a communal act of will, they put the matter of the shirt behind them.

"Let's find Lisa!" Annie whispered.

They started off in single file, out from under the tunnel, Peewee, with unspoken understanding, in the lead.

The rabbi was sitting at his desk going through the bills—the heat, the electricity, they were three months behind on the bills, he would have to ask for donations again or else raise the price of tickets for the High Holy Days.

The knock on the door was soft. "Come in," he said absently. Behind the slowly opening door was a woman, young, slim, on the small side, hair cut shorter than most women wore it, but neat as it framed her face, tiny gold earrings visible on tiny but well-shaped ears—the rabbi was aware he had been aware of such things lately—clear brown eyes, a very small nose, but nice, less lipstick than even Ruthie wore, a necklace of pearls on a suntanned neck. Her face was lightly tanned as well, he realized, though not like the poster girl's. Beneath it a tailored gray suit, a white blouse. He stood behind his desk.

"Rabbi Brunig?"

"Yes?"

"I'm Marion Cole. I hope you got my message."

"Message? No, I don't . . . Wait, a detective? You're not the detective?"

"I'm afraid I am," she said, closing the door behind her. "May I?"

He'd assumed Detective Cole was a man. There were not many lady detectives around.

The rabbi scooted around the desk, pulled up a folding chair, offered it to her. "I'm sorry there's nothing more comfortable," he said. "Funds are a bit short these days."

"This is fine," the detective said, sitting, crossing one knee over the other, smoothing her skirt. Her legs were lovely, he noticed. He returned to his own chair behind the desk.

"You've come about the baby," he said.

"The baby?"

"I've told them all I know, which isn't much. I was up at the parade when it happened."

"I'm afraid I don't understand," the detective said.

"You didn't come about the baby? Lisa Hirsch?"

"Oh, the Hirsch child. Is she related to you?"

"My niece," the rabbi said.

"I'm sorry," the detective said, briefly touching an earring with her hand. "I didn't know that."

"Yes." Leaning back. "They'll find her alive soon, God willing."

The detective smiled. A modest, Meet Miss Subways smile. "I hope so," she said. She uncrossed her legs, crossed them again the other way. "I'm not here about the baby, however." She opened a small purse she was carrying, began to remove a slim gold cigarette case, then thought better of it and put it back.

"That's all right, smoke if you like," the rabbi said.

She nodded and slowly lit a cigarette. "I'm here about the guns," she said.

Louie had a sense that he was falling. He reached forward, steadied his hands on the desk.

"Meaning what?"

"Meaning you've got to stop."

"And if I don't? Am I under arrest, Detective"—he glanced around the desk for the sexton's note "Cole."

The detective put her still-long cigarette in an ashtray on his desk. "Nobody said anything about arrest, Rabbi. This visit is unofficial. All we want you to do is to stop. There won't be any charges, any scandal. Nothing like that."

"And why do you want me to stop?"

"Because what you're doing is against the law."

The rabbi nodded. "Yes, I suppose that's true. I suppose I would have to admit it's against the law.

"And the Germans?" he said. "The Nazis? Wasn't what they did against the law?"

"If you'll excuse an expression of my waitress-mother," the detective said, "that wasn't my station."

"Of course not," Louie said. "No offense. Nothing personal. But it wasn't Roosevelt's station, either. Or Stalin's. Or Churchill's. It wasn't even the pope's station, was it?"

Miss Cole's face flushed slightly. She looked down at her lap.

"No offense," the rabbi said. "Truly. You see, it wasn't my station, either. Me, a rabbi. A Hebrew teacher then. I myself didn't go fight. I was too old to fight. But this," he said, tapping the desk with his forefinger, hard, "this—will you look at me please?—this Palestine, this *Eretz Yisroel*—this *is* my station."

She had looked at him at his command, was frowning now, her lips pressed together, pressed for the moment slightly bloodless, he noticed. She looked again at her lap, again at him, at a loss only momentarily.

"Rabbi," she said, "I sympathize. I truly do. But I'm a policeman. An officer of the law. I can't close my eyes to what I know. I've sworn an oath to uphold the law." She hesitated, then risked it. "You, as a rabbi, a Jew—"

"Don't say it," Louie said. "I know the whole speech." He stood, walked to the stained-glass window, pushed it open, looked out into the vacant lot. "I've even used it myself in sermons." Speaking with his back to her. "As Jews, we must uphold the law, because it is only the law that can save us, that can prevent it from happening here. The hearts and minds of men cannot be trusted. That much the Nazis showed us. Only in the law can we put our faith. You see," he said, turning to face her, "I know the whole speech."

He moved toward his chair, sat again, trying to sort out again his own tangled motives: what part was patriotism toward the future state of Israel; what part some dispersed vicarious aggression, violence against the humdrum parts of his life; what part the tingling pride of merely having such a secret.

"Are you Irish, Miss Cole? Detective?"

"Miss Cole is fine," she said. "Or Marion. Half Irish, half Scottish."

"A nice combination, if you don't mind my saying so. But Catholic."

"Yes."

"Do you believe what Jesus said? Everything?"

She hesitated, decided to allow herself to be led. To see where he was going. "I suppose."

"Do you believe in turning the other cheek, for instance?"

She had the curious image of lying in bed beside this rabbi. He wasn't handsome, but there was an attractive mixture to him, at once gentle and sincere, yet also some authority. This man of God, as her mother called the priests. She certainly did not understand why priests needed to be celibate. All it did was give the ladies dreams.

Rabbi Brunig, she imagined, would be gentle.

"I suppose it depends," she said.

"Yes," Louie said. "It depends. Sooner or later you run out of cheeks. With the Nazis, I think you'll admit, we turned a great many cheeks. Now I help send guns. Can I do any less?"

"You haven't asked me how we know about the guns," she said.

"What difference does it make? An investigation, right? Not a stool pigeon, I hope. Is that the proper word? *Stool pigeon?*"

"Yes. No, not a stool pigeon. Just some neighborly suspicions about the truck. Some complaints. We know about the green trucks."

"So, *nu?* Is that all? I'll tell them to send a blue one next time."

The detective could not help smiling. "Rabbi, it's serious business. I'm not sure you understand. Trafficking with a foreign power. It's a federal offense. The FBI could get involved."

"The Hagganah a foreign power? That's a good one. So how are you involved, then?"

"Transporting illegal weapons. Harboring them without a permit. City violations."

"Violations! Talk about violations! Do you know . . ." His mind was racing with the Nazi atrocities of which he'd read and heard. With an effort he checked himself. "But that's not the issue, is it? The issue is that you have an oath to uphold."

"Yes." She put out the cigarette that was still burning in the ashtray.

"And also that your superiors know. You've already written reports."

She looked down and then at him again. "Yes."

"And this scandal you mentioned before—that was their idea, to say that, right? Not yours."

She nodded, a bit forlorn. She had known he wouldn't be stupid. Not all scholars are stupid.

"Because I'm sure you, personally, understand how nice that would be," he said, feeling more relaxed now, leaning back in his chair, as if somewhere deep inside him without his conscious knowing it he had already come to a decision. " 'Rabbi Defies Authorities: Admits Gunrunning.' You know what that would make me in this neighborhood? A hero, that's what. Not only among the Jews. And to my wife, too." Immediately he regretted that, regretted mentioning Ruthie just now, regretted revealing so much to this cute little Scotch-Irish face. Yet also knowing that he had wanted to. "It wouldn't be a scandal at all."

"I know," she conceded, smiling. She could feel the chemical current, both ways. Who would have thought it?

"The scandal, or at least the dilemma, would be at City Hall," he said. "What would Mayor O'Dwyer do? Sit still while his police department arrests a harmless rabbi, drags him off in handcuffs for helping to ship guns to Palestine? Sit still while he loses maybe five hundred thousand Jewish votes, while his reelection next year goes down the drain? Or would he take action, squash the investigation—interfere with the workings of the police department, for political reasons, as the newspapers would quickly point out—they would find out soon enough, don't worry—and lose the election that way? It would be quite a dilemma, don't you think? For the Irish police department to cost the Irish mayor his job?"

Detective Cole stood, straightened her skirt. "You don't only read the Talmud, do you, Rabbi."

"I live," he said (lying, he told himself), and he too stood.

"I have to be elsewhere," she said. "I don't know what more I can say, except do what you want. I'm sure that's what you'll do, anyway."

"I'll have to think about it," the rabbi said.

She pulled a pad from her purse, jotted something on it, tore off the page and handed it to him. "My number at home," she said. "If you want to discuss the case some more. Unofficially. It would help if you let me know what you decide."

He took the paper, thought of shoving it into his pocket, placed it more or less officially on the desk instead.

"Your mother will answer?" he said.

"No," she said, looking levelly at his face. "I live alone."

"Of course," he said. "A policeman. It wouldn't do for a detective to live with her mother."

"No," she said, her gaze still at his chin, but her eyes averted. "It wouldn't do at all, would it?"

He came around the desk, shook her hand, officially. It fit so nicely in his. From the open stained-glass window the faintest subtle hint of lilacs wafted in on a breeze from the vacant lot. Or was it her perfume?

"Thank you for coming," he said.

"Thank you for your time," she said.

The nothing more to say hung in the air between them. He nodded, showed her to the door, opened it for her.

"No scandal," she said, and then she stepped into the hall, as if out of a shower, and he closed the door softly behind her, neither of them sure what she had meant.

There was a princess, she decided. She looked at the old man's peaceful sleeping face and remembered.

"A princess."

"What you say?" the nigger said.

He had been standing inside the half-open door, hoping for a chance to wangle his way inside. It was going to rain soon, pour down like the blackness of the night, for so it was outside already, dark almost as the night. Not a shower but a day-long New York rain. He did not want to huddle in the doorway in a day-long New York rain. So when she said those *princess* words he took it as an invitation. He left the doorway with his coffee cup in hand, took two steps into the room, and when, lost in another world, she did not object, he stepped back, silently closed the door behind him. He approached, and though there were two chairs in the room, on one of which she was seated looking at the old man, he slid his back down the wall and sat on the floor, leaning, much as he usually sat in the alley. A major step forward in their relationship. It had taken him eighteen months to get inside her place with the door closed behind. A warm glow like whiskey curled inside him. It was different being inside than outside. A bit scary, nervous-making.

"Yes, there was a princess, I'm sure of it now," she said, and the nigger tuned in to listen to a nice fairy tale. Something to lighten things up. He liked this change that had been coming over her ever since she took the baby. Lordy, as his Mama used to say.

"It was that time we walked away from the ghetto," she said, "me and Danielle." Her eyes pointed now at the old man's sleeping face. "We walked till we couldn't walk anymore. I saw a cemetery, Catholic. We crossed the road and climbed the hill and went to sleep in the cemetery. Then I woke up. Footsteps nearby it was that woke me. I grabbed the child's face, so she wouldn't cry out, and huddled behind that tombstone, shivering."

She stopped, hugging herself against the remembered cold, the room itself grown strangely cold in the dark and damp of the day.

"And then?" the nigger prompted.

"And then?" Her remembering was slipping away again, but she snatched at it this time.

"It was this old man," she said.

"It was what old man?"

"It was this old man," she said. "That old man who found us in the cemetery. It was this old man in the bed."

The nigger wasn't sure he understood. He had always assumed the sick old man was her father. Why else tote around a sick old man?

"This old man?"

"This old man," she said. She got up slowly from the straight-back chair and leaned over and touched a lock of hair that hung in sleep on the old man's forehead. "This old man," she said.

She sat on the chair again in the gloomy room and looked at his face.

"What did he do?" the nigger prompted.

Tears were crawling down her cheeks. She hardly knew what they were. Silent water ran down the deep-carved lines in her face like a stream following ancient channels.

"He just stood there looking down at us. He said two words. 'You're Jews.' I nodded my head. I couldn't speak. What was there to say? 'From the ghetto?' Again I nodded my head. Then he said, 'Where are you planning to go?' I saw how old he was. I tried to trust him. 'To escape into the forest,' I said. 'To the partisans.' "

"Who was they?" the nigger said.

The question seemed to startle her. She'd been talking toward the old man's sleeping face, talking toward her own remembering, and looking at the nigger now, she seemed surprised to find him sitting there.

"Freedom fighters," she said distractedly. "Poles who hated the Nazis, who hid out in the forests."

"And this old man helped you find them?" the nigger said.

"*Shah!*" she said. "Listen, if you want to hear."

The nigger pursed his lips. "Sorry," he said. It was not a word he was accustomed to.

"The old man stood there in his boots, looking down at us, looking around at all the tombstones. Then he said, 'That won't do,' and he kneeled on the grass beside us. 'Some of the partisans hate the Jews,' he said. 'As much as the Nazis.' All my hope went away then. There was no more chance of escape. 'You wait here, on the ground. I'll be back after dark.' That was all he said. He stood up and walked away. He had strong, powerful steps for an old man. Strong, powerful steps."

She stopped speaking again, was quiet for a long time, lost in her new remembering. The nigger was not certain whether to urge her on. Before he did she stood, went to the brown door, the door to the coal bin, opened it and disappeared. When she came back after a time she was carrying the baby, the child she called Danielle. She closed the door behind her and sat again in the straight-back chair with the child asleep in her arms. As if this child was living proof of all she was about to tell. Or living comfort, perhaps.

# 3

RUTHIE'S AT HOME with her sorrows, Hindy with hers. Louie's doing (perhaps) God's work. Mickey on the beat, Miriam in her wheelchair, Felice in the Bronx County Hospital. Leave them be for now. There are dark alleys, mean streets to be explored. Peopled with the Kingdom of the Kids.

Peewee, of course, shall lead them. Wearing his Dodgers shirt as if it would ward off evil.

Leaving the tunnel beneath the lowering skies, they follow the scent of his courage, the odorless scent of his fear. The two are commingled in his chest, coiled, like Musial's bat. There is poetry in him this morning working dark and deep.

Along 174th Street they walked, crossing Walton Avenue, crossing Townsend Avenue, down-sloping, passing the residential, passing the commercial, moving toward the dark, brooding stanchions of the el, Peewee in the lead, joined at times by Phil, at times by Beverly, at times by little Annie, the others dropping back a few steps, then hurrying up again. Till at the bottom of the hill they pause, burdened by enough welling fear to turn them back.

"Which way?" Beverly said.

"I don't know," Peewee replied.

"Then maybe," Phil said, looking up one dark, forbidding direction and down the other, "then maybe we shouldn't try it. Maybe we should go back."

"And leave Baby Lisa?" Annie said. "We have to get Baby Lisa."

"You don't even know where we're going," Phil said. "You don't even know who took Lisa."

"Do you?" she asked with mild, not-yet-white-eyed fear.

"Of course we do," Phil said.

"Then who?" she said.

"The Rag Lady," Phil said.

"The R-Rag L-Lady?" she said, stuttering as in the darkest of comedies. "That's where we're g-going?"

Phil nodded vigorously, she at least now sharing his fear. She looked toward Peewee, seeking, also fearing, his confirmation. Peewee would not lie, would not scare her. Peewee, however subtly, nodded as well.

Annie stood dumb, a fairy hand covering her mouth. Phil pressed his advantage. "You know what the Rag Lady does? She steals little children. She cuts them up in little pieces. Then she cooks them up for dinner with turkey gravy, and eats them like chicken wings."

"She does not!" Annie said hopefully.

"She does, I swear it," Phil said.

"With cranberry sauce," Beverly said. Turning to look at her, none of the other three could tell whether she was daring to joke about something as terrible as that or whether rich kids knew something.

"You still want to go get Lisa?" Phil said to his sister.

"All the more reason," she said, "we've got to save her. If she ain't been cut up and ate yet."

They stood in silence in the spark-dropping roar of a train overhead. Peewee took a deep breath, the word *Dodgers* on his chest expanding across the breadth of him. Slowly he let it out, raised a finger, pointed like an illustration of Moses to the promised land he would never see (or was it like Babe Ruth pointing to the distant bleachers; which, unlike Moses, he would reach on the next pitch, if you believed such apocrypha). "I think it's that way," he said, and taking Annie's hand— perhaps really wanting to take Beverly's, but taking Annie's hand—he led them intrepidly across the street, heading south, toward Mt. Eden Avenue. Heading—though he could not be certain of it—toward the real-life home of the Rag Lady.

Down the street they walked, past the radio repair shop with its one television set turned on in the window, a face, a man's face, then a woman's face, glaring at them, this one-eyed monster—not past it because they could not pass it without stopping, pausing, standing in front of the window. Beverly was perhaps the least intrigued, she having access of her own, watching their fascination for a while, then at last speaking out. "We'll never find the baby this way."

"She's right," Peewee said, and led them away, Annie and then Phil the most reluctant: led them across another street, to territory in which none of them had ever been.

At the edge of the abyss they paused. Peewee called a meeting, a huddle on the pitcher's mound.

"Okay," he said. "Her house is a couple of blocks down. I think. But Lisa may not be in her house. The cops said they looked there twice. So we got to start searching now. She could be hidden anywhere."

"Where should we search?" Beverly said, the obedient soldier, comma-haired.

"Every doorway from now on," he said. "Every warehouse. Back of every one."

"But Lisa wouldn't be there alone," Annie said. "She's just a baby."

"She might not be alone," Peewee said. "The Rag Lady might be with her."

They held their breath in startled silence. The Rag Lady had loomed in the future, two blocks away at least, in a house for which there'd be time to prepare an assault, to map a strategy, to stoke each other's courage up. But now here she was, in possibility, the terrifying present, her black-sheathed claws perhaps in back of any door.

And then the worst news. "We got to split up," Peewee said. "We'll meet in ten minutes at the corner. In that food store over there. Ben-Al's."

"Split up?" Annie said.

"Whaddaya mean, split up?" Phil said.

"Uh, Benjamin, uh Peewee, why is it necessary to split up?" This from Beverly, also white-faced now.

"Because there's too many places to look," Peewee said. "Because it would take us all day."

"We got all day," Phil said.

Peewee pretended not to hear. "What's the use of staying together? It only takes one to find her."

All of them studied their shoes.

"But what . . ." Phil said, and gagged a little before he could continue. "But what if we—what if *one* of us—finds her? What do we do if the Rag Lady's there?"

They looked from one to the other, fighting the awful thought. All except Peewee.

"We holler," Peewee said. "We grab hold of her dress and holler for help. And the rest of us from everywhere come running."

They looked at him with baleful eyes: their crazy-mad leader.

"And then?" Phil said. "And then when we got her surrounded?"

"Three of us grabs hold," Peewee said. "Three of us grabs hold and kicks her ankles. While the other takes Lisa and runs."

"Who takes Lisa and runs?" Annie said. "Maybe her big sister should. Who's held her the most. So Lisa wouldn't be scared, I mean."

"A good idea," Peewee said.

"It's a long way to carry her back, running," Phil said. "Maybe the strongest should."

"Another good idea," Peewee said.

"I think the fastest runner," Beverly said. "To get her home quick."

"It can't be me, I got to stay and fight," Peewee said. Thinking: what am I saying, it probably should be the fastest runner, to make sure he gets away. But he couldn't threaten them with that. He couldn't threaten desertion under fire. It was not a shortstop's way.

"I'm the fastest girl in all of Four B," Beverly said. "We had a race in gym."

"They're all good ideas," Peewee said. "The one who gets the best chance grabs her up and runs."

"Another question," Phil said, hating to again acknowledge Peewee's leadership, perhaps also needing to. "What if she's not alone?"

"The Rag Lady?" Peewee said. "She'll be alone, don't worry."

"How do you know?" Annie said.

"Because," he said. "You've seen her. Rag ladies are always alone. Otherwise they aren't rag ladies."

They pondered that a moment. There was undeniable wisdom in that. Maybe that was why he was their leader.

"Okay," he said. Still they didn't move—four children standing on a street corner under the el, under the gray and lowering skies, drawing occasional glances from a nearby worker or a passing pedestrian, none of them knowing, at least at that moment, the fear the children knew; none of them knowing the somber business afoot.

"Okay," he said again. "I'm crossing the street, to check that warehouse over there. You guys split up. Check every doorway, every alley, every garbage can. Every place that's open. If you find anything, holler. If not, we'll meet in that store on the corner. Any questions?"

They racked their frightened brains. They couldn't think of a single other question with which to stall.

"Okay," he said for the third and last time and with it moved to the curb, looked both ways at the oncoming traffic, half the cars with their headlights on, so dark was the morning, and with a sudden burst of speed, like stealing second base—pretending, in fact, that he was stealing second base, the only way to get his thin and now reluctant legs to move—he dashed between the cars across the street. He made it easily, well ahead of the catcher's throw.

The others watched, saw Peewee gathering his strength at the far curb, then resolutely disappearing into the gaping dark of a kidney-bean warehouse with its black metal up-sliding door yawning wide, like the mouth of a red brick dragon. Going of his own volition, so that Phil, the one remaining man now, took command. "I'm going down that alley," he said. "You girls check those stores." And without another word he strode away, turned his hefty body sideways, eased himself down the narrow passageway between two brick walls through which, if the Rag Lady indeed lay at its end, escape would be no small matter. Thinking, I should have sent Annie down here, she could have run with her narrow bones between these walls more easier; and prouder than he'd ever been that he hadn't, that he'd given the easy stores to the girls.

Annie stood on the corner, six years old, her cousin gone, her big brother gone, alone with this intruder, this Beverly. It was time, she decided, to put away jealousies. At least for now. She reached out her hand to shake. Beverly took her hand—perhaps out of misunderstanding, perhaps not—not in a handshake but sideways, like a big sister taking the hand of a littler. Like Peewee taking her hand. Beverly perhaps in this subtle way establishing again her nine-year-old superiority. But perhaps nothing as deep as that. Perhaps just camaraderie in fear. Annie put the better face on it, and smiled gratefully.

"Let's go," Beverly said, and together, holding hands, they started off toward the unknown stores and whatever mysteries they held.

A few minutes later they were gathered in the food store marked Ben-Al's. They moved to the back, past shelves of Del Monte peaches, pears and fruit cocktail, past kosher salt, past boxes of laundry soap, and formed at the rear.

"Okay," Peewee said. The spikes of brown hair that always stuck over his forehead were pasted there with sweat. "Anybody find anything? Any clues?"

"Not me," Phil said.

"Nope," Beverly said.

"Uh uh," Annie said.

Peewee shook his head and frowned. "Me neither."

They stood silently, uncertain what to do next, afraid, perhaps, to go on, till a man with a spare-tire neck came to the back to see what was going on. They all recoiled in fear when he appeared. He wasn't wearing shoes, only white wool socks, and they hadn't heard him coming.

"I want a Devil Dog," Phil said, as if to placate the man with a purchase.

"Anyone else?" the spare tire said.

"Good idea," Peewee said. "Time for a snack break." He looked up at the man above the tire. "Four Devil Dogs," he said.

Annie hesitated, then spoke up. "I want a Yankee Doodle." She didn't like the sound of Devil Dogs just now. She preferred Yankee Doodles, anyway.

"Anyone else?" the spare tire said.

Nobody spoke.

When the man handed over the four wrapped cakes, Peewee fished a quarter from his pocket and gave it to him, Peewee assuming as leader that it was his duty to treat just now. The man rang up the register and handed a nickel back, saying pleasantly at the same time, "What you kids doing out of school?"

Annie didn't hesitate. "We're on a mission," she said.

"What kind of mission is that?"

Peewee wanted to silence her, but before he could, Annie spoke again. "We're looking for the Rag Lady."

Phil and Peewee threw her bitter looks. Annie cringed at the looks, at what she assumed was her mistake. And suddenly found an ally.

"Do you know where she lives?" Beverly said.

"I suppose you mean Mrs. Weed," the spare tire said.

They looked from one to the other. Rag ladies didn't have names.

"An old lady dressed in black," Annie said. "With a sack on her back."

"It's Mrs. Weed you kids call that. She lives on the next block, next to the lumberyard. Comes in every few days, buying her things, her milk and her baby food. Saw her just Saturday, I think."

The phone behind the counter rang. The man with the spare tire turned to answer it. "Thanks," Phil said, and the four of them hurried out of the store, cakes in hand, into the darker day. A fine mist had begun to fall, huddling them against the wall.

"You believe that!" Phil said. "That guy sees her every few days! No wonder his neck is sick like that."

"Never mind that," Peewee said. "She's buying baby food! That means she's got Lisa, all right."

"And it means she's still alive!" Beverly said. "Or at least she was . . ." She stopped.

Peewee finished for her. "On Saturday," he said.

They looked at each other, stuffing their faces with cake. They were proud of themselves. It was good detective work. Better, they thought, than the police had done. Then Peewee choked on his cake at the realization of what lay ahead; what waited just a block away.

The night was long dark when the old man returned. He was carrying a candle that flickered when he walked but stood upright in the still, silent, forest-surrounded night. Under his arm were what she first thought were books. When he came closer, when he told them they could stand now, when they stood and found painful aches in their legs, she saw that they were blankets. She saw, too, glinting in the candle-light, perspiration on his face.

"Come," he said. And, carrying the candle, he led them slowly among the tombstones to the side of the hill. They followed until, as the hill began to drop away, he stopped. Several feet in front of them was a rectangular blackness, darker than the night-black earth.

"Here," he said, turning toward her. "Here, God willing, you will live."

She did not, at first, understand. She reached out her hand for the candle. Cautiously she moved forward, peered down. They were standing near a fresh-dug grave. In its slightly uneven sides the candlelight picked the occasional glint of worms.

The child moved forward, took her hand. Peered down into the grave. The old man came up behind them.

"There, in the day, you will sleep," he said. "I will cover it with boards. With stones. No one will find you. In the night, when all is quiet, you will come out, walk about, eat. But you must go back before light. Into the grave, where you will not be seen."

Still holding the candle, she looked at his face. He was very old to have dug this grave in an hour, perhaps two.

"And then?" she said.

The old man returned her gaze. His eyes were pale blue; his white hair was shot with ancient wheat-shock vestiges of blond.

"What do you mean, 'and then'?"

"Then where do we go?" she said. "The woods you said are full of Jew-haters."

He took the candle from her, held it between them, their eyes glinting points above it. For a moment the candle shivered.

"You will not go," he said. "You will stay. Here, in the grave."

She felt herself grow faint at his words, as if the world were dropping from under her. She looked about for support. The nearest tombstone was several yards away. She clutched the child's hand. The child, not understanding, did not seem afraid.

"In the grave," she repeated mechanically. "We will stay in the grave. Until?"

"Until it's over," he said.

"Until *what* is over?" she demanded, impatient now with him, her savior.

"The war," he said quietly.

"The war? We will live—in a grave—until the war is over?" Hope flooded from her. And urine. The old man was mad. "That could be months!"

The old man nodded. "It could be years," he said.

She looked into his face. She was not crying. She had become accustomed in recent months, with the daily coming of the trains, to not crying. The old man, this Catholic, too, was not crying.

"It's the only way to save you," he said. "To try."

She stared for what seemed like a long time into his pale blue eyes, as he stared back into hers. Probably it was only a moment.

"Why are you doing this?" she said.

He waved his hand in a gesture of nothingness. It reminded her of old Jewish men telling stories in the *shul.* The blankets under his arm fell to the ground. He shrugged, the candle still in one hand. His other hand was shaking. He shoved it into his pocket and looked like a farmer again.

"For eighteen years I've been the caretaker here," he said. "I've seen enough of death."

"If they find us they will kill us," she said.

"Yes."

"They will kill you, too."

"I have lived seventy-eight years," he said. "Perhaps too many already."

She reached out and squeezed his arm. "It will be a *mitzvah.* A good deed. If we can save the child, then Jesus, too, I think, will smile."

"Perhaps," the old man said. "It is time that somebody smiled."

"But food," Madam Wiedkowski said. "If we can really live . . . here . . . where will we get food?"

"Food is no problem," the old man said. "Food the princess will give."

At this the child turned her face upward in the moonlight. They thought she had not been listening.

"The princess?" the child asked.

"The princess Mielcheska," the old man said. He took his hand from his pocket and stroked the child's hair. "The estate beyond that old stone wall is hers."

"And she will give us food?" Madam asked. "Perhaps she will. I played for her once, if she remembers. At the conservatory."

"She will, but she will not know," the old man said. "The princess has left the country for the duration. I am the caretaker."

"I knew it, I knew it, Grandma," the child said. "I used to pray every night that a fairy princess would come and help us. That a fairy princess would stop the trains."

She, too, touched the child's hair. Now, just once, there was a tear on her cheek. It was the last she would remember. After that there would be none; or if that is not true there would be so many she would not remember them.

"The princess has orchards, cows," the old man said. "There will be fruit, milk for the child. For myself, I can spare some bread."

"So we will eat," Madam said. "I am grateful to you, sir . . ."

"Stanislaus," the old man said.

"Stanislaus. But . . ."—aware how already she was taking the food for granted—"to live . . . here . . . in the cemetery . . . in a grave . . . ? Is it possible?"

"When everything else is impossible," he said, shrugging, "then what remains is possible."

"The house?" she asked in a voice both timid and bold. "The princess has a palace?"

"The Germans quarter officers in the palace."

"Yes," Madam said. "Of course." And, turning to the child, or to an unseen God, or both, said, "This, then. This grave provided by the princess—or by this good, strong man—this, then, shall be our palace. Won't that be fun, Danielle? We'll have us a high old time, won't we?"

"Yes, Grandma," the child said.

She looked up at the heavens. She wondered what the stars would make of this. She wondered what the stars made of the trains.

"Shall we—go in now?" she said, pointing.

"Better not to," the old man said. "Better to walk about. Get tired. It is safe at night. You won't be seen as long as you don't leave the cemetery. But at first light you must enter the grave. Sometimes there are dawn patrols. I will cover you; you will stay there all day. It will be hard. You must sleep as much as you can. At dark I'll uncover the grave, let you out, bring food. This will be your life. If you want. Sleeping by day, awake only at night."

"It's like owls, Grandma," the child said.

"Yes."

The old man smiled for the first time. Several of his teeth were missing. "Mielcheska's little owls," he said.

Madam took his hand, thought of kissing it, decided not to. "Stanislaus's owls," she said.

The old man smiled again, nodded his head vigorously. She had the sense that this was a welcome adventure for him, that he had not had an adventure for a long time. For her, she had had adventure enough. The passing of every train was an adventure.

"You were walking long?" he said. "All the way from the ghetto. Perhaps you are hungry now?"

"Yes, sir," the child said.

"I suppose," she said. "If it's no trouble."

He spread the blankets on the ground beside the grave, set the candle on the earth, began to stride off into the dark, saying over his shoulder darkly, "We'll have a picnic perhaps." He glanced upward, said bitterly, "Under the Nazi stars."

When he was gone, they sat on the blankets. The child let her small legs dangle into the dark of the grave. Her grandmother put her arm around her shoulders.

"You understand what's happening, Danielle?"

"Yes, Grandma," the child said.

"They took away Mommy and Daddy on the trains. They took away all your aunties and uncles. We had to run away before they took us away, too. We will try to hide here for as long as we can. Perhaps until the war is over. Until there are no more trains. Until it is safe to go back. You understand all that?"

"Yes, Grandma." She found a glowing worm in the earth at the top of the grave. She picked it up, held it dangling in the air between two fingers. "Only I still don't understand why—why they take us all away in the trains. What did we do to them? That I don't understand."

"Yes," Madam said. She looked out across the invisible road, the invisible forest, the vast invisible night. "That I, too, do not understand. That no one understands. Maybe someday, if we live long enough, we shall."

The child was holding the worm over the candle, idly at first, then watching it try to twist and turn and writhe in the air, watching it dry out, lose its glow, watching its bottom part begin to char and become crisp in the flame. Madam Wiedkowski, returning her attention from the night, looked at the child and saw what she was doing. She felt herself start to scream but held back. She felt her hand wanting to lash out, wanting to smack the child, but held back. Instead she turned away, shut her eyes, held her breath as long as she could; as if this would stifle the sound of the child's giggle.

She did not open her eyes, did not turn back, till she heard the sound of the old man's footsteps returning through the grass. When she did, the child was sitting as before, dreamy-eyed and innocent, looking off across the cemetery.

Peewee did not understand the courage of catchers. He had taken his turn as catcher in stickball games a few times. He could, if the batter didn't swing, handle the fastball down the middle, handle with no more trouble the breaking curve. He could even handle the drop, throwing his body in front to block it if it broke too sharply down into the asphalt. He could handle just about any pitch—the high-rising fastball being the hardest—if the batter didn't swing. But if the batter swung, he blinked. He couldn't help himself. And in that instant of terror, he lost it. If the batter hit the ball squarely, there was no problem. Nobody noticed his blink (though he himself knew). But if the batter popped it straight up, or behind the plate, or fouled toward first or third, he lost in that momentary closed-eyed blink the instant when it was best to find the ball. And if the batter missed the ball entirely, then he Peewee the blinking catcher was at the mercy of fate. If he was lucky, if God was being kind, the ball would lodge in his glove anyway, in the pocket or at least the webbing. But if God was not being kind, then he would get struck by the ball in the chest, or arm, or thigh or, once or twice, in the nose. Or, worse, he would not be struck at all. The ball would go sailing by him, would hurtle away down the street, one sewer, two, till, losing velocity, it would veer to one side or the other, in and among the parked cars, with Peewee in not so swift pursuit, while the other players waited, groaned. These were the worst moments: the future shortstop of the Dodgers, the next Pee Wee Reese, groveling under the cars in search of the ball he could not catch: the punishment for his blink. And yet he couldn't help it, try as he did. He tried to tell himself sometimes that in the majors he wouldn't blink. That if he were a real catcher like Bruce Edwards, he would have a mask, a chest protector, shin guards: the tools of ignorance, as the announcers jokingly called them. But he knew that a hardball was a whole lot harder, too. A foul tip would hurt like hell. What he needed was not a lot more tools, he knew. What he needed was a lot more ignorance. Without it, he was doomed to keep on blinking. The grace of shortstops, he hoped, would be his passport to the majors. But sometimes, deep inside, he longed for this other, too. He longed for the courage of catchers.

He did not know if it was possible to have both. Most of the time he accepted, with a certain amount of despair, that it was not.

Now, standing outside the fence of the lumberyard, half a block from the house of the Rag Lady, he searched inside himself for courage. It did not seem to be there. He found instead that the blood was throbbing in his temples, in the veins of his arms. His stomach felt loose. He hated himself for being so afraid. He looked at the others, saw their uncertainty, their fear, and was determined that they should not see his.

With a casual air he studied the stacks of lumber behind the black wire fence till Beverly asked, "What next?" Beverly buying his act, accepting his leadership. Dear graceful Beverly.

"The cops said the baby isn't in the Rag Lady's house," he said as the others closed around him. "Maybe she is, maybe she ain't. It could be she's somewhere here in the lumberyard. Could be that's where the Rag Lady hides her. Somewhere in all these stacks."

Seeing the faces of the others, he wiped his lips with his hand to remove any errant whipped cream or sticking crumbs. Some band of rescuers they made, he thought: faces smeared with bits of Devil Dog. The others, seeing his motion, copied it, like a band of cowboy robbers pulling their neckerchiefs up over their mouths.

"I think we got to search it," he said, wondering if he really thought that or if this was merely his lack of courage stalling.

They moved along the fence in the eerie dark morning toward the double-wide and unchained opening. At the curb alongside, a great flatbed truck was parked, its great flat bed piled high with thick, round trees. The truck with great difficulty it seemed would be backed into the lumberyard to be unloaded, the great trees to be unchained, but first another truck already inside, piled high with flat-board lumber white in the morning dark, had to with somewhat less difficulty move on out. They watched the first half of this operation, unnoticed as any children would be, and then, unhindered as one truck pulled away and the other ground its gears to begin the backing and filling of moving in, they slipped through the gate and into the yard.

There was no talk now of splitting up. Not this close to The House. They could see its gray boards not a hundred yards away yet barely visible in the thickening fog, the presumably unoccupied upper story nosing at the bottom of the el. As they looked, a train came rumbling along. It had its headlights on.

The train did not seem to scream as loud as usual. Perhaps the thickening mist muted the scream. The whine of the saw, too, seemed muted, as if in the now almost impenetrable mist it was cutting up not trees but . . . babies? This would be the place to live, Peewee thought, if your job was to kidnap children and cut them up. The scent of trees, of distant forests, of the vast countryside that seemed so far away, filled the space inside the black metal fence, between the tall stacks of piled lumber, with sweetness that would cover any more suspicious smells. The great trucks that moved in and out, unsearched, could carry off any strange cargo. The screams of the trains, the screams of the saw, would blot out the death screams of kids. All this whirled through his mind in a flash, a flash that ignited a pain in his teeth, inspired perhaps by the similarity between the sound of electric saws and dentists' drills. Which reminded him of Dr. Greenberg, and then Felice, who had not been watching when the baby was taken away. Who'd been carted off to a crazy house instead. Pretty Mrs. Greenberg with the long blond hair.

All this passed in double time through Peewee's brain, the way he'd heard you see your life pass before you when you drown. This lumberyard perhaps their final place. The Ebbets Field of child slayers.

Idle, frantic thoughts as they moved slowly past the innocent lumber stacks, idle glances revealing nothing. Until, coming out of a passageway between two high stacks that blocked what little light there was in the lowering skies, they came to a clearing and then, looking across it, huddled back against the stacks in horror. Across the clearing, near the rear of the yard, were piled, quite clearly now yet hidden from the street, not raw, unused and innocent fresh made boards but row after row of ominous ocher coffins.

They pressed against the boards until their shoulder blades hurt. Peewee, feeling his knees begin to weaken now, summoned up what grace he could, tried desperately to make a joke.

"I think we're getting warm," he said.

He waited for laughter that didn't come.

This, then, would be the place, he thought. They would die in a lumberyard, be shipped out in coffins to sites unknown. His mother and father would cry. The whole block would cry. Even Brooklyn, perhaps, would cry, he thought; though Brooklyn did not yet know who he was.

"She could be in one of those boxes," he said, heart pounding.

"But then she'd be dead," Beverly said.

"Maybe she is," Phil said.

"But we know that she isn't," Beverly said. "Or at least she wasn't on Saturday."

"It don't take long to get killed," Phil said. "I think maybe we should go."

"We can't go, Philip," Annie said. "We come this far. We got to find Baby Lisa. One way or another."

Peewee looked at his little cousin, marveled at the words. The courage of catchers in a pint-sized six-year-old. A girl. He placed his hand on top of her head, squeezed it, as if to encourage her, seeking perhaps to absorb through his fingertips some of her strength.

"Annie's right," he said "We come this far. We might as well find out."

He gazed at the boxes piled across the clearing. "She can't be in those high-up ones," he said. "The Rag Lady couldn't reach that high. And she can't be near the bottom of the pile, 'cause the Rag Lady couldn't pile the others on top. So the only place is those ones over there." And he pointed to three lone coffins resting on the ground beside the piles. Two were full-size, for adults. The other one was smaller, for a child.

"You mean," Phil said as he looked around the lumberyard in the haze, hoping perhaps some workmen would come, would chase them away right now, "that we're gonna go over and open up them coffins? And see what's inside?"

Then Peewee found his inspiration, which without knowing it he had been seeking all morning.

"It's not us that's gonna do it," he said.

"It's not?" Phil said hopefully.

"Then who?" Annie said.

He filled his chest with air, expanding his Dodgers shirt, and let it out. "Becky Thatcher here is gonna do it," he said, at the same time tapping Beverly on the shoulder. "And Tom Sawyer," he said, poking Phil's ample belly. "And me, Huckleberry Finn."

They looked from one to the other, as they had been doing at critical moments all morning. In the sudden melting or at least diminishing of fear, they were all trying not to smile. All except Annie, who looked pained.

"Hey, what about me?" she said. "I want to be Becky Catcher."

"It's Thatcher, stupid," Phil said.

"Hey, no fighting," Peewee said. "We'll have two Becky Thatchers. Becky Thatcher One"—putting his palm on the top of Annie's head, at the same time shrugging for understanding from Beverly—"and Becky Thatcher Two"—squeezing Beverly's hand with a warmth and strength that made her smile and blush, a blush that somehow washed all fear from Peewee's thin body.

"And the only thing we got to worry about," he added, "is Injun Joe."

"The hell with Injun Joe," Phil said, emboldened now. He was Tom Sawyer, all right.

"I'll kick him in the ankle, like you said," Annie said.

"I'll kick him in the nuts," Phil said. And glanced at Beverly and saw her still-blushing face.

Beverly did not say what she would do with Injun Joe.

"Okay," Peewee said. "Keep a careful lookout." And with him, Huck, in the lead, they crept across the clearing, crept with hearts pounding in their chests, toward the high-piled coffins and the three that lay beneath, Peewee hearing in his mind the shrill voice of Aunt Polly—or was it Aunt Hindy?—warning Tom to keep away from there; warning Tom not to play with that no-good rapscallion Huck Finn.

In the front of the lumberyard the flatbed truck was grinding its gears, backing in with its load of dead forest. The workmen were there to unload the murdered trees. No workers guarded the coffins. Coffins are scary enough to guard themselves, Peewee thought.

Six more steps and they were there. Three coffins lined up before them, as if only one of them would escape alive.

"Okay, Tom," Peewee said, trying his best to sound brave. "You open up the first one."

Phil didn't move.

"Hey, Tom," Peewee said in the mist. "You open up that first one there."

Phil didn't move.

"Hey, Philip," Annie said, at the same time elbowing him in the ribs. "That means you. You're Tom."

"I know it means me," Phil whispered. "I don't wanna be first."

They paused on the edge, uncertain how to proceed, till Beverly broke the spell. "I'll be first," she said.

"You hear that?" Peewee said. "You gonna let a girl be less scared than you?"

Phil hesitated. It's okay with me, his head was screaming. But aloud he said, "Okay, okay, I'll be first, goddamnit." Making a mental note from now on never to begrudge Peewee the starring role.

With great, fat trepidation he moved forward, placed both hands on the coffin's lid. His hands were trembling. His whole body was trembling. "Aunt Polly is right," he thought. "Why am I playing Huck Finn's games?" And then he remembered what he was really looking for, and he wanted to throw up. His dead sister might be inside. Or the black living skirts of the Rag Lady.

He thrust aside the coffin lid.

Nothing happened.

No foul demons rose up to envelop him.

Nothing.

"Well," Peewee said impatiently.

"Well what?" Phil managed to croak.

"Look inside," Peewee said. "Is there anything inside?"

"Oh," Phil tried to say, but the word didn't make it past his throat. He touched his fingers to his eyes and realized only now that they were closed. With all his powers concentrated on not retching, he opened his eyes and looked in the box. There was nothing there, nothing but the white insides. "Ain't nothing in this one," he said, as nonchalant as could be.

Then it was Peewee's turn. He approached the second large coffin, figuring with eight-year-old gallantry that he ought to leave the little one for the girls. He stood before the coffin, poised, as if in the batter's box, thinking that this was sort of like Russian roulette, except that if you lost, instead of being dead you had to look at a dead person instead. Which, he thought, probably was worse.

Russian roulette made him think of the old roulette wheel dried out and buried for so long as if in a coffin in the drawer in the back room. And thinking of that, he ripped off the lid of the coffin.

Nothing but woodsmell emerged. Nothing but a few stray woodcurls nestled in the box.

"Nothing in this one," he said, which they could already tell from the relief on his face.

The others pressed closer and looked inside, knowing there was nothing to fear. Still, it took a certain bravery to look inside a coffin, even an empty one. They used this bravery to prepare for the next: the little coffin beside.

"How come that one's so small?" asked Annie.

"To keep dead babies in," Phil said.

"Why do babies die?" asked Annie.

"Why is the pope Catholic?" Phil said. He wasn't sure what he meant. It was just something he'd heard people say.

"You think someday there'll be a Jewish pope?" Peewee said.

"Maybe a lady Jewish pope," Beverly said. "It's something to shoot for, anyway."

Across the mist of the lumberyard, the whining saw stopped. "Someone might be coming," said Beverly, and she stepped forward and with no further hesitation, though perhaps holding her breath, she lifted the lid off the baby coffin.

There was nothing in that one, either.

"Let's get out of here," she said, and she ran off across the yard toward the opening in the fence, the others in sudden swift and pale pursuit, mistaking her action, thinking she'd seen something awful in the box. She was, Peewee thought, without doubt the fastest-running girl in 4B. In the country of baseball, a female pinch-runner, perhaps. Go from first to third on a single every time. Get the tying run to third.

They stuttered to a stop near the curb, the fog dripping like raindrops off the el, a long rectangular dry spot on the cobblestones from which the great flatbed truck had departed, long, rectangular and enormous, like the coffin mark of a dead or sleeping giant.

"What was it?" Peewee said, breathless.

"Lisa's dead," Annie said, starting to cry. "Lisa was in the box, wasn't she!"

"No," Beverly said, holding both Annie's shoulders, looking her hard in the face. "Nothing was in the box."

"Nothing?" Peewee said.

"Then why'd you run like that?" Phil said.

Beverly stood catching her breath, her future breasts heaving under her tucked-in white blouse. "To get away from there," she said. "It was getting spooky in there."

"It sure was that," Phil said. "For a girl."

"You sure the box was empty?" Annie said.

"Positive," Beverly said.

"Then I guess there's nothing left to do," Phil said, "except to go on home."

Peewee looked at his sneakers, kicked twice with one of them at the curb, as if kicking at the pitching rubber during a conference on the mound, giving good old reliable Hugh Casey more time to get ready in the bullpen down the right-field line.

"I guess there's nothing left to do," he said, "except go to the Rag Lady's house."

The others didn't answer. Not a word. Peewee said nothing, too. It was, he understood—they all understood, but he perhaps more than the others—not a game anymore.

*Go to the Rag Lady's house.* It was an action that, after all the years of running from her approach, of hiding under the bed at the sight of her, they could hardly comprehend. Not even in their most terrifying dreams did they approach the Rag Lady's house.

"But the Rag Lady kills children," Annie said, looking with pleading at Peewee's face.

"And cuts them in little pieces," Phil said, looking at Peewee with pain in his eyes.

"And eats them," Beverly said, biting hard on her upper lip, not wanting to cry in front of Peewee, yet also somehow wanting to.

Peewee looked at the ground, waiting for help from the bullpen that wouldn't come.

"I know," he said quietly.

They all stood that way then, looking at the ground, saying nothing. Through the mist they heard a scream, a scream that made them shiver, that prickled the skin on their arms, that started their breath racing, until they realized what it was: the scream of the electric saw starting up.

When their pounding terror had passed, Peewee spoke. "I guess we should take a vote," he said.

He waited and they waited while a rumble began in the distance and turned into the familiar scream of a train rounding the curve of the el. When it was gone, he knew he'd better speak first.

"I vote to go to her house," he said.

The others looked at the ground, as if the answer to some hard test question were written there in blood. Each waited for the others to speak.

"Me, too," Annie said, at last.

"Me, too," Beverly said.

And then Phil, too, could wait no longer. "It was half my idea in the first place," he said.

The nigger was spellbound as he listened to her story. He felt as if her tale of horror had cast an actual spell over him. He had heard as a child his mother's mother's tales of horror, of slave days, of lynchings. But he had heard from a first-person mouth no other tales quite so awful till today. In the spell she cast, they had become one woman, his grandmammy and Mrs. Weed, as he called her: one singular old woman who'd seen it all and lived to tell the tale.

He did not interrupt her story. He did not speak as, the sleeping child heavy in her arms, she stood in pain ignored and carried it through the brown rear door to its resting place, and returned, gazing at the sleeping old man, and sat again. He, too, craning his neck, looked at the old man's face. This sleeping lump. This savior. He had the sudden premonition that the old man would die today, now that his tale had been told.

Without the child in her arms, she sat in the straight-back chair more primly now, more erect, her hands clasped in her lap, like the lady she once had been. It was as if by telling her story she had ransomed strength from the past. But how long she could resurrect this old and long-forgotten persona, how long they would war within her, which would triumph in the end, the nigger had no idea. Though he had some sandlot baseball in his own bleak ancient, disintegrated past, he no longer remembered what he considered victory, and what defeat. Perhaps, he thought, surviving was the only victory: except that in the end you lost. In the final end everybody lost. Bottom of the ninth and that was it. There weren't no ties—no extra innings—no games-to-be-completed-at-a-later-date—in the playing fields of the Lord.

And yet, he thought now, maybe there was. This Mrs. Weed's story:

you'd have to call that extra innings, how she and the child had actually done it, had lived in a grave for twenty-two months, until the war was over.

Living like groundhogs, they'd seen the seasons change from a hole in the earth, the leaves on the tops of the trees turning red and yellow and brown, slightly visible through a slit in the boards above them; snow covering the ground, crunchy and speckled in the moonlight, but the child not allowed to run and play in it, because someone the next day or the day after that might wonder about the footprints; the grave in winter lined for warmth with animal hides the old man had found in a barn on the estate of the princess. Other furs he'd fashioned into robes for them. The coming of spring they'd heard but not seen in the early chirping of birds, birds that competed with the child for the worms.

Summer had been better, the earth cool but not cold, and up top the nights a joy. That was how she remembered them, the nights among the tombstones, eating bread and peaches and melons brought by the old man: a joy compared to the days.

Six months, a year, eighteen months, and still the fear they might be found out, be taken away and shot, along with the old man. And so, weeping or talking or merely passing by on the road below, people had become hateful to her. At first there had been patrols, the old man had said, looking for her and the little girl. But after several days the patrols had stopped. It was assumed they had gone into the forest, where quite likely they would be killed by partisans. In any case, they were gone, as surely as the people loaded on the trains like cattle were gone; and just as soon forgotten. They had disappeared, living, into the earth, as the others had disappeared into ovens; into smoke.

What saved her sanity was the music: the music she could play in her head, recalling every concert note by note. With the music, too, she tried to save the child. She asked the old man after a time for a board, of which he had plenty, and for two small cans of paint and a brush, which were harder to come by but which he managed to find. In the yellow light of a full moon she painted on the board the keys of a piano, the white keys and the black. This board they took into the grave, and on this silent board she taught the child to play, softly humming the sounds of middle C on up, till the child could imitate.

This one blessing God had given them, she soon discovered: the child, like her, had almost perfect pitch.

She taught her in the wan light of the grave the sound of each note, and the proper fingering, and the child, with no distractions, learned quickly. Before many months they were playing and humming duets.

One night, in the moonlight, the old man having mentioned that his eightieth birthday had come and gone that day, they played a concert for him. It was the only gift they had.

The old man, seated on the ground near them, soon turned away to hide his tears and listened with his back to them.

The music saved her, but in between the music one question troubled her more and more: why bother to be saved? What was the point of living like this? In the end, whether now or later, there would be death. Why not now? Why fight and struggle and squirm like a worm in a flame? Better, she began to think, for the old man to cover them, to seal the grave, to let them die and get it over with. He could put up an appropriate marker if he wished. That alone would be enough. The others, she had guessed, had none. But though she wanted at times to die, she lived on. She owed it to the child, she felt. The child must be saved for long enough to make her own decisions of life or death. And she owed it, she soon came to feel, to the old man. All that they could give him was their survival. That would be his triumph, his victory over everything.

And so, not wanting to, she lived on. She remembered better times: people throwing roses after concerts; sailboats on black lakes; picnics on green lawns; white wicker chairs on verandas overlooking vistas that swept away to the sea. But her remembering began to slip, to get confused with her dreams. Only the grave in which they lived was real.

And so to the grave she clung, to the child she clung, the child growing old in a grave, though she was still so young; and to the old man, this Jesus, who seemed to acquire a certain light about him as he brought their food each night; and to the music she clung, the music in her head with which she tried to drown her stifled screams.

That was all she remembered, even now. The rest was hazy, vague. In time, endless time, the war had ended. There had been soldiers, trains, a boat, the child holding her left hand, the old man at her right, always in the midst of crowds. Everyone in the crowd had a story. There were too many stories to tell. Before the boat there had been a delay. She had gone to a shop, had asked a craftsman to carve a marker for her. On it she had him paint in Hebrew letters, in black, the names of her dead parents, her dead husband, her dead daughter, her dead brothers and sisters. That was the marker, there, on the dresser, she said. It was the only marker they had.

"And the child?" the nigger asked. "What happened to the child? To Danielle?"

"Danielle is there, asleep in the coal bin," she said.

"Now, you know that ain't Danielle," the nigger said. "I mean the real Danielle. The one you brought across. The one that all that survivin' was for."

The Rag Lady stood and moved closer to the bed, gazing at the old man. "Who knows?" she said. "We came to America. They took the child. I wasn't fit to take care of her, they said. The old man, I said. The old man I have to take care of, too. The old man take, they said."

"You mean after all that," the nigger said, "after all that time in the grave, you don't know what happened to the child?"

The Rag Lady shook her head. "It was a long time ago," she said. "Two years. Three years, maybe."

The nigger shook his head, stood up from his place against the wall. He began to pace the room. "Man," he said. "Man."

She stood for a long time in silence. Then she motioned to the nigger, who came and stood beside her. Together they looked at the pallid face, at the chest no longer rising or falling under the soiled yellow blanket.

The nigger looked at her. She did not turn her face from the old man. He took the old man's wrist, looking for a pulse, then after many seconds laid it down again on the bed.

"I think he's dead," the nigger said.

The Rag Lady didn't flinch, didn't weep. Her face remained expressionless.

"Yes," she said calmly. "He's dead."

They stood again for a time in silence, as if at the side of the only grave he would know, until her bandaged legs ached enough, bearing in their brittle muscles all the memories. Then she sat for relief in the chair, and pondered what to do. She would not, she decided, prowl the garbage cans today. This she would forego, in his honor.

# 4

BLOOMSDAY.

The word has stuck in Ruthie's head ever since she thought of it the night before.

It is just another day, Bloomsday, of no special consequence. Another tedious boring Monday the start of another week of agony. Nothing of consequence will happen today. Nothing of consequence will ever happen again. Not till Mickey is dead and gone from her.

I hate Peewee, she thinks or rather does not think but hears in that little voice that slithers into her head like a tiny snake. I do not, she retorts with all the power of her maternal chest, and the snake slithers away and then returns again to whisper in her brain: she hates her son. Why do I hate him, she asks, and knows the answer before the snake speaks: because he got in the way. Because of him I had to give up Mickey. Because he was picking up on something; as if not Lou Gehrig but he—little Benny in his baseball uniform—was looking down on the Concourse Plaza bed. The way he'd say to Mickey, go home, the way he'd say to Mickey, why do you come here so much, the way he'd say to Mickey, you're not my daddy, you know. All this only after the affair had begun. As if with some secret antenna he could search them out. Until in her panic of what it would do to him if he really found out, of what it would do to all the family, hers and Hindy's both, she'd cut it out, with all the ease of sticking a bread knife in her chest. She hated Mickey for the agony that was their residue, while the snake in her head kept whispering: I hate Peewee. The son she loved the most. Who needed her more than Eli ever did.

She doesn't know how to kill this snake.

To stop the buzzing in her head she vacuums the living room.

She takes apart the sofa, does a thorough job. Hindy is not on the sofa today. Hindy had come to the door soon after the children left for school, had said she would not be coming in today. Someplace to go, she'd muttered. Some errand. Ruthie had been thrilled: a day without the sickness of Hindy growing on the sofa like a tumor. Thrilled for her little sister. It was the first day since the theft of the child that Hindy was going out. Perhaps she was recovering; perhaps she was adapting, at last. And thrilled for herself: first, for a day alone. Second, for the vague belief that if Hindy could recover in less than three weeks from the theft of her child, then surely she, Ruthie, the strong one, still desperate after three months from the withdrawal of passion, would one day perhaps recover from it, even though just now she saw no end.

Bloomsday, she thinks again, coiling the vacuum back into the closet. Bloomsday and she is alone, Lou over at the *shul*, the kids in school, Mama asleep in the back, Hindy for once not there. And she gets an idea. She will write. She will write to relieve the pressure. And instantly she knows what she will write, and where she will write it: where she will pour it out.

She makes sure that Mama, slowly recovering, is still asleep. She with some difficulty pushes open the door of the dark back room, this room where Lou works at the battered desk sometimes, where the children play hide-and-seek sometimes, but which she has hardly entered for more years than she can remember.

She finds the diary in the place where she remembered, in the bottom drawer of the desk, under some faded pink clothes—she had made a dress for Benjamin, she remembers, thinking he would be a girl—the first girl shortstop, she thinks—under also the battered roulette wheel, gift from Papa Max. Once she had dived fully clothed into the Atlantic at Le Havre to save the stupid wheel, she recalls. She cannot remember having been so young. She remembers Lou blanching at the dripping sight of her. How would he blanch now, if he knew?

The rabbi's wife.

She finds the diary and on the desk one of his pens, and sits in the spiny swivel chair and leans into the circle of yellow light from the gooseneck lamp. Idly she glances at the early pages of the diary, but she is not really interested, not now. Her chest is throbbing with the excitement of what she will write: with letting it out. All this time she could not tell it to a soul, but now this inspiration: she could write it down. Perhaps it would relieve the pressure, the agony: some of it at least.

She flips diary pages, gilt-edged, till she comes to the empty ones; flips more pages till she reaches the ones near the back. They are delicate now in the circle of gooseneck light. She turns thin pages one at a time till she finds a page that suits her. Here she will begin it. Here she will write her own soliloquy.

She does not remember, exactly, how it begins: her old secret heroine's final thrust. No matter. She will write her own version, pour it out. Only one thing will be different from Molly Bloom's. All the *yeses* will be *nos*.

She takes up the pen as once she had taken up a pen to write about the war. Now she will write much closer to the heart, closer to the gut of things. This one day at least she will tell it all, to the Wanamaker Diary, 1922.

She thinks for a moment with the pen beside her cheek. Then she begins to write.

She writes and writes. Hours pass without her noticing till, worn and exhausted, she closes the diary, too worn to reread it now, and places it back where it was, and lays the pen on the desk and snaps off the gooseneck lamp, and feeling dizzy, gropes her way past the boxes and closes again the door to the dark back room.

She feels much better for the writing. She makes herself a cup of coffee. She sits at the kitchen table drinking coffee and smoking a cigarette. The Pall Malls, she notices, haven't tasted this good in months.

She sips the coffee and smokes, and wonders what Mickey is up to today.

It was an hour perhaps since the detective had left the office. The number of thoughts he realized again that can flit and flash through the human brain in only one hour defies the imagination: the guns and the Hagganah and the Nazis and the poster girl and the cute *goy* detective and the Mt. Eden Center and Ruthie, Peewee, Eli, the missing Baby Lisa, all in his brain at once, a pinball lighting up first one and then another, sometimes several at once. It was terrible about the missing baby, a terrible thing for Mickey and Hindy to go through. He was glad at least that except for himself, his own family was at peace: strong Ruthie secure in her role as wife and mother and protector of all her clan; Eli intent on his future in astronomy; Peewee content to be the at-least-for-now future shortstop of the Dodgers, till in time he would find his true calling. Only he, the rabbi, was in turmoil, with his secret gunrunning and his uncertainty over his true motives, with his fantasies about Rebecca, the poster girl, and his sudden new uncertain imaginings about the very real Miss Cole, with the offer from the Mt. Eden Center, which he must accept or reject this week, and the uncertainty of his motives about that. He must make the decisions now, he decided; he must act and clear his mind, and be once more at peace with himself, and so at one with his family. Perhaps that was why God had sent the detective, he thought: to force him to act. The angel didn't force him to act; the angel only led him around and around. The angel was a messenger from the world of the imagination, the world of the Jew. The detective spoke of streets and twisted sheets, of the *goyische* world that was real.

He tried to contradict himself. The guns in the boxes were real. The freedom fighters dying in Palestine were real. He had spent his own nights in twisted sheets: Eli and Benjamin were proof of that. (But how many times, really, and with how many women, really, and how long ago and far away and unreal even that seemed. The kids were his because of God's will. It had little to do with vague and distant temporary passion.) Mickey, for instance, with his flying the Hump and his walking the streets as a cop and his hardly secret affairs with shopgirls, Mickey lived out front in the *goyische* world. Mickey was hard to think of as a Jew. Jewish fathers, for instance, didn't let their babies get stolen: though he knew that that was an absurd and irrational and absolutely unfair thing to say. It wasn't Mickey's fault, after all.

And then there had been the ghettos, the concentration camps, the barbed wire, the naked-bones bodies, the piles of hair and teeth, the striped uniforms, the shaved heads, the forced labor, the brutal experiments on living women, on living men, the gas chambers, the ovens, the smoke. Those weren't Jewish imaginings. Those had been all too real. Into what category did those things fit?

Those were beyond categories. Those were beyond everything.

His own problems were so puny in comparison. Only his imagination could make them large enough.

And so, at times, it did. That, perhaps, was why the angel mocked and did not take him seriously; and disappeared.

All this he thought as the subway train hurtled downtown, the lights blinking at times as if they had something in their eye, the cars mostly empty in late morning, only a few housewives going downtown, shopping, no doubt.

Grand Central Station, Thirty-third Street, Union Square. Most of the shoppers got off. The rabbi stayed on the train, feeling overdressed in his raincoat in the trapped and humid air but not bothering to take it off. He was still wearing it, still carrying the furled black umbrella with its curved wooden handle, when he reached his stop, got off and climbed the stairs, walked the two blocks to the ordinary-looking tenement where he had been just once before. Where the redheaded Hagganah contact had been. And the poster of Rebecca.

The woman in the outer office seemed to be the same, he thought, but when he explained who he was and was led into the rear room, the redheaded boy wasn't there. An older man with rimless glasses and graying temples was there. This man looks like a communist, the rabbi decided, though he did not know why he thought so. The communists, following Russia's lead, were against the state of Israel.

He asked where the younger man was, the redheaded boy. The new man did not know to whom he was referring. "We move around, we get new assignments," the man said. "It's safer that way."

The rabbi took a seat, explained who he was, what he had been doing. The man stood, went to a gray filing cabinet in the corner, pulled out a folder, sat again at his desk. He opened the folder, looked at a list of some kind, took a pen and drew a line through a single item on the list.

"The police have found out," the rabbi said.

"Yes, that's why you're here," the new man said. "I just crossed you off the list."

"I've thought a lot about it," the rabbi said. "It's a difficult decision to make. But I'm afraid I will have to bow out."

"Yes, I know; I've already crossed you off the list, as you saw. Is there anything else?"

The rabbi was confused, momentarily dizzy even. Just like that, he thought. So easy. Not even any thanks.

"It happens all the time," the man said, as if reading his mind. "We have to keep moving around. Your services have been invaluable, of course, Rabbi."

"Yes," the rabbi muttered. "Of course."

Is there anything else, the man had said. Yes, there was. It swam in his mind like a blur. He was not embarrassed when he spoke; it was as if he was talking to himself. The man at the desk was bloodless, a cipher.

"There used to be a picture," he said. "On that wall. A poster. How come there is no more poster?"

The man looked blankly at the blanker wall. "I've only been here a few weeks. There was no poster. What has a poster to do with anything?"

The rabbi smiled. Perhaps there had never been a poster. Perhaps he had made it all up.

"Yes," he said. "What has a poster to do with anything?"

He stood, shook hands with the communist-looking man and left the room in a daze. That was it, then. The end of his adventure. The end of Louie Brunig's heroism. How quickly the end had come. He did not understand how it had ended so fast.

On the dark subway platform a teenage Negro boy grabbed his wrist, held a knife near his belly, asked for his wallet. Louie, startled momentarily out of his daze, calmly handed it over without a fight. The Negro took it, put his knife away, ran quickly up the stairs in high-top sneakers.

On the train grinding uptown, the rabbi's shoulders slumped beneath the raincoat's weight. So much for courage, he thought. If the poster had been there, if Rebecca had been there, then perhaps he would not have handed over his wallet so easily. Not without a fight.

"And what good would that have done?" the angel said, standing above him, hanging onto a strap. "Gotten you a knife in the belly, left you bleeding on the platform? Dead, perhaps? What good would that have done?"

Louie shrugged and shut his eyes. "You tell me," he murmured.

The sky had grown as dark as it could become and still be called day. Cars and trucks that moved under the el had their headlights on, beams diffusing softly in the white-falling mist that was lighter than the sky. The traffic lights, red and green, reflected in oily rivulets on the cobblestones. The stores and warehouses that lined both sides of the avenue had their lights on, too, as if it were night. Only the streetlights had not been turned on: a civic oversight.

The children had left the lumberyard with its coffins for parents and kids. They were walking slowly along its outer fence toward the gray wooden house they could barely see in the mist: the house in whose basement, the man with the sick neck had said, the Rag Lady lived. They would storm the house, Peewee imagined; they would outnumber her four to one; they would swipe Baby Lisa and run.

But something in the thought disturbed him, deep in his child's gut. Running away was not the way to win. And this thought led to another: outnumbering her four to one was not the way to win. He must do this alone. Outnumbered four to one, the Rag Lady might panic, might kill the baby out of fear, or spite. Alone, unarmed, he wouldn't frighten her. They could talk.

And if that didn't work . . . *then* he could swipe the baby and run.

The impending scene was impossible for him to envision: walking down the dark, sloping alley to the basement door alone; entering the basement alone; meeting the Rag Lady alone. He could not imagine finding the courage to do that; and yet he knew it must be done.

They were not more than fifty feet from the edge of the gray house when he held out his arm to stop them.

"Okay," he said in a whisper that he could barely make heard. "You guys are gonna wait here."

The others looked at each other, not understanding. "What do you mean, we're gonna wait here?" Phil said.

"I mean I'm going in alone."

Their faces looked like ghosts.

"Alone?" Annie said.

"Alone," Peewee said.

On the el above they heard a train moving, from uptown, going down. They could not see it, so thick had the fog become. From its sound it was moving very slowly; perhaps, too, because of the fog. At that speed it did not scream.

Beverly took Peewee's hand. He held her hand as she held his. They were not self-conscious, even in front of the others. A moment before he would not have thought this possible.

He glanced from Beverly's face to Annie's. Annie did not seem to mind that they were holding hands.

From the lumberyard, which they had not quite left behind, came the distant, fog-shrouded whine of the saw. Holding Beverly's hand, he noticed, made the sound less threatening.

"You're crying," Annie said. With a look of defiance at Beverly, she took hold of his other hand. Peewee squeezed hers, too, at the same time lifting his shoulder and wiping his face on his shirt.

"It's just the rain," he said.

His hands were sweating, though his face felt cool in the mist. He let go of the others, wiped his hands on his pants. He wiped his right hand again, across the red-lettered *Dodgers* printed in felt on his shirt.

He stood, taking deep breaths, his heart tolling wildly, like a bell gone mad. He tried to hide his fear behind generalship. "Wait here for ten minutes," he said. "If I'm not out in ten minutes, you better come take a look."

"Come take a look?" Phil said. "Maybe in ten minutes we should go get help."

"There's no one to get," Beverly said. She squeezed Peewee's hand. "Ten minutes. We'll be there."

He looked at them and could think of nothing more to say. He took two steps away from them, then turned back. "If anything happens," he said, looking at Phil, "you get my baseball cards." Then, before they could grasp his meaning, he was gone, disappearing along the fence into the fog.

Slowly, with the stealth of Pee Wee Reese taking a lead off first, he inched along toward the looming gray house, sometimes with his weight on his back foot, ready to scoot back at the slightest startlement. He took in his breath sharply as he reached the end of the lumberyard fence and found himself touching wood instead of iron; found himself touching her house.

Ten feet in front of him he saw brick steps leading to the front door of the house. Beyond the house was an alley, he could see. There, at the bottom of the alley, would be a door that led to the basement, just as there was in his own house five blocks away. There in the dark beside what was probably a coal bin, the Rag Lady would live.

And there—the thought came unbidden, ferociously—someone would die.

He tried to conquer the fear, to find within himself the courage of catchers. And couldn't find it anywhere. And then he thought: the grace of shortstops; the leap over flying spikes. The grace of shortstops was in part doing what must be done, no matter how afraid you were. And, thinking this, he moved past the stoop, inched along to the far edge of the house, felt the point of the wood in his palm. Around the edge of the house, he could see the alley sloping away.

He dared not pause long. With another deep breath, he began the dim descent. It was, he thought, like walking off the edge of the earth. It was, he felt, like walking into a grave.

The distance down to the door was thirty feet. It took him only a second to cover it. It took him only forever. And then he was beside it, his back pressed hard against the side of the house.

For several long seconds he remained that way, pressed against the wall, his very being pounding inside him. He was terrified, alone in the world. Far behind him he could hear again the distant whine of the saw. And then, with an unexpected wrenching, tearing motion, he found himself in front of the door. He found his small, thin, shortstop's fist knocking.

For a time there was no answer. Half of him hoped that no one would be home. But then from inside he heard shuffling; and then, to his horror, voices. There was more than one of them! He saw in his mind's eye phalanxes of rag ladies, marching in their black dresses and bandaged legs in row after endless row down the Grand Concourse. Could it be? he wondered. Could there be more than one?

He had started to turn, was about to flee from this endless parade of dark-clad witches when with a squeaking sound the door was slowly pulled open from within. In the doorway of the dark interior, like a ghost in the mist, stood not the Rag Lady but a Negro man. He must be, Peewee thought, the strongest, bravest man in the world, to spend his time in there, with her! Maybe it's the wrong house, he thought.

The man looked down at Peewee. He said over his shoulder into the dim interior, "It ain't them." Then he looked at Peewee again.

"What do you want, little boy?"

Peewee thought his chest would burst.

"I want the baby," he blurted. And found himself shivering.

The Negro didn't move, didn't flinch. He stared down at Peewee silently, as if sizing him up. Then he said, "You wait here," and he closed the door and left Peewee standing where he was. The mist had grown still thicker. He could feel it now beginning to soak his hair.

He didn't know how long he waited there. Probably it was only a few seconds. He was somewhat calmer now, because he had boldly stated his mission. Calmer, too, because the Negro was there. The Negro, he felt, if necessary, would save him from the Rag Lady. He did not know why he felt this way. If the thing he feared most in the world was the Rag Lady, then his second worst fear was niggers. Niggers liked the taste of blood. Niggers cut you up for fun. This he had absorbed from Uncle Mickey. And yet there it was, a feeling inescapable: if necessary, the nigger would save him; would save him from the witch.

The thought sickened him. He thought he might throw up. But the feeling left when the door was pulled open again and the Negro, standing there in his stained pants and his faded plaid shirt, said, "Mrs. Weed says I should let you in."

He hesitated in the doorway. He could not make out anything in the dim interior. He felt as if he were leaping into a pit in whose bottom there might be tigers; from which there was no way out. He had scarcely heard the Negro's words—who was this Mrs. Weed? All he knew was he was supposed to go in.

"Well, make up your mind, Peewee," the Negro said. "Does you want to come in or doesn't you?"

He looked up at the dark face in almost speechless alarm. "How did you know my name?" he managed to say.

"Well, if you is a Dodger, like it's writ there on your shirt," the Negro said, "a sprout like you, you must be Pee Wee Reese. Now am I right, or am I right?"

Peewee wanted to smile, or thought he wanted to smile, but found himself incapable of that. All he could do was nod.

"Well come on in then," the Negro said; and just as the man was about to take his arm, Peewee walked in by himself.

He moved slowly, letting his eyes adjust to the dim light, picking out the contents of the room: plotting his route of escape. Inside the door piles of old newspapers; on one side an old sink, an old stove, a narrow bed unmade, a small battered dresser. In the middle of the room a straight-back chair, closer to the other side another, and beside it a slightly larger bed, with a dead body lying on it. That was what it looked like at first, a dead body, so still it was, and his heart momentarily clutched; but then he saw or told himself that it was nothing more scary than an old man sleeping; no scarier than his father, except that this man didn't snore.

At the rear there were two doors, both brown. He couldn't tell where they went. A closet and a bathroom, he supposed. There was no way out that he could see, except the same way he'd come in. As the Negro closed the door behind them, he moved farther away, into the center of the room. There was no sign of anyone else.

"You can sit if you want," the Negro said, and he sat on the straight-back chair that was farthest from the bed. He had the uneasy sensation again that the man in the bed was dead, but he didn't really believe this or he would have gotten sick. Nobody lived with a dead man in the house—maybe the Rag Lady did, he thought for one horrible instant—but certainly not this unexpected friendly Negro who knew of Pee Wee Reese.

He sat in the straight-back chair with his hands clasped in his lap, as if he were in school. He didn't know what was supposed to happen. He tried to appear calm. His eyes in his motionless head roamed the room. There was no sign of Baby Lisa.

Beside him, the Negro now stood. He, too, seemed puzzled, uncertain what was to happen next. He, too, did not seem to know where the Rag Lady was.

Then they heard sounds, rustling, behind one of the doors. The brown door on the left slowly opened and framed in its opening was: what? A lady, much like the Rag Lady, except in reverse. Her dress was white, not black. It was as wrinkled as the other, her legs still were bandaged, her battered shoes black, her gray stringy hair unkempt, her face as wrinkled as the dress. But the dress itself was white, with a little yellow in it; as white as the other had been black with a fading of gray in it. He did not know what to make of this. He was pretty sure it was her. The different dress just made her a little less scary. He didn't know if that was enough.

He held his breath as she came out of the dingy bathroom into the larger room. As she moved slightly closer, he bolted, leaped from the chair and stood behind it, putting the chair between him and her. When she saw him jump she stopped, waited.

He looked as hard as he could at her face. He had never seen her face this close. He couldn't be sure if it was she. This uncertainty, perhaps, helped calm him.

As she stood there, breaking her lips in what was supposed to be a smile, she reminded him of his grandma, somehow; his grandma after the stroke.

"Are you the Rag Lady?" he said.

Her lips broke farther still. She closed her eyes for a moment, as if in remembered pain. When she opened them again she spoke in a hoarse voice.

"My name is Mrs. Weed. Though I have heard"—the attempted smile gone—"that some of you children call me that."

To Peewee's ear, her voice was more of a croak. He realized he had never heard it before. He realized he hadn't been certain if she could speak at all.

He realized, too, that it was she.

She stood there silently then, waiting for him to speak. He didn't know what to say; how to accuse. All he could think of to say was that the man in the bed looked dead. But he didn't think that was proper, somehow, since the man surely wasn't dead. Instead he said, "I like your pretty dress."

Her lips broke into a smile, more of a real smile this time. "Why, thank you," the Rag Lady said.

Standing behind the chair, gripping it as if at any moment he might have to pick it up to defend himself, he could not believe what was happening: him saying nice things to the Rag Lady about her dress; the Rag Lady thanking him. Something felt wrong; as if it wasn't supposed to be this way; as if there was *supposed* to be fear, terror, hate. It was the white dress that had changed things, somehow. And then he remembered something he'd seen in *Life* magazine: people were often buried in white things; there was a name for them; shrouds, they were called.

"I ain't never seen that before," the Negro said to her. "Where in heck you ever find that?"

"It's my dress for entertaining guests," the Rag Lady said. "I suppose this young man is my first guest."

"I know!" the Negro said. "It's your piano-playing dress. You had it somewhere all this time."

Peewee moved his eyes from one to the other as they spoke, trying to understand. He didn't see any guests, though he thought that she meant him. He didn't see a piano anywhere. The only strange things he saw were a pointed thing on the dresser that had writing on it, writing that looked almost Hebrew, and the old man in the bed who looked dead.

"How come," he blurted, unable to stop himself, "how come that old man looks dead?"

" 'Cause he dead," the Negro said.

In an instant his growing calm was gone. He ran to a corner away from them, pressed himself into its shadows, eyed the closed door through which he would have to escape. Back was the Rag Lady dressed all in black, hobbling down the street with the dirty sack on her back, the sack in which she stole little children, Peewee watching her pass through venetian blinds; or else not watching at all, hiding under the bed. They had killed the old man, murdered him, were living here now with his body. God knows what they'd done with Lisa. The white dress she wore was a trap.

"He won't hurt you 'cause he's dead," the Negro said, looking at Peewee in the corner. "Ain't you never seen a dead person before?"

"He's dead!" Peewee blurted. "You killed him! The two of you!"

"Now calm down, Pee Wee Reese," the Negro said. "Ain't nobody killed nobody. The old man died not ten minutes ago. We was figuring what to do, who to git, when who but you knocks on the door."

The Rag Lady in her white dress moved toward the bed, touched the old man's forehead with her fingers, proving without doubt she was a witch.

"He was a saint," she said.

Then, touching her hand for an instant to his lips, she pulled the blanket over his head. Under the blanket was only lumps now.

"There, is that better?" the Negro said.

"You killed him!" Peewee half-shouted, crying. "You killed him like you killed Baby Lisa!"

"Now you calm down," the Negro said, "or your shouting will wake the dead."

Peewee, breathing heavily, kept quiet, sniffling in his tears. If there was one thing he didn't need now it was that. If there was one thing he didn't need now it was to see the dead old man rising under the blanket.

Pressed against the wall in the corner, he didn't know whether to run to the door or stay. He looked around the room again, seeking escape. There was none. On the dresser beside him he could see quite clearly the white pointed thing. The writing on it was Hebrew, all right. It gave him pause; it made him wonder. It almost seemed to offer hope.

For many seconds they remained that way, a motionless tableau: Peewee pressed into the corner, the Rag Lady in her wrinkled white dress across the room, the two of them watching each other warily, like cat and dog; the Negro watching the two of them, the third point in a triangle; behind him the old man, dead in the bed under the soiled blanket. The room was subtly beginning to lighten under its one high window, as if the mist outside was lifting, the low skies giving way. It was as if some total stalemate had been reached: a rift, a gap, a tear in the march of time. Until, in her croaking half-voice, never taking her eyes off Peewee, the Rag Lady spoke.

"You've come to take the child," she said.

He could not force air into his chest. He could not make his vocal cords vibrate. All he could do was nod his head. Yes.

The Rag Lady lowered her gaze and looked at the floor. What thoughts were in her mind he couldn't tell. He could only watch without a word as she turned, as she shuffled on her broken shoes to the other brown door and opened it.

Behind the door was only black: dull black of no light; shiny black of coal. Into the black the Rag Lady vanished: shoes, hair, legs, wrinkled dress. Peewee, watching fearfully from his corner, half thought he would never see her again. She would disappear out the unseen back through some secret passageway, or into the air itself. Rag ladies could do those things, he'd heard. Rag ladies had tricks. He wished he'd been a better general, wished he'd posted the other kids out back, where they could watch. But thinking that was too late now. Now he could only wait, prepared to run.

It did not take long. It was as if Mrs. Weed, having made up her mind, was now prepared to act, to get it over with. She emerged in a little while from behind the door. Her white dress was smeared black with coal. Cradled in her arms in a soft, smudged blanket was the child: smiling, gurgling happily.

Peewee could not believe it—dared not believe it—that this was Baby Lisa, alive.

The Rag Lady was crying, he thought, but of this he could not be sure. The tear he thought he saw was quickly lost in the wrinkles of her face. She moved now to the straight-back chair in the center and softly sat. The child in her arms made not a sound.

Peewee remained where he was, pressed against the wall in the corner, watching suspiciously. It was as if he suspected a trick. It was as if he expected at any moment the baby in her arms to leap up, to turn into a monster of one kind or another, to fly at his throat. His hands, his shortstop's hands, were ready to protect his face. But nothing happened; nothing changed. The baby remained as she was, where she was. Slowly he forced himself from the corner, moved across the room. From several feet away, still afraid the Rag Lady might grab him, still afraid that all this was a trick, he looked at the baby's face. He could not be positive it was Lisa. He had never, he realized, truly looked at Lisa. All babies looked alike. He must, he decided, assume it was. But still he did not go closer. He moved instead toward the open brown door. He peered into the bin of coal. There were no lurking monsters that he could see. No reserves. Only a pile of wavy coal, a couple of cats near a small cellar window and a dark wooden box he could just make out. Hesitantly he started to climb the coal. It slipped under his sneakers, clattered. He scrabbled with his arms on the pile, feeling the coal pressed against his shirt. His Dodger shirt. When the clattering stopped, he scrambled up again and reached the box. In it was another soft blanket. A blanket inside, he recognized now, a coffin. A coffin the size of a child, brother to the one in the lumberyard. Fear clutched him again for a moment, till he told himself there was nothing to fear from wood. Without the dead in it, it was just a box. He pondered how she had done it: why the cops had not found this. He clambered down the coal to ask, wiping the sweat from his face with his hands, smearing as he did without realizing it the black coal dust across his cheeks, his temples, his nose; and returned to the room he had left a moment before as a clean Jewish boy looking now like an urchin of the streets.

Without realizing it he was black as she, as the coal dust on her dress. He moved toward the chair where she sat holding the baby, stopped only three feet away.

"How come the cops didn't find her?" he said. "How come nobody heard her cry?"

The Rag Lady looked at him. "The trains, they scream and cry," she said. "The lumberyard, it screams and cries. The cats, even the cats scream and cry. Nobody hears a small child cry." She nudged the blanket from where it had begun to creep up over Baby Lisa's chin. "She's a good baby," she said. "She doesn't cry much, anyhow."

To live with the Rag Lady and not cry! Of this the baby would have some explaining to do, he thought.

"But the cops," he said. "They came here and looked. Twice. Even my uncle Mickey came."

The Rag Lady shrugged and after a moment motioned to the Negro. The Negro shuffled over beside him, paused, indicated he should follow. He did as the Negro entered the coal bin, scrambled up the coal with an agility that Peewee would not have believed from the way he walked, dislodging less coal than Peewee, following, did. At the high rear of the pile they knelt beside the coffin on the coal. Inside the coffin under the pale blue blanket was a stick. The Negro propped the stick up in the coffin, then closed the lid. The stick held up one end of the lid by two inches. Peewee wasn't certain what this meant till the Negro with both blackened hands began shoveling coal over the coffin. He pushed the coal around until the coffin was hidden beneath. All that was visible was a two-inch space where the stick was holding open the coffin lid. For air, Peewee understood. From a few feet away there was no way to tell that there was anything there at all.

"You helped her?" Peewee said. "Bring the baby up and down, I mean."

"Only when she was working," the Negro said.

Side by side on the coal they sat. The Negro brushed the coal from the coffin, exposing it again. Peewee needed to know something else.

"That thing on her dresser. It has Jewish writing on it. Do you know what it is?"

"A monument," the Negro said. "To her family killed in the concentration camps."

Peewee looked puzzled, shook his head. "But . . ." He didn't understand. "She isn't Jewish."

The Negro shrugged, made an uncertain face in the dark. "It seems that she is," he said.

Peewee looked at him, at the coffin, at the coal, at a cat crouching high in the corner. He felt that he should be amazed, dumbfounded, but he was in a place beyond amazement. Here he was, sitting with a nigger, in a coal pile, near a coffin, in the Rag Lady's house, with an old man dead in a bed, and the Rag Lady seated below. So the Rag Lady was Jewish. It didn't seem to matter; as if he was beyond surprise. Someday there'd be a Jewish shortstop, too.

They sat in silence for a time, till Peewee said, "But why? Why did she steal Baby Lisa?"

"It's a long story," the Negro said.

"And why is she giving her back? To me instead of the cops."

"I guess you happened to come at the right time," the Negro said. "It's a long story."

Peewee remembered again what his mother had said that time about something she wouldn't forget as long as she lived. This was one of those moments, he knew. As if it weren't happening at all. And yet he knew he wouldn't forget it as long as he lived.

They sat in silence again, he and the nigger. Then slowly they climbed down the coal. The Rag Lady—or Mrs. Weed, he thought he ought to start calling her—was sitting where they had left her, holding the child. He went and sat across from her. Neither spoke; neither stirred. Then Mrs. Weed stood stiffly from her chair and came to him and handed him the child. He cradled her in his arms, against his chest, as he had seen Aunt Hindy do many times. Against his coal-smeared Dodger shirt.

"Her name is Danielle," Mrs. Weed said.

"Uh uh," Peewee said, looking down at the gurgling baby face. "Her name is Lisa."

Mrs. Weed touched the child's hair with her scarred fingers. Peewee didn't flinch. "Lisa," she said. "A pretty name. Like Danielle."

He had never held her before. He had never held any baby before. She smelled soft and clean, as if she was freshly bathed. As if perhaps she had, despite the dim and dirty surroundings, been bathed with care every day in the rust-stained sink on the wall.

"She's pretty," Peewee said, looking up at Mrs. Weed and then past her at the Negro, who was standing behind, peering at both of them with a great broad smile in his face, a smile like a benediction.

"A lovely chile," the Negro agreed.

They were still in those positions, all of them breathing deeply, content, when they heard a commotion in the alley outside—footsteps, yelling, squealing. And just as they turned to look, the door burst open with a clatter, and in came not the police, not the Nazis, but three more children: Annie, Phil and Beverly.

The children paused at the open door, burst into the room with three more steps, then stopped short at the sight that confronted them. They hesitated, not knowing what to make of this, having overcome their own fear to come bursting in like this, to save Peewee's life perhaps, and finding he didn't need their help. He didn't need saving at all. They stood that way, hesitant still, afraid perhaps it was some kind of trick, and heard the Negro man speak first.

"Well, well, well," he said. "It looks like we're havin' a party, doesn't it?"

Still they hesitated, and Phil called out to Peewee, as if across a broad wide canyon; "Are you all right?"

Peewee nodded, unable to speak for the choking in his chest, and as if by way of answering held up the baby in his arms.

"Is she all right?" Annie called across the gulf.

Peewee nodded again. And then, with no sign of danger from either the Negro or the Rag Lady, Beverly crossed the gulf, came farther into the room, came right up to Peewee's chair, Phil and Annie following quietly behind.

"You got her back," Beverly said.

Peewee, cradling the child against him with one hand, reached out and squeezed Beverly's wrist with the other. He thought he was going to cry and did not want to cry and instead tried to think what Huck Finn would say at a time like this. And then he said it.

"Course I got her back," he said. "That's what we came for, ain't it?"

The rest would be a blur afterward: how they sat on the floor around him because there weren't any more chairs, and passed the baby gently and slowly around, so each could take a turn holding her; so each could claim a part in the rescue; how the Rag Lady talked to the Negro in the corner and gave him something from her purse, and the Negro left through the open door out into the brightening light, and the Rag Lady produced a container from the small battered refrigerator and served them each a glass of milk, in six-sided glasses they knew had once held *yahrzeit* candles for the dead. They drank the milk, getting child's white mustaches; all except Peewee, who declined, who liked only chocolate milk unless there was cake or cookies to eat with it, who preferred to hold the baby while the others drank. Till the Negro returned with a bag, a bag of chocolate-chip cookies from the Ben-Al store, and gave the children cookies to eat with their milk. And Peewee, seeing the cookies, wanting milk and cookies now, too, hesitated, holding the child, and finally stood and went to where the Rag Lady was sitting and, hesitating only an instant, handed the baby back to her.

"You'll give it back?" he said, and Mrs. Weed, taking the child in her arms for perhaps one last time, said, "Drink your milk, eat your cookies, *bubbeluh.* I'll give her back. You don't have to worry." And he sat on the floor and ate and drank with his friends, who, eating and drinking, still at times looked wide-eyed at the Negro standing watching them with a grin and at the Rag Lady they feared so much holding Baby Lisa in her arms, much as any mother would. In time, idly, one and the other looked around the room without moving from their places on the floor, seeing nothing much of interest except for Phil, who tugged Peewee's arm and said, "What's that lumpy thing on the bed?" Peewee almost spilled his milk at the impact of the question—he had forgotten about the dead old man in the bed—and decided, though some of his old fear was returning, that he shouldn't say anything about the dead man now. "I'll tell you later," he whispered, nodding toward the girls, as if it wasn't something girls should know about, and Phil, glad to be part again with Peewee of a boys-only conspiracy, was content to let it go at that.

The rest would be a blur—the finishing of milk and cookies, the wiping of mouths on sleeves, the thank yous and the good-byes: good-byes from each of them to the Negro and to the Rag Lady both, as if they had known them all their lives, as if they had always been friends.

Peewee held both arms out in front of him, and the Rag Lady settled the baby in. With another round of good-byes they moved in single file toward the door and out into the alley, up and out into the fast-lightening mist, dripping, the Negro and the Rag Lady standing in the doorway, watching them go. Up the street they went, past the house and the lumberyard, past Ben-Al's food store where the man with the sick neck came out to watch them pass, to see what the commotion was as

they laughed and skipped and joked, all except Peewee, who was careful
to hold the baby right—he thought for a moment of his father holding
the Torah on the High Holy Days—past the hardware store, the warehouses, the radio repair shop, people on this slow day coming out of
each to stand in the doorways and watch them pass, not knowing who
it was they were seeing, who this baby was. Up the block they walked,
the mist rising rapidly now, the weak sun breaking through, growing
stronger every moment, as if by some outrageous grand design, sharpening the outline of the el, sharpening everything, as they reached the
next corner, turned away from Jerome Avenue into Clifford Place, up
one block and then turning left, into Townsend Avenue. Going home.
Bringing Baby Lisa home. Peewee imagined that he saw flags waving,
saw flags hanging from the windows, that he heard bands playing,
drum-and-bugle songs, that he saw majorettes in brisk red skirts and
tunics with silver buttons tossing batons way up in the air, so high that
they gleamed in the sun; that he saw people lining the streets on both
sides, clapping, cheering.

Past the Hirsch house they marched, because there was never anyone home there these days, Hindy always plopped on the sofa at
Ruthie's, past the next house to the Brunigs, up the four brick steps
and into the little hallway, the four of them marching in, down the
corridor to the living room.

Ruthie was there alone, Hindy having gone out on an errand this
day, Grandma Lester asleep in Eli's room with the door closed, Ruthie
with a dust rag in one hand and a pale blue spray bottle of Windex in
the other, cleaning the fingerprints off the picture frames. Keeping
busy. She was wiping the glass of a new Vermeer print—a soldier talking to a woman, with a map of the world and the world itself visible
through a window behind them—when, hearing the commotion, she
turned, heard and then saw the kids come marching in.

"What's going on here? What time is it? Why aren't you kids in
school?" she said, seeing Peewee, Phil, Annie, another girl she didn't
know. Not at first seeing what Peewee held in his arms.

"We got something to show you," Peewee said, seeing that his
mother didn't see, and he stepped forward, half turned, pulled down
the top of the baby-blue blanket that was creeping up over the child's
face. At first nothing seemed to register on Ruth. Then her eyes themselves seemed almost to drop open.

"What?" she said. "Who—where—" And she looked at the infant, looked at the four children, swooped her arms down and took Baby Lisa and hugged her to her breast. "I—oh my God—"—swaying the child back and forth in her arms, hugging her again. "Where in the world did you find her?" And all of them bursting out at once then. "The Rag Lady—the basement—Jerome Avenue—the man with the sick neck—this Negro man—she gave us milk and cookies, right there on the floor." This outburst of chatter that made no sense at all to Ruthie, that didn't matter at all. They had gotten the baby back.

"Where's Mommy?" Annie said in a moment's pause. "We've got to show Mommy." And Ruthie saying, "Yes, Hindy, we've got to tell Hindy, she went out somewhere today, I don't know where, she should be back soon, wouldn't you know it she ups and goes out the one day the baby is found."

And just then, as if on schedule, the telephone rings in the kitchen. Ruthie, still holding the child, goes into the kitchen to answer it. The kids in the living room look at each other with smiles on their faces. Wait till Hindy sees! And Mickey—Mickey who is a cop—and Louie, and Eli, and everyone in the whole neighborhood. Wait! And Ruthie on the telephone in the kitchen, barely heard, saying "Who? . . . Yes, this is she . . . Dr. who? . . . Yes, Doctor . . . She what? . . . Oh my God, she didn't!" The doctor telling how her sister Hindy had come to the hospital, had walked down the corridors opening every door till she came to Felice Greenberg's room, had entered the room and with no warning but a stream of epithets had hurled herself on Mrs. Greenberg in her bed, had tried to throttle her, Mrs. Greenberg fighting back after recovering her breath, the two women scratching, pulling hair, screaming at one another, till orderlies hearing the commotion in the hall had hurried in and pulled them apart. Yes, no damage had been done, just some facial scratches. Mrs. Greenberg was under sedation now, Hindy in his outer office, where he'd had her for half an hour, calming down. No, he didn't think there needed to be charges, but she had better come and get her sister. He didn't want Mrs. Hirsch going home alone. Ruthie saying my God, of all days. Tell Hindy—tell my sister—no, better not tell her anything just yet. I'll tell her myself. Yes, Doctor, thank you for calling, I'll be there as soon as I can. Hanging up the phone, returning to the living room, pale, shaken, thinking, Thank God: it could have been worse.

"What's wrong?" Peewee said, seeing her face.

"What? Oh, nothing. Nothing's wrong," she said.

Ruthie looked around the room, at the sofa, at the picture whose glass she'd been cleaning, then down at the infant in her arms, as if surprised to discover she was still there.

"I have to go out for a little while," she said, half to them, half to herself. "To bring your mother home."

"My mother?" Phil said.

"Yes, don't worry, she's fine," Ruthie said. "But I can't take the baby. Who can we get to mind the baby?"

"We can do it," Peewee said.

"What, you?" his mother said, and then, calming, as if stepping back, she looked for a long time at each of them—this here is Beverly, Peewee saying—oh yes, pleased to meet you, Ruthie saying, Peewee has talked about you—Peewee turning red at this—looked at them in a new light, as if seeing each of them for the first time. And saying, after a time, "Yes. Yes, I suppose you can. We'll put her in the bed inside." And with the kids trailing behind her like obedient soldiers, she walked through the bedroom, glancing for a moment at her own bed in the middle of the room, then continuing into Peewee's smaller room, where his bed touched the wall on three sides. "We'll put her in your bed," she said, laying the wrapped child in the center. "Now you take care of her. Make sure she doesn't fall off. I'll be back in twenty minutes at the most. With your mom with me," she added, touching first Annie's hair, then Phil's. And looking at them one more time— kneeling and hugging Peewee—she said for them to be careful, and then she hurried to the kitchen to get her handbag, and on the way out to the street looked in on them one more time. "I'll be back in a little while," she said again, "and then you can tell us all about it. Then you can tell us everything." And then she was gone. They could see her through the window, hurrying down the street toward Clifford Place. They watched till she was out of sight, and then they turned. The baby in the bed was fast asleep.

They shushed each other's chatter. They sat down on the floor, the four of them in a row. And looked at her.

## IV

# *The Seventh Day*

The idiot of music finished his song, and the
president of forgetting spread his arms and
cried, "Children, life is happiness!"

Milan Kundera,
*The Book of Laughter
and Forgetting*

# 1

THE SUBWAY SERIES, they called it, because in theory you could for only a nickel shuttle back and forth on the subway between the two diamonds in question, Ebbets Field in Brooklyn and Yankee Stadium in the Bronx. On this seventh day of the Subway Series, with the celebrating barely begun in one borough and the mourning barely begun in the other, the very stanchions of the el itself, at a place just twelve blocks up from the stadium, near the home (or former home) of the Rag Lady, would begin to melt. Such were the passions unleashed in the city that day.

Peewee, as we shall see, was instrumental; though no one else knew it at the time.

The Dodgers had clinched the pennant by seven and a half games over the Cardinals two days before Yom Kippur, rewarding Peewee, he sometimes thought, for his faith; rewarding him, he thought at other times, for saving Baby Lisa. The hated Yankees had won *their* pennant a week earlier.

The Series, with the Yankees as heavy favorites, was the most exciting ever played. The Series through the first six games had seen the Dodgers twice with almost biblical miracles bounce back from the brink of annihilation to where today, the day of the seventh game, they stood an even chance of winning their first world championship in the history of the universe.

On the seventh day, of course, God rested. But the certainty of that was still hours away as the cool October morning spread across the city of dreams.

"Excited?" Ruthie said, pouring herself a cup of coffee and joining them at the kitchen table.

Peewee and his father both nodded, each assuming the question had been addressed to him. For Peewee it referred to the seventh game of the Series. For Lou it referred to his first day of work as rabbi of the Mt. Eden Center. (Eli had left earlier; Eli in his third week at Taft High School had an eight o'clock class on Mondays.)

"The Dodgers are gonna win," Peewee said flatly. "They ought to let us out of school to listen, don't you think?"

"At least they give you the score every inning," his father said. "That's better than nothing."

"Yeah," Peewee said.

"That's *yes*," his mother said. "Don't say yeah."

Peewee, eating his toast and drinking his chocolate milk, reviewed in his mind yet again the Series to date. It had begun disastrously, the Yankees taking the opener at the stadium 5 to 3, and then destroying them in the second game, 10 to 3. The Yankees in four straight was what everyone was saying, and even he with a sickening feeling in his stomach had begun to believe that maybe they were right. "The Dodgers are gonna win the Series," he kept chanting to himself in bed at night, but he knew his faith was wavering. Then had come the third game, in Brooklyn, a classic everyone called it, the Dodgers hanging on to win, 9 to 8, as Hugh Casey in relief stopped the Yankees with the bases full in the ninth.

But that was just the beginning. The classic was yet to come.

The classic was the fourth game: Bill Bevens of the Yankees hurling a no-hitter through two out in the ninth. The first no-hitter in World Series history it would be. The Yanks leading 2 to 1, the Bums having scored on walks, and now in the bottom of the ninth with no hits and one out left, they had two men on base, again on walks, runners on first and second. Al Gionfriddo running for Furillo had stolen second with two out, an incredible move, and then with the count three and one on Pistol Pete Reiser, the Yanks had walked him on purpose, another incredible move, putting the winning run on base. And then Cookie Lavagetto, the passed-over third baseman, had been sent up to bat for

Stanky. He swung viciously at the first pitch and missed. Then he swung again and the ball went sailing out toward right field. Tommy Henrich raced for it frantically but the ball hit the wall over his head and caromed away. Gionfriddo scored from second. Eddie Miksis, running for the lame Reiser, scored from first. Just like that, with one mighty swing of the bat, the no-hitter was over, the game was over, the Bums had won instead of lost, the Series was even at two–two. Peewee, listening to the game in his room, had raced down the hall and out into the street, and found that Phil, running from his house, had beat him there. He never figured out how fat Phil had beat him into the street that day, the moment that Cookie Lavagetto became, in the way that baseball sometimes could make you, immortal.

"Ruthie?"

It was Grandma Lester's weak voice coming down the hall. Ruthie went to see. Grandma Lester, though she was still bedridden or wheelchair-ridden most of the time, had begun to talk more of late. Not a lot, but some. Mostly to call attention to her needs.

"She wants her tea," Ruthie said, returning, and began to fix it at the stove.

In the bed Miriam twisted onto her side. This she had been able to do in recent weeks for the first time since the stroke. On the wall where the sun wouldn't shine till late afternoon the angel danced in shadow. She could see him from the pillow; she didn't have to raise her head.

"So, *nu?*" she said. "How come today you're dancing?"

"No reason," the angel said, and continued dancing on like Fred Astaire.

"No reason?" Miriam said. "I never saw you dance for no reason."

"How come you've been feeling better lately?" the angel asked.

Miriam closed her eyes. Both of them were working again. She could not recall when this had happened. Certainly not why.

"No reason," she said.

It was the closest she could come to the truth. Many times of late she had had vague images in her head of death coming dressed in black to steal her soul away. Always these would fade into the sharper image of an old lady dressed in black who was taking a child away. There had been talk in the house, she thought, of a real child being stolen, and then some time later of a real child coming back. She somehow felt responsible for this, without knowing why.

"Something's going on," she said to the angel, opening her eyes. "Something's going on today. That's why you're dancing like that."

"My lips are sealed," the angel said.

"Maybe in heaven," she said. "Maybe something's happening in heaven. Something with Max, no?"

The angel did not respond. His frown told her that nothing was happening in heaven. Nothing more was happening with Max. Max knew the truth, Max had known it all along. Max at last was dead. And Alex, too.

She lay there thinking till Ruthie brought her tea. She managed to raise herself. Ruthie fixed the pillows behind her.

"What's happening today?" she asked.

"Today?" Ruthie said, pausing while fluffing a pillow. "Lou takes over at the Mt. Eden Center today."

"Yah," Miriam said. "That's good. But that's not it, I think."

"That's not what?"

"What else goes on today?"

Ruthie looked closely at her mother, still holding the pillow. "Let me see. The World Series. Benjamin's all excited about that."

"Benjy," Miriam said. "Maybe it has to do with Benjy. But not this . . ." Her voice trailed off as she couldn't find the word.

"Baseball?" Ruthie prompted. She set the pillow in place.

"Yah," Miriam said. "Not this baseball. Something else, I think."

"Something else what?" Ruthie said. She sat on the edge of the bed and took her mother's hand. "What is it, Mama? What is it you're trying to think of?"

Miriam looked annoyed. "If I knew I wouldn't have to think. Something I think that hasn't happened yet."

Ruthie squeezed her hand, then stood. It was frustrating when this happened: Miriam coming so close to lucidity, then trailing off again, into her own vague and irrational world. Her comeback had been remarkable, but it was always like this: three steps forward, one step back.

"Drink your tea before it gets cold," she said. She leaned over and kissed her mother's forehead and left the room.

"A book," Miriam said, and she thought she saw the angel on the wall jump. "Yah, it has to do with a book." But she didn't know what book, or anything more about it, and Ruthie, who probably would not have known either, was too far down the hallway to hear.

"How is she today?" Lou asked.

"Good, I think," Ruth said. "Good and then lapsing. As always."

Like the Dodgers, Peewee thought. After those two good victories—one of them great and the other incredible—they had been tamed in the fifth. Frank Shea had set them down, 2 to 1. They seemed to be out of heroics. The Yankees led the Series three games to two and needed only one more win as they shifted back to Yankee Stadium. It was all going to be for nothing. And then had come yesterday. "One of the most extraordinary games ever played," the *Times* said in the morning. Three hours and nineteen minutes, the longest World Series game ever. High-scoring, the Dodgers going into the bottom of the sixth with an 8 to 5 lead. And then, with two men on base, Joltin' Joe DiMaggio—revoltin' Joe DiMaggio—had blasted the ball into the bullpen, 415 feet away, for a homer that would have tied the game. Except that this day it didn't. On this particular Sunday, with God looking down, and with the same little rookie outfielder who had stolen that base the other day, 5-foot-6-inch Al Gionfriddo, in center field, for reasons of whim or defense, the ball had never quite landed. At the crack of the bat the little reserve center fielder had turned his back to home plate and started running. He did not turn around again until he reached the bullpen fence, where, his glove stretched out behind him at a peculiar angle, as if he had a broken arm, he caught the ball waist-high as it settled over the fence, and converted his name with his glove —as two days before Cookie Lavagetto had done with his bat—into a permanent part of baseball myth. "Gionfriddo's catch." It was almost an afterthought when, with the Dodgers leading 8 to 6 in the bottom of the ninth, and the Yankees having filled the bases again, Hugh Casey, who already had credit for both Dodger victories, kept the Yankees away once more. Good old reliable Hugh. And so the Series was even again, three to three, and today the Brooks for the first time ever could take it all.

Peewee kissed his father and then his mother on the cheek, went to his room for his books and his zippered jacket, hurried out the door. At the Hirsches' he rang the bell and waited, and a moment later Phil came clomping down the steps, followed by Annie. Together they walked to the corner and up Clifford Place toward school, Phil and Peewee discussing the Series, Annie off in her little-girl's world.

As they neared the Lewis Morris, Peewee's mind wandered from Phil's discourse. His eyes flickered up toward the penthouse, where he had fantasized at times during the summer about watching this World Series through the miracle of television: the first one ever televised. But it was not to be. Beverly's father had gotten a new job with another company, and the Rosenthals had moved away in August, to someplace called Delaware.

Peewee returned his gaze to the sunny October street. She had promised that she would write to him, but she never had.

At the bottom of the gray stone steps Louie paused—a ritual moment, he was extremely conscious of this—and looked up at the three-story building. An *edifice:* that was the only word for it.

He climbed the steps and entered the great temple. He was tempted to go into the main synagogue in its weekday emptiness, to stop at the altar perhaps and say a prayer. But this, he decided, would be too formal, too sacramental. Too Catholic. He might be a rabbi, a teacher, but he was also an administrator. He had, he knew, in his new position, to consciously retain his modesty.

Mrs. Skolsky, Goldenbaum's matronly secretary, whom he had retained at least for the time being, was not at her desk, though her coat was on a rack in the corner. He entered the inner office and hung up his own coat, and sat for the first time at the large, rich, oiled oak desk; more of a thick table, actually, its top now bare and inviting, awaiting the first official papers of Rabbi Louis A. Brunig of the Mt. Eden Center; New York; U.S.A. He ran his palms along the oak and thought of the lady detective. He had been, after that first interview, politely formal with Miss Cole. He had called her the next day, had told her he would stop with the guns; had thanked her for her interest, for the discreet way in which she'd handled it. She had thanked him for the call, had suggested, perhaps innocently, that they continue to discuss relative moralities over lunch one day. He had said that would be very nice, but he'd left it up in the air. And he hadn't called again. There was no point.

There had been a hollowness in his chest ever since he gave up the guns. In a curious way it made him feel hungry all the time: as if mere food could fill the hole. Sometimes the hollowness was so vast it made him shudder, it made him want to cry out for a sign from God. This hollowness, he supposed, he would have to try and fill with scholarship. He didn't know if it would work, but he'd have to try. Perhaps, he hoped, like the hollow of lost love, it would heal with time. For love of a sort it no doubt had been: L. Brunig, Gunrunner.

In Palestine the Hagganah seemed to be doing all right without him: there was talk of a Jewish state by early next year.

He was contemplating the implications of this when there was a knock on the door and the matronly Mrs. Skolsky bustled in, over-dressed for secretarial work in a flowered dress, and overwhelming perfume. She was carrying a small plant with a "Best Wishes" card attached—Good morning Rabbi welcome to the center this just came to the side door, from Rabbi Goldenbaum—and she set it on the windowsill and returned to her own office and then back again, a stack of mail in each hand. These are addressed to you, she said, setting them on the desk, and these still to Rabbi Goldenbaum. Shall I forward them? Yes, of course. Is there anything you need just now? No, thank you, perhaps I'll look at the mail and we can answer them later, try to keep the desk clear, at least for a while. And she saying oh yes, and producing from somewhere in the folds of her dress a yellow telegram. It came earlier. I opened it, I hope you don't mind, a telegram, I thought it might be an emergency, you know, that I might have to call you at home. And he saying that's quite all right, taking it from her hand, and she saying it's awfully sweet, I think, don't you, and he reading the telegram:

BEST OF LUCK
FROM THE
NEW YORK CITY POLICE DEPARTMENT

Feeling warmth flooding, trying to fill the hole in his chest; saying, without looking up from the yellow paper, yes, Mrs. Skolsky, I think it's very nice. Very nice indeed.

Thinking that perhaps he will ask her to have it framed, put it up in the office, a memento of his first day on the job, thinking then that perhaps that is not a good idea, that he had better think about it. Thinking there it is again, too much thinking: a lifelong flaw; a professional flaw; perhaps even a racial one.

Mrs. Skolsky bustling from the office—if you need me, just holler—

leaving her perfume behind, and he picking up the telegram, reading it again.

Knowing, despite the rekindled excitement inside him, that he will of course do nothing.

Sitting, waiting, she remembers. Most things she remembers clearly now.

Faces, she remembers. Faces carved by the hard, uncaring knife of existence. Lean faces and bloated ones, bearded and stubbled, blotched and scarred, blotched red Times Square faces. And she among them in her soiled white dress like an elderly fallen angel, her burlap sack held tightly at her side.

And when in time she chose a doorway to call her own, they gravitated toward her like children. Perhaps it was the soiled white dress: she did not know why. At first it was the men, who came to paw her, while the women looked on jealously from entryways across the busy street. But when she managed to chase the first foul man with shoves and screams, and when the second man was strongly and more lewdly persistent and she, lulling him to relax for a moment, reached into her sack for the obelisk and with all her gathered strength crushed it into the side of his head, the smelly being, blood flowing now from his temple, reaching up his fingers and getting sticky with it, crawled away from her in fear and disbelief, the others, men and women both, all cheered, for he had been a bully of sorts. After that instead of pawing her they protected her. Men and women both, they sat around her, sat at her feet, the monument no longer in her sack but at her side, the ivory obelisk like a talisman for all of them. Beside it, they asked for stories, stories from undreamed-of worlds, and these she gave to them: all the stories she could recall.

Till one day after several weeks of this, sipping tea for a nickel as she did sometimes in the Automat on Broadway, turning the pages of a newspaper left behind on a table, the small black words leaped out at her like the bold writing of God:

WARSAW GHETTO
SURVIVORS TO MEET

And she with hands trembling taking the newspaper, placing it carefully in her sack, under the obelisk. The newspaper perhaps her most prized possession now, she read it twenty times a day for three days, till the day itself came, and at the appropriate time she walked to the Hotel Taft where the meeting was to be, a walk of only four blocks, which she had made twenty times since she found the newspaper. And when at the door a man in a maroon uniform with gold braids on the shoulders barred her way, she straightened her own shoulders grandly, as Madam Wiedkowski would have done, and grandly, without begging, showed him first the newspaper and then the monument, and, still clutching her sack, swept fearfully inside, with all the false grandeur she could muster. She mustered it till she found the room where they were meeting, and there, once inside, seeing the others milling about, waiting, signing their names in a book, seeing all these unknown faces, unknown and yet her own, seeing all of these, she collapsed at last.

This she remembers, finishing her tea in her apartment in Crown Heights. The coming-to, the swapping of stories, the comparing, the remembering. The handshakes of strangers. The hugs of strangers. The tears. All of them much better dressed than she. In dark suits and white shirts and ties, in simple dark dresses, some of them with pearls, with gloves. This she remembers thinking then, and thinks again now: at least we still take care of our own.

Finishing her tea, she walks to the kitchen, rinses the glass, returns to the living room. She straightens the doilies on the sofa, sits in a straight-back chair, crosses her unbandaged legs. Waiting for Monday's child.

The nigger lying awake under his blanket of newspapers got up at last and staggered wearily inside. He put water in the kettle and lit the burner. Waiting for the water to boil he sat on the edge of the bed, spread his fingers behind him on its softness. Tonight, he told himself. Tonight I will sleep inside. Tonight I will sleep in her bed.

He has made this decision every day for several weeks now, as the nights have gotten colder, but he has continued to sleep on the pavement outside the door. "I swear it," he says this time, looking at the ceiling. "Tonight I will sleep inside."

For the first time, he believes that he will.

# 2

NEEDLESS TO SAY, he couldn't concentrate. When you are eight years old and the Dodgers are in the World Series for the first time in your conscious life, in the seventh game of the Series, against the hated Yankees no less, what could anyone expect? He squirmed and fidgeted and looked out the window into the cloudless sky and tried to listen to the teacher, a sullen old lady named Mrs. Rich, who cared no more about baseball than she did about the moon. Her favorite subject in life was long division.

She had written some numbers on the blackboard and asked who knew the answer, and when no one raised a hand, she said, "Benjamin, do you know the answer? Perhaps it's written there in the sky." He had looked at the blackboard and seen the mysterious problem and wanted to say he didn't care, but was about to say he didn't know, when static and squawking out of the brown box above her head saved him from replying. The voice of the principal came on—he was no Red Barber, but it would have to do—explaining about the game, as if anyone didn't know (though some of the girls actually didn't seem to). He wondered if Beverly cared, somewhere in Delaware. The voice said that the first inning now was over. In the top half of the first inning Eddie Stanky of the Dodgers had led off with a single to right off Frank (Specs) Shea. Peewee's heart began to exult. The Dodgers were gonna win the Series. On the first pitch to Pee Wee Reese, Stanky was out trying to steal. (That was okay, the Brooks were taking control, taking the initiative.) Reese batting second, of course, where he had belonged all along, having raised his average forty points, all the way to .281 by the season's end, once they moved him there. Reese walked, the principal continued—no emotion at all in his voice, you couldn't tell which side he was rooting for—and Robinson lined to Henrich in left. After Dixie Walker narrowly missed a home run into the lower right field stands, Reese was out stealing. No runs, one hit, no errors, none left. Damn, Peewee thought, almost a two-run homer. Still, a pretty good start.

In the bottom of the first Hal Gregg set the Yankees down in order, and by the time the principal said so, Mrs. Rich had forgotten that Peewee had not yet answered her question. She called on someone else.

The clock on the wall moved slowly through its paces, five minutes, ten, fifteen—fifteen minutes, a goddamn long inning, the Brooks must be pouring it on—and then he realized the principal was doing it only inning by inning, it could just as well be the Yankees rallying. Mrs. Rich babbling on till the principal's voice cut her off. A triple by Hermanski, a single by Edwards, a single by Furillo, a double by Jorgensen. Two runs! His joy was diminished only slightly when in the bottom half the Yankees got a run of their own.

With the Dodgers clinging to that one-run lead, his joy continued through the end of arithmetic and into the start of spelling. Then the voice announced through the dark brown speaker that in the bottom of the fourth the Yankees had scored twice. The Yankees had taken the lead, 3 to 2. It was about that time that Peewee began to feel sick. And when, in the bottom of the sixth, the Yankees scored again, making it 4 to 2 just as the three o'clock bell rang, the steps going down and out of school seemed to move about under his feet with a Jello-like life of their own.

He met Phil in the yard and they hurried home together to pray for a Dodger rally. By the time the radio came on it was the end of the seventh. The Yanks had increased their lead to 5 to 2.

"I'm going up to Fordham Road to shop," his mother said. "You look in on Grandma once in a while."

In the top of the eighth the Dodgers had the top of the order coming up. This was it, Peewee thought. But Stanky flied out. So did Reese. So did Robinson. No runs, no hits, no errors. Phil's middle finger where he had been biting the nail began to bleed.

The Yankees didn't score, and then it was the ninth. Last chance.

Peewee couldn't sit still. He stood and paced about in the kitchen. He felt a personal sense of helplessness before the news of the weak Dodger bats. He wanted to help so much. And there was nothing he could do.

Dixie Walker grounded to second. Peewee sat, found himself glaring at Phil, as if it were Phil's fault that his hero hadn't gotten on base. As if, if Phil himself were in better shape, then Dixie Walker might have gotten a hit.

Eddie Miksis filling in for Reiser singled to center. "Way to go," Phil said. Peewee raised a fist of determination. And then before they could grasp what happened in the roaring from the yellow radio, Bruce Edwards had hit into a double play, Rizzuto to Stirnweiss to McQuinn. The inning was over. The game was over. The World Series was over. The fucking Yankees had won. The Dodgers had lost. All of baseball was gone till next year. Life for that moment had lost its point.

They sat in silence, dazed, as the radio babbled on. Eli came home from school, saw them sitting in the kitchen.

"The Dodgers lost, huh," he said.

Peewee only nodded, trying to keep the tears from spilling out, tears anchored weightily in his chest.

A moment later Eli passed the other way. "I'm goin' to the schoolyard to play basketball," he said.

What was it that drew them then to the dark back room? Fate, destiny, some predetermined act of God or of the devil, something to which Peewee's entire young life had been leading? Or was it merely happenstance, the nearness to his grandmother's room?

Suffice it to say that Peewee, wanting to be away even from Phil, walked down the hallway and opened his Grandma's door to check on her, as his mother had told him to do. Miriam was in bed, propped up high on the pillows. She turned her head at his approach.

"Your ball game is over?" she said.

Peewee only nodded.

"Your team won?" she said.

Peewee shook his head.

"Ah, well, *bubbeluh*," she said. "Maybe tomorrow. Tomorrow your team will win."

He wanted to explain to her, but he didn't have the stomach for it. Instead he shrugged his shoulders.

He stood looking at the linoleum a moment, at the strip of naked wood where second base used to be. Then he looked at her. Her face had returned almost to normal by now. Or else he had gotten used to it.

"You need anything?" he asked.

"No, *bubbeluh*, go play," she said. "I'm fine. Just leave the door open, in case I want to call."

He nodded again and squeezed her hand where it rested on the blanket, and she with her returning strength squeezed back. Leaving the door open, he stepped over the missing base, and then because he wanted to be alone—or perhaps simply because the door was there—he did not return to the kitchen. Instead he pushed open the cocoa-brown door; pushed his way, fumbling for the switch, into the dark.

The cardboard cartons in the dim overhead light were piled as always at crazy angles. The battered wooden desk sat between them at one end of the room like an altarpiece in a cave. Peewee walked between the piled boxes and sat on the floor near the desk. He drew his knees up in front of him, his arms resting on them. It was as if here he hoped the dead feeling inside him, the deadness over the Dodgers' loss—this real (if temporary) tragedy, for that was how it felt to him—that here in the dark back room perhaps it would begin to drain away. He wondered idly how he would fall asleep. No more The Dodgers are gonna win the pennant; no more The Dodgers are gonna win the Series; not till next April, at least.

Idly he pulled open the bottom drawer, threw a fistful of colored cloths disconsolately aside, took out the old roulette wheel, which, as he had heard, his grandma's uncle had given her in Russia long ago. The wheel still didn't turn, but the old wooden ball was still there. Idly he flicked the ball with his index finger, watched it run around the groove of the stationary wheel, watched it come to rest on green, double zero. House wins, he knew, but he wasn't sure what that meant. Idly he flicked the ball, again, again, watched it run around inside the groove, small as a baseball shrunk by headhunters, the kind they showed about every other week in *Life* magazine. Again he flicked the ball, his eyes blurring as he stared at it. After a time Phil knocked on the open door, came in, sat beside him near the desk. He didn't ask what Peewee was doing. He seemed to know.

Together they sat in the gloom of the Dodgers' loss, the only sound the faint whirr of the ball as Peewee flicked it again around the groove. Phil, noticing in the open drawer what looked like some kind of book, idly reached in and pulled it out. Peewee was hardly aware of what he was doing as Phil with vague interest flipped through the pages, reading to himself a line here and there.

"Whose book is this?" he asked in time.

Idly, with the ball still spinning in its track like a planet around the sun, Peewee glanced at what Phil was holding. "Just some old diary my mother wrote," he said.

"Any good stuff in it?"

Peewee, spinning the ball, shook his head.

The ball ran around and around. Phil with his fat fingers flipped the pages. There was no joy in Mudville. Then abruptly Phil stopped flipping, turned a few pages back. He began to read intently, leaning forward slightly as he did.

"You sure this is your mother's book?" he said, not taking his eyes off the page.

"Uh huh," Peewee said, his blurred eyes still on the ball.

"I don't think so," Phil said.

"Why not?" Peewee said, not at all interested in this conversation, his eyes still on the ball, his mind, try as he would to wrench it away, still lost in Yankee Stadium.

"Here's why," Phil said. "Listen." And he began to read aloud.

What Ruth had written in the back of the old diary that Monday in June, that Bloomsday when nothing much was going to happen, had confessed in the only place she could confess, was this:

*No I am not Aunt Truth but Aunt Ruthless perhaps Ruthless in the total devotion to my own selfish pleasure whether it be his cock inside me thrusting and pressing home or the power the others give me over their lives their decisions given me by default perhaps not sought but power nonetheless and taken willfully by me nonetheless so there must be somewhere inside a pleasure motive like the time I jumped fully clothed into the cold waters near Le Havre when the suitcase fell in what need did I have for that old roulette wheel after all a gift from Papa so what it was the pleasure of shocking them I think shocking Lou and all the others on the boat how brave they said how gay and reckless they said it was none of that of course it was the selfish pleasure of seeing the looks on their faces just as that first time he took me to the concourse plaza we had no sooner undressed each other no sooner lay down on the double bed beneath that framed gray picture of Lou Gehrig than before he could even touch me I squirmed down and took his cock in my mouth not to give him pleasure oh that would come soon of course but the quickness of it the eagerness of it of me to do such a thing brought such a look of shock more shock I think than pleasure to his face at first that I warmed inside Everybody's Aunt Truth doing this, someone has got to know me he at least was going to know me he at least*

*My hair falling all over his belly sucking sucking his hands then on my breasts nipples firm and then sitting astride him him filling me up so I miss it so I miss it so I want to die and yet it shall never be again right Mickey right Mickey No it shall never be again Ruthless in my fear that he is finding out that Benjamin somehow is sensing divining it all I cannot let that happen so Ruthless in my devotion to my own like a Tiger Mother I Ruthlessly send Mickey away send both our souls to the very fires of hell for the pure selfish pleasure of Doing the Right Thing which if that was the truth I should never have started at all not for his sake and not for mine not to end leaving us hanging in hell like this and knowing i have done this to him i hate him so and for what i have done to myself i want to die*

*That night we got engaged and coming home and not telling them Papa so excited about his foot using this as an excuse to not tell them and making him suffer so Lou I mean when Papa's news could have kept compared to mine the truth is I cherished it I cherished knowing what others didn't I cherished having untold news like a journalist gone mad a secret i had we had and i cherished it i cherished in that crowded household having at least a secret from all of them it gave me new life it gave me pleasure knowing something no one else knew*

*Like that time with the ice skates I saved up for so long for skates and then when one of them didn't fit the martyr I was the benefactor giving them to Hindy like that so selflessly as everyone said what a nice image it helped to build for me when the Truth was i hated skating anyway i never wanted to be a skater on ice it was more as if deep down i knew already that someday in some way unforeseen Hindy would pay me back*

*Mickey Mickey Mickey Prickey Mickey what shall we do all these months gone by and still it lives in my head and i think in yours our passion our illusion our madness though we never speak of it of course it would not do to bitch and complain still i think it lives in you as much as it lives in me that you hate me as much as i hate you while in the living room together of necessity we carry on these charades or does it have you fucking Felice upstairs fucked our memory to smithereens would that I could do it but it would not do to pick up some stranger off the street such randomness wouldn't do for the rabbi's wife and so a little bit more each day I die and you alone know who I really am and the possessor of such secret knowledge I want to love and you I hate because together with the help of god we have made it so we have made us hate each other for loss of love*

*And who is Alex then who is Mama's Alex then i cannot ask her and will not ask her for fear of another stroke but who is it who was it who is Alex then there is only one answer i think dear Mickey Alex was Mama's you Alex was Mama's Mickey way back there somewhere in Russia Alex was Mama's you for sooner or later in life I think that everyone has a deep dark Mickey or else as they go to the grave except for children of course it is not or was not life this endless eternal damnation this suffering that maybe lasts forever though god i hope not i cannot bear it sometimes and yet i fear it's true it lasts forever until another comes along and you simply cannot have another if you are the rabbi's wife though why it must be so i do not know except for this that God is Aunt Ruthless too*

*Lou not knowing passionless and smug in his ignorance a good man Lou a baby a good match we made they said very near the perfect couple they said and it was true but where Mama from where did this passion come please in your silence tell me Mama from where did this passion come and where Mama tell me Mama how i can make it go i think i know the answer mama tell me Mama tell me before you die who was Alex and what were you to him and he to you that you should take a vow of silence for him are you the same Mama the same as me or i should say am i the same as you are you too Mama through all these years a keeper of secret passions a keeper of secret flames can it be so Mama can it be so does the poisoned apple fall that close to the tree is all human life a repetition a tired joke retold and nothing more*

*Did Alex have red hair, Mama*

*Do secrets like murder always out Perhaps and yet murder doesn't always and perhaps secrets don't always out either but who is to say for who knows what secrets are taken to the grave by the sad diviners of secrets*

*Do I need you Mickey boorish Mickey cloddish Mickey selfish Mickey No No No No No No No*

*Yes*

*No!*

They didn't read all of it, of course. Not Phil reading aloud, sniggering, skipping to interesting sentences ("Hey, listen to this, listen to this!") and not Peewee when he grabbed the book from him to read himself.

*"No I am not Aunt Truth,"* Phil read aloud *"but . . .* wait a minute, here, listen to this *. . . my own selfish pleasure whether it be his cock inside me thrusting and pressing home or . . .* wait, there's better stuff later, here: *Before he could even touch me I squirmed down and took his cock in my mouth not to give him pleasure oh that would come soon of course . . ."* He had, of course, Peewee's attention now. Peewee was trying to grab the book from him, to see for himself, but Phil held it tight. Phil wouldn't let go and read even faster, even louder: *"My hair falling all over his belly sucking sucking his hands then on my breasts nipples firm and then sitting astride him . . ."* Peewee wrenching at the book then, tearing it to get it away from him, Phil holding tight.

"What do you think it is?" Phil said. "Who do you think wrote that stuff?"

"I don't know, I don't know," Peewee screamed, pulling at the book, but the stronger Phil held tight, tried to read again, and then said, "Hey, wait a minute. My dad's name is in here too." And skimming the page, *"Mickey Mickey* it says," and then skimming farther, turning the page, reads, *"Mickey Mickey Prickey Mickey what shall we do . . . our passion our illusion our madness though we never speak of it of course . . . or have you . . .* Look, here's Mrs. Greenberg *. . . fucking Felice upstairs fucked our memory to smithereens would that I could . . .* wait, there's more *. . . you alone know who I really am . . . I want to love and you I hate . . ."*

*"Stop it!"* Peewee screamed.

Phil stopped, shocked by the outburst. He let Peewee take the book this time, he let Peewee read, let him see he wasn't making it up. Peewee read and the ink ran under his eyes, blurred, solidified into a blot. He watched the blot spread, spread across the book, spread over the book and into his lap. He slammed the book at Phil as hard as he could, catching him harmlessly on the elbow, the book tearing some more and then in the flick of an instant slammed his fist into Phil's fat mouth, cutting his knuckle on Phil's fat teeth, Phil's fat lip beginning to bleed. "Hey," Phil saying. "What the hell—" but couldn't finish it as Peewee jumped on him, punched him as hard as he could in the stomach, punched him again in the face, Peewee on top of him pummeling him now, Phil only then beginning to be able to fight back, struggling to push Peewee off, trying to talk "What the hell—you gone crazy?" but not able to finish a sentence between Peewee's fisted blows, only Peewee getting out sentences between hot breathless sobs.

"Your father was fucking my mother! You fuck! That's what it says in there, goddamnit, your father was fucking my mother, you fuck!" Punching and punching till, exhausted, his wild punches losing strength, Phil the stronger of the two managed to shove him off, managed to grab Peewee's arms and pin them behind his back.

"If that's true," Phil said, huffing, puffing, holding Peewee's squirming arms, their red faces only inches apart, glaring with hatred at one another, "if that's true it's cause your mother wanted it. Sucking his cock, like she said."

The two of them pinned together between the boxes, cousins, best friends, glaring, till Peewee in a moment of Phil's relaxation wrenched free and punched him in the mouth again.

"You fuck!" Phil screamed. He got to his feet and kicked Peewee as hard as he could in the knee, and ran, past the old lady staggering with a cane into the room, almost knocking her over as he passed, out from among the boxes, down the hallway past the living room and out of this hated house, slamming the door behind him as he did. Out into the street he ran, down the block toward his own house and then past it— I'll never go in that fucking house again, he thought—ran to the corner and up Clifford Place away from the el and toward the vacant lot. In the lot he ran to the rocks, and there among them he sat behind a boulder on the earth, his fat chest heaving, heaving with hatred for— he didn't know. For his father, for his aunt Ruth, for Peewee—for the whole fucking world. There behind the boulder he sat, touching the cut on his lip, trying to catch his breath.

While in the room Peewee, too, sat, sat on the floor amid the cardboard boxes, several of which had tumbled down in the fight. There were cuts on the skin of his knuckle from Phil's teeth. He sucked at the blood coming out, ate warm blood while hot tears rolled and a broken machine pumped in his chest, pumped out irregular sobs. He tried to think of baseball, to blot out the images he'd read—his mother, Mickey —it couldn't be but there it was. His head was aching now as if a Joe Page fastball had caught him square in the temple, but he couldn't think of it. The sobs wrenched loudly in his gut, making him want to vomit, him not at first seeing, hearing, his frail grandmother standing in her nightgown, holding on to a box with one hand, her black wooden cane with the other. Saying, *"Bubbeluh. Bubbeluh. Bubbeluh."* Not even telling him not to cry.

# 3

OUTSIDE THE STADIUM, where he has spent the afternoon listening to the roars of the crowd, the nigger watches the streams of mostly happy people emerge. In the busy street car horns are honking in celebration. The bars under the el are overflowing with laughing men.

A vendor is selling Yankee pennants for fifty cents. Dodger ones he is giving away free. The nigger takes a Dodger pennant. It is the team of Jackie Robinson.

Walking alone through the crowd, he thinks: I can put this Dodger banner on the wall. Then it will be mine.

He likes the idea of his new home. A few blocks from the Stadium he reaches into his pocket. He finds a quarter there. He goes into a crowded bar, and he orders himself a beer, to celebrate.

Across two rivers a strange quiet has fallen over the universe. Mrs. Wiedkowski, looking out the living-room window of her second-floor apartment, notices it. The window is open in the late afternoon. A breeze is blowing in, nudging the lace curtains, but on the breeze there are no sounds of laughter or yelling, no sounds of children at play, no sounds of radios that have been incessant this past week. Waiting for the child, she leans out the window, looks up and down the block. There are no children anywhere. For a moment she feels dizzy, grasps the side of the window frame, pulls her head back in. The dizziness passes, followed by a moment of anxiety, of remembering, that passes through her veins, her brain. She gathers her strength in an instant, fights it off. The sick moment passes. They have been easier to fight off, these attacks, and they have happened less and less, as more and more children have come to her. She wonders for a moment why it happened just now, and thinks it must be because of the strange quiet, the absence of children in the street. Like then. But then she remembers what the doctor had said; there is no point to think what causes it; it is caused in a place beyond thought. To get through the moment, to get on with life, is all. Hopefully it will happen less and less.

As if to demonstrate her strength to herself, she opens the door to the hall, rides the elevator down to the lobby, goes out into the strangely quiet afternoon street. The children must be home from school by now. She cannot imagine what has happened to the children. Where their games have gone. She is conscious of the children's daily games, especially of the boys playing ball in the street, because they are noisier than the girls, and their games drifting in through the windows give her joy. The laughter of children is music, and only in the midst of lessons does she close the window to shut it out. But now in the street there are no children.

Puzzled but not afraid—thinking, this, too, shall pass—she takes a tissue from her pocket and wipes a smudge, a fingerprint, from the brass plate beside the building's front door. One has the name of a doctor on it, another of a dentist, and then hers: PIANO LESSONS—OLGA WIEDKOWSKI. She returns the tissue to the pocket of her dress and looks up and down in the emptiness. In the two months since they helped her find the apartment, she has never seen, heard, such quiet. Then around the corner she sees her four o'clock coming, in a plaid skirt and white blouse and white socks and little red shoes. Sharon is this one's name. Eight years old she is. A friend of the daughter of one of the other survivors. More and more their friends are coming now.

She greets the little girl and takes her hand, leads her into the elevator and up to the apartment. Sets out milk and cookies for her, as she always does before the lesson. She encourages the child to chatter on, afraid to broach the subject. Till at last she does.

"Where are the other children?" she asks. "Where are the little boys playing ball?"

The child shrugs but replies. "Nobody is very happy right now. The Brooklyns lost, you know."

"Ah, yes," she replies. "The football."

"Baseball," Sharon says.

Football, baseball, what is the difference, Mrs. Wiedkowski thinks. She nods and puts the glass in the sink and leads the girl to the piano. As the child begins her exercises, her scales, she goes out of habit to close the window against the shouts of the boys. But there are still no sounds from the street; the street is empty.

She inhales the stillness for a time, then walks to the piano and sits beside the child. "Not like that," she says. "Like this."

There is arthritis in her fingers, but it doesn't bother her when, for the children, she plays.

For Louie in late afternoon his first day as rabbi of the Mt. Eden Center felt vaguely disappointing.

He did not at first know why. Most of the mail had been congratulatory, and with the help of Mrs. Skolsky he had answered it appropriately. There had been numerous phone calls—residents and Jewish organizations wishing him well—and to these, too, he had responded with modest thanks. Reporters had called from the *Times*, the *Herald-Tribune* and the *Post*, making him feel for a moment—he wondered if Peewee would agree—that he was in the big leagues now. With all of them he had declined interviews, feeling that personal aggrandisement was not the way to start, not the way to achieve his goals. He suggested instead that it would be more appropriate for them to cover his first sermon on Saturday. Why he did that, beyond politeness, he wasn't sure. He had no idea what he was going to say.

In a curious way the highlight of his day had been the telegram from the lady detective, which he had filed appropriately with the others. And that, he suddenly understood, was what was bothering him. Everything had been so perfectly appropriate. In the cluttered dingy rooms of Beth Shalom he hadn't worried about appropriate. From Beth Shalom he'd run guns. It was perhaps the one inappropriate thing he had done in his life, and it, more than any other act, had made him feel truly alive.

"Patience," he said aloud, behind his still-blank table. "It's only the first day."

"Patience," he was startled to hear the angel reply, "is what some people are saying as they're lowered into the grave. As the clumps of earth begin to fall."

He looked around wearily. He was not sure he wanted to speak with the angel just now. He found him hanging from the chandelier above the desk.

"The board of directors urges patience," Louie said.

"That's why they're the board of directors," the angel said. "You're the rabbi. So it says on that nice brass plate outside. You've noticed it, perhaps, immodestly?"

"I've noticed it," Louie said.

He waited to hear what more the angel had to say—what specifics; what reasons. And then in the silence looked up at the chandelier. All he saw was the bulbs; the light.

He stood and paced about in the spacious office, twice the size of the one at Beth Shalom, thinking, Perhaps I'll have to grow to fill this. He had grown internally, he felt, with the running of guns, illegal though it was. Perhaps it was a rule of life: grow or die, regardless of the risks involved. His fantasy of the past few weeks came back to him with new insistence. The first time the fantasy had appeared in daylight: to circumvent the board of directors entirely, now, his first week on the job. To go over their heads, as it were, to the congregation. To announce on Saturday, in his very first sermon, his dream for the Mt. Eden Center —but not a dream: a plan—to make it into a leading center for Jewish scholarship. There would be grumbling backstairs, but who could oppose it publicly? And with the press perhaps there—even the New York *Times* perhaps there—it would become de facto an official statement, read throughout the city, read in Jewish circles throughout the land. Who knows, there might even be editorials lauding the idea: for who, indeed, could find fault? And what, then, could the directors do? Fire him for such a plan? Hardly likely. They'd have to support him, in public at least; and then to save the reputation of the center they'd have to raise the money to make it come true.

He sat at the desk and found a yellow legal pad in a drawer and, conscious of his own internal drama, took a pen from his pocket and began to make notes: sentences: paragraphs: to outline his dream in the reality of blue-black ink. Before he was done he picked up the telephone, called the man at the *Times*, apologized about the interview but urged him to come on Saturday. "I think it will be newsworthy," he said, and heard his own voice like an eavesdropper, saw a boy of twelve who had not yet learned much English schlepping cases filled with work clothes through the streets of the Lower East Side.

The *Times* man said he would come. Louie hung up the phone and continued making notes on the yellow pad, a small part of his brain thinking at the same time, Why does this feel so good? And after a time working it out: because his gunrunning, however important, was secret, there was no one he had to oppose. And at the first hint of opposition, from Miss Cole representing the police, he had quietly folded his tent. Whereas this would be an open challenge to the majority of the directors. He, Louie Brunig, would be opposing his will to theirs. There could be a private strength to be gained, he was just beginning to understand, from the public use of power.

He exulted at this new feeling as he wrote. He wanted to call someone and tell of his decision—call up a woman and tell her of his decision—call up, in fact, Miss Cole and tell her—but he decided he could not do that. Over dinner he would tell Ruthie instead. He heard in the corridor outside Mrs. Skolsky's door some of the children arriving for Hebrew school, which made him think of Benny. Benny would need some comforting tonight. The Dodgers had lost the Series.

Still he wrote on, and when he was finished put the pad in the drawer—he would read it over, polish it, all week—and leaned back in his brown leather swivel chair and placed both hands on top of his head, on top of his yarmulke, relaxing, feeling good, and then in this exposed position it occurred to him—as something in good moments so often did—that perhaps it was all an excuse, his sermon-dream. For hadn't he planned, actually, to make his very first sermon about the holocaust? About which he didn't know what to say?

Dejected, he dropped his hands to his lap. Thirty minutes, he thought. Perhaps thirty minutes of happiness we are permitted, every week or so. If that. He rubbed his cheeks, his eyes. The day had been tiring, after all. He rubbed them again and then, opening his eyes, between the red spots dancing he saw the angel perched on his desk.

"Hey, not to worry," the angel said. "The holocaust won't go away."

The rabbi thought a moment, smiled ruefully, reached out to touch the angel as if he were a toy.

"No, I suppose not," he said. "The holocaust won't go away."

He stood again, measured again the large new office with his paces;

sat again, opened the drawer, took out the yellow pad; began once more to write. Perfection in his sermons might well be his new goal, if he could not find happiness in life.

The way of the artist, he thought.

He had never before envisioned himself that way.

The child, on the floor, cries. The cries fill his nose, his mouth, rack his body with spasms, make him choke. Leaning on her cane, watching, grasping with the other hand an unsturdy cardboard box, she thinks, Soon he will vomit: his childhood innocence he's spitting up.

The child throws himself prone, his cheek on the wooden floor, and pounds the floor. Watching, she thinks, Let him be. Let him, for a few minutes, be.

He is on his back now, his hands covering his eyes, as if in some biblical scene he has just turned around and seen the forbidden. He is kicking the heels of his brown-scuffed shoes on the floor. There is, she imagines, only one thing he realizes now, and that is pain.

Watching as at last his energy drains, as the kicking stops except for an occasional spasm, as the sobbing stops except for an occasional hiccuplike cry, as his tears are broken only by sniffles now, she thinks, So this is what it was for. All the months of not being allowed to die. For this they—He—Someone—was keeping me. To be here now. To see the *kinder* through this.

And do I, she asks, in the end, have the strength?

She waits: waits till he is finished crying, or almost so, for perhaps he will never now be finished crying. Waits till, taking his hands from his eyes, sitting up, he sees her, an apparition, and clearly does not at first understand—his grandma Lester, standing up; for the first time in many months, standing up by herself. It is almost as if, she sees in his eyes, he doesn't know who she is; as she, after the stroke, at first did not know him. Perhaps this it was for, she thinks again, this moment: all of it—Alex, Max, the children, the sewing, even the stroke, perhaps: all of it for her to be here, this moment. To give to the child her strength.

Leaning on her cane, she lets go of the cardboard box, finds that she can balance. She reaches out her hand to him. Slowly the wildness drains from the child's eyes. Slowly there is recognition. Sitting on the floor, he reaches up and takes her hand. This he has not done with such child-need, child-love, in years. This he has not done in such a way, in fact, since Max. Since Max used to take him to the park.

Ruthie's boy.

His little hand is warm, moist.

"Do good," she hears a voice say, from somewhere among the boxes, above and behind. She cannot see who it is, but she knows. This time it's not the angel. It's Max himself.

With strength she can hardly remember, she hardens her hand. The child, feeling this, pulls himself up. In the dim light, holding hands, they move together through the narrow path left by the boxes, the child shoving aside one that had fallen. In this way she leads him or he leads her or they lead each other out of the room, across the space where second base used to be, and side by side they sit on the edge of her bed.

They do not speak. The child in pain looks imploringly at her eyes. He sees from the pain in her eyes, the pain reflecting his, that she has heard. He opens his mouth, tries to talk, but cannot. The tears start again, and he buries his face in the lap of her faded robe and lets them come. She feels even through the robe, even through the nightgown, the heat of his cheek. With her hand she rubs the hair on the back of his head. Even now it will not stay in place. She pulls from it a dust ball from the floor, tries to throw it away, but it clings to her hand. She rubs it off on the bed.

He circles her waist with his arms, clings tight. She rests her frail hand on his back, can feel his chest heaving beneath. Holding him, she thinks of what she's heard. Of what they read. Of Ruthie: fiery hair and blood-red heart. Alex's.

Who is she to condemn? She is too old to judge. Life's only true lesson, she thinks: we none of us can judge.

Rubbing the child's hair again, listening to his tears, she thinks, Is this, too, a gift from Alex?

She lifts his head from her lap as the sobbing slows, pulls it to her ancient breast. *"Bubbeluh,"* she says. "Enough now, *bubbeluh."*

In time he runs out of tears. And what is she to say? And how shall she begin?

The child himself provides the answer. "I'm gonna tell my daddy," he says, between left-over sobs. "He'll beat Uncle Mickey up."

She touches the wetness of his face, finds water in her own healed eyes. She knows what she must say, for better or worse.

"Listen to me, Benny," she says. "Listen carefully to what I say."

The child lets go, stands beside her. He takes her hand, lets it go, keeps it nearby.

"Things happen to people," she says. "Things happen between people. Sometimes they have no control." She takes one of his fingers in hers. "There are forces inside us sometimes—forces we maybe don't want, but they're there anyway. I don't know why. Nobody knows why. But they are. And sometimes they're stronger than we are, and we do things we know are wrong. But we do them anyway. You understand?"

The child looked at the floor. "Like when I skip Hebrew school?"

"Yes. And what happens when you skip Hebrew school?"

"My daddy spanks me."

"But sometimes you do it anyway."

Eyes still on the floor, he nodded, sniffling.

"What happened is something like that," she said. "Your mother perhaps did something she shouldn't. And she is paying for it, I can tell you that. She has been in great pain ever since, sorry for what she did. That's why she wrote it down, I think. To try and make the pain go away. I'll bet she cries about it a lot when she's alone. She has a secret, and it hurts and hurts. You understand?"

She looks at his face, sees only the redness, the hurt now his, and also puzzlement.

"The important thing is this," she says, squeezing his hand tightly now. "Whatever happened with your mother and Mickey is over. Done with. It ended a long time ago. You understand?"

He nods under the bombarding of words. She can only guess at his thoughts.

"And because it's over," she continues, "—are you listening? Because it's over, the only thing to do is to forget. To let it be. You said before you would tell your daddy. Do you know what that would do? It would hurt your daddy very much. You don't want to do that, do you? It could make a lot of trouble, it could hurt a lot of people: your mama, and Eli, and Hindy, and Philip, and Annie. You don't want to hurt all those people, do you? Who didn't do anything wrong?"

He shakes his head uncertainly. "I hate my mommy," he says.

She feels the tears on her own face now. She pulls him to her breast.

"I know you do," she says. "I know you do, right now. But that feeling will pass, in time." I hope, she adds silently.

She feels like she is slipping, unequal to the task. She feels that she is losing him. She lifts his face, hugs him, looks at him again in desperation.

"You know what you found out in that book," she says. "It has nothing to do with your mother and Uncle Mickey. That concerns only them. That's important only to them. What you found out is that grown-ups have secrets. The more years you live, the more secrets you have. In a way, it's your secrets that make you you. You understand?"

He said nothing.

"I know it's hard to understand," she said. "You're too young to understand. Someday you will. But in the meantime just think of this. Your mother has a secret, and Uncle Mickey. And now it's your secret, too. And that's the important thing. To keep it always a secret, for all of you. To make believe you don't even know."

"You mean I should never tell anybody?" he said.

"Nobody," she said. "Never. And the first thing you should do is throw away that book. So nobody sees it, ever again."

He looked up into her face. "But it's Mommy's," he said.

"Your mother doesn't need it anymore."

"And if she does it's tough titty!" he said, with a hint of strength returning to his voice.

"Right," she said, feeling her face flush. "If she does, it's too bad for her. And you know what? That will be our secret, mine and yours. That you were the one who threw away the book. Okay?"

"Okay," he said, sniffling.

She hugs him again and looks over his head across to the window, across the yard to the warehouse wall beyond. She does not know if she has said the right things. She doesn't know what else to say. The getting rid of the book, she sees, seems to at least have taken his mind from what was in it. At least for now.

"Maybe you should do it now," she says. "Get the book and throw it away now. Before anyone else comes home."

He stands and looks at her. She shakes her head. She doesn't know what else to say. The water in her eyes is melting snow. Melting Russian snow.

"Only you're my friend, Grandma," he says. He hugs her tightly, kisses her on the cheek.

"Now I'll get the book," he says. "Before anyone else comes home."

And he goes once more to the room where the dim bulb burns forlornly overhead and the broken diary waits on the floor.

The diary feels hot as coal as he picks it up: so hot it will burn his fingers. Perhaps this triggers the idea.

It is hanging almost in two pieces now from the fight and he thinks to look inside it again, to read the words again, but doesn't do this, shuts it tight instead. With his other hand he puts the roulette wheel back in the drawer, and the box on top, and closes it. He comes to the front of the room and turns off the light.

He carries the diary past second base, down the hallway, then all the way to his room. He will throw it in the garbage, he thinks, so no one will ever read the words again. But in the garbage someone might find it and everyone will know his secret. His very own secret. The Rag Lady might find it, he thinks, and take it away and give it to some stranger who will read it and then will know. The Rag Lady has not come around since the day he brought the baby back. Perhaps this memory triggers the idea.

Perhaps he should rip it apart, he thinks. Tear out the pages one by one and go somewhere tall and windy and scatter all the pages to the wind. Climb the rocks in the empty lot near the tunnel and one by one let the pages fly away. But however far they fly on the wind, they eventually will fall to earth. One of them might fall to earth on the sidewalk near the tunnel from which his father will emerge on his way home from the Mt. Eden Center and pick it up and read it all. So that is no good. It must be someplace where his father doesn't go.

His mother and Mickey. His mother and Mickey. He must get away from that. He must go back before that, before the ashes that seem now in his mind to blacken his mother's face. And then he knows what he must do and where he must go.

He puts on his zippered jacket. He goes into the kitchen and opens a closet and takes out the small can of lighter fluid his mother keeps to fill the table Ronson in the living room, which is squat and silver and feels like a baseball in your hand. He slips the can of fluid into his pocket easily, and a batch of wooden matches from the stove. He goes back to his room and zips his jacket halfway up and slips the diary inside. Then he zips the jacket all the way up. He goes past his parents' bedroom, wondering if they ever did it here, goes past it quickly, not looking, afraid of what leftover ghosts he might see, and down the hall and out the door, not even telling Grandma where he's going. This part he has decided will be his secret, his alone.

The diary trapped between his jacket and his chest beats like a frantic bird with a heart of its own. To the right he walks, past the fall-dusty hedges from in front of which Baby Lisa was stolen; past the alleyway that leads to their punchball field; past Phil's house and Annie's and Mickey's. At the corner he turns right again, down Clifford Place to the el. If he looked back he could have seen the Lewis Morris towering a block behind, but he does not look back. He hates Beverly Rosenthal, too. He hates Beverly Rosenthal as much as he hates his mother just now. On the el overhead a train passes, noisy with revelers from the stadium. He hears this and remembers that less than an hour ago the Dodgers lost the Series. And walks on.

Everywhere, it seems, there are celebrants. The thick-armed men in navy wool caps loading the trucks in front of the warehouses are talking about the Yanks. In front of the radio repair shop in whose window the small television is, a knot of joking men are talking about the Yanks. The man from the linoleum store is standing in the doorway with a big dirty smile on his face. Even in front of Ben-Al's food store men are joking as they pass around a small white card. Peewee, unthinking but led perhaps by the diary beating in his chest, asks them what's so funny. One of the men shows him the card. It is a small white card with a black border on it, and tiny letters in the center spelling two words: BROOKLYN DODGERS.

"What's it mean?" Peewee says to the man holding the card.

"It's a death notice," the well-dressed man says. "It means the Bums is dead."

The others laugh and whoop. Peewee walks away. He crosses the street where once he felt he was crossing into another country, leaving his own behind, but now it feels overpoweringly the reverse. Now he is leaving behind an alien land, the land of the Bronx and the winning Yanks, the land of Mickey and his mother; crossing as if a river to where he belongs: to the land of Baby Lisa and the nigger; to the land of the Rag Lady herself.

From the lumberyard the last trucks of the day are leaving. The great electric saw is still. The men are straggling out, locking the gate behind. Going to drink some beer for the Yanks. He watches from afar, standing near a lamppost on the corner, as they go. In his chest the diary is beating with a new rhythm now. No longer a bird, it is going clackety-clack, clackety-clack, like the spikes of the ball players on the cement runway leading from the locker room in all the John R. Tunis books he has read: *The Kid From Tomkinsville, Keystone Kids, World Series* and all the rest. Clackety-clack, clackety-clack, like the telegraph in the background of away games, bringing in the news; spreading the news to everyone: that Mommy and Uncle Mickey used to fuck.

Whatever that means.

In the prison of his knowledge, he waits. Waits till the last of the lumbermen have left the street, till a few stray pedestrians have passed. Till between trains the street in the dying afternoon is quiet as a cemetery. When all is quiet, the diary pumping now like a machine in his chest leads him on. Past the lumberyard's long gate. Past the front of the Rag Lady's house. Down the alley beside. The nigger may be there, he remembers. He doesn't know what he will do if the nigger is there. But the nigger is not there on the crate in the alley and when, knocking on the paint-eroded door, there is no answer, he knows the nigger isn't there.

The door is not locked, not even fully closed. He is about to push it open when he remembers: the dead man in the bed. The nigger isn't there but the dead man in the bed may be. His heart begins to beat like the diary, but then he remembers: that was months ago. The dead man couldn't still be there. Calling up his courage with the strange new notion that it doesn't matter anyway, he pushes open the door and goes inside. It is mostly as he'd seen it before, except that both beds are empty. The dead man has left or been taken away or whatever happens to dead people.

He remembers the terror he felt that day, confronting the Rag Lady. And the exultant triumph of getting the baby back. He knows no terror now, not from this place. The place has become in some indescribable way his second home, a place he will always cherish. But he knows no triumph, either, at this unexpected familiarity. It is as if he will never know total triumph again: will from this day forth spend his life perhaps in its pursuit.

After a brief glance around he pulls out the diary and sets it on a dresser top where once a monument was. Beside it he sets the matches and the fluid, like some pint-sized priest preparing a consecration. Or like Abraham, perhaps, preparing to sacrifice his son. (Though for this diary Peewee will feel no loss. Would that he could.) Thinking then of the dark coal dust, he takes off his jacket and drapes it over a chair to keep it clean. Takes off his jacket like good old reliable Hugh Casey striding toward the mound. And then, diary in one hand, lighter fluid and matches in the other, he crosses the room, pulls open the dark brown door, scrabbles up the mound of coal.

The coffin is where he'd seen it last, untouched since then, half-buried in the coal. Beside it the lid, the stick. He thinks again to open the diary, to read the words again, but fears they will make him sick. Instead, still closed, he stands it in the coffin; stands it because he somehow knows it will burn much better that way. Slowly he opens the lighter fluid, the sacred oil, and pours it onto the book, soaking the book as best he can. The rest he continues to pour into the coffin. His hand is shaking now. Some of it goes into the coffin, some on the coal beside. When there are no more drops to drip, he tosses the can away. Only the matches are left in his hand. Wooden matches, much more fun than paper ones. Like a Louisville Slugger made to your own size. Pee Wee Reese, he knows, grew up in Louisville. Bat city.

For a long time he hesitates, looking at the offering. There is guilt in him, but he doesn't know why. Grandma said his mother wouldn't need the book anymore. The fear that shook his hand begins to shake his arms, his chest. He must do it now, he thinks, or leave. With sudden resolution he takes a match, strikes it on the side of the coffin. When it flares bright orange, he lets the flame settle, for an instant is hypnotized by it. Then he drops it in.

The fluid flares. He feels the instant warmth, the smell, and draws his head back. From atop the coal a sleeping cat he hadn't noticed rouses, cries, leaps out through the open coal door. He watches as the flame changes color, as the diary itself catches, smolders, begins to burn. The book falls open slightly, separate pages curl, brown, blacken into ash and die. Suddenly he is aware of the smoke: that it is getting hard to breathe. A moment longer, holding his breath, he watches the diary burn, taking all its secrets to the grave. Then, as the flames on the fluid leap higher, he scrabbles down the coal, out into the pale apartment. There is coal dust on his hands, and he runs the water from the faucet and washes them, and wipes them on a pillow on the bed. Then, with flickering light visible through the door to the coal bin, as all secrets seem to their keepers to give off a flickering, betraying light, he pulls on his zippered jacket and walks to the basement door and steps outside.

At the top of the alley he looks both ways to make sure that no one will see him leave. When he's certain the stands are empty, he walks away. Past the lumberyard, toward home.

**4**

H E   D O E S   N O T , however, go straight home. His mother may be home from shopping, and he doesn't want to look at her. He doesn't want to see her, ever again. On Clifford Place he continues up the slope a block to the base of the Lewis Morris, and then to the empty lot beside. He hopes perhaps the big kids will be playing ball and he can sit on the rocks and watch. But the sky is clouding over; the afternoon is fading toward evening, and there is no game going on now. All he can see in the scruffy lot is a lone figure sitting against a boulder. From far away it looks like Phil.

Peewee stopped. If he did not want to see his mother ever again, then he did not want to see Phil, either. But there was, he decided, something to be done. With slow, disconsolate steps, wanting as he always did to kick at empty cans or loose stones, but no longer having the energy to, he crossed the lot. Phil, hearing footsteps, glanced up to see who was coming and then looked down again. There were no more tears in his face; only the redness they had left. Peewee approached wordlessly. He did not greet Phil and Phil did not greet him and as he passed he wanted for a moment to keep on walking, out of the empty lot, through the gray tunnel, across the Bronx. All the way to Brooklyn, perhaps. Instead he stopped and sat, leaning against the rocks, not beside Phil but ten feet away. He, too, with his elbows on his knees, looked at the ground between his feet. From across the lot they resembled bookends, one fat, the other thin.

They sat that way for many minutes. Once the year before they had strung a waxed cord between their two houses, with waxed paper cups on the ends, through which to talk. It had not worked very well. Nor did it now. Every few minutes the ground beneath them shook as the D train shuddered under the tunnel. The D train was the train you took to Brooklyn. Now disgorging people into the failing light, ground shaking, it echoed in the outer world the invisible shaking in their limbs. It did not, however, close the gap between. They were for the first time in their lives on opposing teams.

How long they sat in silence they couldn't say. It was Peewee who spoke first, his face and words pointed at the ground.

"We have to keep it a secret," he said.

Phil, hearing the words, did not reply but slowly lifted his head and looked at him. In his face, though it was still rotund with baby fat, there was for the first time unmistakable weariness. Peewee, looking, saw this, and felt the bond still there. The face was a mirror of his soul.

"Grandma Lester said so," he said. "To keep the peace in the family. So everyone doesn't get hurt."

Tears appeared in Phil's eyes. He looked at the ground so Peewee wouldn't see; though he half wanted him to see. To accept his regrets.

"Grandma Lester talked?" he asked.

Peewee did not reply directly. It was not the first time she had talked.

"It has to be a secret," Peewee said. "Forever."

Phil picked up a small rock at his side, threw it angrily across the lot. It skipped and bounced across the distant sidewalk and almost hit a man from the subway walking by, and slammed with a loud ping into the hubcap of a car at the curb. The man looked to see who had thrown the rock and yelled something nasty that they couldn't quite hear.

"It's in the goddamn book," Phil said. "Someone else could find the book."

Peewee started to say *I burned it*, but something, he didn't know what, made him pause, made him change direction. "No one else will see it," he said. "I threw the book away."

Phil looked across at him as if to make sure he was telling the whole truth. They both held the look a long time, and then Phil looked at the ground. To both it seemed that they had a lot to talk about. But with the book thrown away, then that was it. They must make believe it hadn't happened.

In the street people were pouring from the subway. The rush hour was coming on strong. All these strangers. Peewee took several deep breaths. Then he pushed himself up, hurting his hand for a moment on a rock, and stood and moved over, and sat again on the ground, his back against the boulders, next to Phil. They did not shake hands, or even speak; but merely sat there, side by side.

He did not, at first, see the flames. His eyes were downcast on the pale city earth between his legs. Phil's silent presence beside him had the inert bulk of a boulder, nothing more. Only the pain was with him, part of him, like knives hollowing his chest. Seeing a boy emerging from the tunnel with a forgotten yarmulke still on his head, he realized he had not gone to Hebrew school, had totally forgotten it today. His father the new rabbi would be mad.

The images insinuated: his mother and Mickey, Mickey and his mother. Like the dirty gray postcards Phil had once brought home from school. Men and women sucking each other's things. He imagined such postcards circulating through the schoolyard: Mickey and his mother.

He slammed his fist on the rocky earth, again and again, ignoring Phil's presence, till it hurt. Phil, he could tell, was looking at him but saying nothing, out of respect. *Why?* he wanted to scream. Not *why them?* but *why him?* Why had he gone to the back room today? Why had he opened the drawer? To play with the roulette, he remembered: to play with the goddamn broken roulette. If it had not been there, then he would not have gone in there and Phil would have not come in after and opened the book. What was it Grandma had said about the roulette? A gift from Alex, she'd said. A gift from Alex it was. He thought, Who the fuck was Alex, anyway? And then he put it together with himself, his middle name. Benjamin Alexander Brunig. In some stupid crazy way this Alex was part of him.

The shortstop for the Dodgers. He screwed his lips together. If the Dodgers had won the game, had won the Series, he would have run out into the street with Phil. They would have found the other kids, would have taunted the Yankee fans. Then probably they would have gotten their gloves and played some ball, with happiness in their chests. So there was guilt enough to spread to everyone. If the Dodgers had won, he would not have gone to the back room to sulk. If the Dodgers had won, they wouldn't have read the book.

The Dodgers are gonna win the pennant: his nightly affirmation, his nightly prayer, all spring, all summer. And they had won, had made it to the World Series. And if they had not? If they had not, after all, won the pennant, would he then have read the book?

There is dizziness in him, dizziness that makes him think for a moment that the boulders piled above, boulders that reach to the Concourse above, are beginning to cascade, to crash upon his head in an avalanche, like the boxes. He ducks his head, his neck, instinctively, to avoid their crush. The world settles momentarily; the boulders do not come. Still the sensation has scared him, leaving aftershocks.

"Hey, look!" Phil says, and he ducks again, waiting for the crush, and then when it does not come looks upward. The boulders haven't moved.

"Over there," Phil says, pointing. "Look at all that smoke. Must be a fire somewhere."

He looks where Phil is pointing. In the clouding evening a great gray ocean of smoke is spreading across the sky, is perhaps more responsible for the darkening than the night. It is billowing up from a source they cannot see, flattening like a lid over the Bronx. On the underside of the gray in the center is a pale wash of orange, a mirror, no doubt, of the flames running wild at the source.

"Let's go see what it is!" Phil says, standing, restless now to be off as Peewee still sits, as Peewee then slowly stands. It is as if the seductive fire has driven from Phil all deeper, desperate thoughts. Peewee stands and follows Phil across the lot in the direction of the smoke: the smoke that with uncanny speed is coming to meet them now. He follows slowly, as if he knows this: there is little left for flames to destroy.

Fire engines. Little boys were supposed to say at that time in that place when asked what they wanted to be when they grew up: a fireman. Not Pee Wee Reese. Who the hell was Pee Wee Reese? And now suddenly they are on all sides, fire engines fire-engine red, careening through the streets. Silver bells clanging urgently on the rears of truncated trucks, on the rears of hook and ladders. Bells clanging beneath the wail of sirens, police cars too converging, dark green and white. All

other traffic has pulled to the side, has stopped, the streets first a block
and then two blocks away from the source clogged with equipment
now.

They left their quick-walking and ran, down Clifford Place to the el,
then left toward where, nearly two blocks away, the smoke was funnel-
ing up. New engines, black-clad firemen running up behind them,
passed them the wrong way uncaringly down one-way streets. Under
the el they ran past stores unnoticed now, toward where they could see
the flames that fed the smoke, bright orange and roaring uncitylike, the
shopkeepers in front of each store looking at the flames, the last straggling warehouse loaders looking at the flames, rush-hour departees from
the el above gathered in knots, looking. They ran their way through the
gathering crowds till in front of Ben-Al's food store they were stopped
by wooden barricades, police lines, keep back, you've got to move back,
police saying, and across the street the lumberyard, the tall piles of
lumber at this end still standing tall, the tall piles of lumber at the
other end a great giant bonfire of flames, the flames that produce the
smoke that blots the sky.

"It's the goddamn lumberyard," Phil says, breathless and redundant,
and Peewee, staring, staring at and then through the flames, sees behind the burning lumber at the far end the dark black skeleteon of a
house, the charred still-standing (but barely) remains of the gray frame
house in whose basement the Rag Lady lived; or used to live until she
disappeared. In whose basement perhaps the nigger still lives.

Sickness fills his chest. There was nobody there when he went and
burned the book. The nigger was not inside. The nigger was not inside!

Ill thoughts obliterated then by the commotion, great streams of
water from great long hoses arcing through the air onto the white-
orange flames. Fire trucks hampered by the stanchions of the el filling
three blocks now; four. Red fire cars crawling between them like bugs: a
deputy, a chief. More hoses shooting water skyward.

"Looks like a goddamn pissing contest," Phil says.

Blood cousins still, in spite of everything.

Peewee stared into the flames that seemed to be growing ever higher
despite the best efforts of the firemen, that seemed to be sweeping
across the lumberyard as if it were a forest to be crossed.

"How do you think it started?" Phil said.

Torn from the fire, Peewee glares at his cousin. He can feel the heat of the flames on his face now, and the burning heat of his fury, his guilt.

"How the fuck should I know?" he says.

Phil looks at him, squinting to see his cousin in the fast-falling dark against the blinding, flickering light, his own face hotter too from the angry response. And lets it go. The flames are roaring now like a rushing train; from all sides sirens still converge; talking has to be shouted now. He lets it go.

Peewee isn't listening anyhow. Peewee, caught up in the roaring train, the roaring waterfall, sees in the flames his hero dropping his bat at the ball at the last second, bunting for a hit, laying it down beautifully toward third, crossing the bag at first. The third baseman didn't even bother to throw. Peewee almost without realizing it is moving back, moving back, edged back in the growing crowd by a fireman— back up, back up, the fireman is saying, they need more room to run hoses on this side. Peewee then hearing, seeing the fireman with his fireman's hat and a silver badge in the center, finds himself almost without knowing it thinking, All these firemen once were little boys who wanted to grow up and be firemen.

Tears, perhaps from the dry heat or perhaps not, roll down his cheeks as in the flames he sees Pee Wee Reese stealing second. A great jump on the pitcher, a straight dash to the bag, a straight slide in ahead of the throw. Over and over again the bright-clad image dashes through the flames, like a hero rescuing a child: Pee Wee Reese in his home Dodger whites and blue cap sliding straight and true into second base. Down the linoleum corridor and into the wooden board that is second base. Over and over Pee Wee Reese runs. Over and over Pee Wee Reese slides.

Phil, confused and worn but sounding like a big brother now, grabs his arm just above the elbow. "What are you crying for?" he says.

Peewee hadn't realized he was crying.

The flames are growing everywhere like wild orange leaves. The evening sky is darker at the ground than up above, where orange light is caught by the hanging smoke. On the ground the streetlights, the store lights, all manmade lights have gone out. The streets are lit by the burning lumberyard. In distant windows candles can be seen, pale substitutes for the shorted incandescence. In nearby windows the lumber-yard fire dances off the glass.

Firemen in wet black slickers move among the hoses like glistening bugs. Behind police barricades on all sides, half a block or more from the fire, the crowd is six or eight deep, watches, most of the neighborhood there. A few have radios in their hands, over which the news comes crackling. "A five-alarm fire . . . every piece of equipment from the Bronx is at the scene . . . the mayor is on his way . . . Firehouses in Manhattan are on alert in case they too are needed . . . electricity in much of the west Bronx has gone dark . . . the Transit Authority has stopped all rush-hour train traffic on the Jerome Avenue el for fear that the blazing fire has weakened the iron stanchions . . . flames can be seen spreading to some of the wooden ties of the el . . . the fire appears to have started in an abandoned house beside the lumberyard . . . the cause is not yet known . . ."

All this Peewee hears from radios that crackle. Phil is beside him in the crush of the front row. For a moment he thought he had seen his father's portly figure moving across the street, his briefcase in his hand. But a fire truck had edged by, and when it passed, his father was gone. He thought for a time he heard Eli and his friends yelling and joking somewhere in the back of the crowd behind him, but there was no room to turn around to see.

"The one small bright spot," an announcer was saying on a radio, "was that the fire did not break out an hour earlier, when the trains passing on the weakened tracks above would have been jammed to capacity with fans from Yankee Stadium twelve blocks to the south, going home to celebrate the Yankees' World Series win."

The wind has spread the flames. The entire lumberyard has caught. The firemen have given up on the lumberyard and on the coffin plant in the rear They are playing their hoses on the buildings across the streets now, trying to contain the damage, to stop the wind-lashed flames from leaping across the streets, to the stores and the warehouses. The smoke is acrid now to the nose, the eyes.

"You don't think the Rag Lady lives there anymore?" Phil shouted into Peewee's face above the noise of the flames, the water.

Peewee, hot-faced, shouted back in his face. "Couldn't be! We ain't seen her since she gave Baby Lisa back! Your father went looking for her. Remember?"

Phil nods, eyes tearing from the flames, and then, speak of the devil, a policeman is in front of them, in front of all of them, urging them to please move back. It is Mickey, Uncle Mickey, blue uniform black in the fire night, saying please move back it's getting too hot over here, they have to move the barricades back. Mickey and then some other policemen lift the barricades, not even noticing Peewee and Phil right under their noses, gently urging the barricades back.

"Hey, Dad!" Phil yells, but Mickey cannot hear him in the noise. Peewee sees him and says or yells nothing, his throat dry from the smoke, but looks at the black that covers Mickey's face, soot from the smoke where he's been up close with the firemen. The barricades are shoved back a few feet, and then Mickey pausing, Phil reaches out and grabs his arm. "Hey, Dad!"

Mickey, startled, looks down, wipes his forehead with his arm, smiles at his son.Then he goes to where he's needed somewhere else. Peewee watches his back.

The crowd has hardly thinned. The crowd will stay for the duration. The most excitement in the Bronx since Decoration Day, when the President came to the parade. Check that, Peewee concedes. The most excitement in the Bronx since the Yankees won the Series. Four or five hours ago.

And then he sees her. The crowd must have thinned some; there must have been some movement, like waters lapping at a beach. Because there across Jerome Avenue in the front row of the crowd on the other side he suddenly picks her out in the light of the leaping flames.

His mother.

There is a tightening in his stomach. More tears well behind his eyes. At first he is not sure it is she. His mother used to be prettier.

He wants to scream with rage, but does not. He wants to run to her, throw his arms around her waist, to nuzzle his face into her chest. But does not. He stands and looks at her, one face in the crowd across the street. Her face is flickering in and out in the light of the flames, like an image on a television screen. He is very conscious of watching his mother from a distance, something he has never consciously done before. A strange thought flits through his mind: he wonders it if is possible to hug someone without touching her.

How lucky he was, he used to think, to have for a mother the prettiest lady in the world.

He wonders what has happened to her face.

He turns away and doesn't look across the street again. He stares with blurring eyes into the flames. Pee Wee Reese is still cavorting there. His uniform is catching fire now. Pee Wee dashing, leaping, while flames break out in his Brooklyn Dodger grays. There's a looping pop fly to left. Pee Wee turns his back and races out. The left fielder is charging in, the center fielder is charging in, but Pee Wee keeps going, his back to the plate, the blue number 1 leaping out on his back in the orange flames. He dives for the ball with his back to the plate. He lands outstretched on the grass, facedown, the ball nestled in his glove. It's the last out of the game; the others go trotting by in victory. But Pee Wee doesn't get up. Pee Wee Reese lies facedown in the grass. He faced the charge of the inrushing outfielders, he made the play himself, he made the catch with arm impossibly stretched. He saved the victory, he won the game. But now he doesn't get up. Unnoticed and alone, he lies on the empty field in the flames. Ever so slowly his uniform turns to ash. Pee Wee Reese is burning.